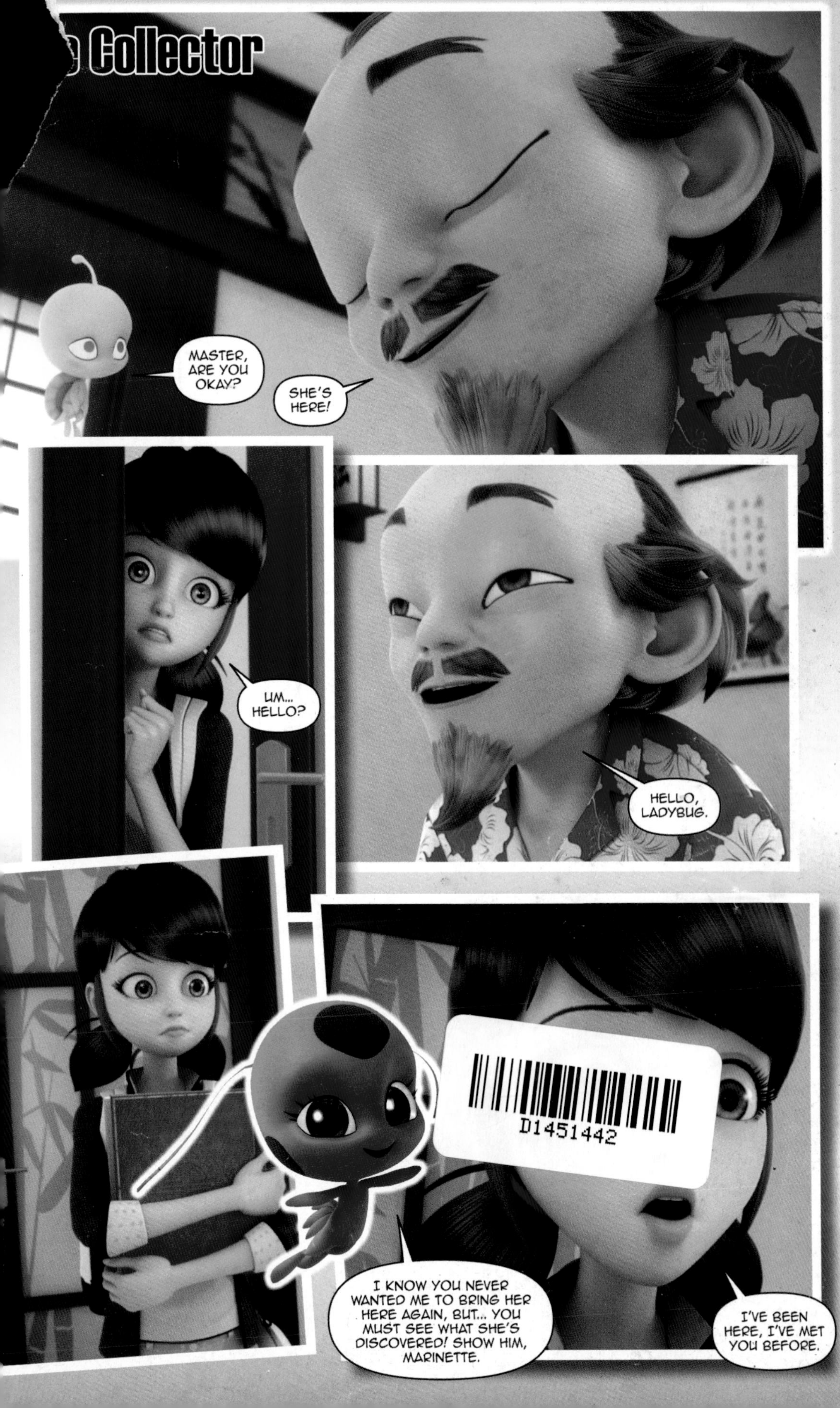
Collector
MASTER, ARE YOU OKAY?
SHE'S HERE!
UM... HELLO?
HELLO, LADYBUG.
I KNOW YOU NEVER WANTED ME TO BRING HER HERE AGAIN, BUT... YOU MUST SEE WHAT SHE'S DISCOVERED! SHOW HIM, MARINETTE.
I'VE BEEN HERE, I'VE MET YOU BEFORE.

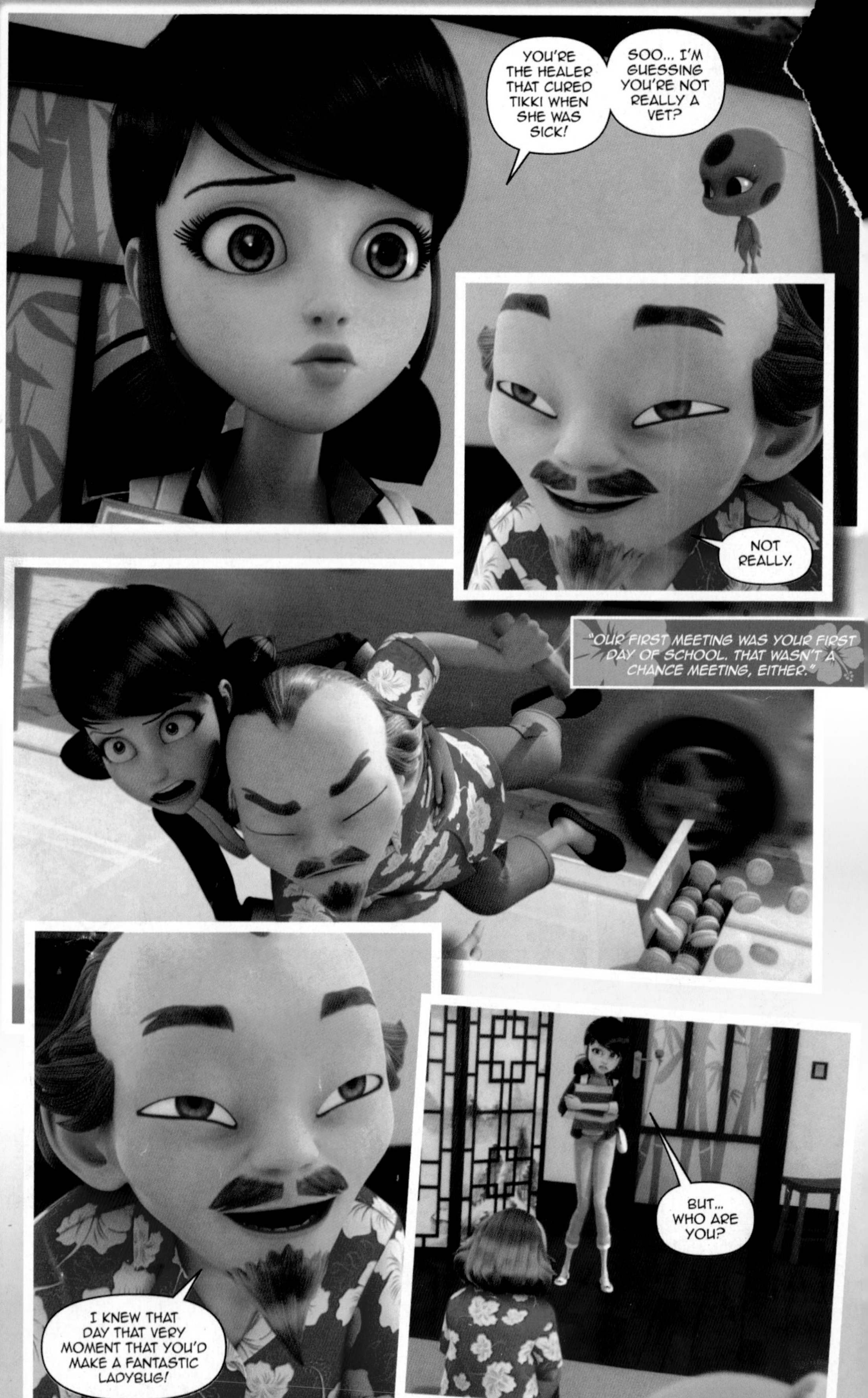
YOU'RE THE HEALER THAT CURED TIKKI WHEN SHE WAS SICK!
SOO... I'M GUESSING YOU'RE NOT REALLY A VET?
NOT REALLY.
"OUR FIRST MEETING WAS YOUR FIRST DAY OF SCHOOL. THAT WASN'T A CHANCE MEETING, EITHER."
I KNEW THAT DAY THAT VERY MOMENT THAT YOU'D MAKE A FANTASTIC LADYBUG!
BUT... WHO ARE YOU?

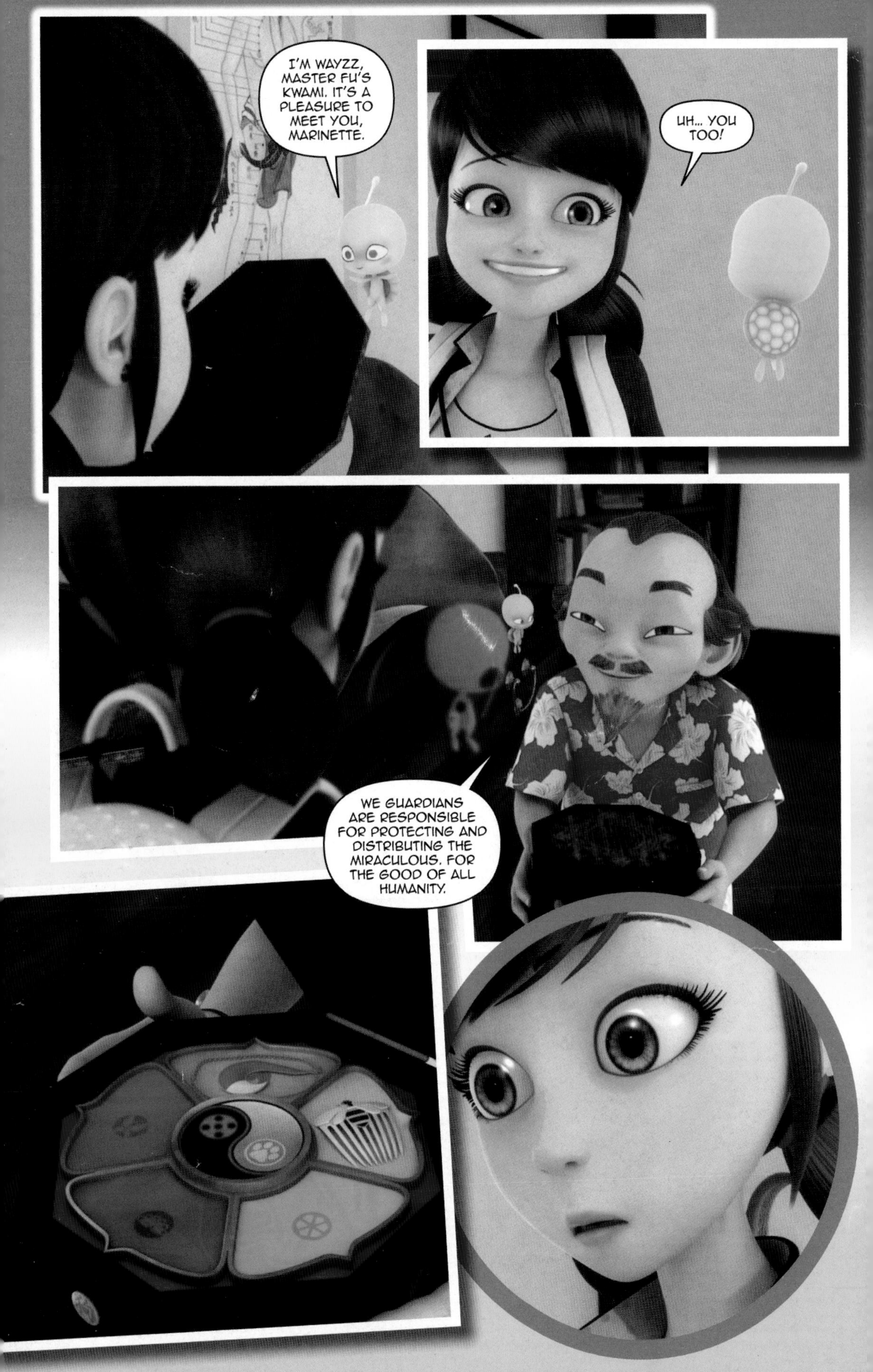
I'M WAYZZ, MASTER FU'S KWAMI. IT'S A PLEASURE TO MEET YOU, MARINETTE.
UH... YOU TOO!
WE GUARDIANS ARE RESPONSIBLE FOR PROTECTING AND DISTRIBUTING THE MIRACULOUS. FOR THE GOOD OF ALL HUMANITY.

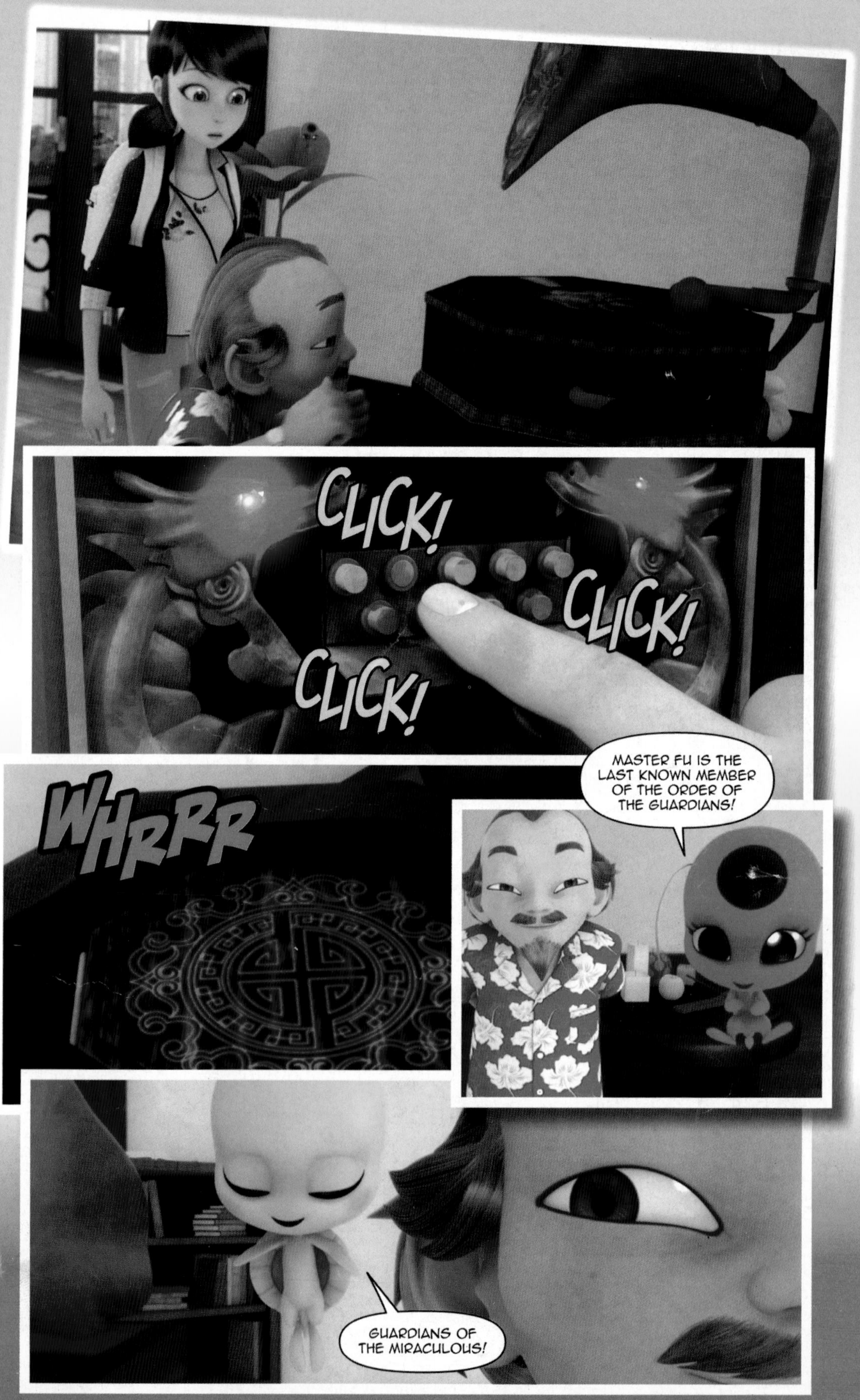
CLICK!
CLICK!
CLICK!
WHRRR
MASTER FU IS THE LAST KNOWN MEMBER OF THE ORDER OF THE GUARDIANS!
GUARDIANS OF THE MIRACULOUS!

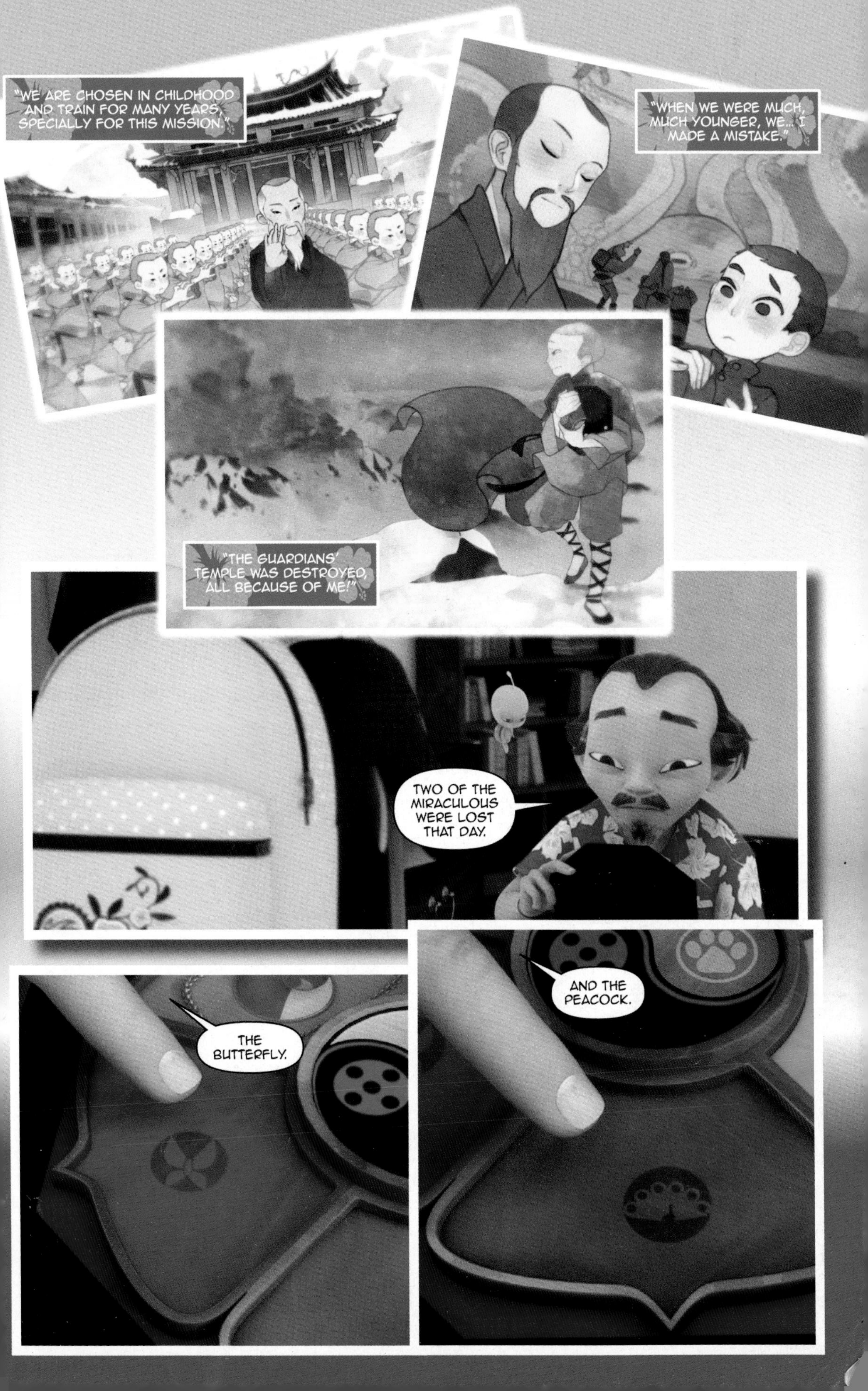
"WE ARE CHOSEN IN CHILDHOOD AND TRAIN FOR MANY YEARS, SPECIALLY FOR THIS MISSION."
"WHEN WE WERE MUCH, MUCH YOUNGER, WE... I MADE A MISTAKE."
"THE GUARDIANS' TEMPLE WAS DESTROYED, ALL BECAUSE OF ME!"
TWO OF THE MIRACULOUS WERE LOST THAT DAY.
THE BUTTERFLY.
AND THE PEACOCK.

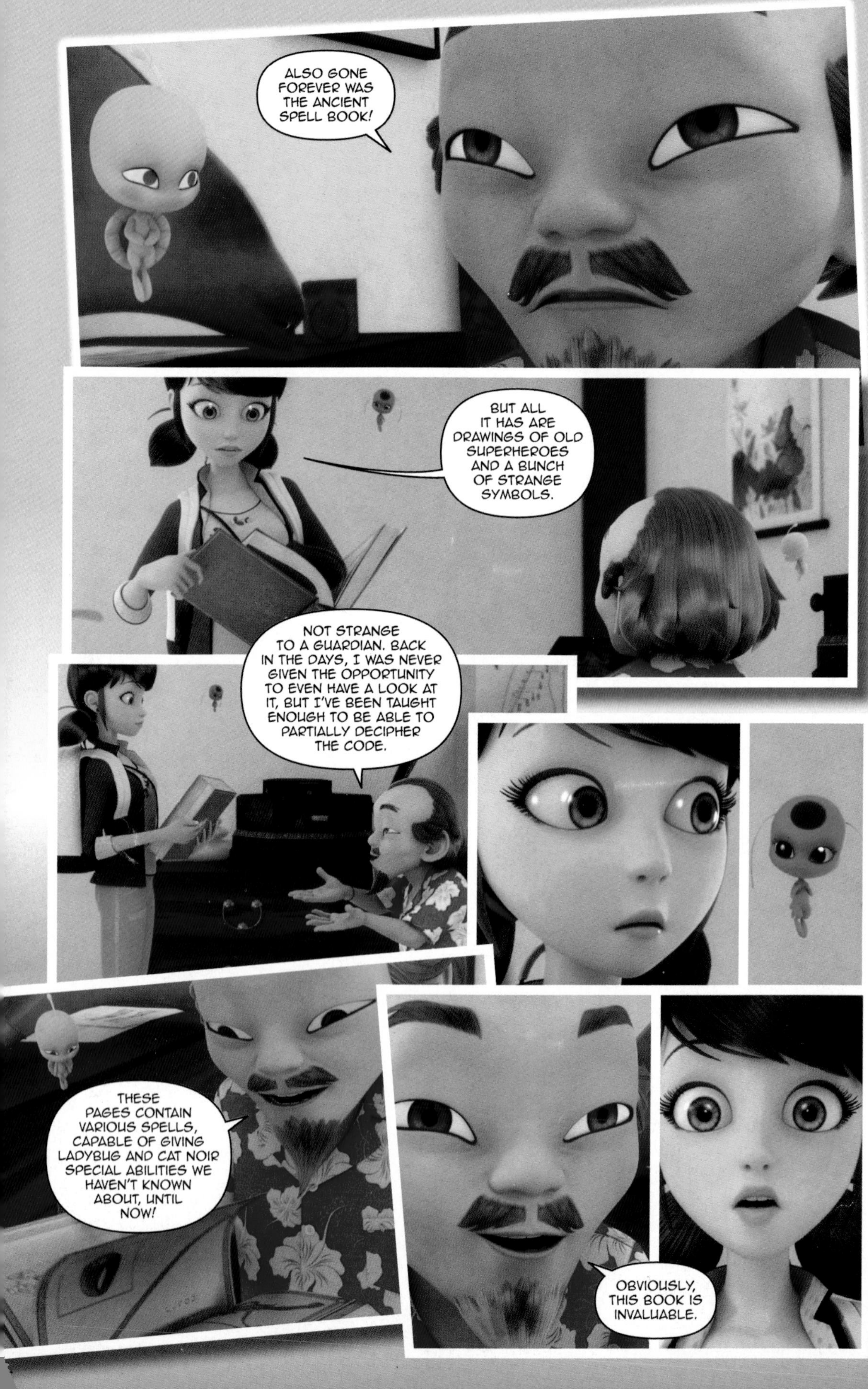
ALSO GONE FOREVER WAS THE ANCIENT SPELL BOOK!
BUT ALL IT HAS ARE DRAWINGS OF OLD SUPERHEROES AND A BUNCH OF STRANGE SYMBOLS.
NOT STRANGE TO A GUARDIAN. BACK IN THE DAYS, I WAS NEVER GIVEN THE OPPORTUNITY TO EVEN HAVE A LOOK AT IT, BUT I'VE BEEN TAUGHT ENOUGH TO BE ABLE TO PARTIALLY DECIPHER THE CODE.
THESE PAGES CONTAIN VARIOUS SPELLS, CAPABLE OF GIVING LADYBUG AND CAT NOIR SPECIAL ABILITIES WE HAVEN'T KNOWN ABOUT, UNTIL NOW!
OBVIOUSLY, THIS BOOK IS INVALUABLE.

I'VE ALWAYS BELIEVED THAT WHOEVER POSSESSED THIS SPELL BOOK MUST ALSO HAVE THE PEACOCK AND THE BUTTERFLY MIRACULOUS.

WAIT A SEC...

...YOU MEAN WHOEVER OWNED THE SPELL BOOK COULD BE HAWK MOTH?

HOW DID YOU DISCOVER THIS BOOK, MARINETTE?

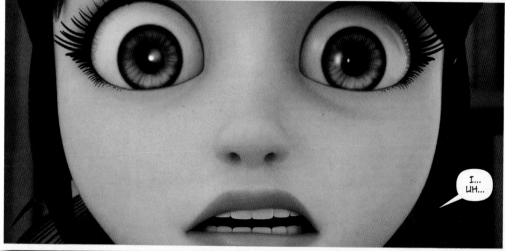

I... UH...

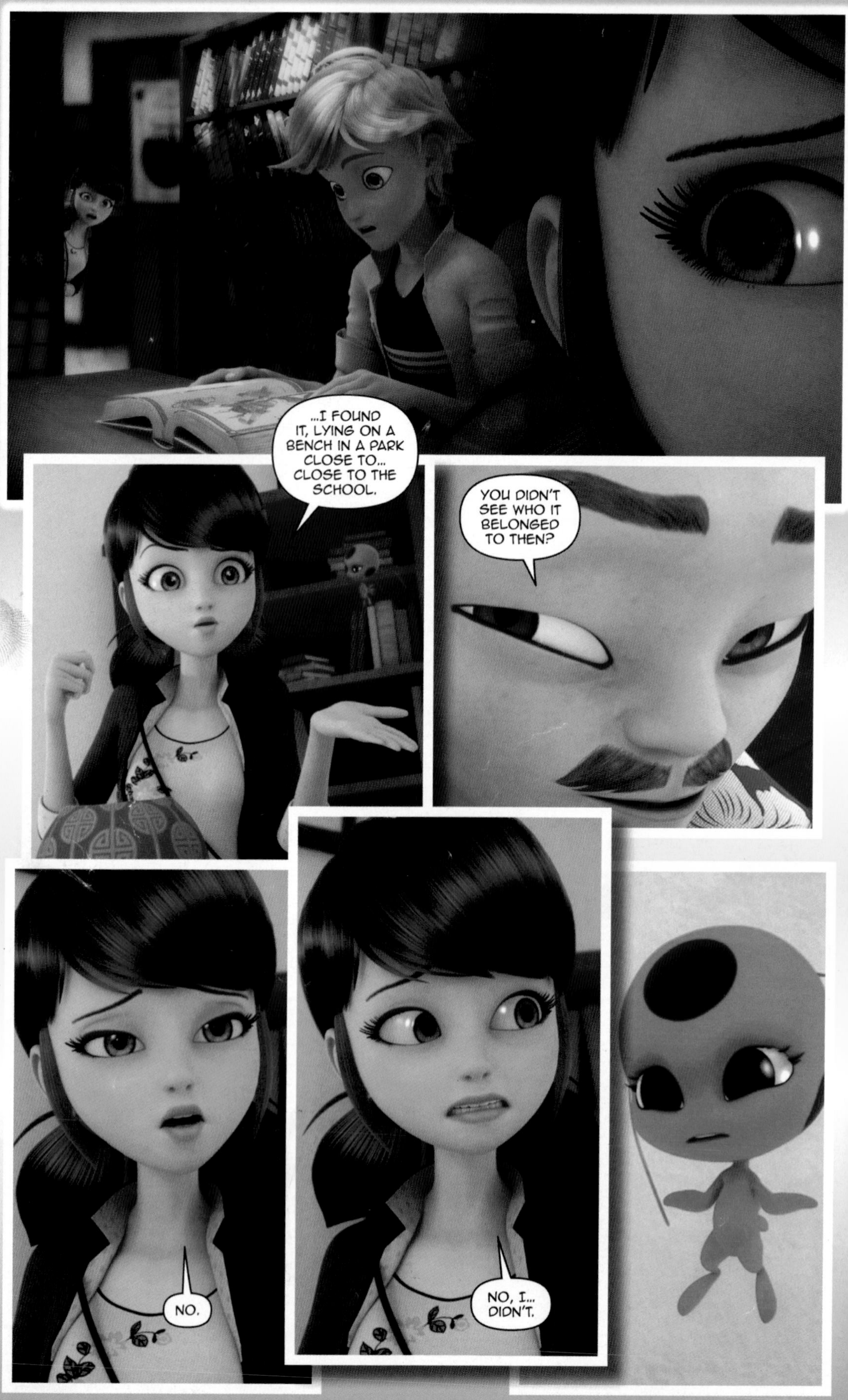
...I FOUND IT, LYING ON A BENCH IN A PARK CLOSE TO... CLOSE TO THE SCHOOL.
YOU DIDN'T SEE WHO IT BELONGED TO THEN?
NO.
NO, I... DIDN'T.

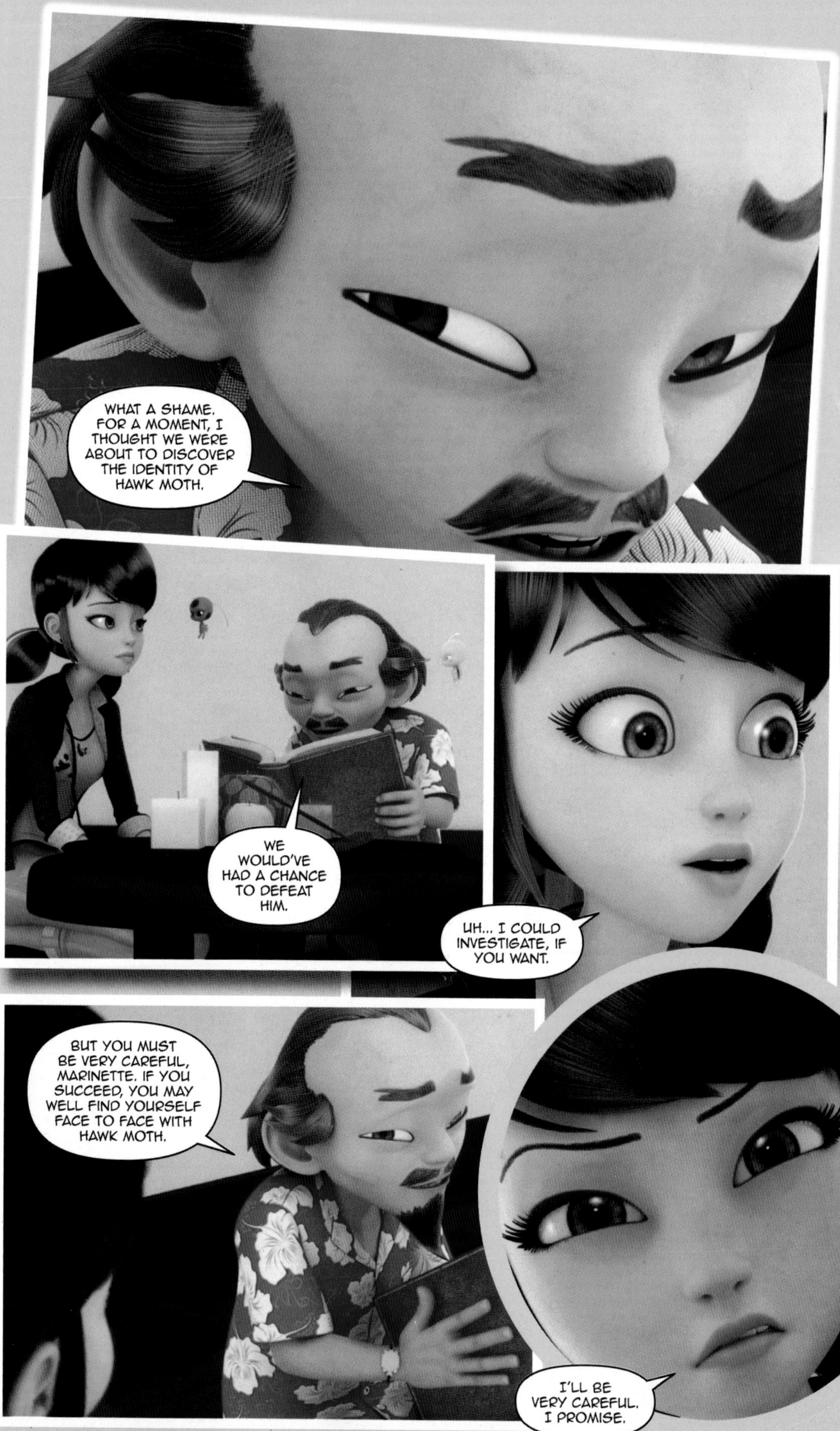
WHAT A SHAME. FOR A MOMENT, I THOUGHT WE WERE ABOUT TO DISCOVER THE IDENTITY OF HAWK MOTH.
WE WOULD'VE HAD A CHANCE TO DEFEAT HIM.
UH... I COULD INVESTIGATE, IF YOU WANT.
BUT YOU MUST BE VERY CAREFUL, MARINETTE. IF YOU SUCCEED, YOU MAY WELL FIND YOURSELF FACE TO FACE WITH HAWK MOTH.
I'LL BE VERY CAREFUL. I PROMISE.

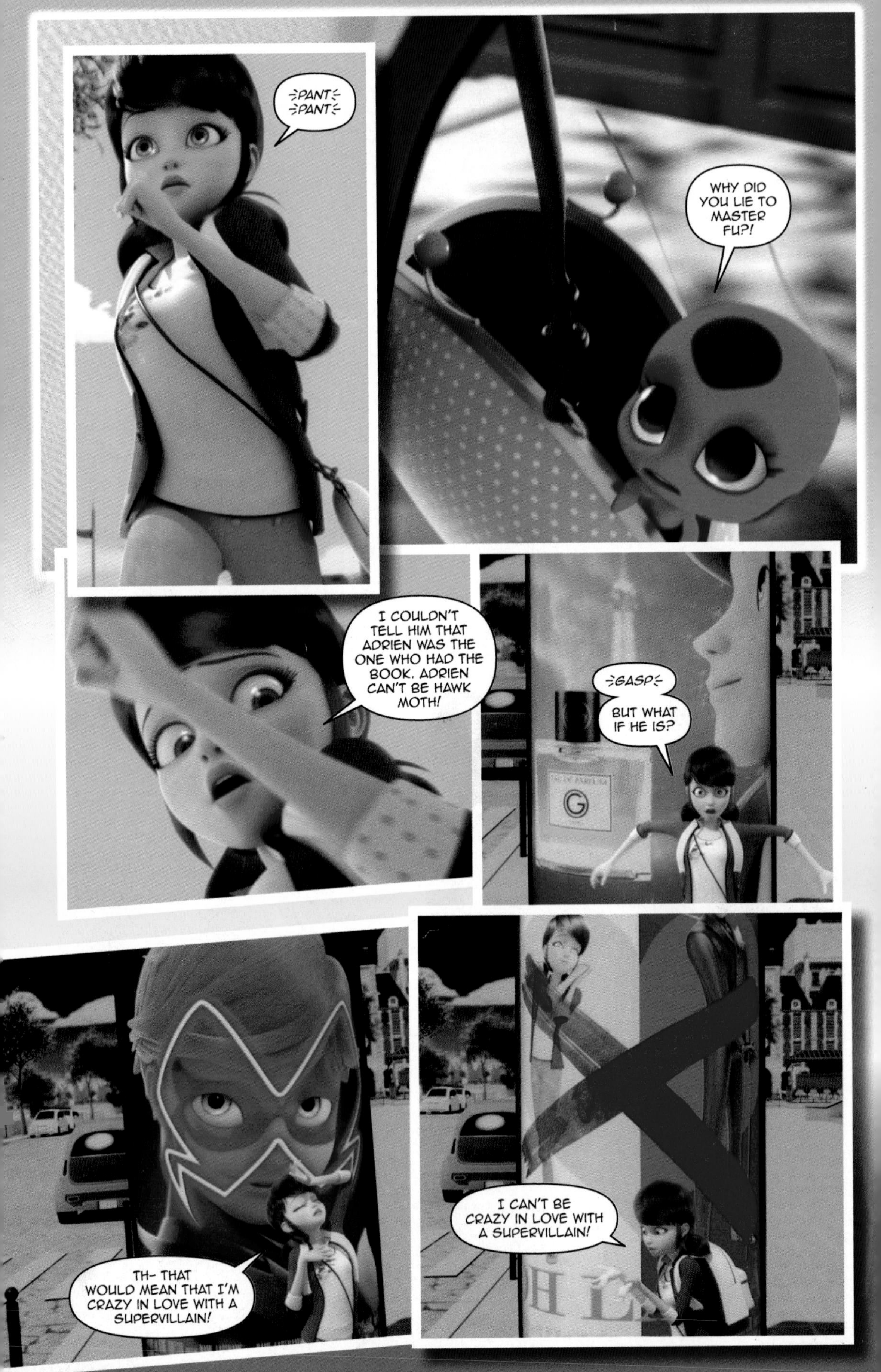
PANT PANT
WHY DID YOU LIE TO MASTER FU?!
I COULDN'T TELL HIM THAT ADRIEN WAS THE ONE WHO HAD THE BOOK. ADRIEN CAN'T BE HAWK MOTH!
GASP
BUT WHAT IF HE IS?
EAU DE PARFUM
TH- THAT WOULD MEAN THAT I'M CRAZY IN LOVE WITH A SUPERVILLAIN!
I CAN'T BE CRAZY IN LOVE WITH A SUPERVILLAIN!

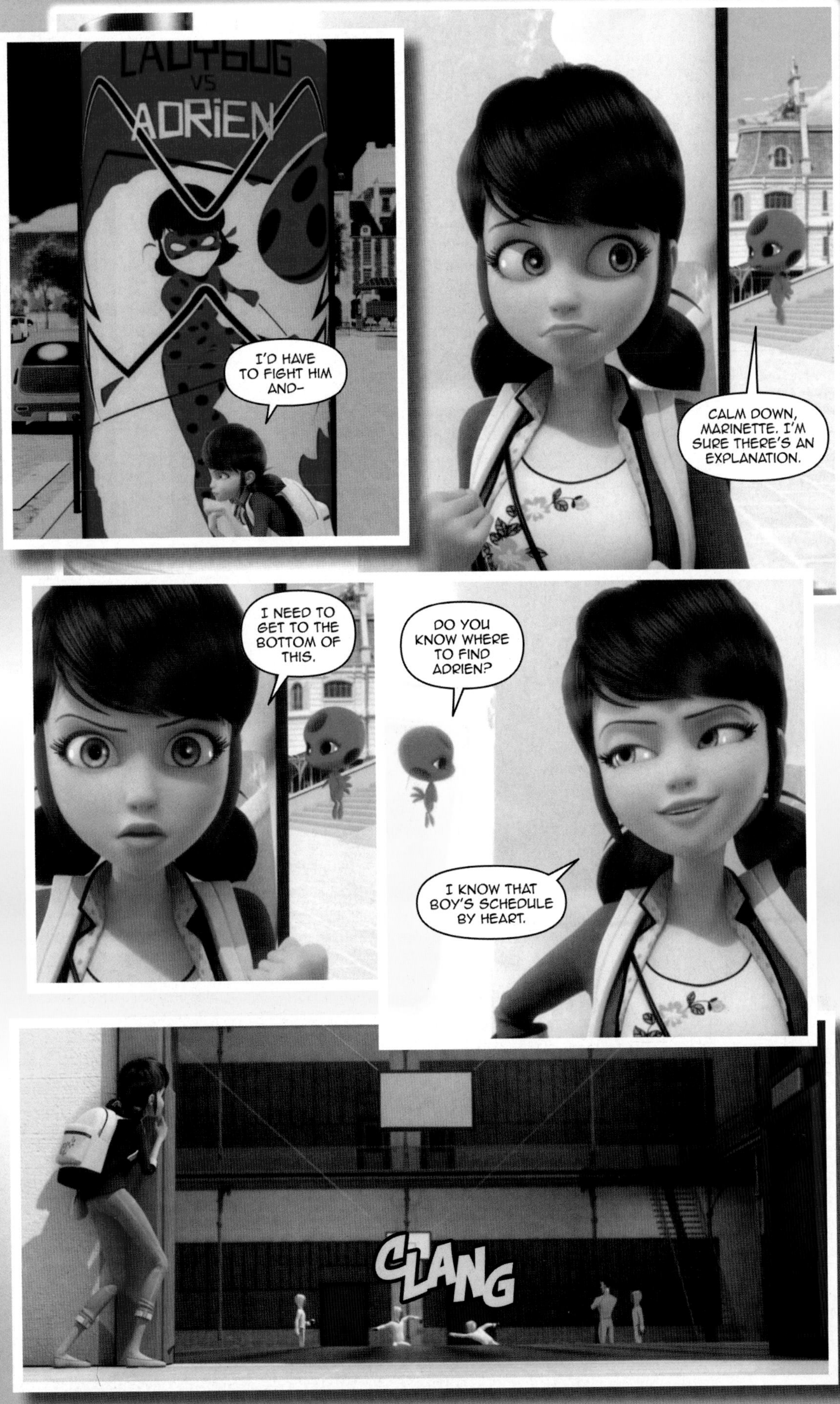
LADYBUG VS ADRIEN
I'D HAVE TO FIGHT HIM AND-
CALM DOWN, MARINETTE. I'M SURE THERE'S AN EXPLANATION.
I NEED TO GET TO THE BOTTOM OF THIS.
DO YOU KNOW WHERE TO FIND ADRIEN?
I KNOW THAT BOY'S SCHEDULE BY HEART.
CLANG

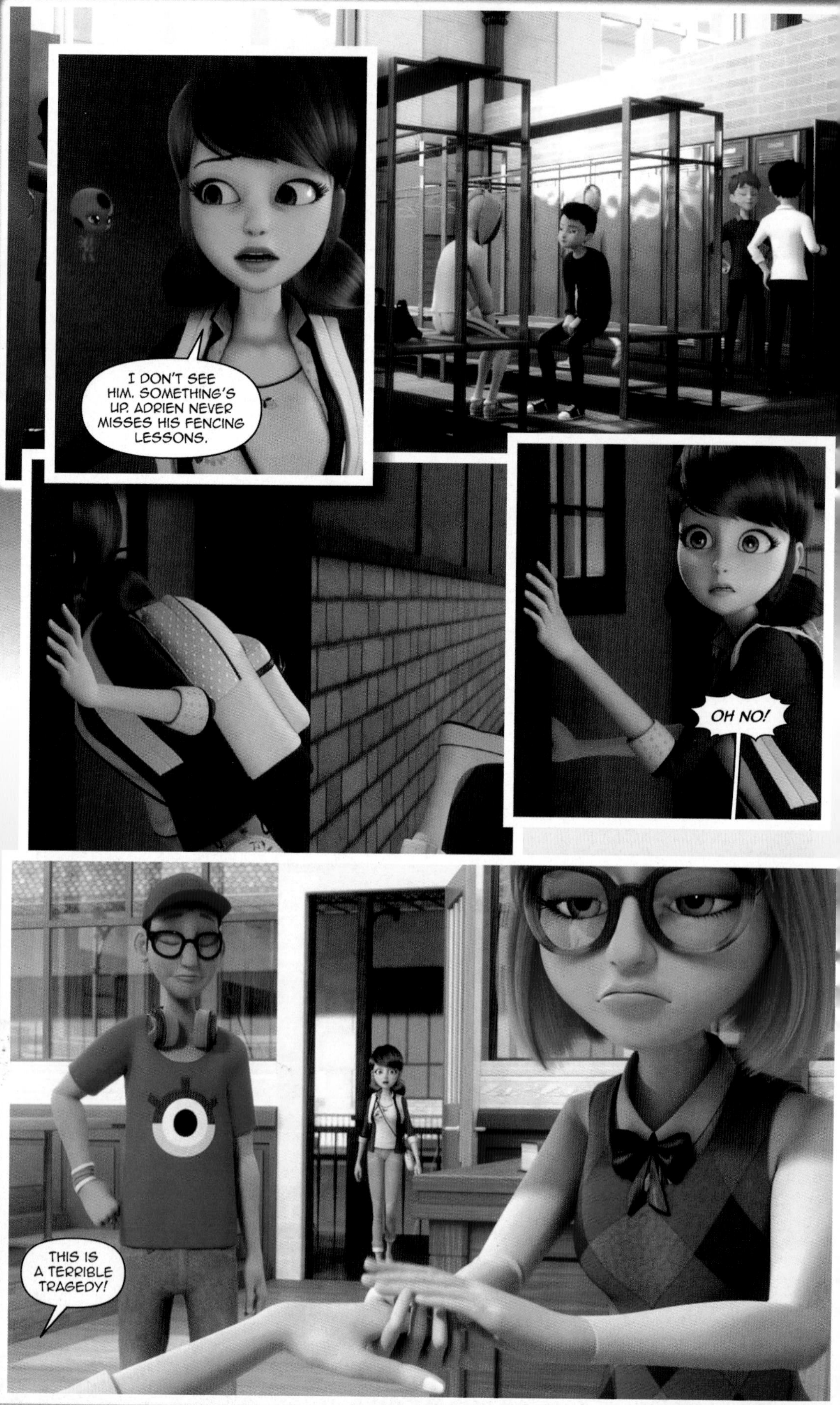
I DON'T SEE HIM. SOMETHING'S UP. ADRIEN NEVER MISSES HIS FENCING LESSONS.
OH NO!
THIS IS A TERRIBLE TRAGEDY!

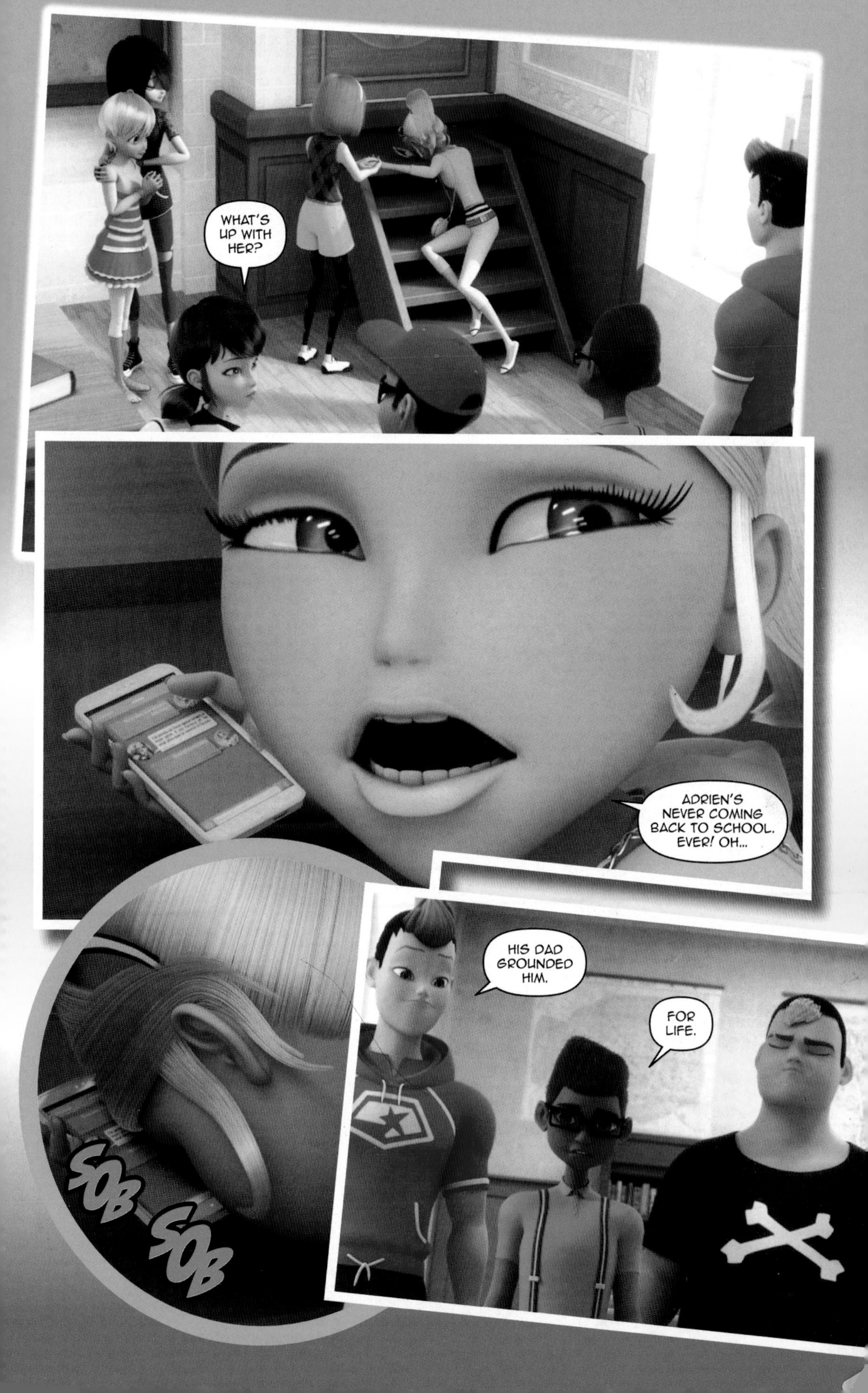
WHAT'S UP WITH HER?
ADRIEN'S NEVER COMING BACK TO SCHOOL. EVER! OH...
SOB SOB
HIS DAD GROUNDED HIM.
FOR LIFE.

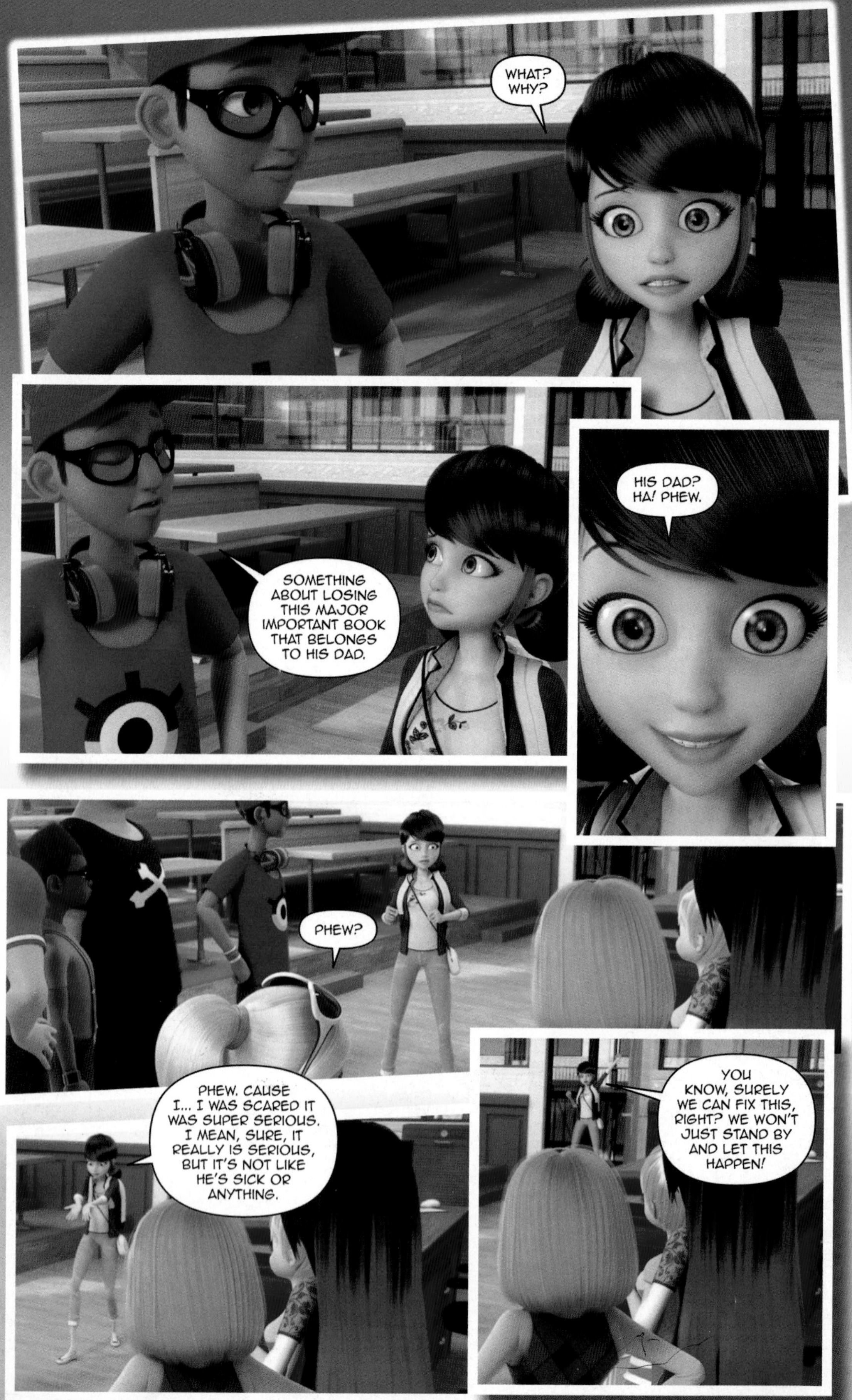
WHAT? WHY?
SOMETHING ABOUT LOSING THIS MAJOR IMPORTANT BOOK THAT BELONGS TO HIS DAD.
HIS DAD? HA! PHEW.
PHEW?
PHEW. CAUSE I... I WAS SCARED IT WAS SUPER SERIOUS. I MEAN, SURE, IT REALLY IS SERIOUS, BUT IT'S NOT LIKE HE'S SICK OR ANYTHING.
YOU KNOW, SURELY WE CAN FIX THIS, RIGHT? WE WON'T JUST STAND BY AND LET THIS HAPPEN!

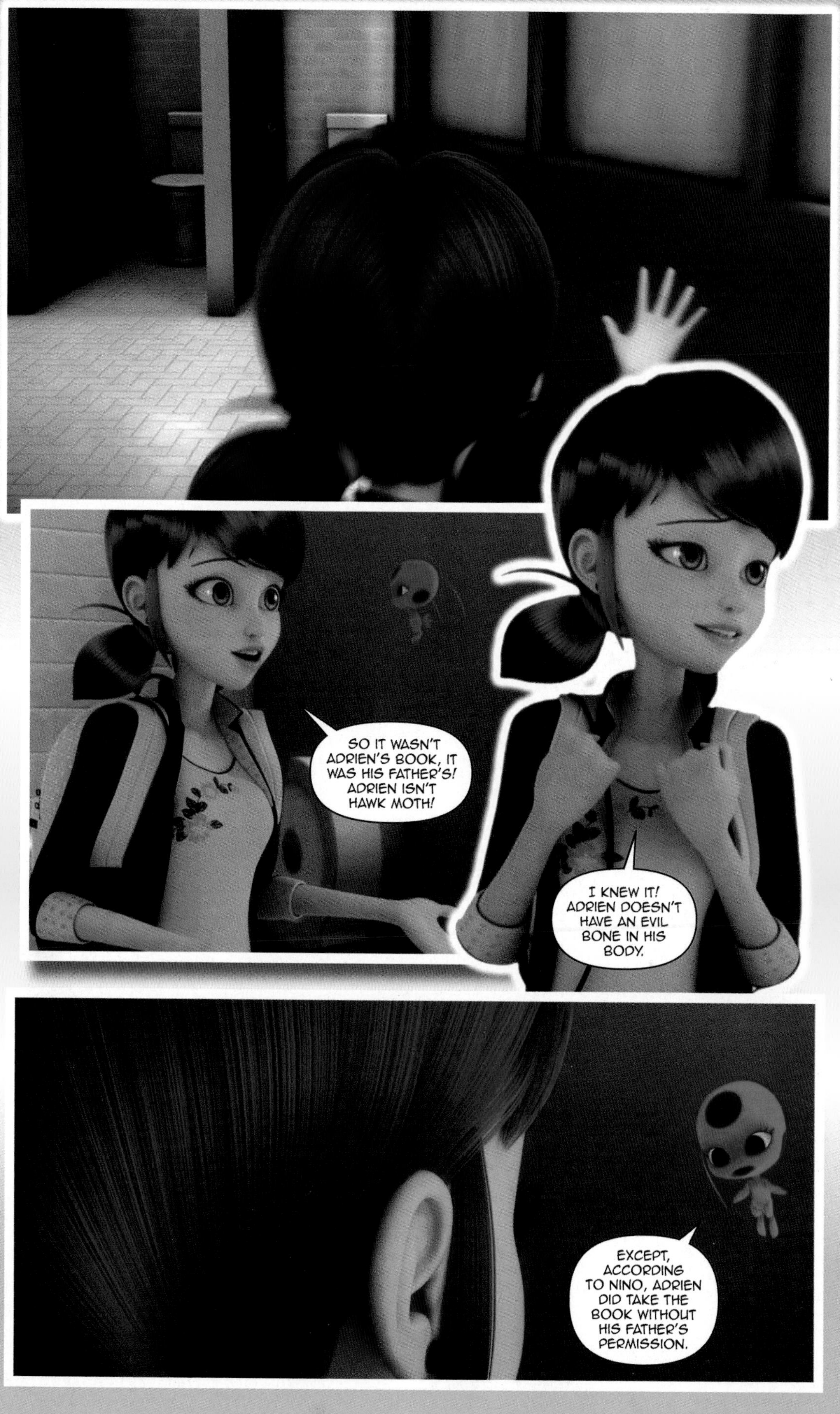
SO IT WASN'T ADRIEN'S BOOK, IT WAS HIS FATHER'S! ADRIEN ISN'T HAWK MOTH!
I KNEW IT! ADRIEN DOESN'T HAVE AN EVIL BONE IN HIS BODY.
EXCEPT, ACCORDING TO NINO, ADRIEN DID TAKE THE BOOK WITHOUT HIS FATHER'S PERMISSION.

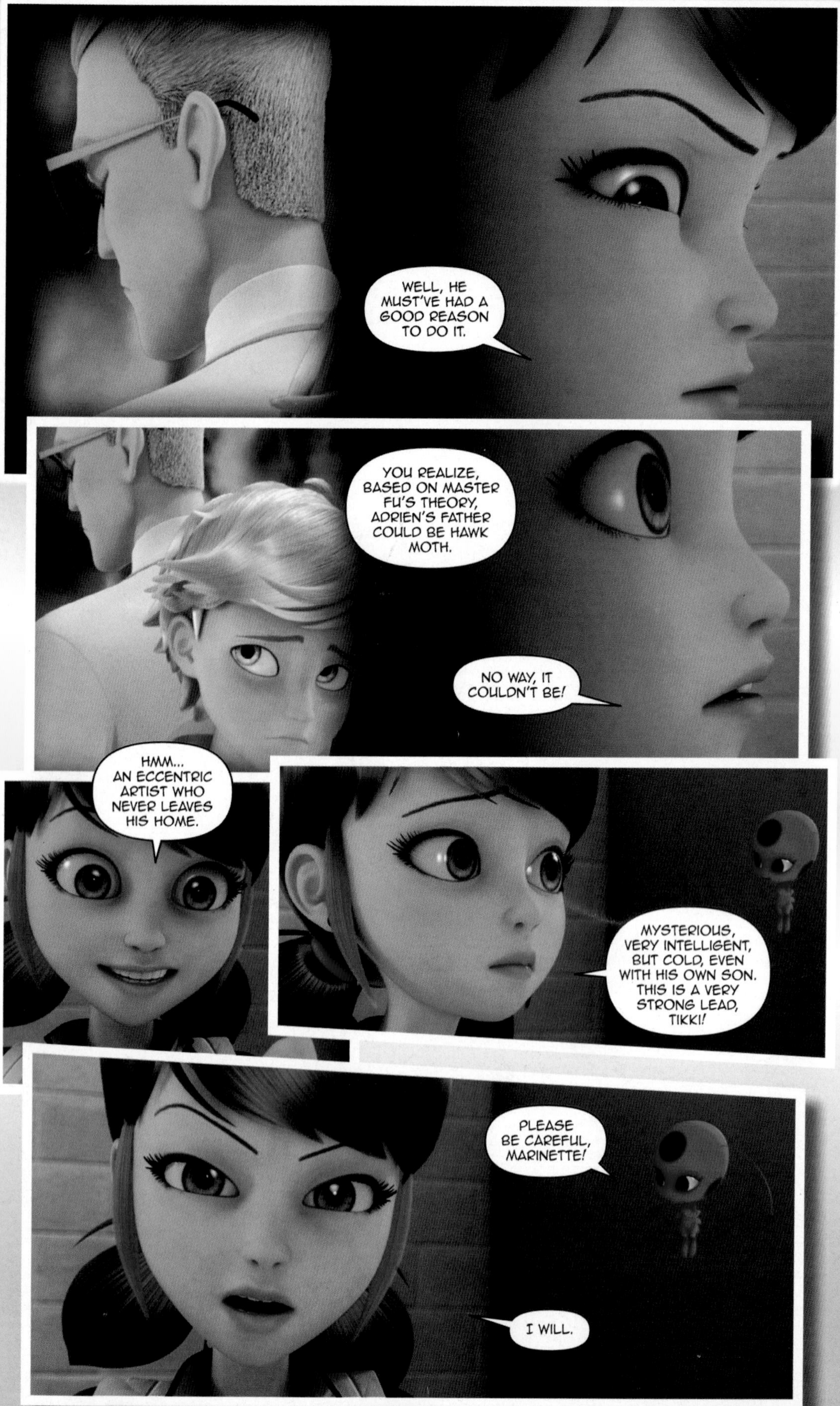
WELL, HE MUST'VE HAD A GOOD REASON TO DO IT.
YOU REALIZE, BASED ON MASTER FU'S THEORY, ADRIEN'S FATHER COULD BE HAWK MOTH.
NO WAY, IT COULDN'T BE!
HMM... AN ECCENTRIC ARTIST WHO NEVER LEAVES HIS HOME.
MYSTERIOUS, VERY INTELLIGENT, BUT COLD, EVEN WITH HIS OWN SON. THIS IS A VERY STRONG LEAD, TIKKI!
PLEASE BE CAREFUL, MARINETTE!
I WILL.

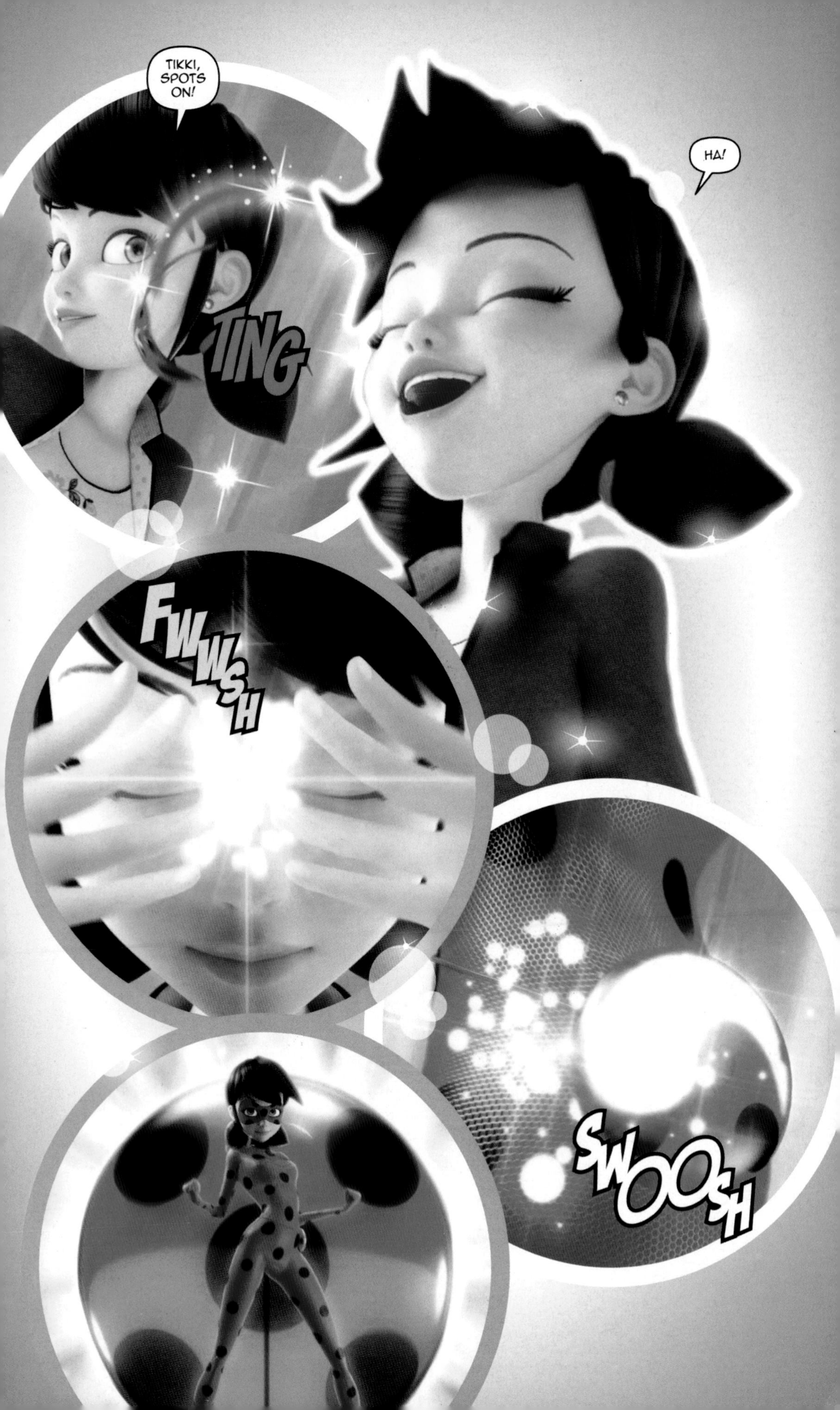
TIKKI, SPOTS ON!
TING
HA!
FWWSH
SWOOSH

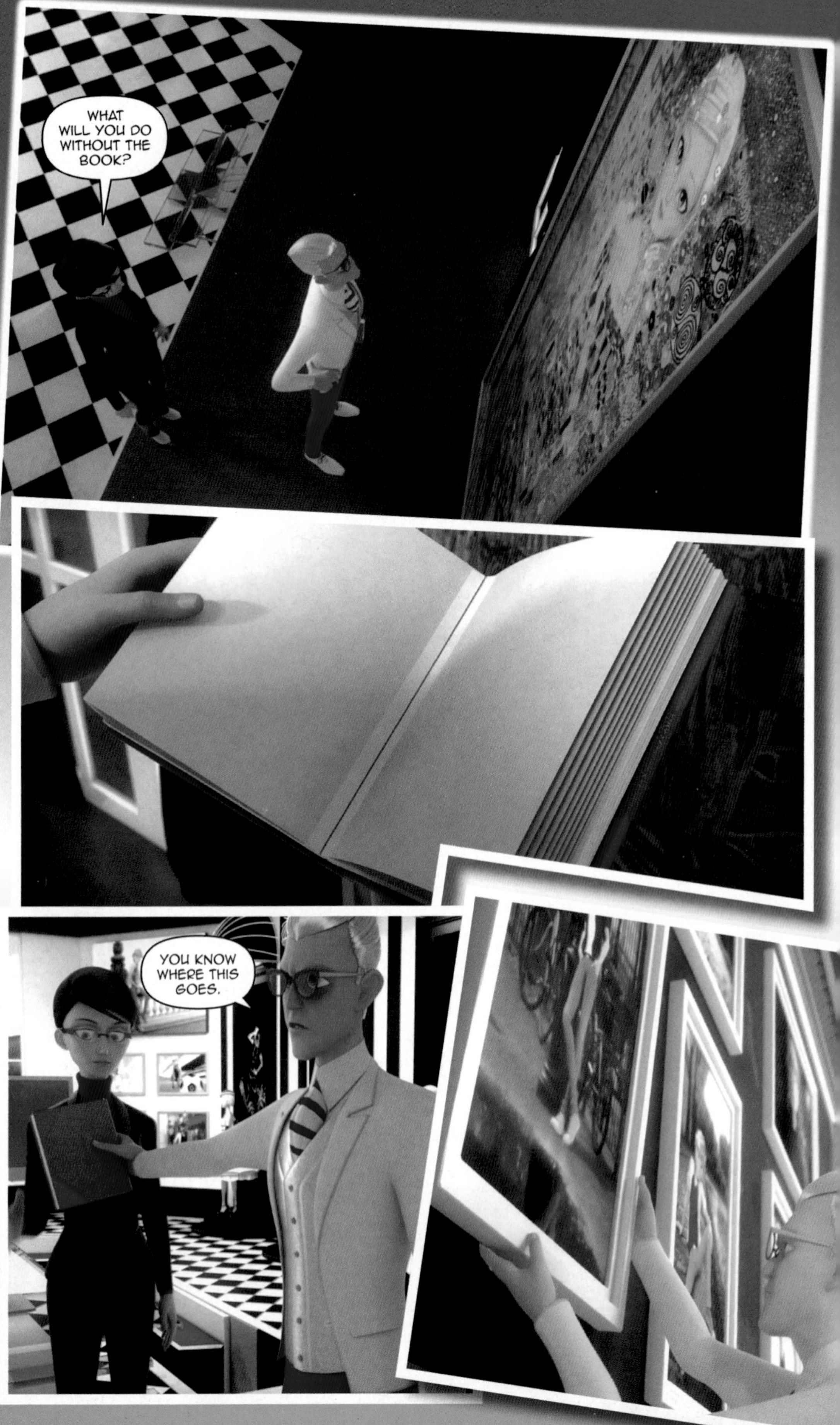
WHAT WILL YOU DO WITHOUT THE BOOK?
YOU KNOW WHERE THIS GOES.

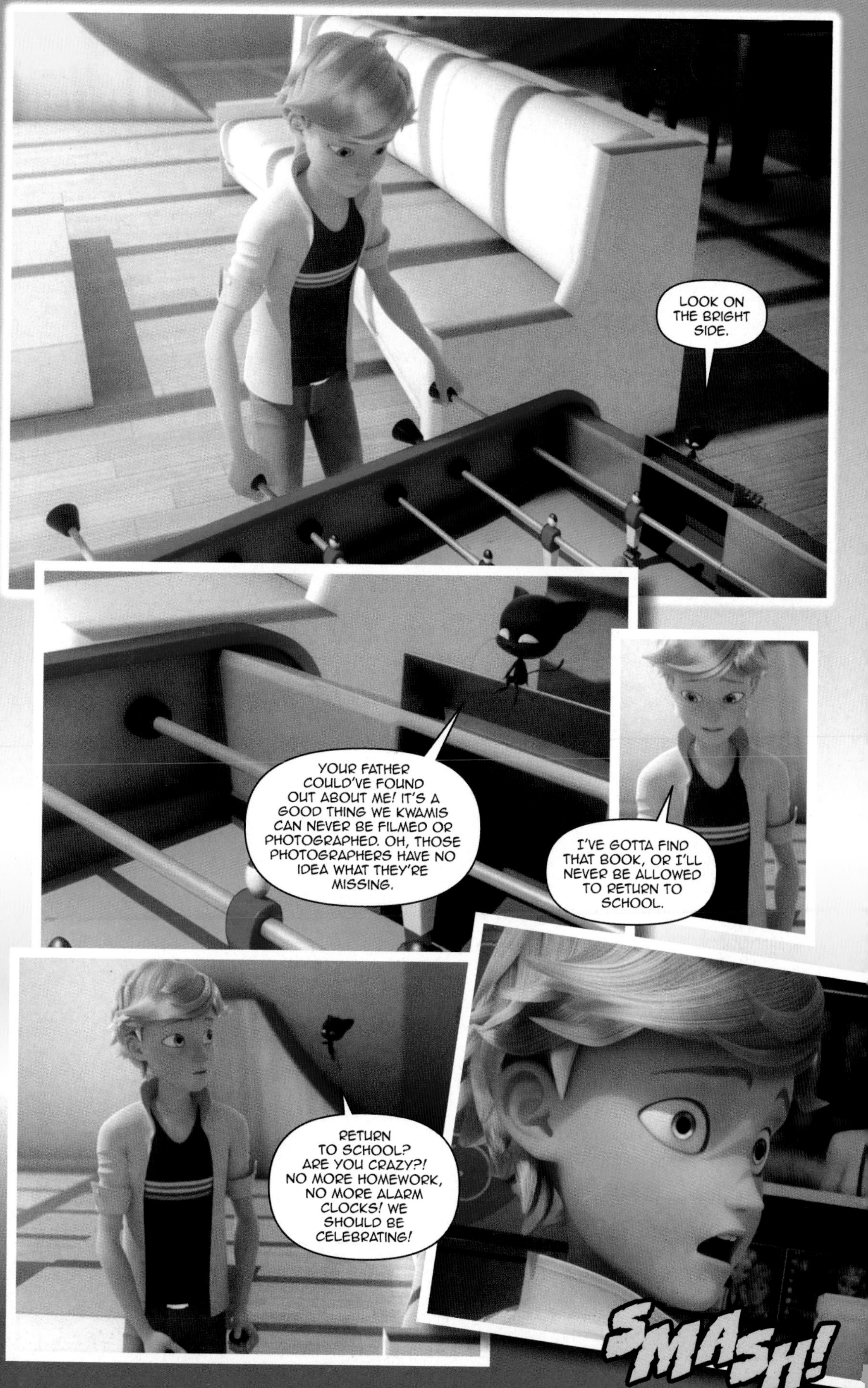
LOOK ON THE BRIGHT SIDE.
YOUR FATHER COULD'VE FOUND OUT ABOUT ME! IT'S A GOOD THING WE KWAMIS CAN NEVER BE FILMED OR PHOTOGRAPHED. OH, THOSE PHOTOGRAPHERS HAVE NO IDEA WHAT THEY'RE MISSING.
I'VE GOTTA FIND THAT BOOK, OR I'LL NEVER BE ALLOWED TO RETURN TO SCHOOL.
RETURN TO SCHOOL? ARE YOU CRAZY?! NO MORE HOMEWORK, NO MORE ALARM CLOCKS! WE SHOULD BE CELEBRATING!
SMASH!

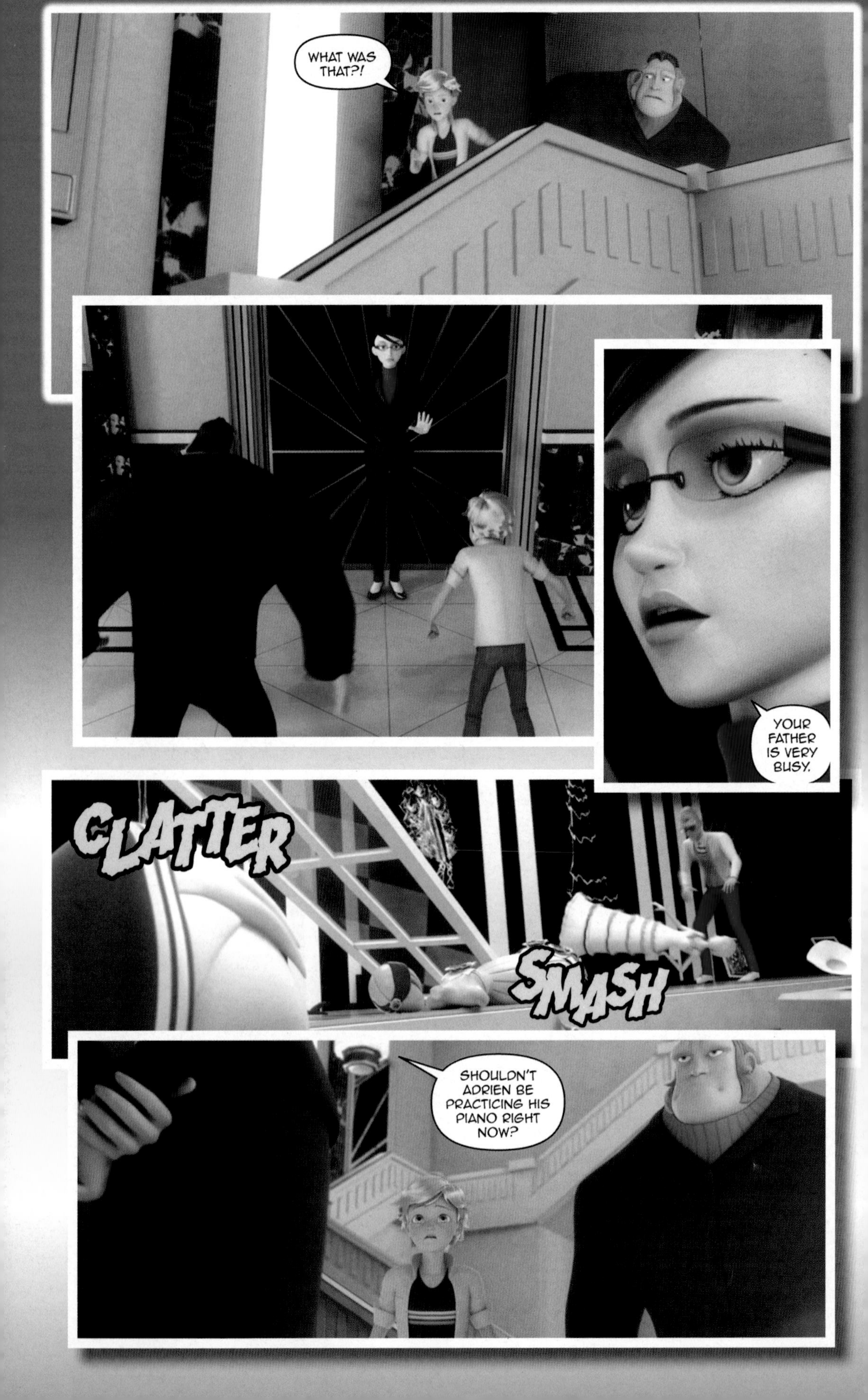
WHAT WAS THAT?!
YOUR FATHER IS VERY BUSY.
CLATTER
SMASH
SHOULDN'T ADRIEN BE PRACTICING HIS PIANO RIGHT NOW?

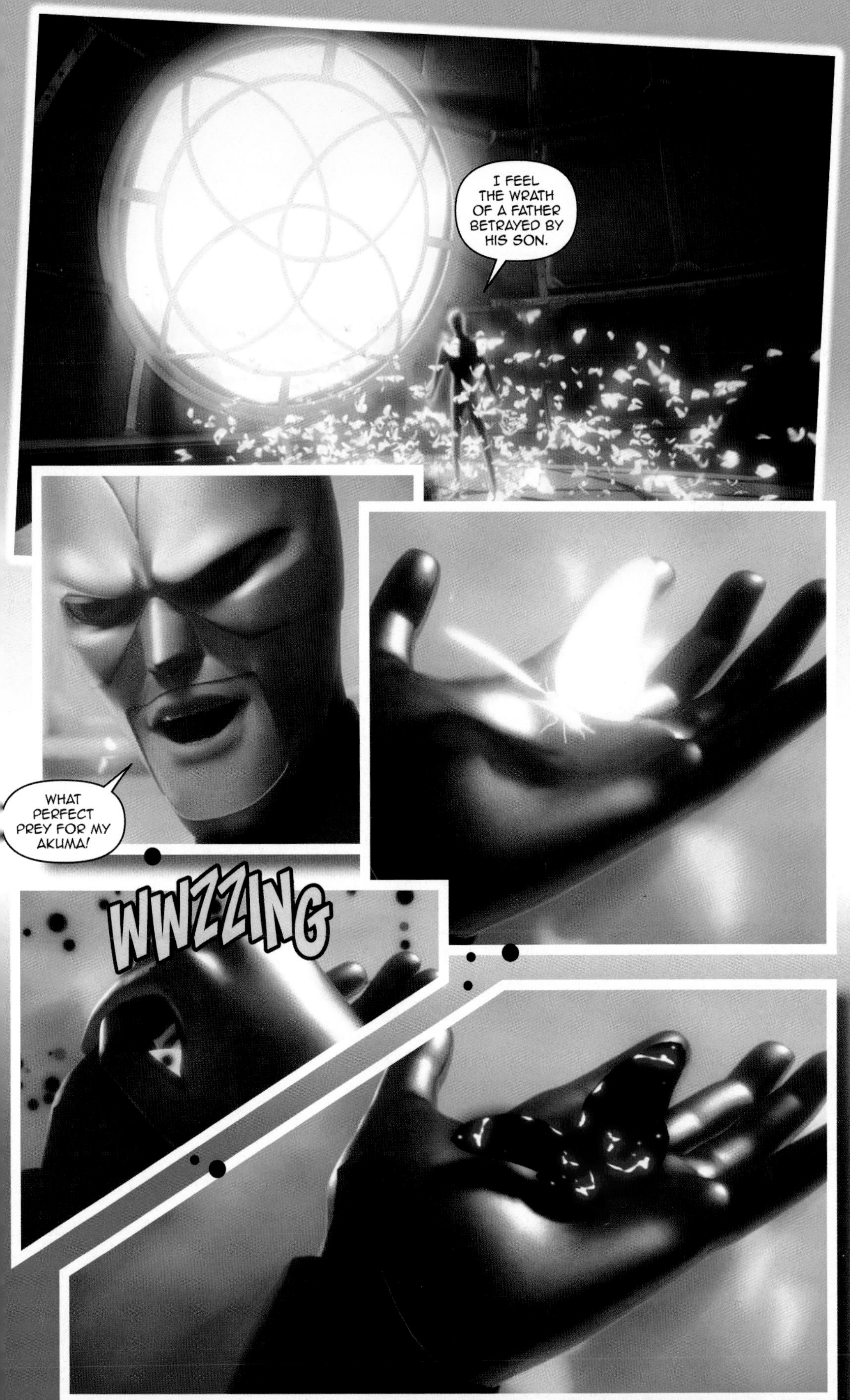
I FEEL THE WRATH OF A FATHER BETRAYED BY HIS SON.
WHAT PERFECT PREY FOR MY AKUMA!
WWZZING

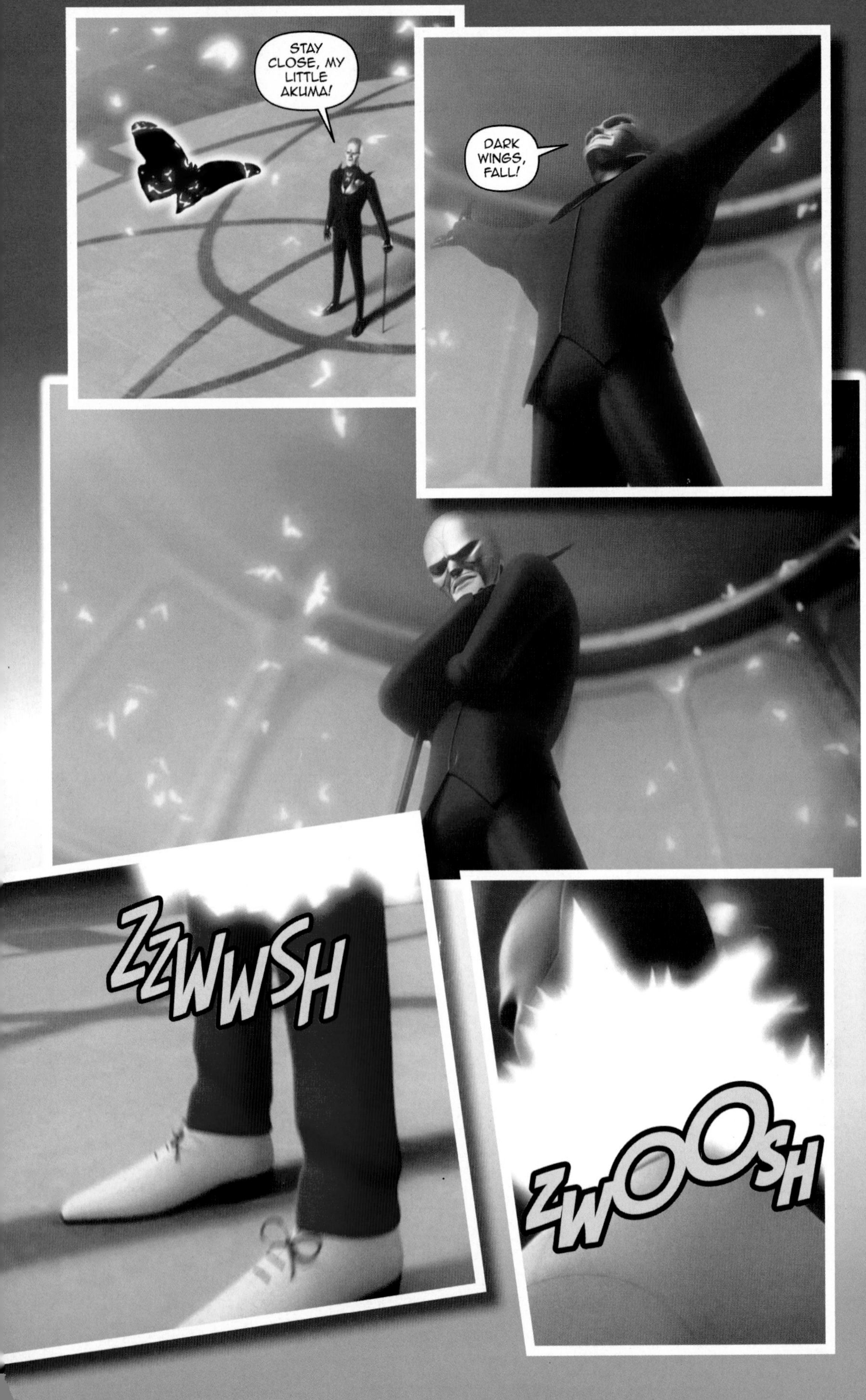
STAY CLOSE, MY LITTLE AKUMA!
DARK WINGS, FALL!
ZZWWSH
ZWOOSH

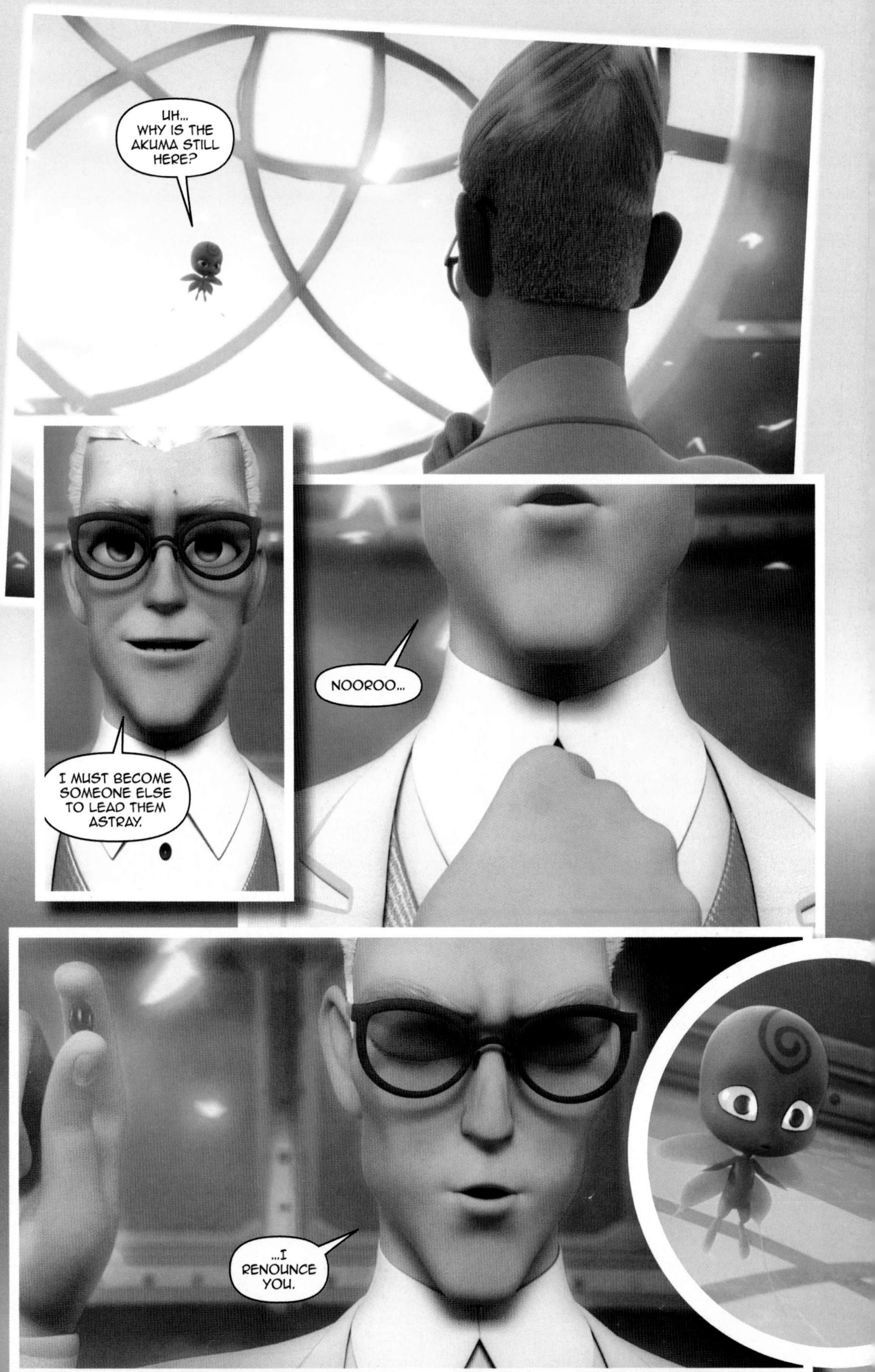
UH... WHY IS THE AKUMA STILL HERE?
I MUST BECOME SOMEONE ELSE TO LEAD THEM ASTRAY.
NOOROO...
...I RENOUNCE YOU.

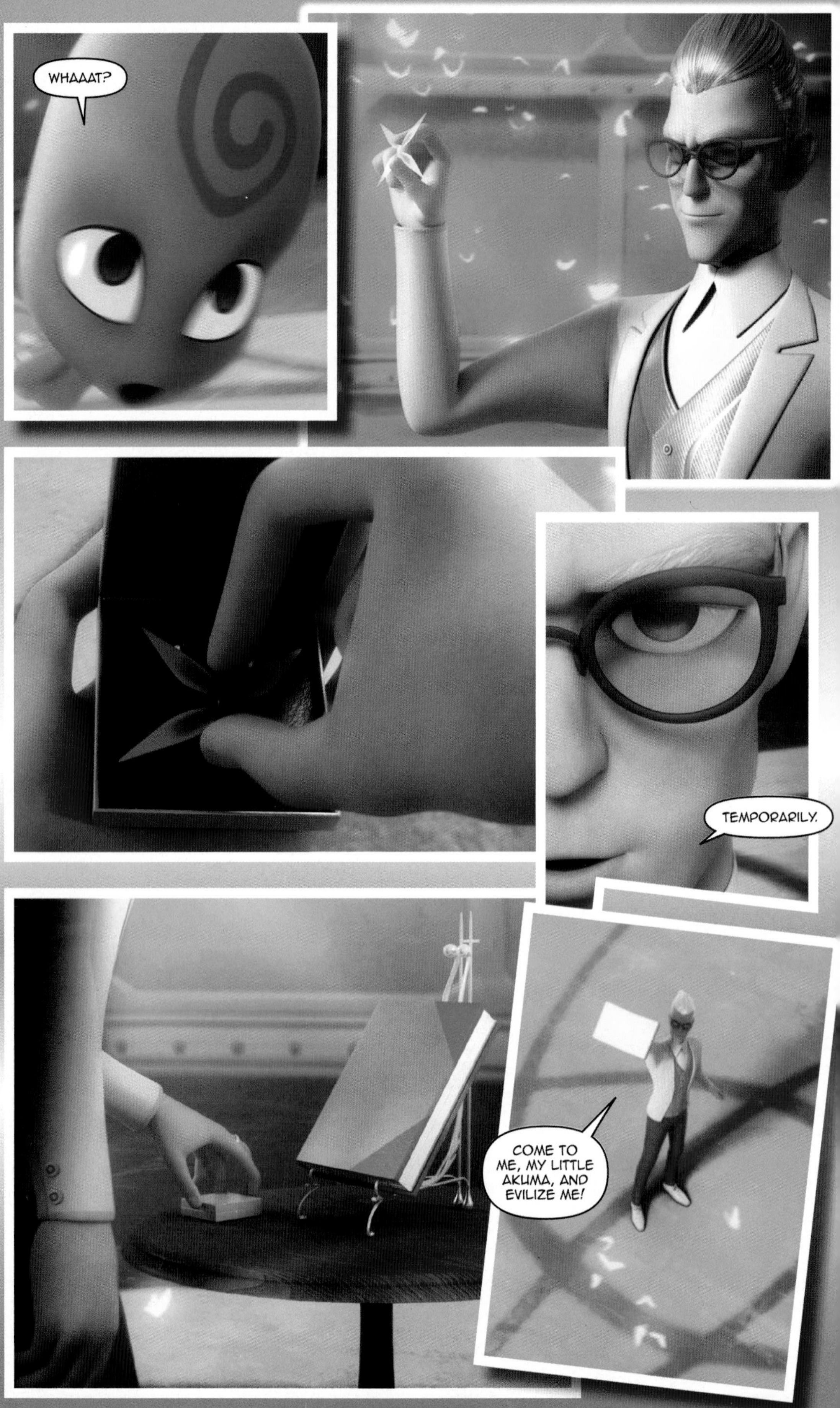
WHAAAT?
TEMPORARILY.
COME TO ME, MY LITTLE AKUMA, AND EVILIZE ME!

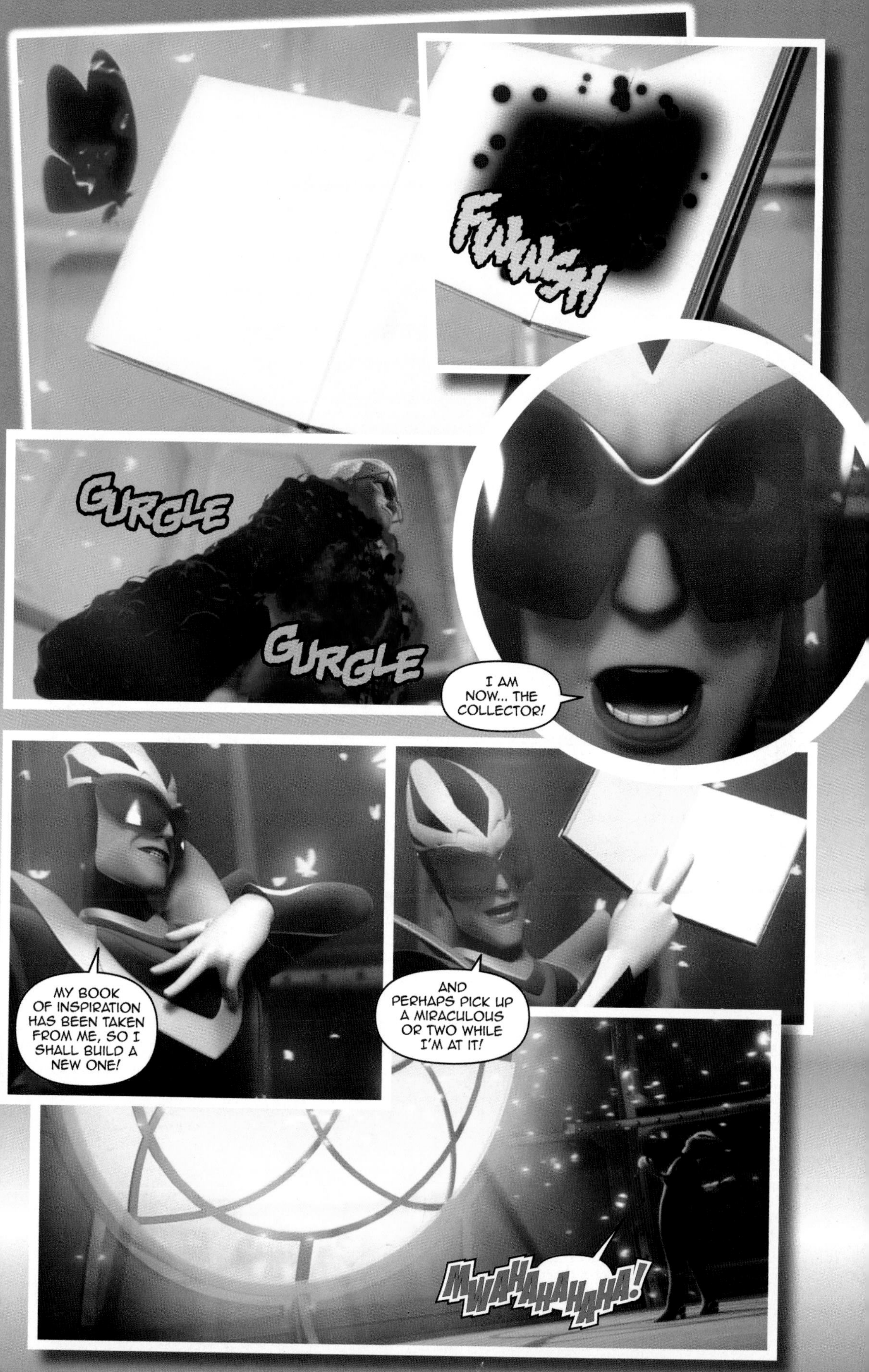
FWWSH
GURGLE
GURGLE
I AM NOW... THE COLLECTOR!
MY BOOK OF INSPIRATION HAS BEEN TAKEN FROM ME, SO I SHALL BUILD A NEW ONE!
AND PERHAPS PICK UP A MIRACULOUS OR TWO WHILE I'M AT IT!
MWAHAHAHAHAHA!

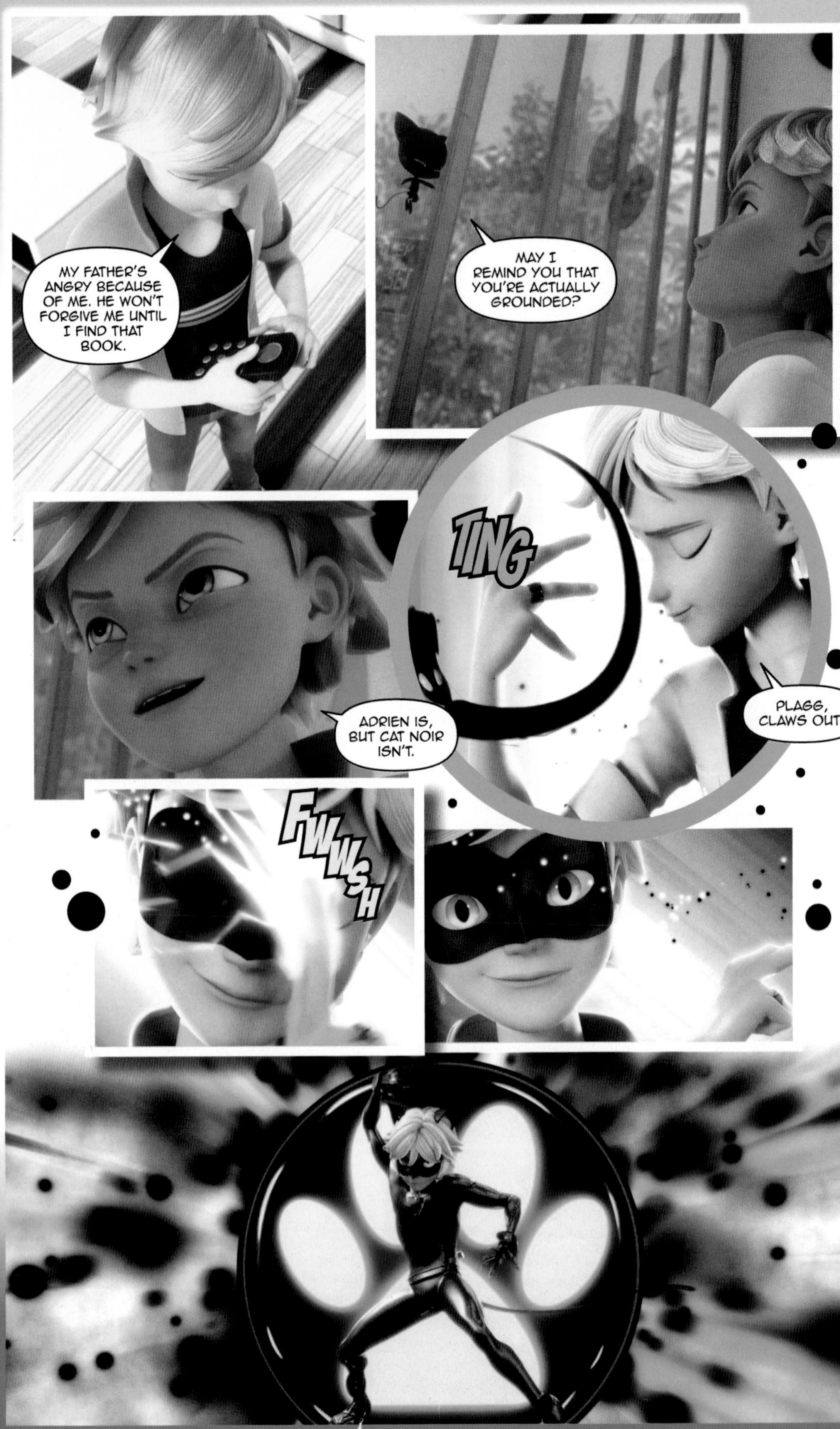
MY FATHER'S ANGRY BECAUSE OF ME. HE WON'T FORGIVE ME UNTIL I FIND THAT BOOK.
MAY I REMIND YOU THAT YOU'RE ACTUALLY GROUNDED?
ADRIEN IS, BUT CAT NOIR ISN'T.
TING
PLAGG, CLAWS OUT!
FWWSH

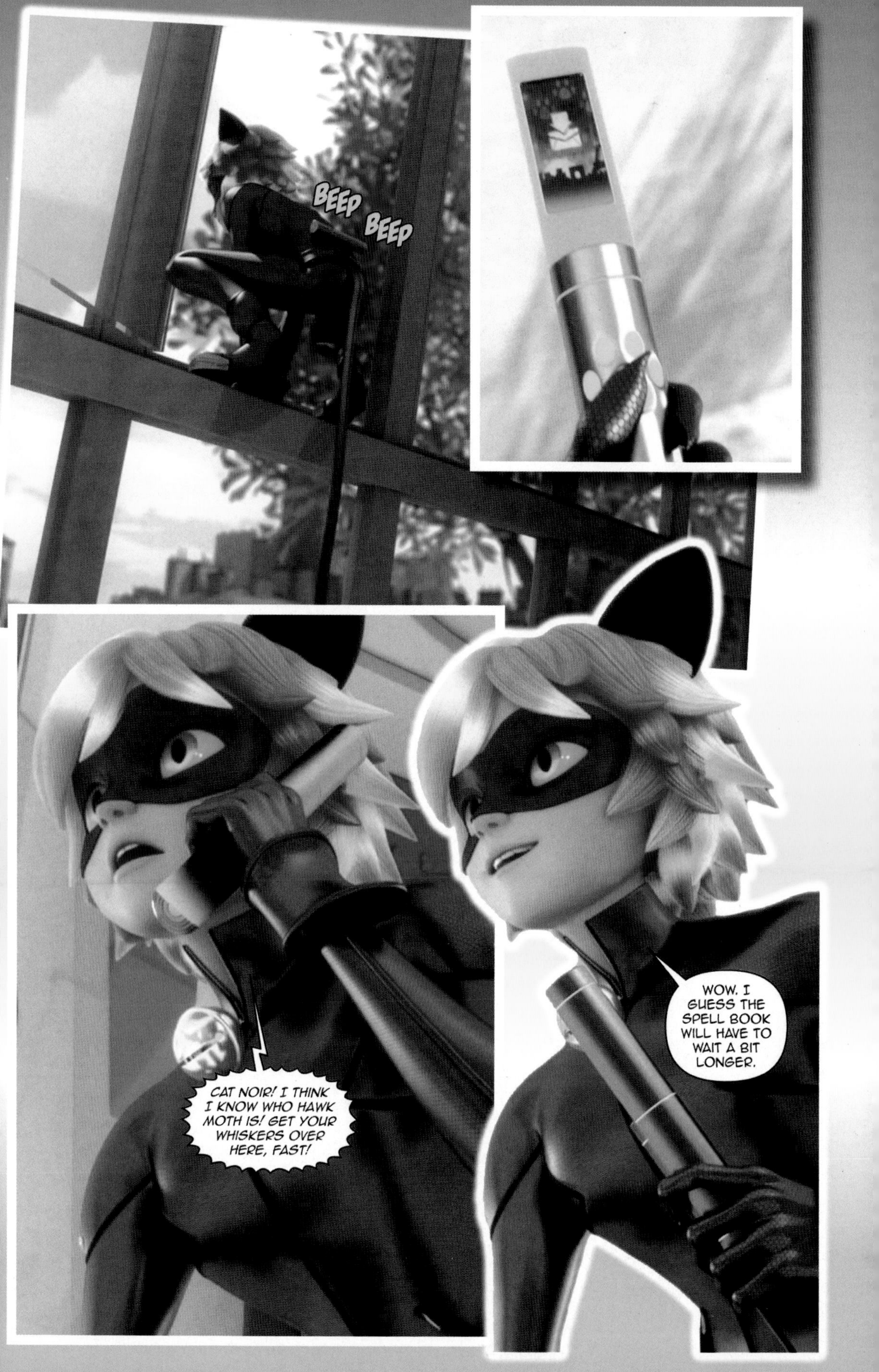
BEEP
BEEP
CAT NOIR! I THINK I KNOW WHO HAWK MOTH IS! GET YOUR WHISKERS OVER HERE, FAST!
WOW. I GUESS THE SPELL BOOK WILL HAVE TO WAIT A BIT LONGER.

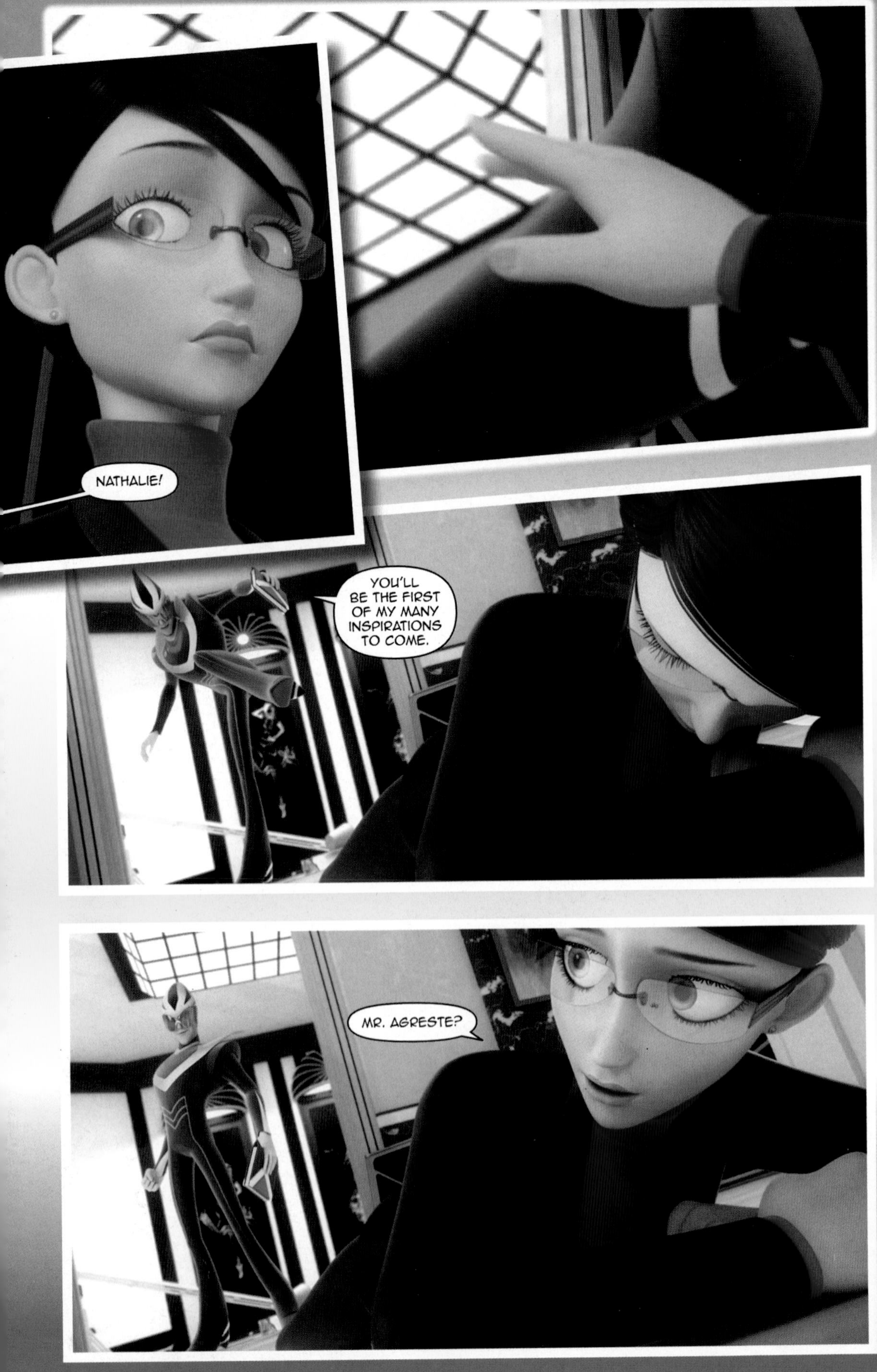
NATHALIE!
YOU'LL BE THE FIRST OF MY MANY INSPIRATIONS TO COME.
MR. AGRESTE?

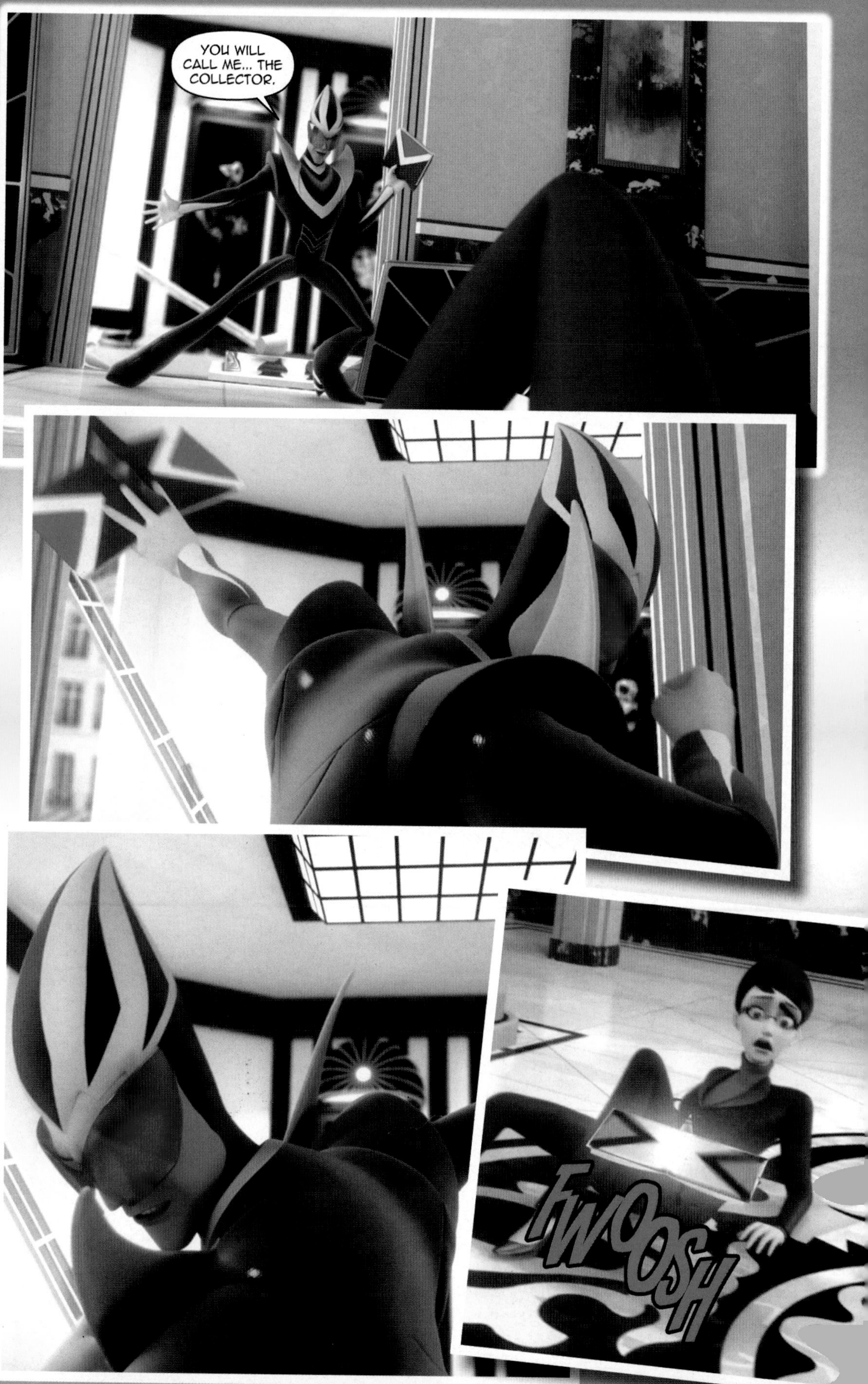
YOU WILL CALL ME... THE COLLECTOR.
FWOOSH

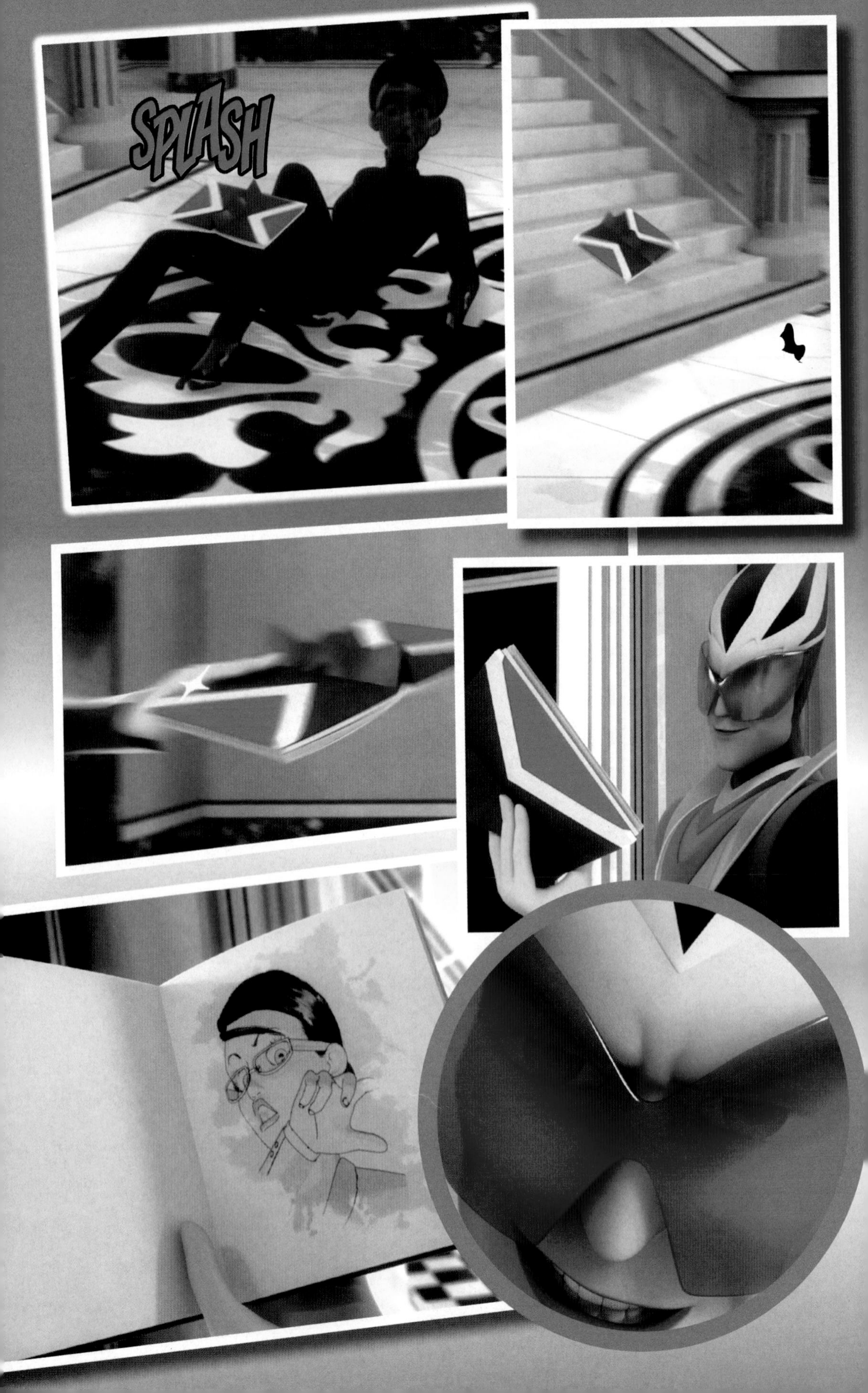
SPLASH

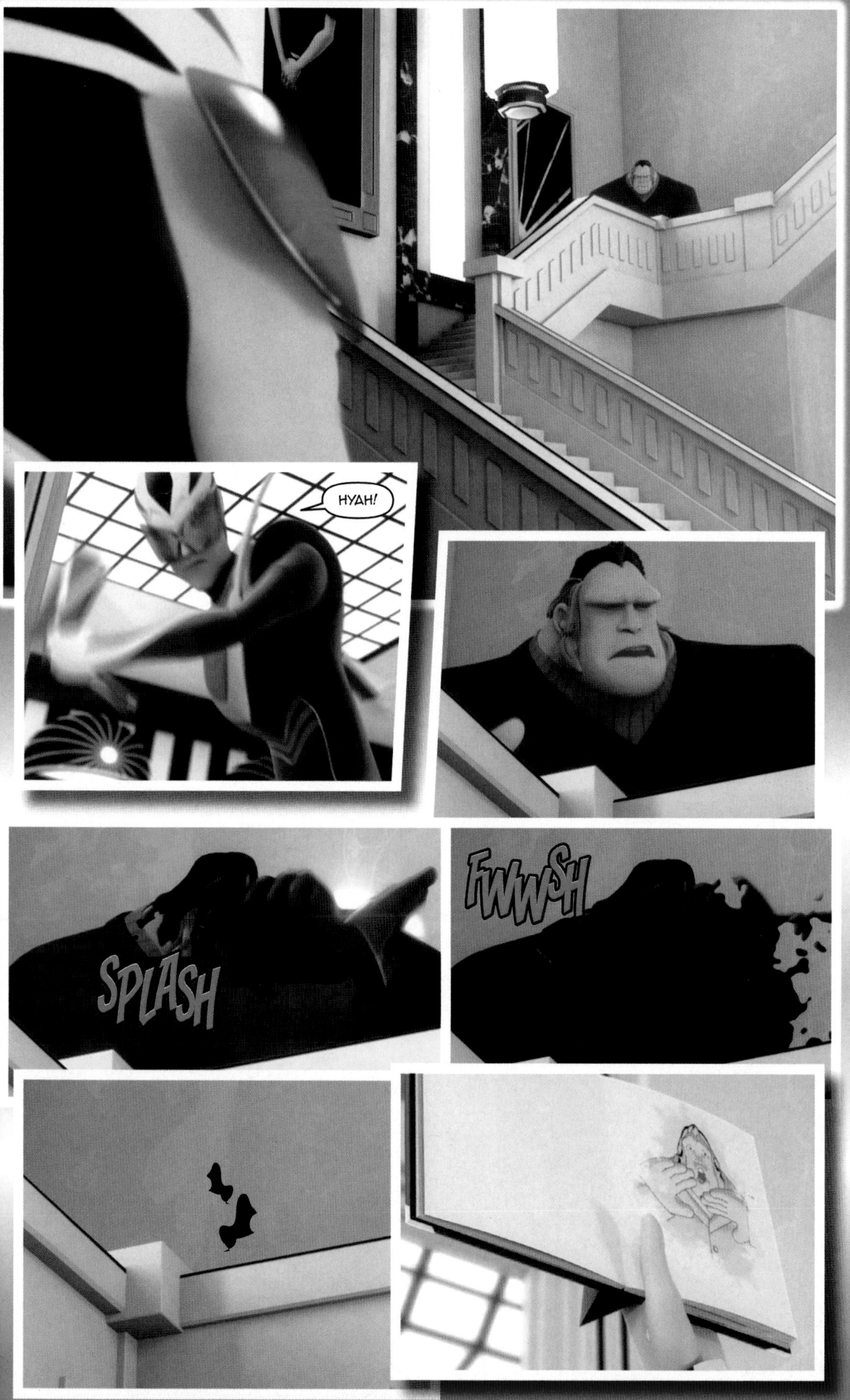
HYAH!
SPLASH
FWWSH

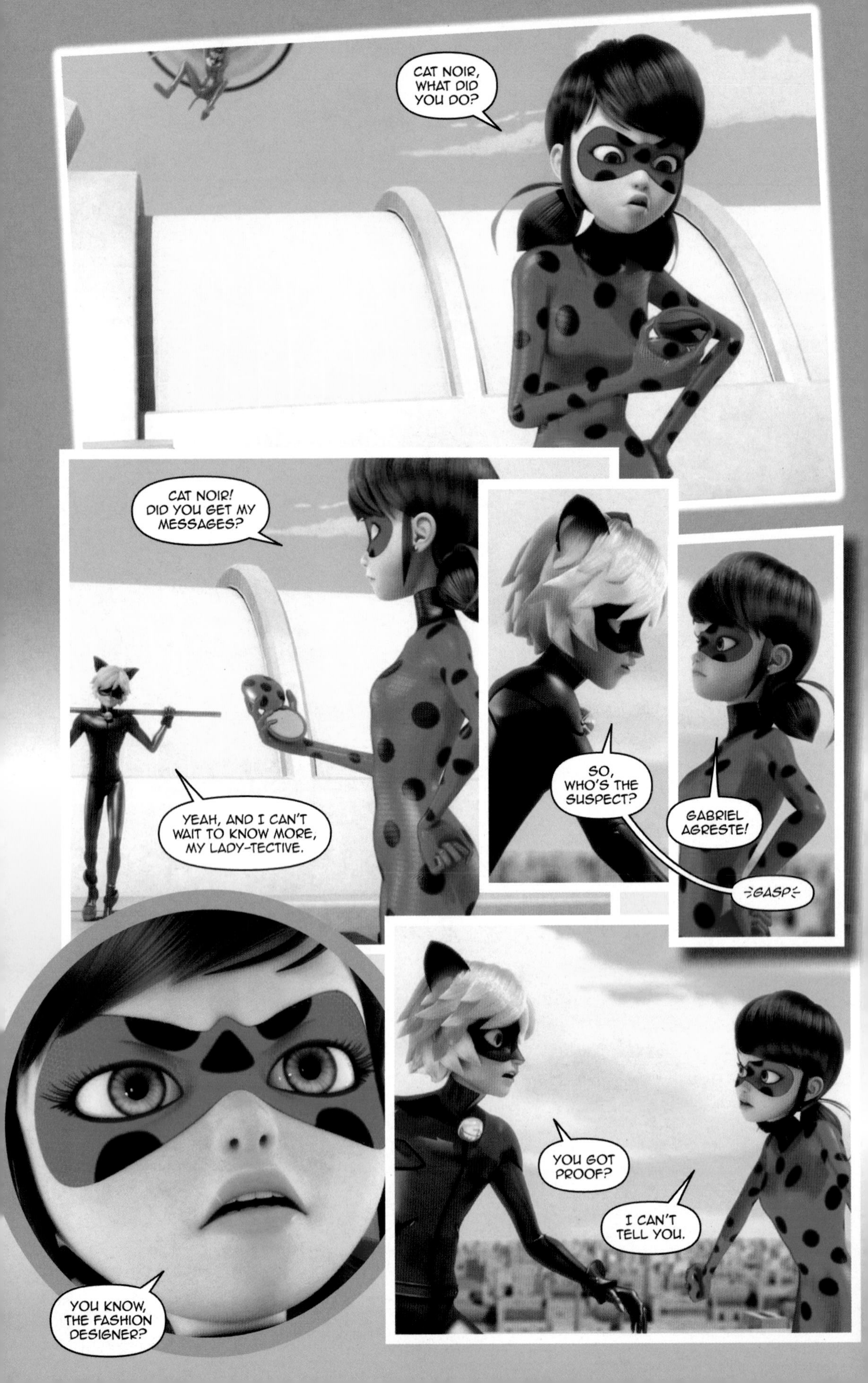
CAT NOIR, WHAT DID YOU DO?
CAT NOIR! DID YOU GET MY MESSAGES?
YEAH, AND I CAN'T WAIT TO KNOW MORE, MY LADY-TECTIVE.
SO, WHO'S THE SUSPECT?
GABRIEL AGRESTE!
GASP
YOU KNOW, THE FASHION DESIGNER?
YOU GOT PROOF?
I CAN'T TELL YOU.

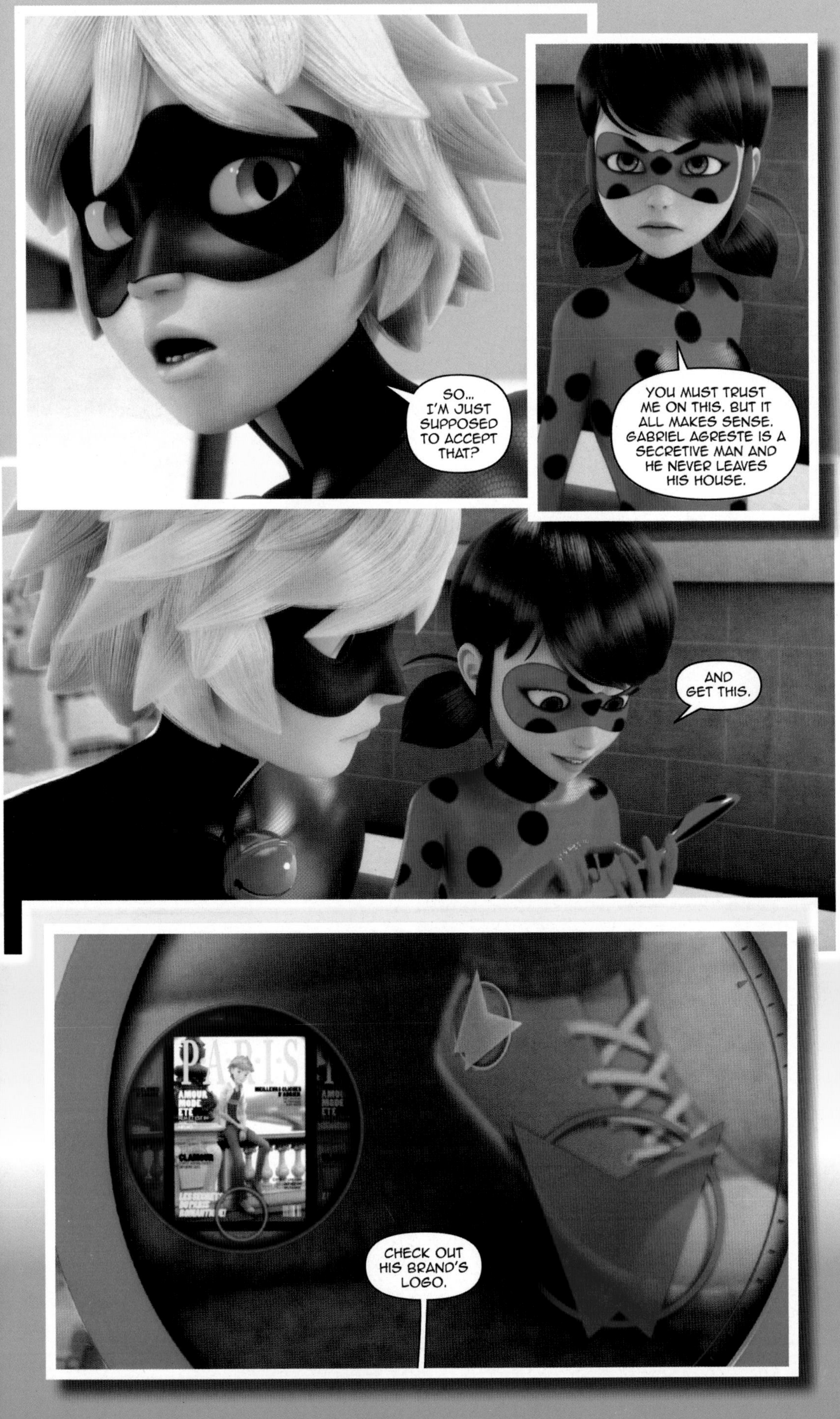
SO... I'M JUST SUPPOSED TO ACCEPT THAT?
YOU MUST TRUST ME ON THIS. BUT IT ALL MAKES SENSE. GABRIEL AGRESTE IS A SECRETIVE MAN AND HE NEVER LEAVES HIS HOUSE.
AND GET THIS.
PARIS
CHECK OUT HIS BRAND'S LOGO.

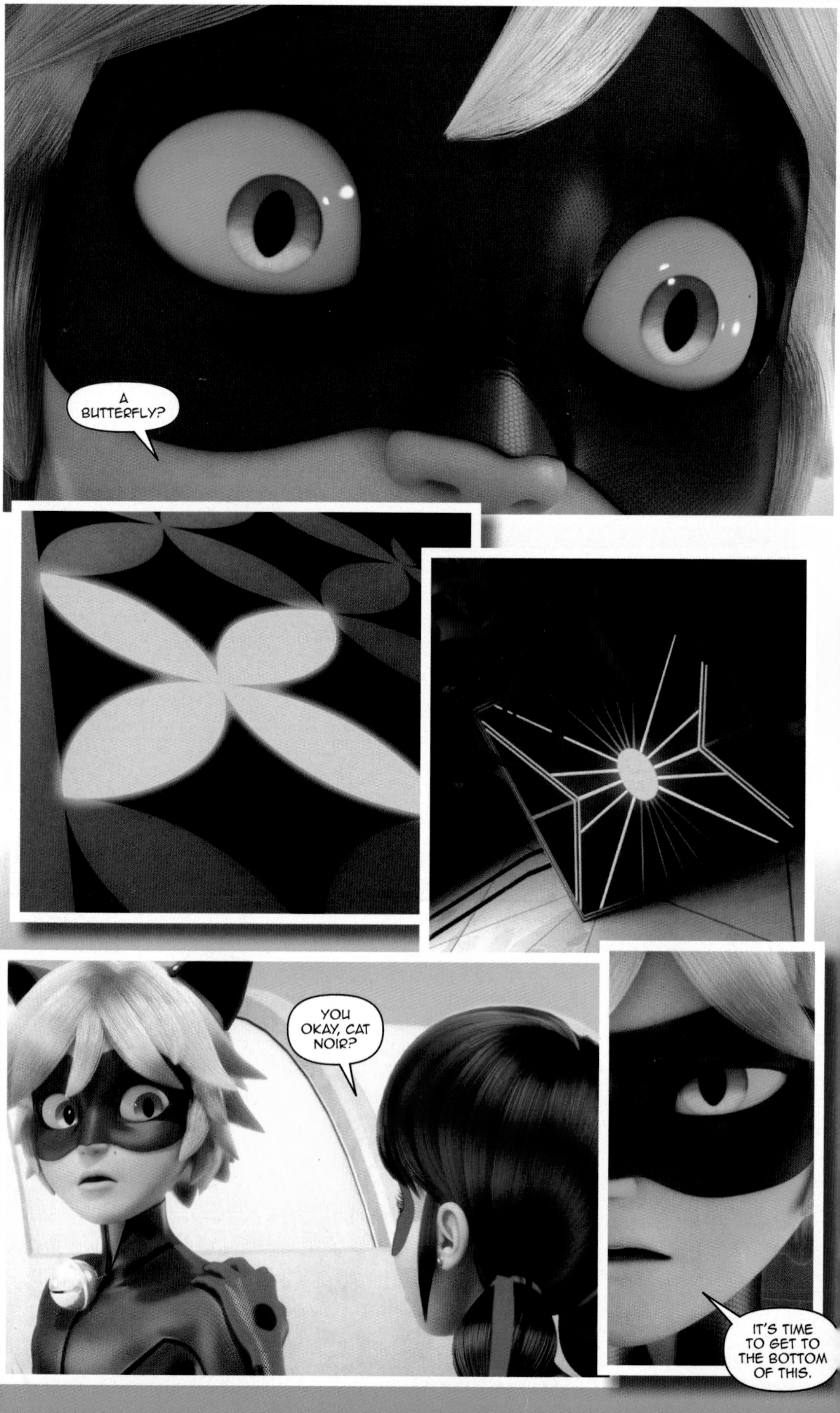
A BUTTERFLY?
YOU OKAY, CAT NOIR?
IT'S TIME TO GET TO THE BOTTOM OF THIS.

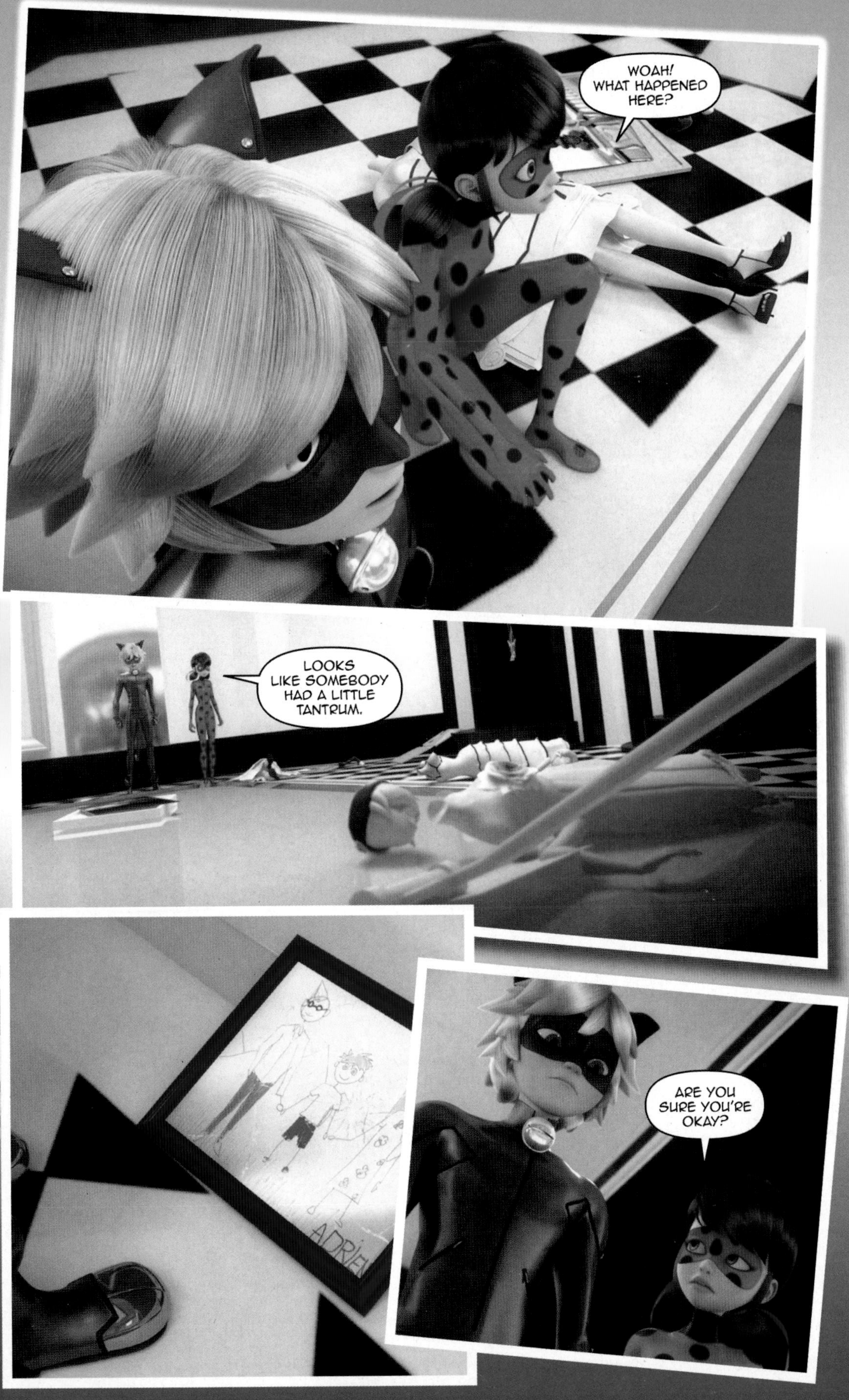
WOAH! WHAT HAPPENED HERE?
LOOKS LIKE SOMEBODY HAD A LITTLE TANTRUM.
ADRI
ARE YOU SURE YOU'RE OKAY?

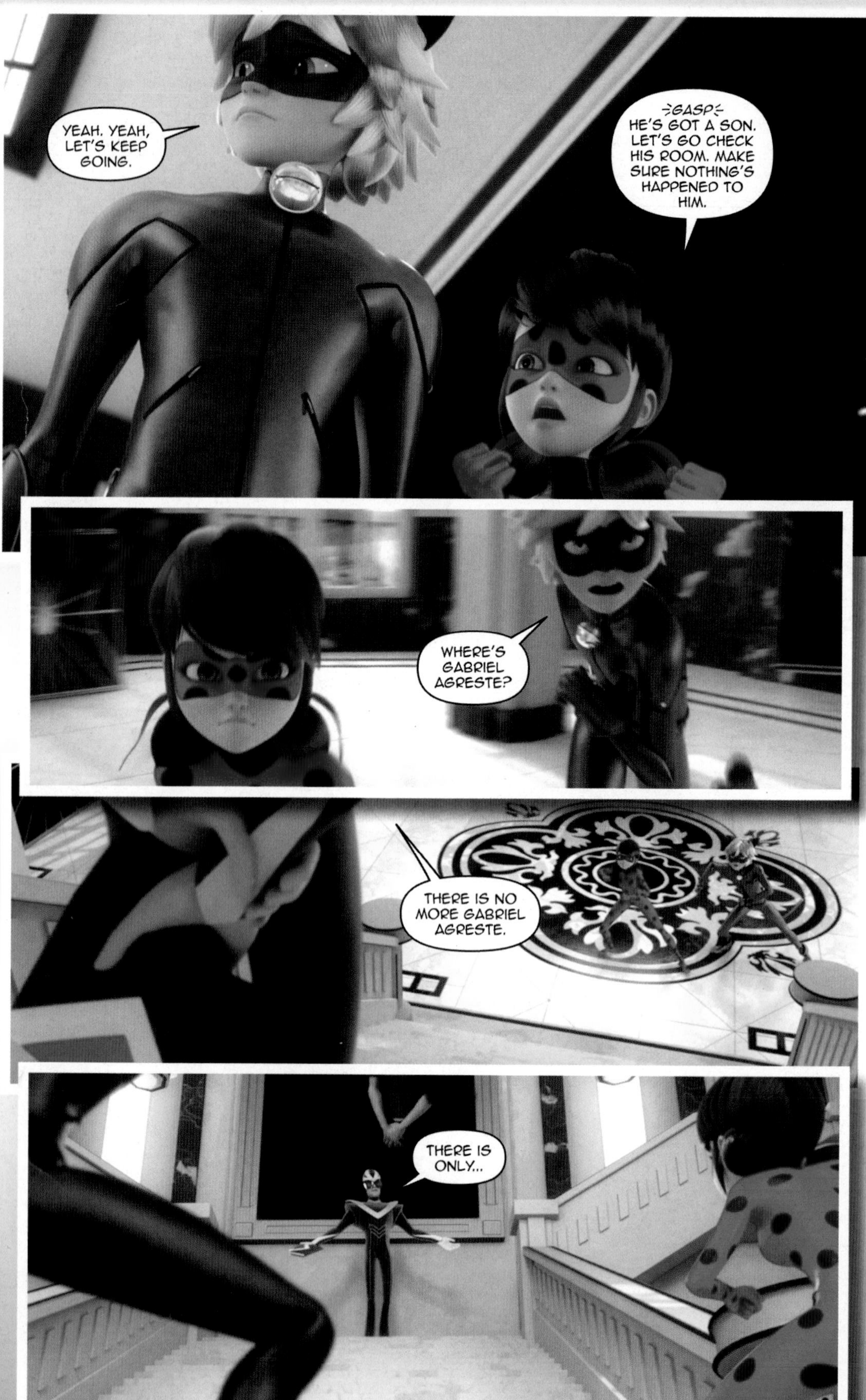
YEAH. YEAH, LET'S KEEP GOING.
⇒GASP⇐
HE'S GOT A SON. LET'S GO CHECK HIS ROOM. MAKE SURE NOTHING'S HAPPENED TO HIM.
WHERE'S GABRIEL AGRESTE?
THERE IS NO MORE GABRIEL AGRESTE.
THERE IS ONLY...

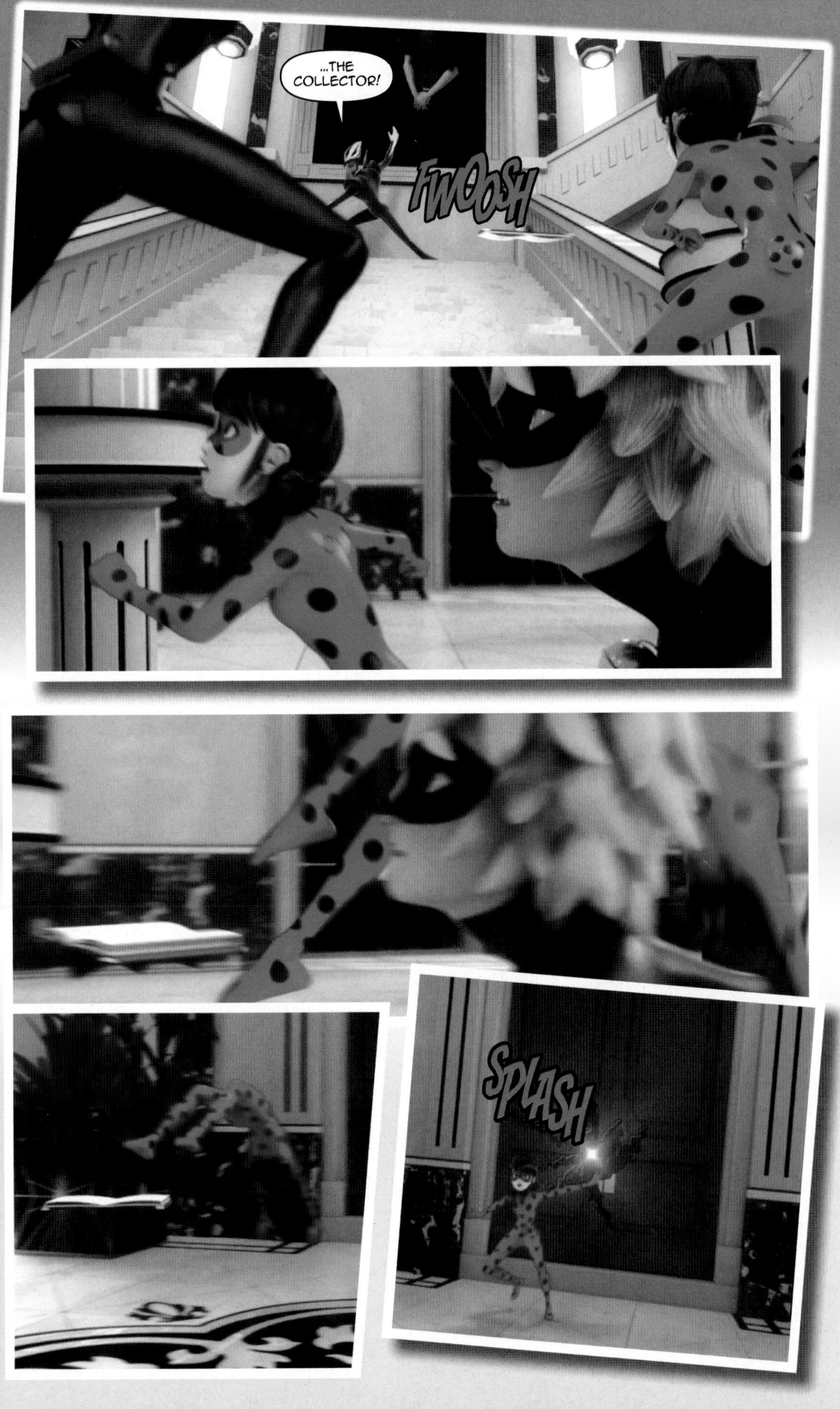
...THE COLLECTOR!
FWOOSH
SPLASH

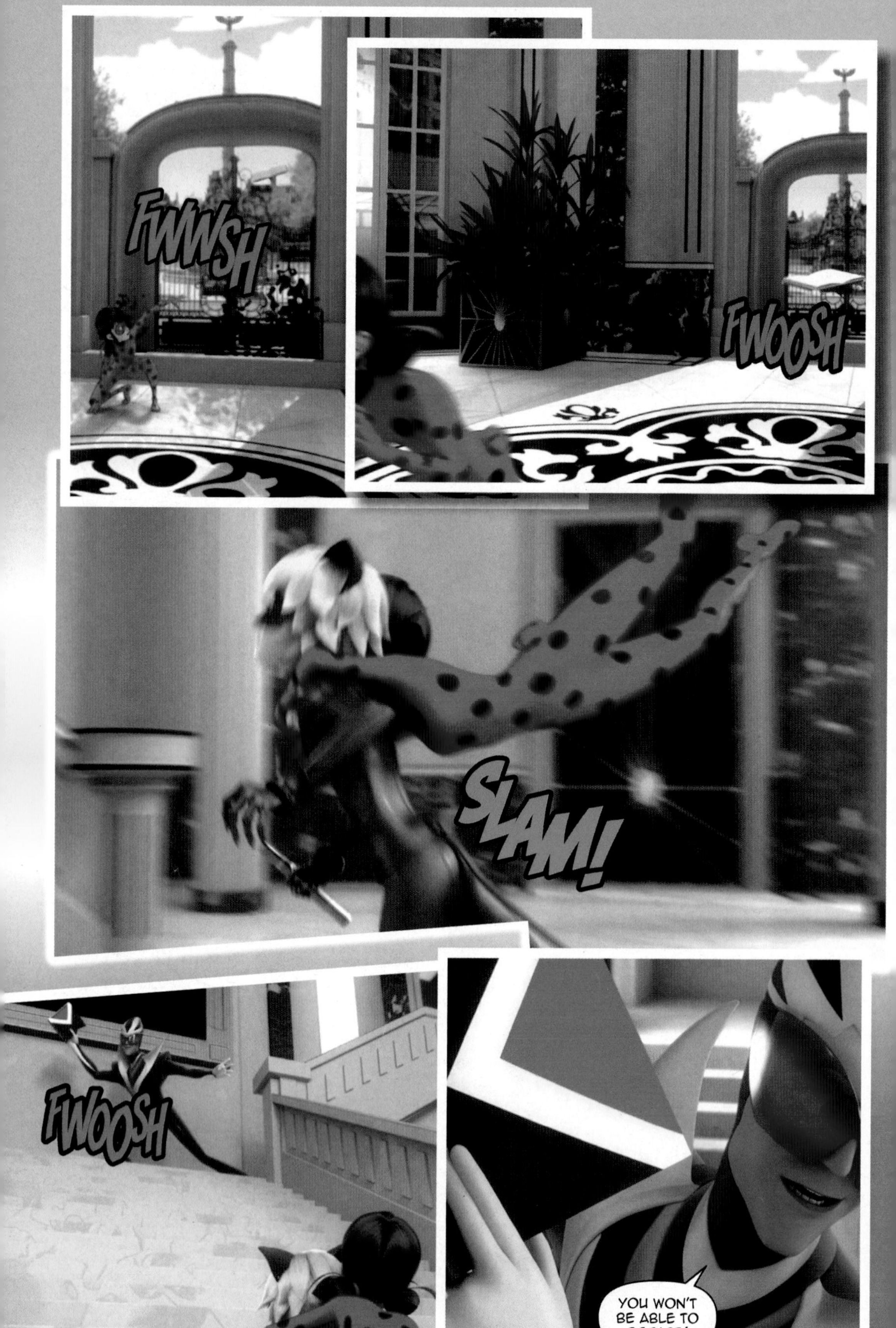
FWWSH
FWOOSH
SLAM!
FWOOSH
YOU WON'T BE ABLE TO ESCAPE!

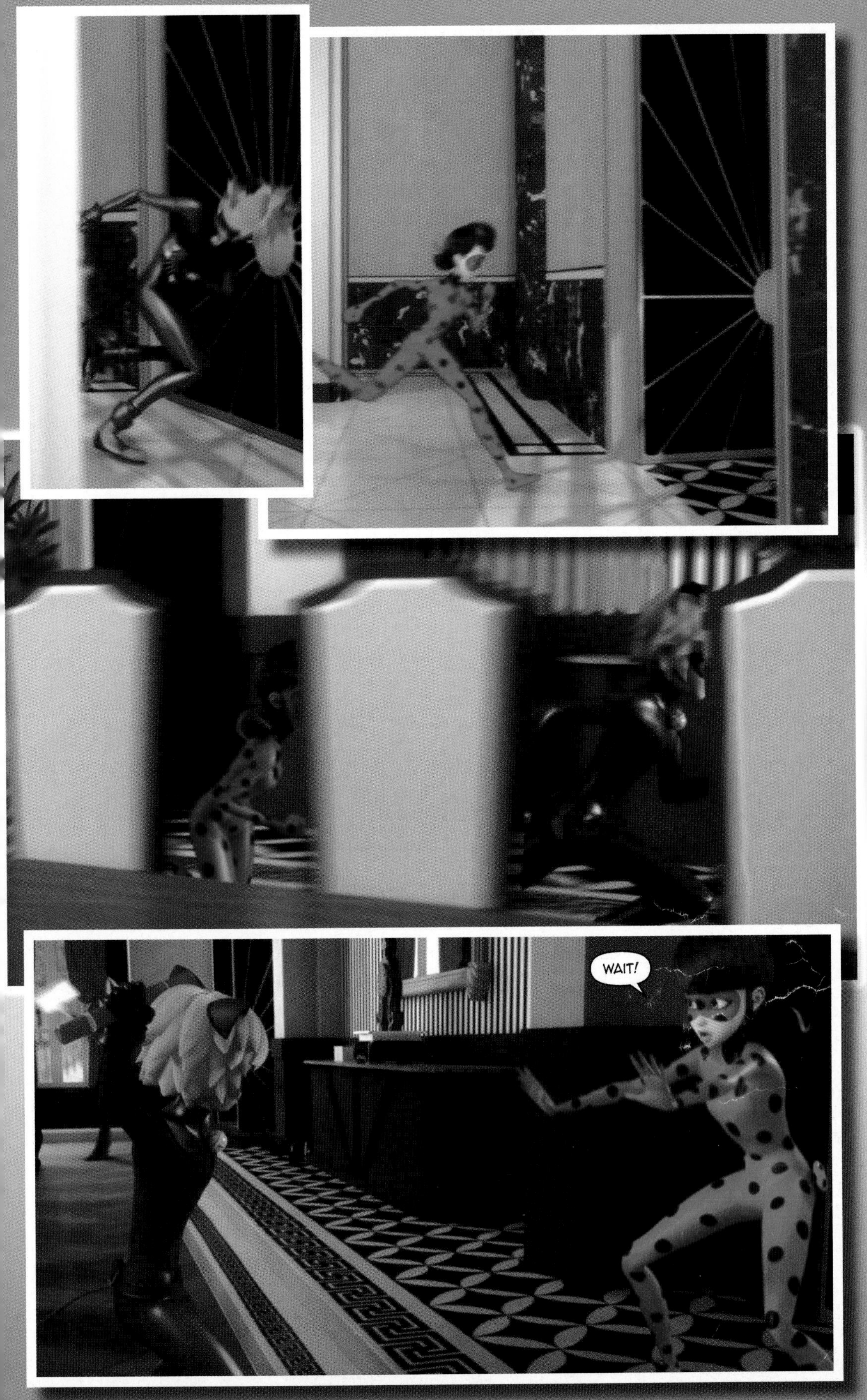
WAIT!

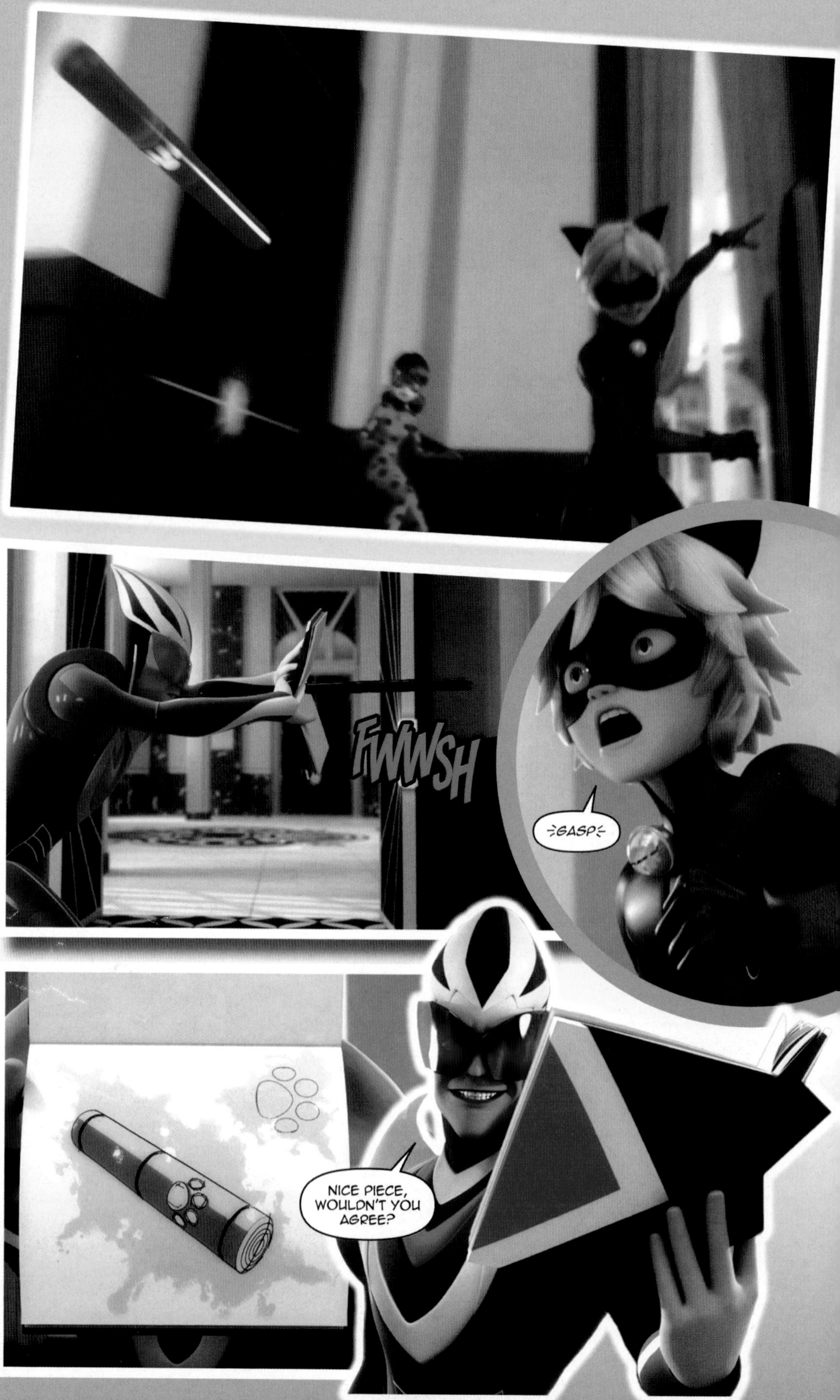
FWWSH
GASP
NICE PIECE, WOULDN'T YOU AGREE?

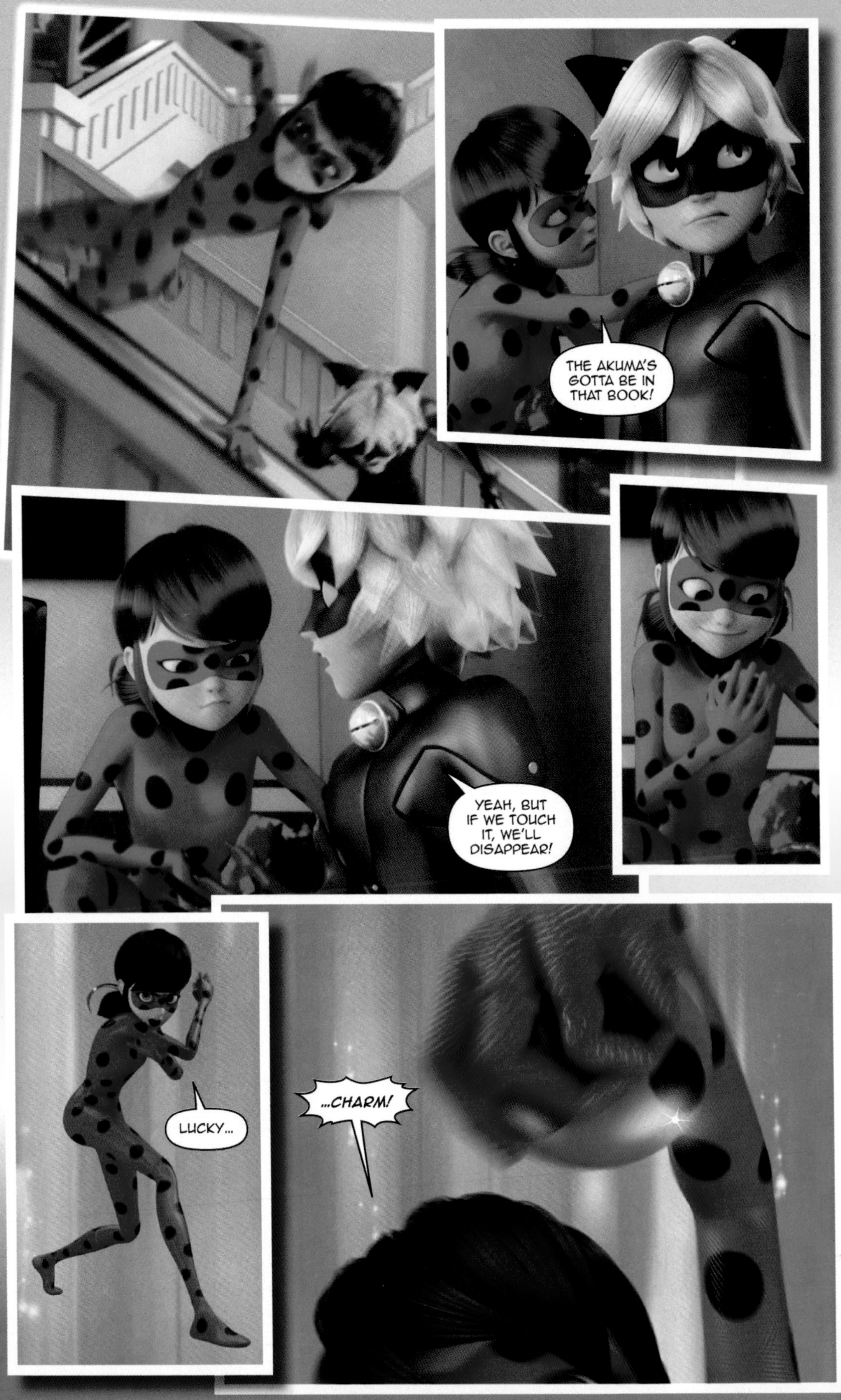
THE AKUMA'S GOTTA BE IN THAT BOOK!
YEAH, BUT IF WE TOUCH IT, WE'LL DISAPPEAR!
LUCKY...
...CHARM!

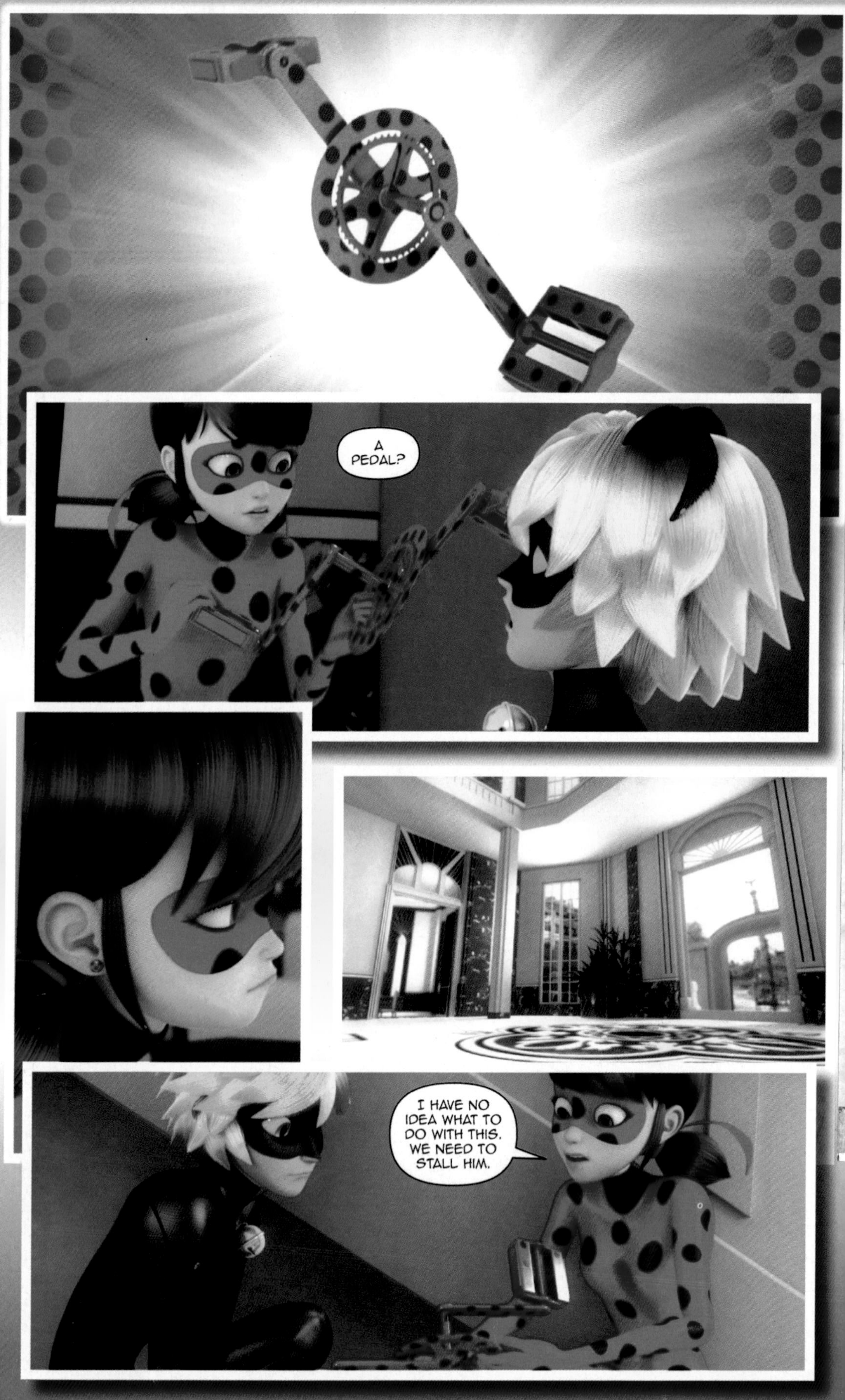
A PEDAL?
I HAVE NO IDEA WHAT TO DO WITH THIS. WE NEED TO STALL HIM.

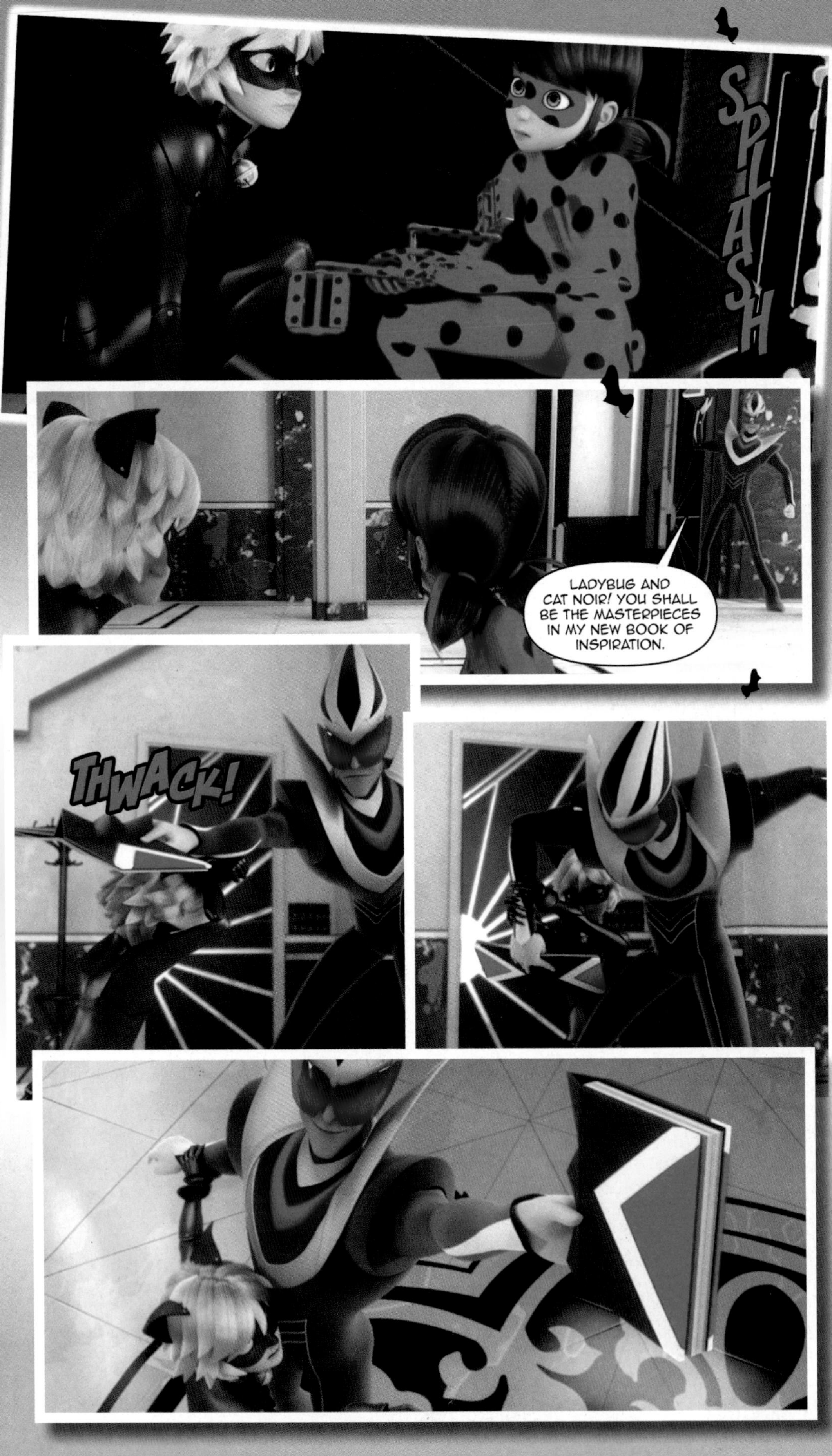
SPLASH
LADYBUG AND CAT NOIR! YOU SHALL BE THE MASTERPIECES IN MY NEW BOOK OF INSPIRATION.
THWACK!

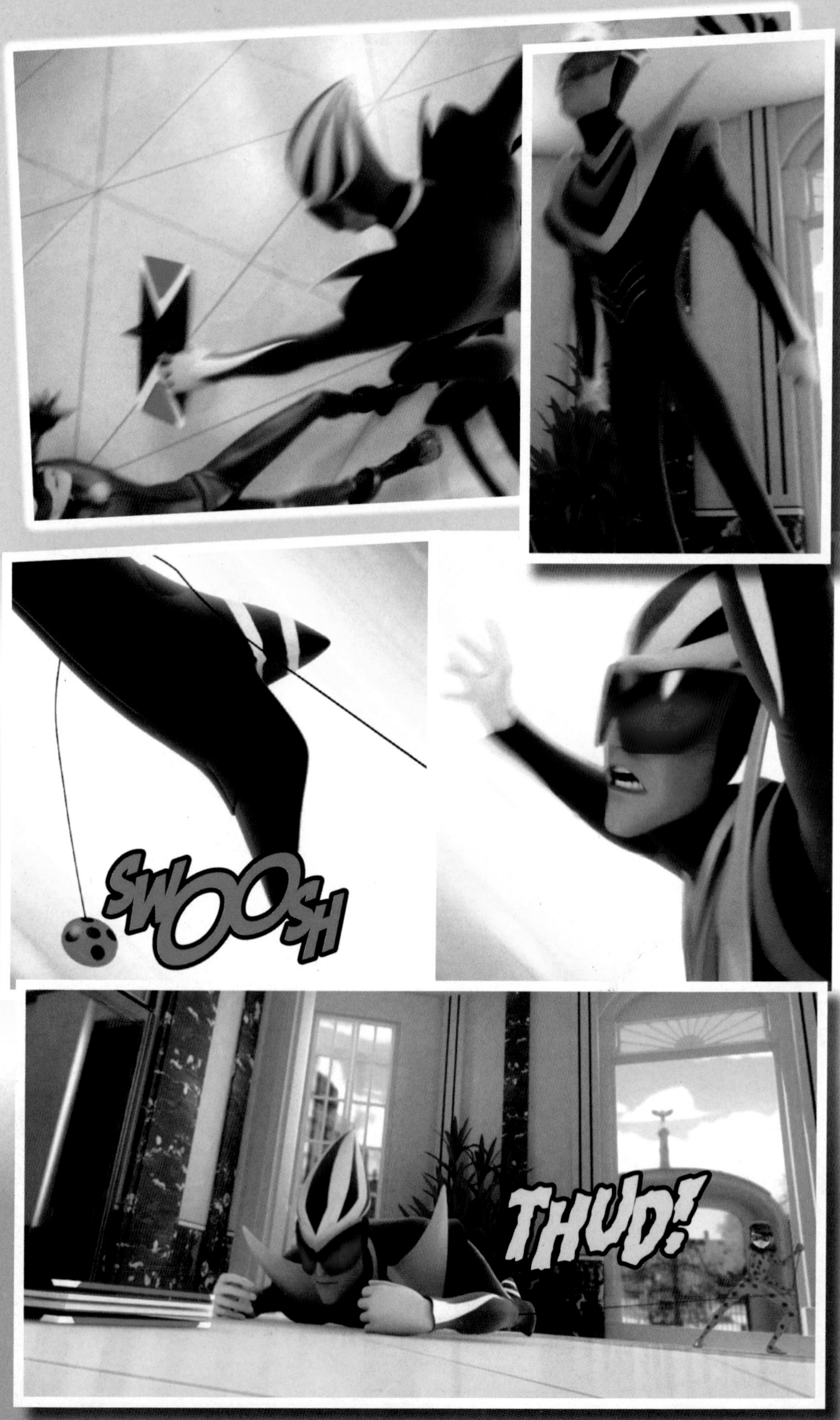
SWOOSH
THUD!

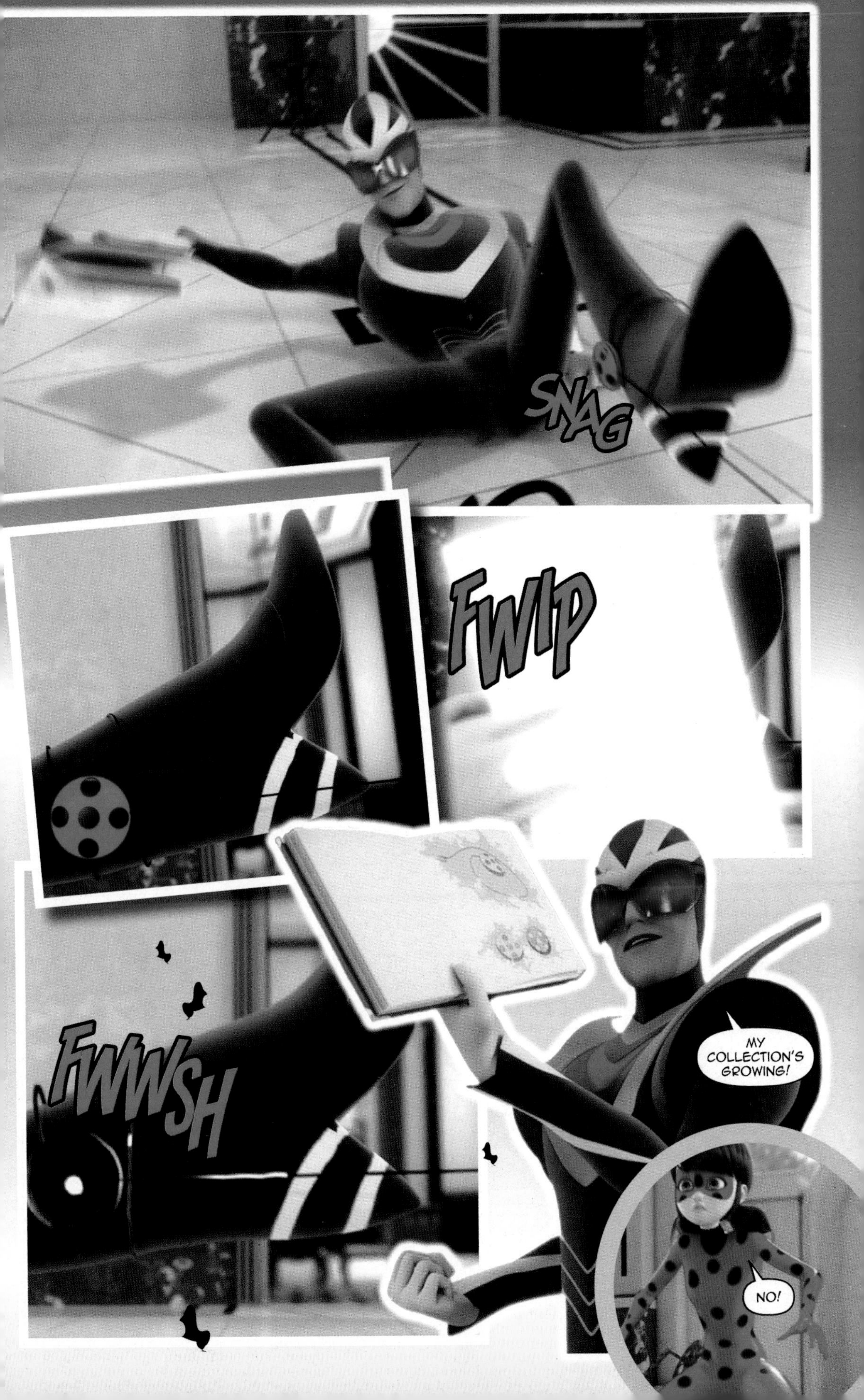
SNAG
FWIP
FWWSH
MY COLLECTION'S GROWING!
NO!

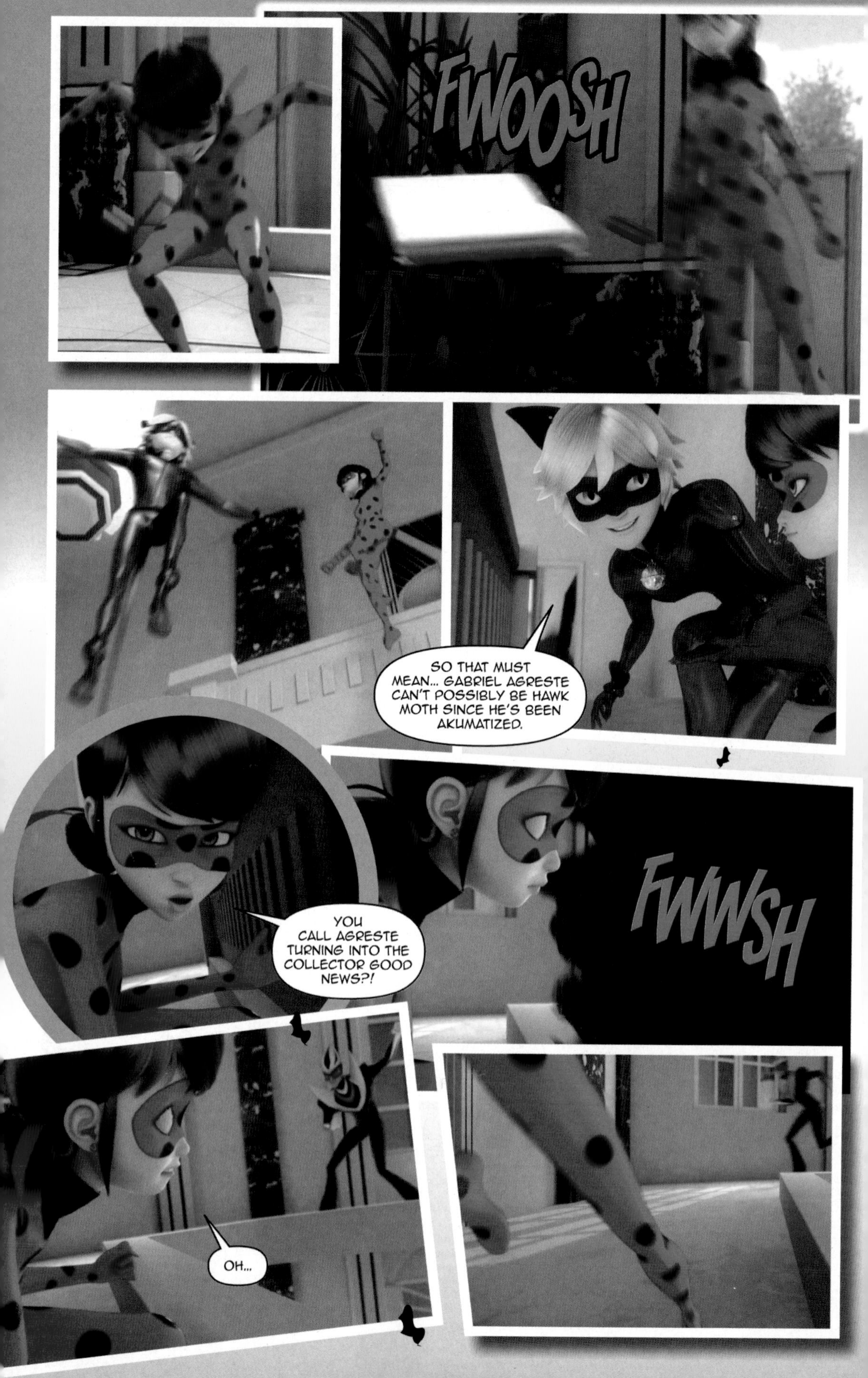
FWOOSH
SO THAT MUST MEAN... GABRIEL AGRESTE CAN'T POSSIBLY BE HAWK MOTH SINCE HE'S BEEN AKUMATIZED.
YOU CALL AGRESTE TURNING INTO THE COLLECTOR GOOD NEWS?!
FWWSH
OH...

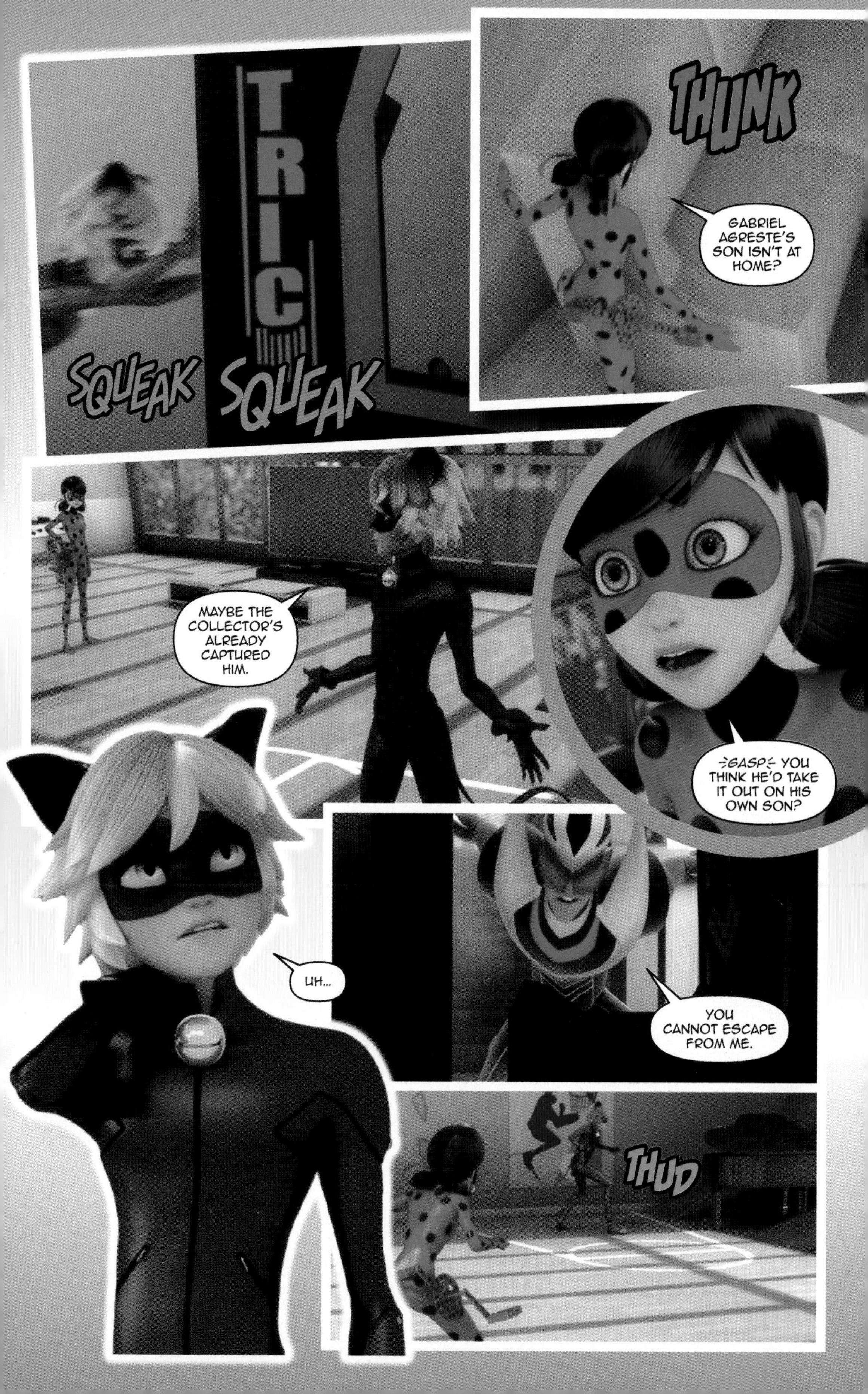
TRIC
SQUEAK SQUEAK
THUNK
GABRIEL AGRESTE'S SON ISN'T AT HOME?
MAYBE THE COLLECTOR'S ALREADY CAPTURED HIM.
⪡GASP⪢ YOU THINK HE'D TAKE IT OUT ON HIS OWN SON?
UH...
YOU CANNOT ESCAPE FROM ME.
THUD

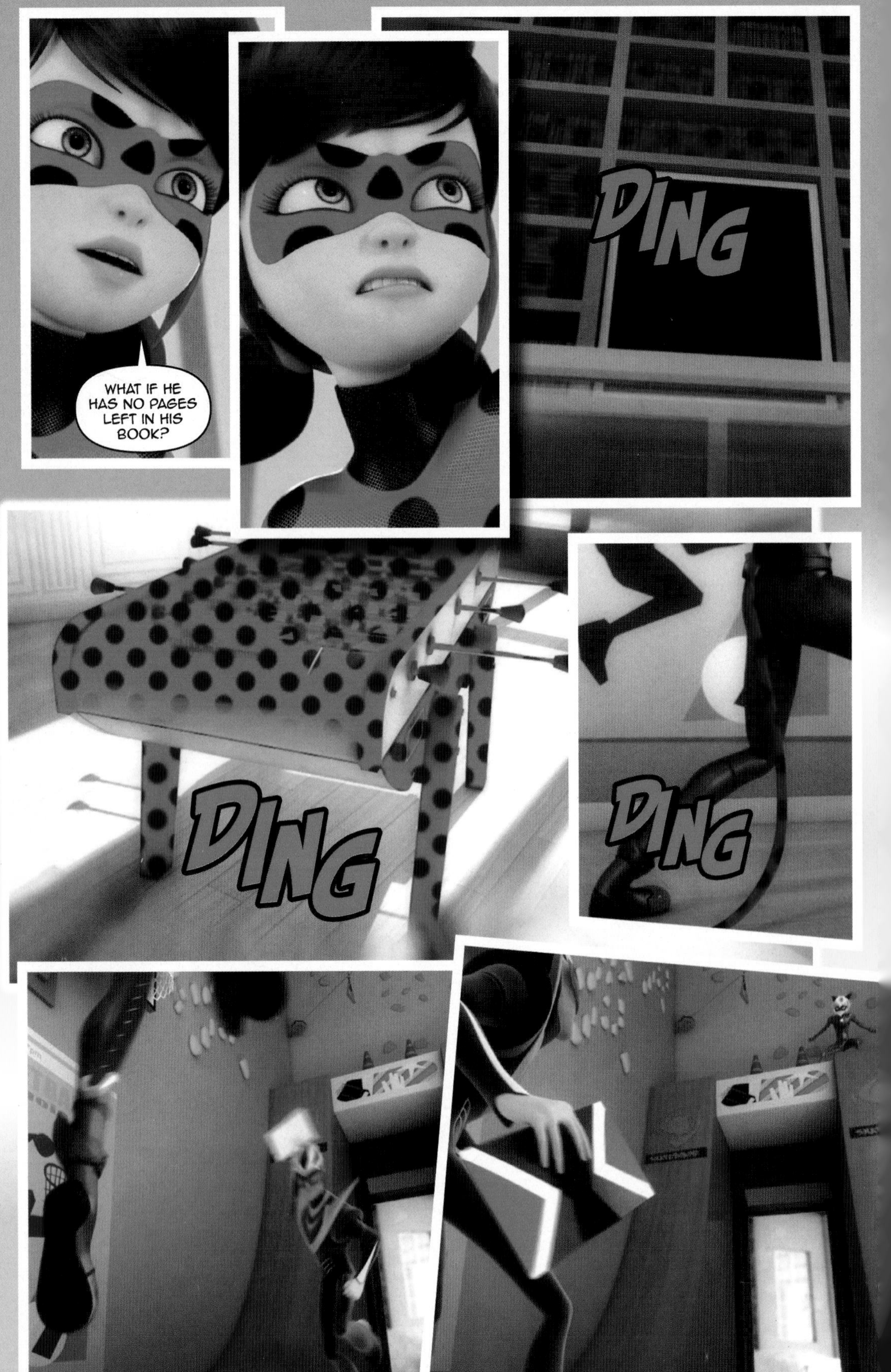
WHAT IF HE HAS NO PAGES LEFT IN HIS BOOK?
DING
DING
DING

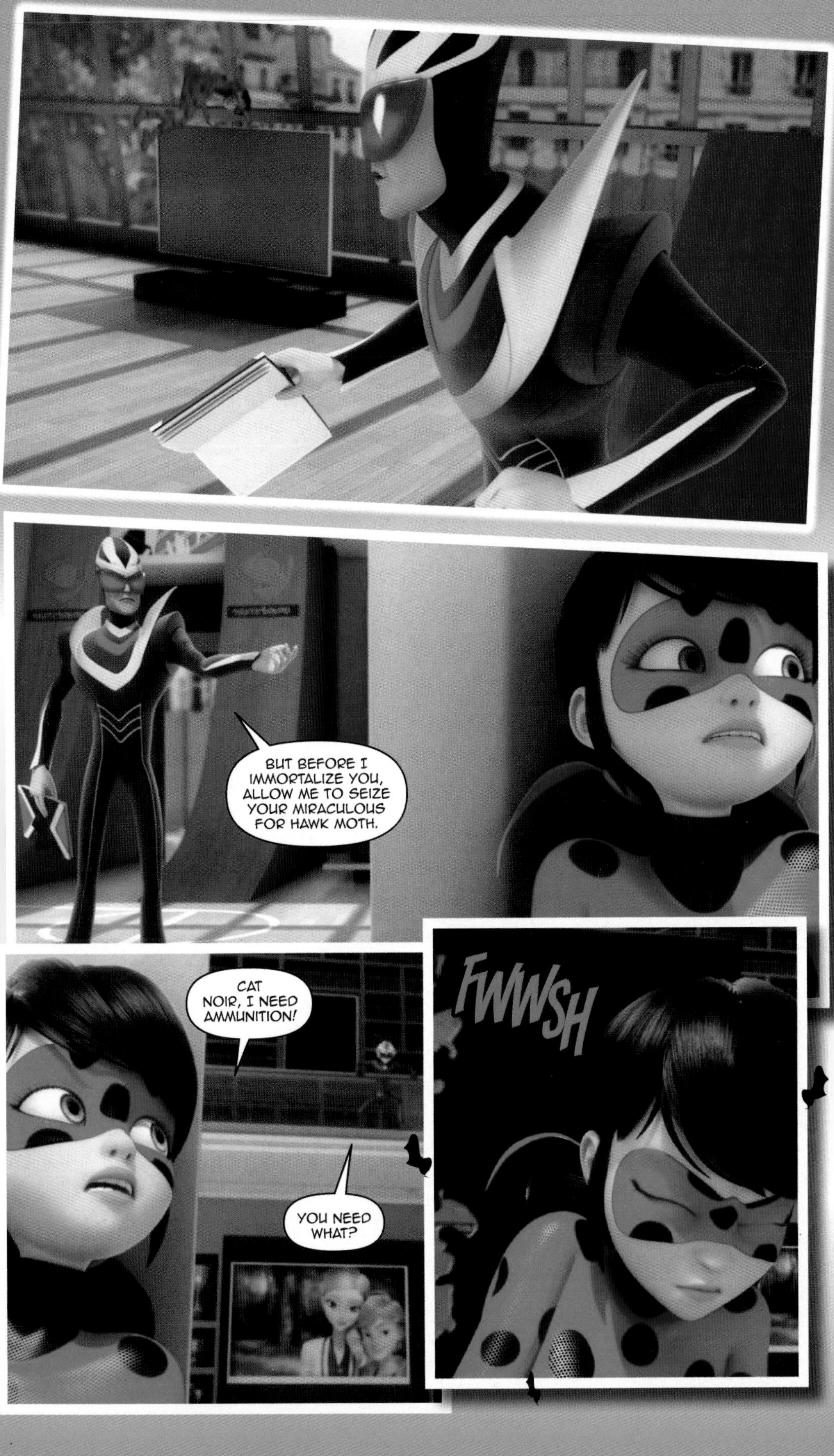
BUT BEFORE I IMMORTALIZE YOU, ALLOW ME TO SEIZE YOUR MIRACULOUS FOR HAWK MOTH.
CAT NOIR, I NEED AMMUNITION!
YOU NEED WHAT?
FWWSH

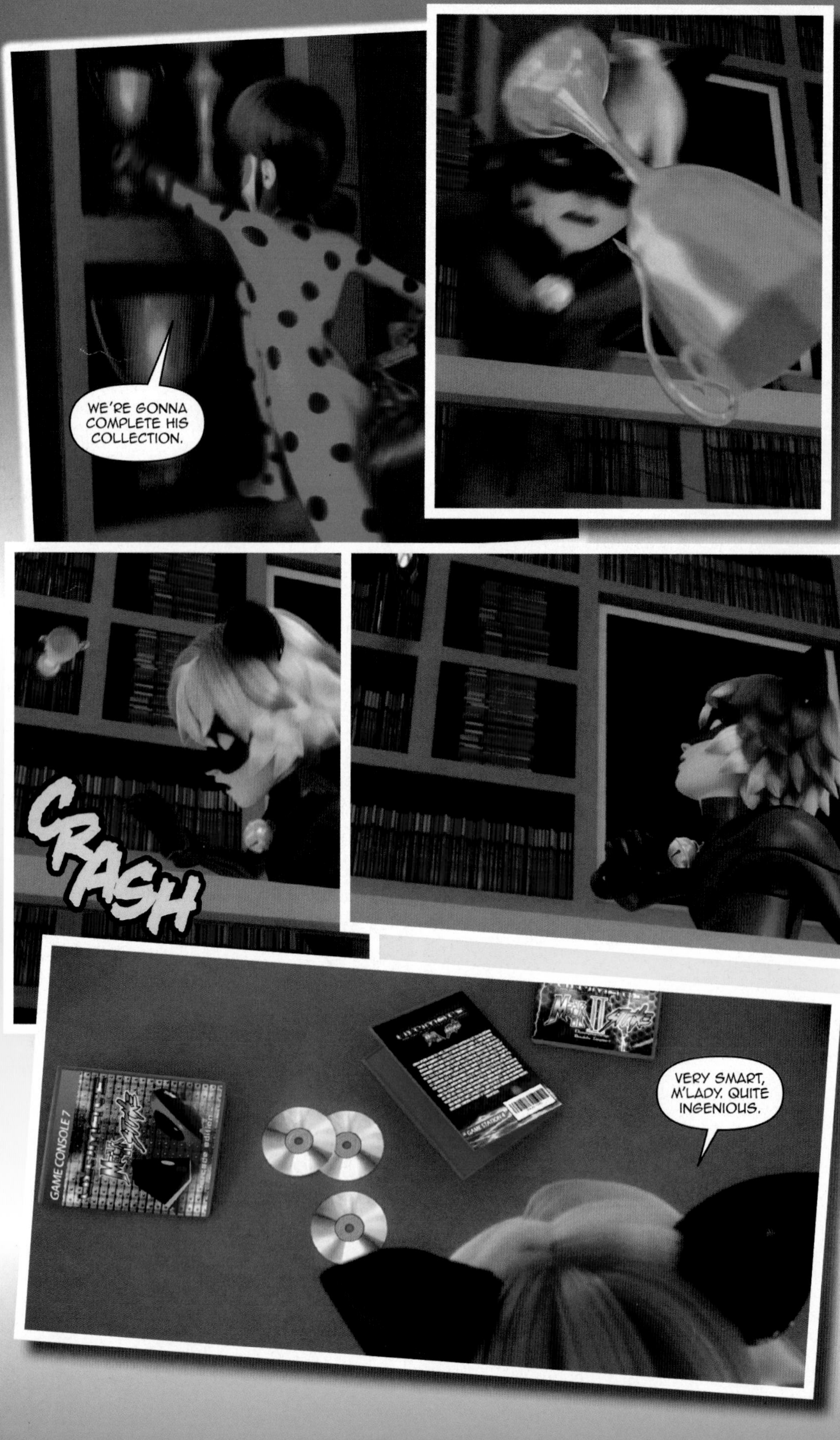
WE'RE GONNA COMPLETE HIS COLLECTION.
CRASH
VERY SMART, M'LADY. QUITE INGENIOUS.
GAME CONSOLE 7

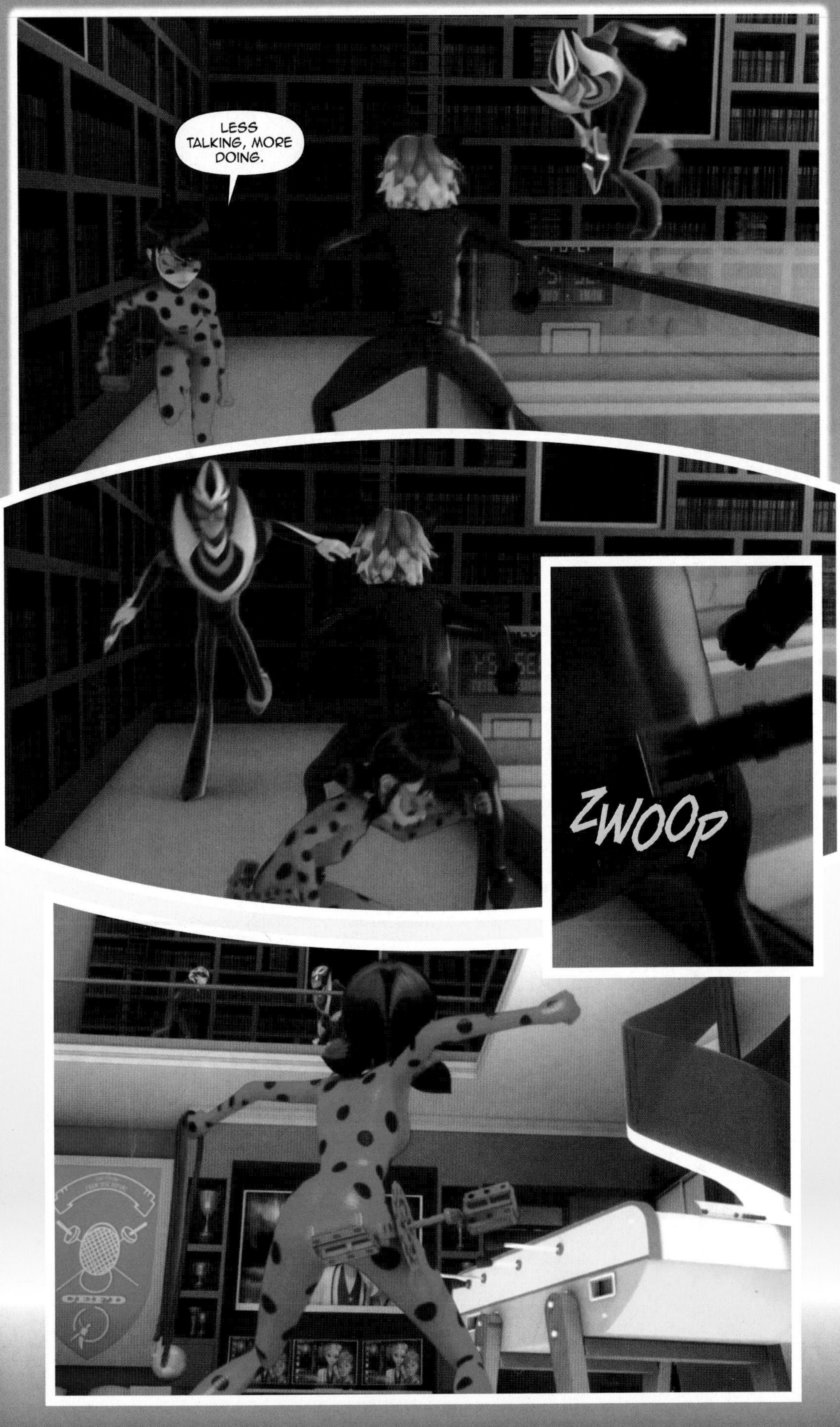
LESS TALKING, MORE DOING.
ZWOOP

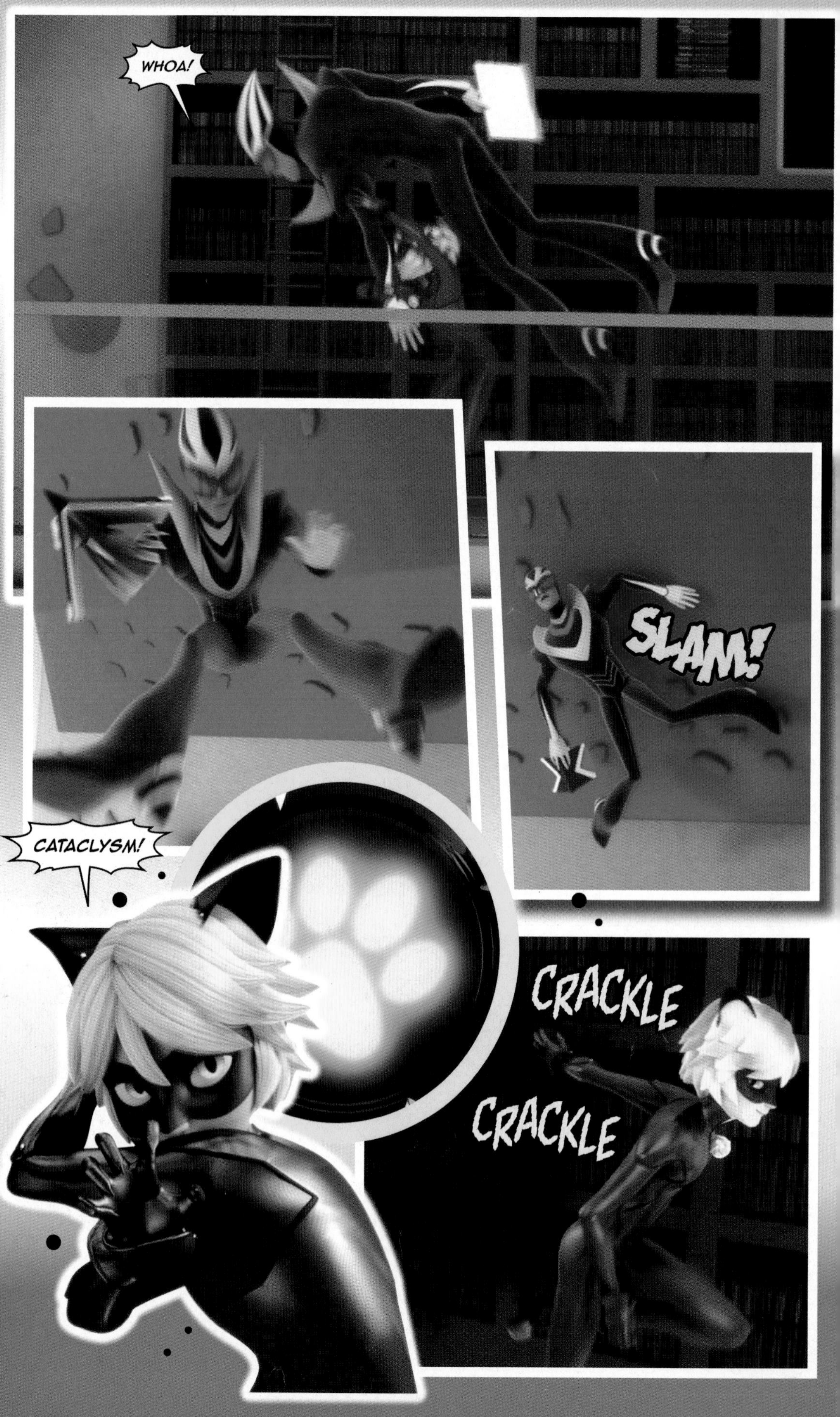
WHOA!
SLAM!
CATACLYSM!
CRACKLE
CRACKLE

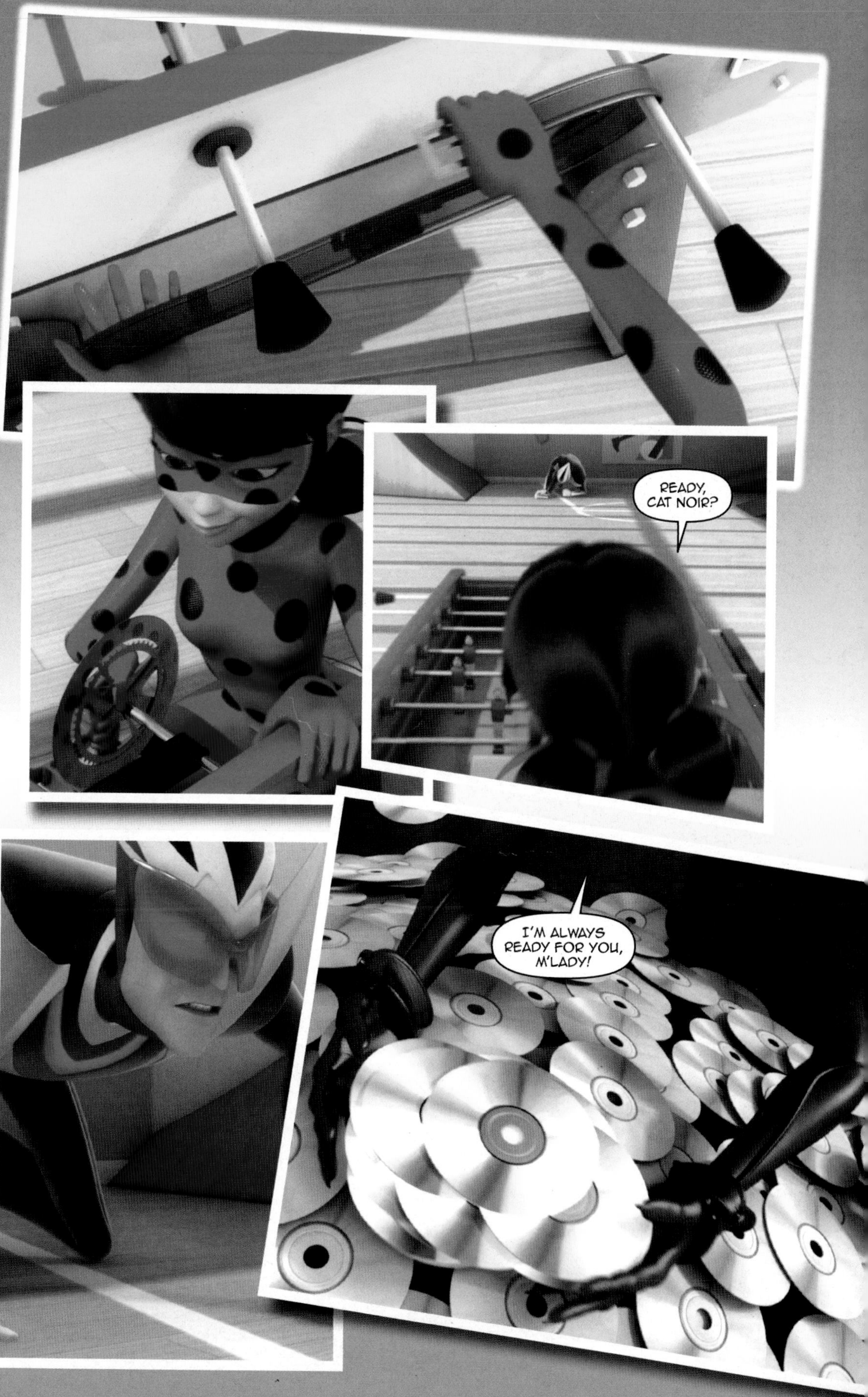
READY, CAT NOIR?
I'M ALWAYS READY FOR YOU, M'LADY!

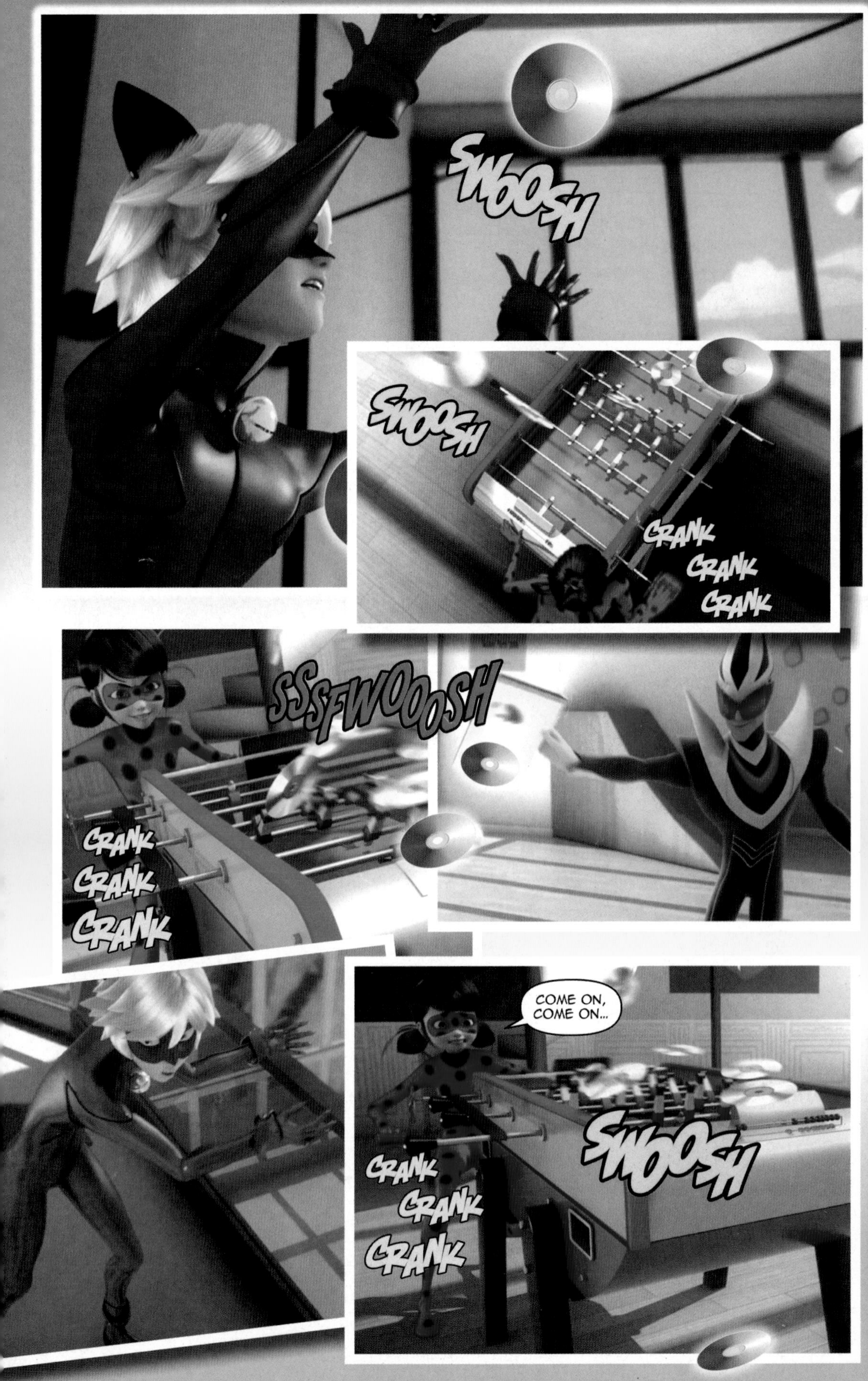
SWOOSH
SWOOSH
CRANK
CRANK
CRANK
SSSFWOOOSH
CRANK
CRANK
CRANK
COME ON,
COME ON...
SWOOSH
CRANK
CRANK
CRANK

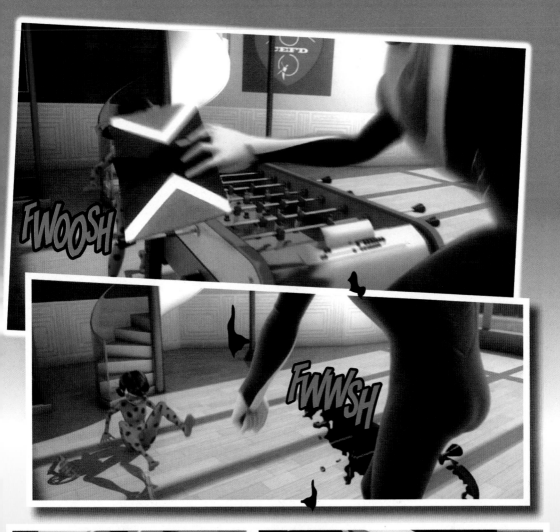

FWOOSH

FWWSH

÷GASP÷

HUH?
IT'S ALREADY
FULL!

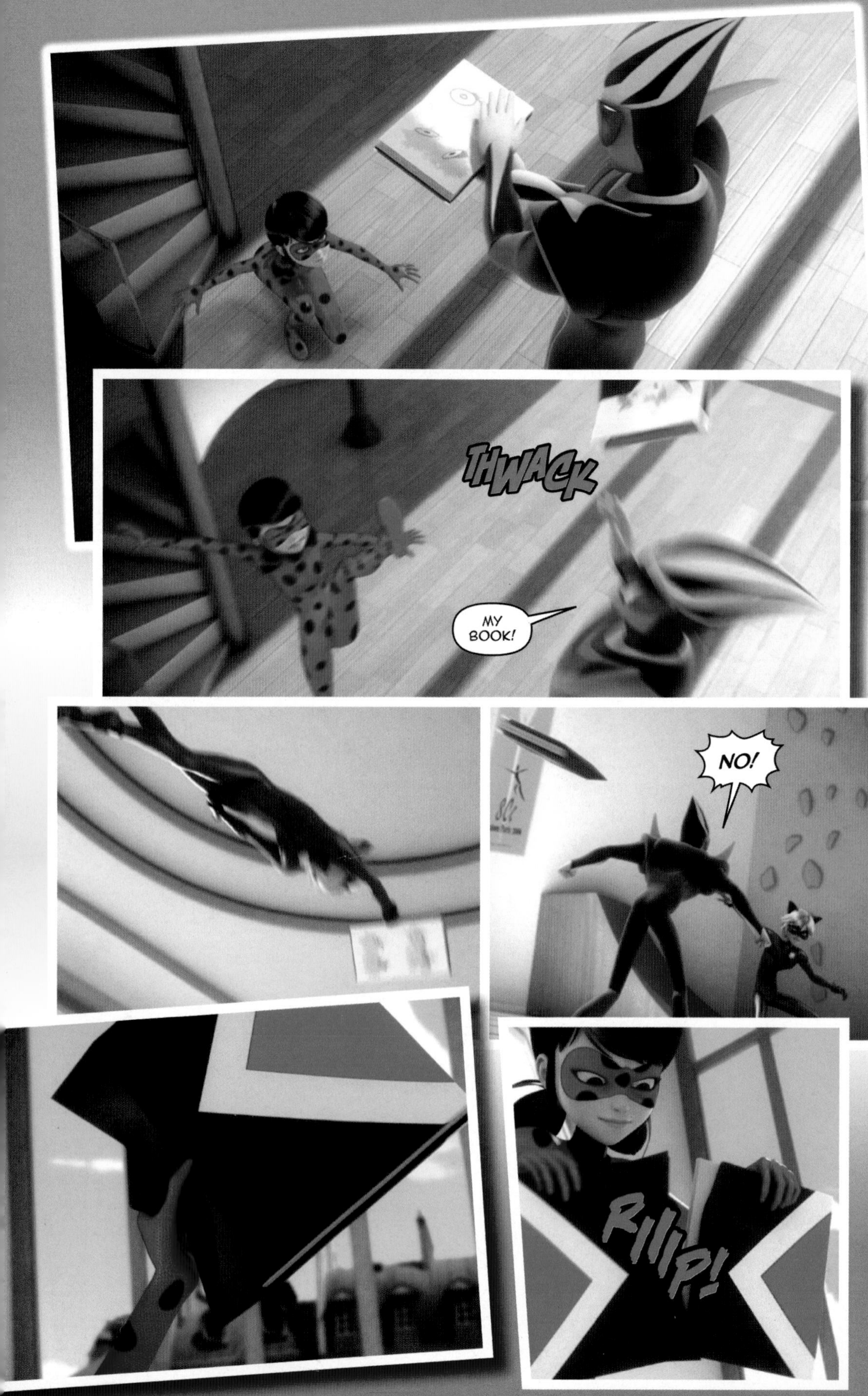
THWACK
MY BOOK!
NO!
RIIIP!

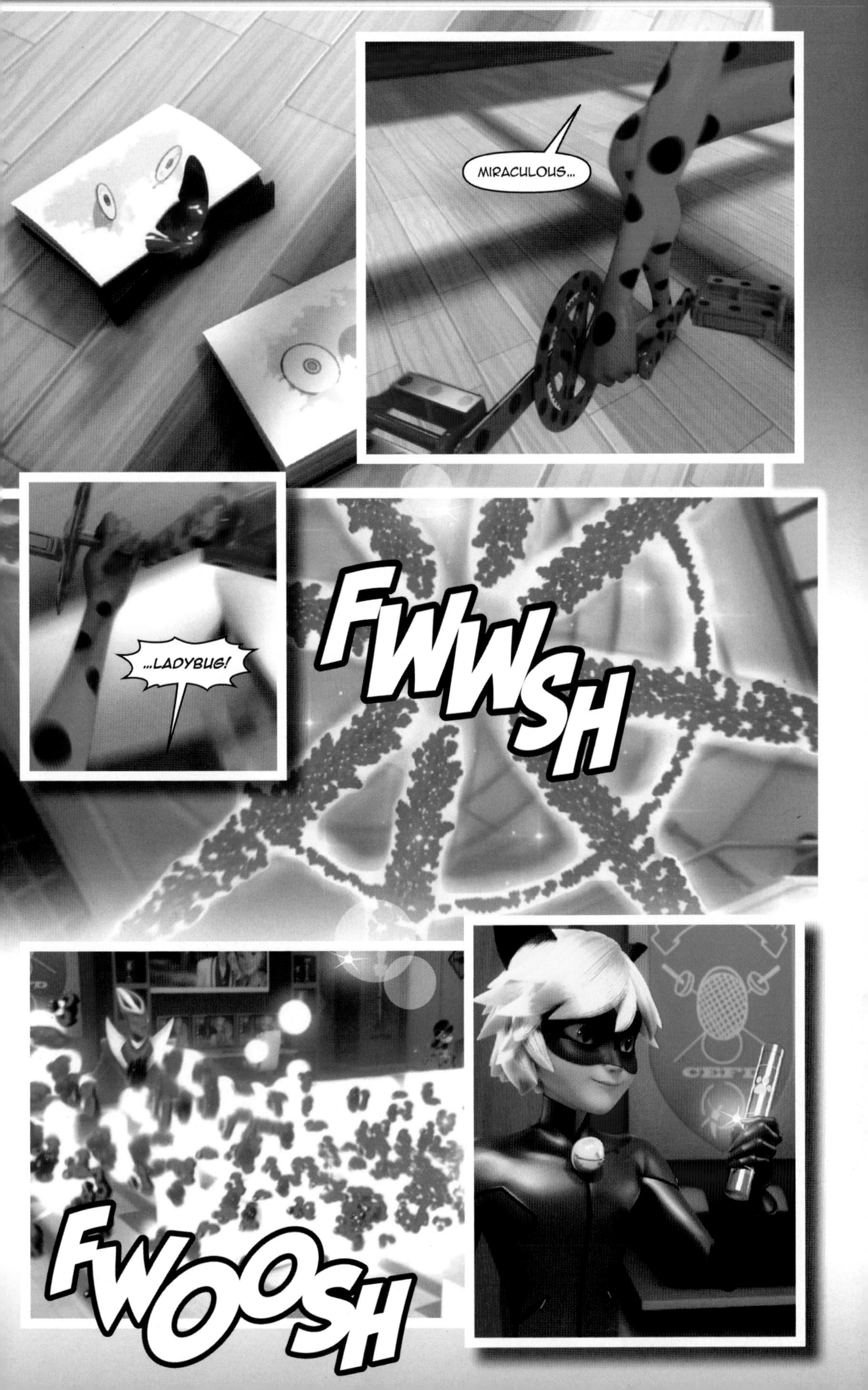
MIRACULOUS...
...LADYBUG!
FWWSH
FWOOSH

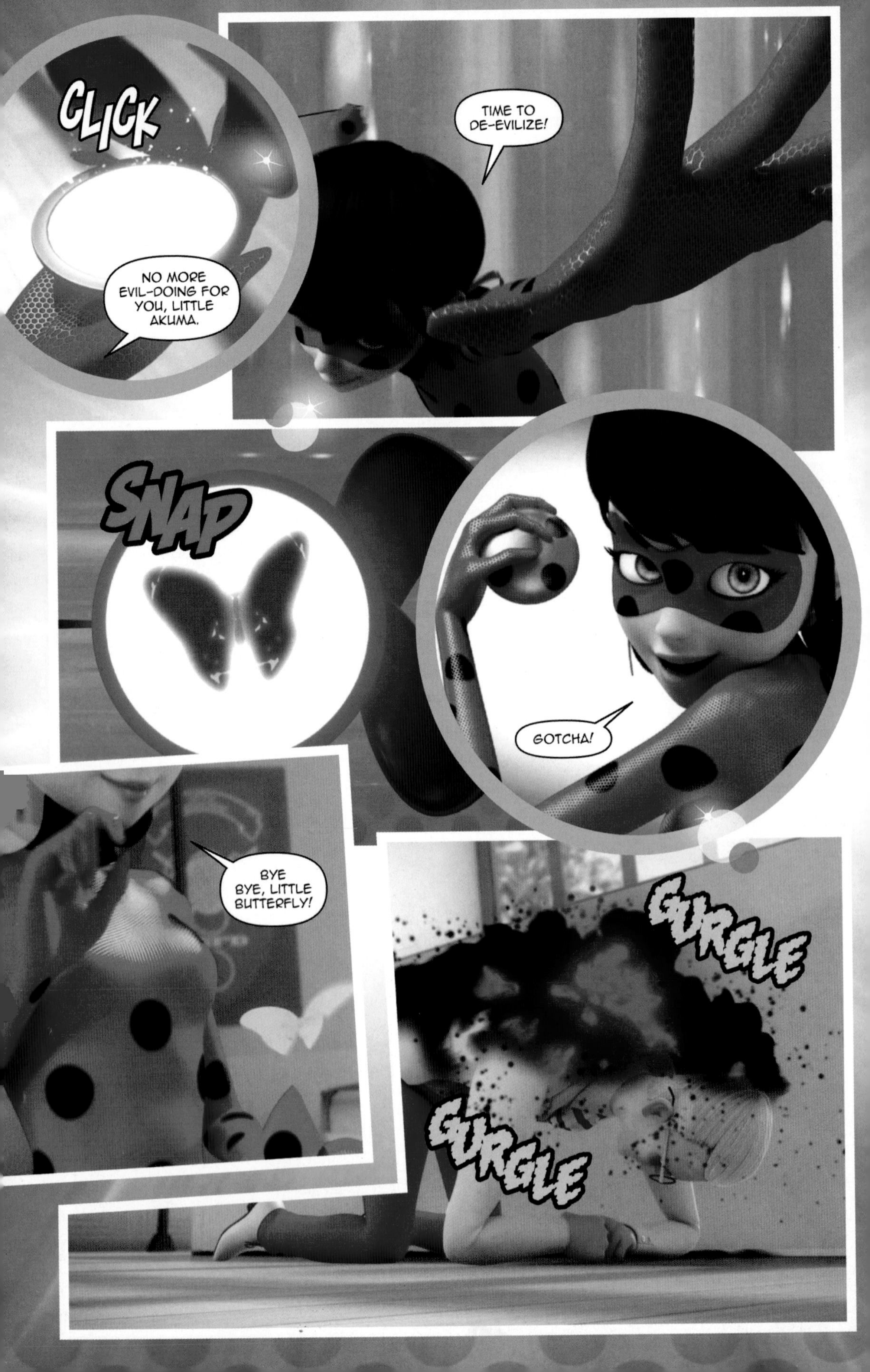
CLICK
NO MORE EVIL-DOING FOR YOU, LITTLE AKUMA.
TIME TO DE-EVILIZE!
SNAP
GOTCHA!
BYE BYE, LITTLE BUTTERFLY!
GURGLE
GURGLE

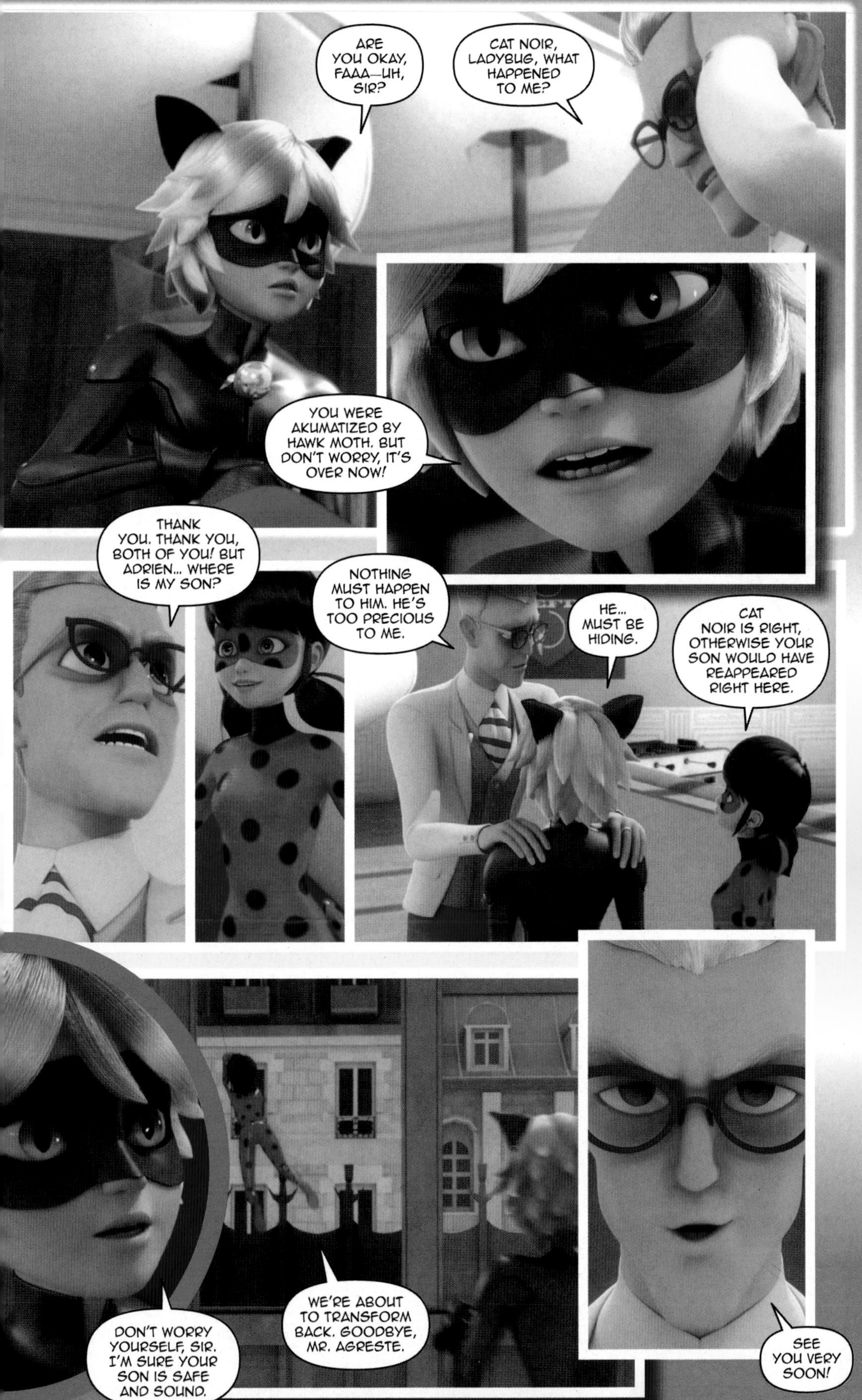
ARE YOU OKAY, FAAA—UH, SIR?
CAT NOIR, LADYBUG, WHAT HAPPENED TO ME?
YOU WERE AKUMATIZED BY HAWK MOTH. BUT DON'T WORRY, IT'S OVER NOW!
THANK YOU. THANK YOU, BOTH OF YOU! BUT ADRIEN... WHERE IS MY SON?
NOTHING MUST HAPPEN TO HIM. HE'S TOO PRECIOUS TO ME.
HE... MUST BE HIDING.
CAT NOIR IS RIGHT, OTHERWISE YOUR SON WOULD HAVE REAPPEARED RIGHT HERE.
DON'T WORRY YOURSELF, SIR. I'M SURE YOUR SON IS SAFE AND SOUND.
WE'RE ABOUT TO TRANSFORM BACK. GOODBYE, MR. AGRESTE.
SEE YOU VERY SOON!

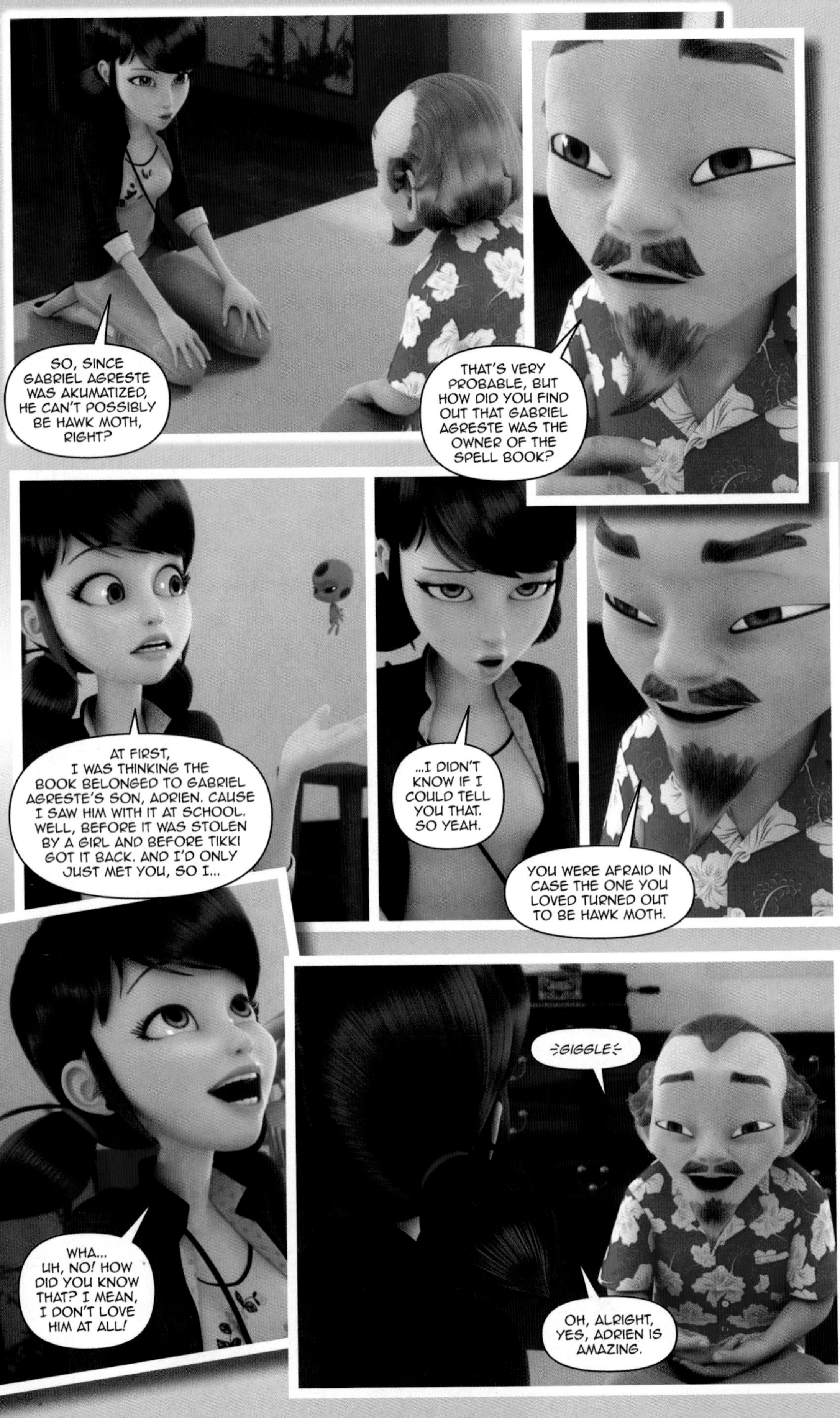

SO, SINCE GABRIEL AGRESTE WAS AKUMATIZED, HE CAN'T POSSIBLY BE HAWK MOTH, RIGHT?
THAT'S VERY PROBABLE, BUT HOW DID YOU FIND OUT THAT GABRIEL AGRESTE WAS THE OWNER OF THE SPELL BOOK?
AT FIRST, I WAS THINKING THE BOOK BELONGED TO GABRIEL AGRESTE'S SON, ADRIEN. CAUSE I SAW HIM WITH IT AT SCHOOL. WELL, BEFORE IT WAS STOLEN BY A GIRL AND BEFORE TIKKI GOT IT BACK. AND I'D ONLY JUST MET YOU, SO I...
...I DIDN'T KNOW IF I COULD TELL YOU THAT. SO YEAH.
YOU WERE AFRAID IN CASE THE ONE YOU LOVED TURNED OUT TO BE HAWK MOTH.
WHA... UH, NO! HOW DID YOU KNOW THAT? I MEAN, I DON'T LOVE HIM AT ALL!
GIGGLE
OH, ALRIGHT, YES, ADRIEN IS AMAZING.

YOU KNOW, MARINETTE, IF WE WANT TO BE STRONGER THAN HAWK MOTH, WE HAVE TO TRUST EACH OTHER.

I COULDN'T STAND THE THOUGHT OF HIM BEING A SUPERVILLAIN.

I KNOW, BUT NOW, ADRIEN WILL NEVER BE ABLE TO COME BACK TO SCHOOL BECAUSE I CAN NEVER GIVE HIM THAT BOOK BACK. I'LL NEVER EVER SEE HIM AGAIN.

THERE ISN'T A SINGLE PROBLEM THAT CAN'T BE SOLVED, MARINETTE.

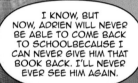

SNAP!

THESE MODERN INVENTIONS REALLY ARE QUITE INCREDIBLE.

SNAP!
SNAP!

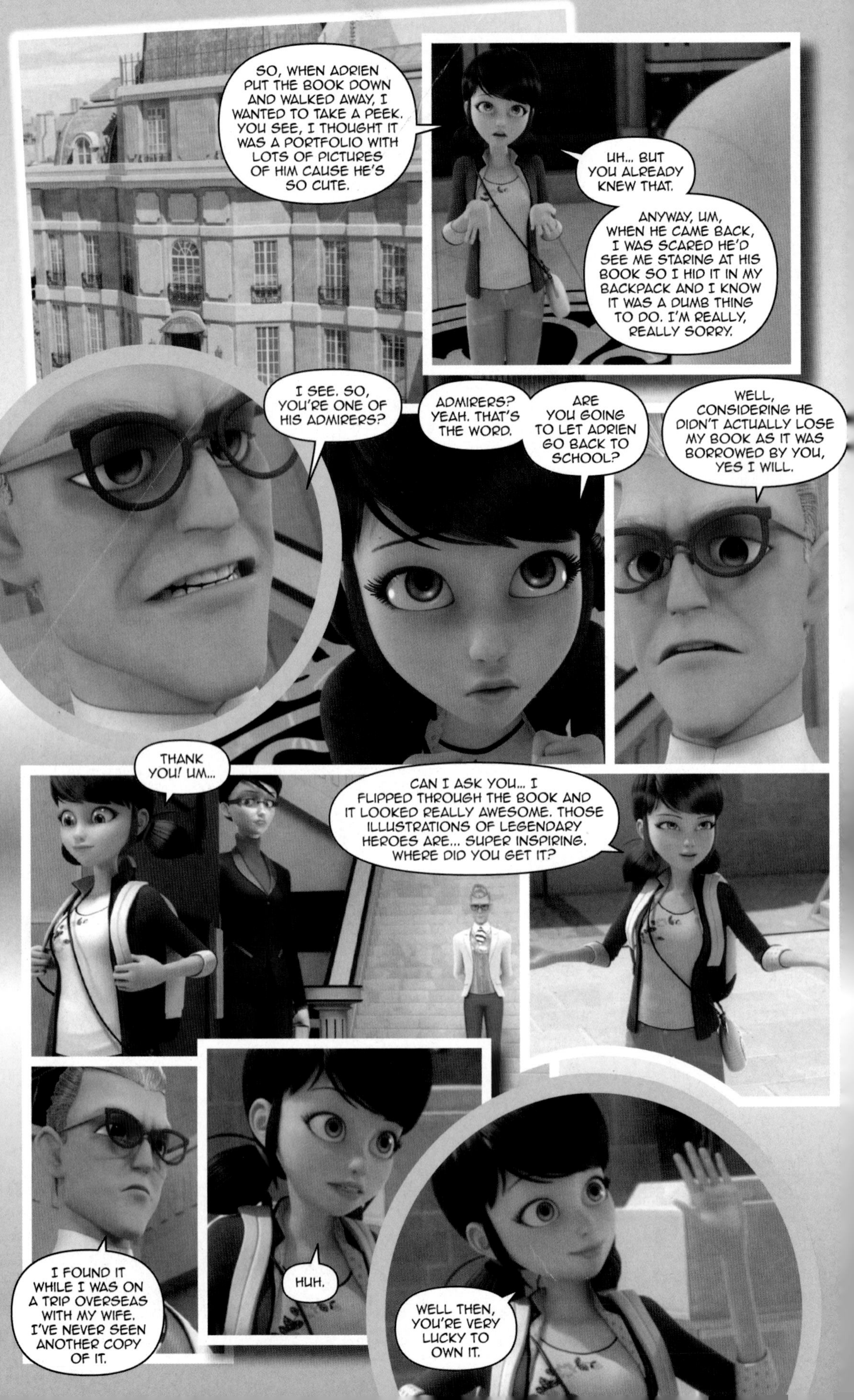
SO, WHEN ADRIEN PUT THE BOOK DOWN AND WALKED AWAY, I WANTED TO TAKE A PEEK. YOU SEE, I THOUGHT IT WAS A PORTFOLIO WITH LOTS OF PICTURES OF HIM CAUSE HE'S SO CUTE.
UH... BUT YOU ALREADY KNEW THAT.
ANYWAY, UM, WHEN HE CAME BACK, I WAS SCARED HE'D SEE ME STARING AT HIS BOOK SO I HID IT IN MY BACKPACK AND I KNOW IT WAS A DUMB THING TO DO. I'M REALLY, REALLY SORRY.
I SEE. SO, YOU'RE ONE OF HIS ADMIRERS?
ADMIRERS? YEAH. THAT'S THE WORD.
ARE YOU GOING TO LET ADRIEN GO BACK TO SCHOOL?
WELL, CONSIDERING HE DIDN'T ACTUALLY LOSE MY BOOK AS IT WAS BORROWED BY YOU, YES I WILL.
THANK YOU! UM...
CAN I ASK YOU... I FLIPPED THROUGH THE BOOK AND IT LOOKED REALLY AWESOME. THOSE ILLUSTRATIONS OF LEGENDARY HEROES ARE... SUPER INSPIRING. WHERE DID YOU GET IT?
I FOUND IT WHILE I WAS ON A TRIP OVERSEAS WITH MY WIFE. I'VE NEVER SEEN ANOTHER COPY OF IT.
HUH.
WELL THEN, YOU'RE VERY LUCKY TO OWN IT.

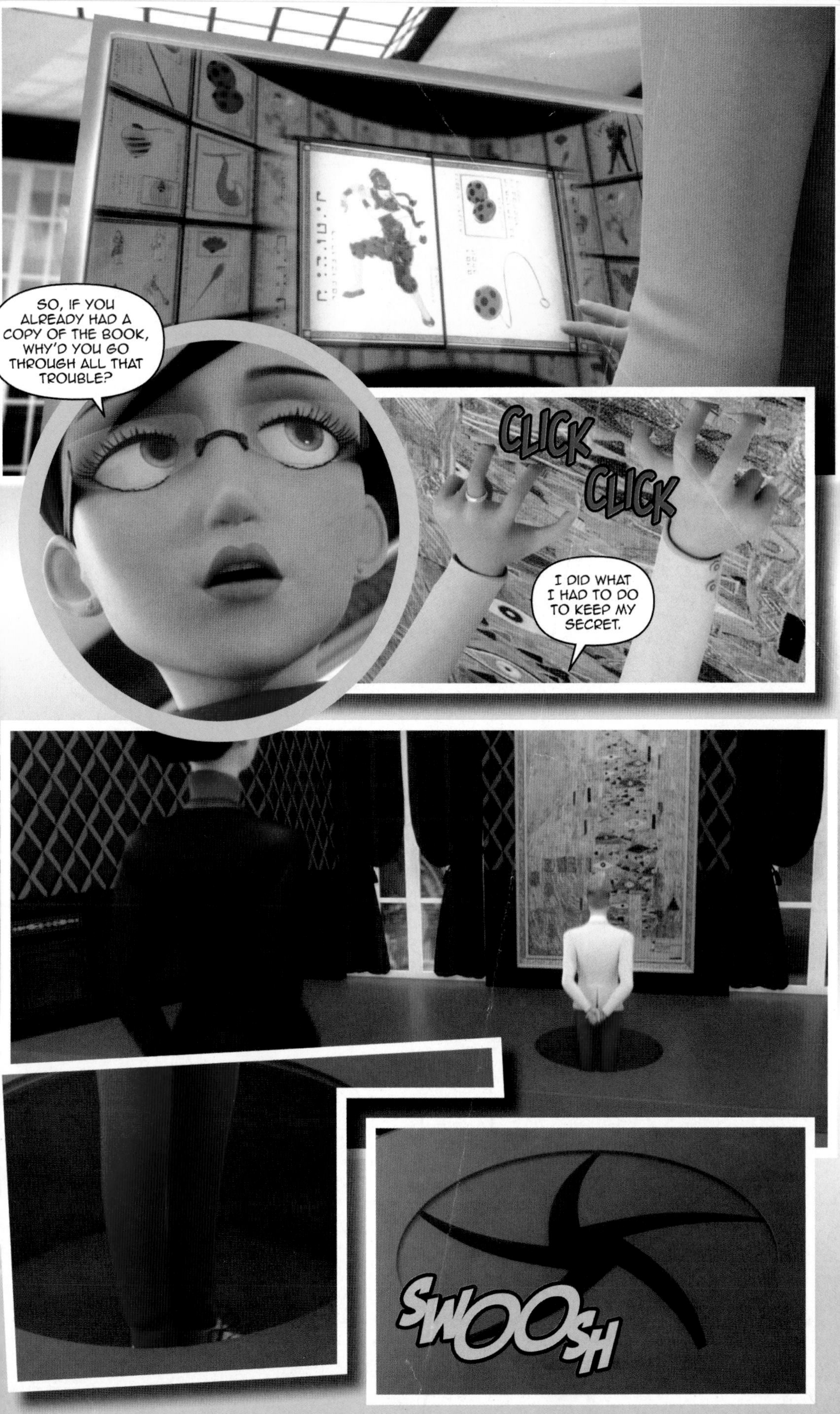
SO, IF YOU ALREADY HAD A COPY OF THE BOOK, WHY'D YOU GO THROUGH ALL THAT TROUBLE?
CLICK
CLICK
I DID WHAT I HAD TO DO TO KEEP MY SECRET.
SWOOSH

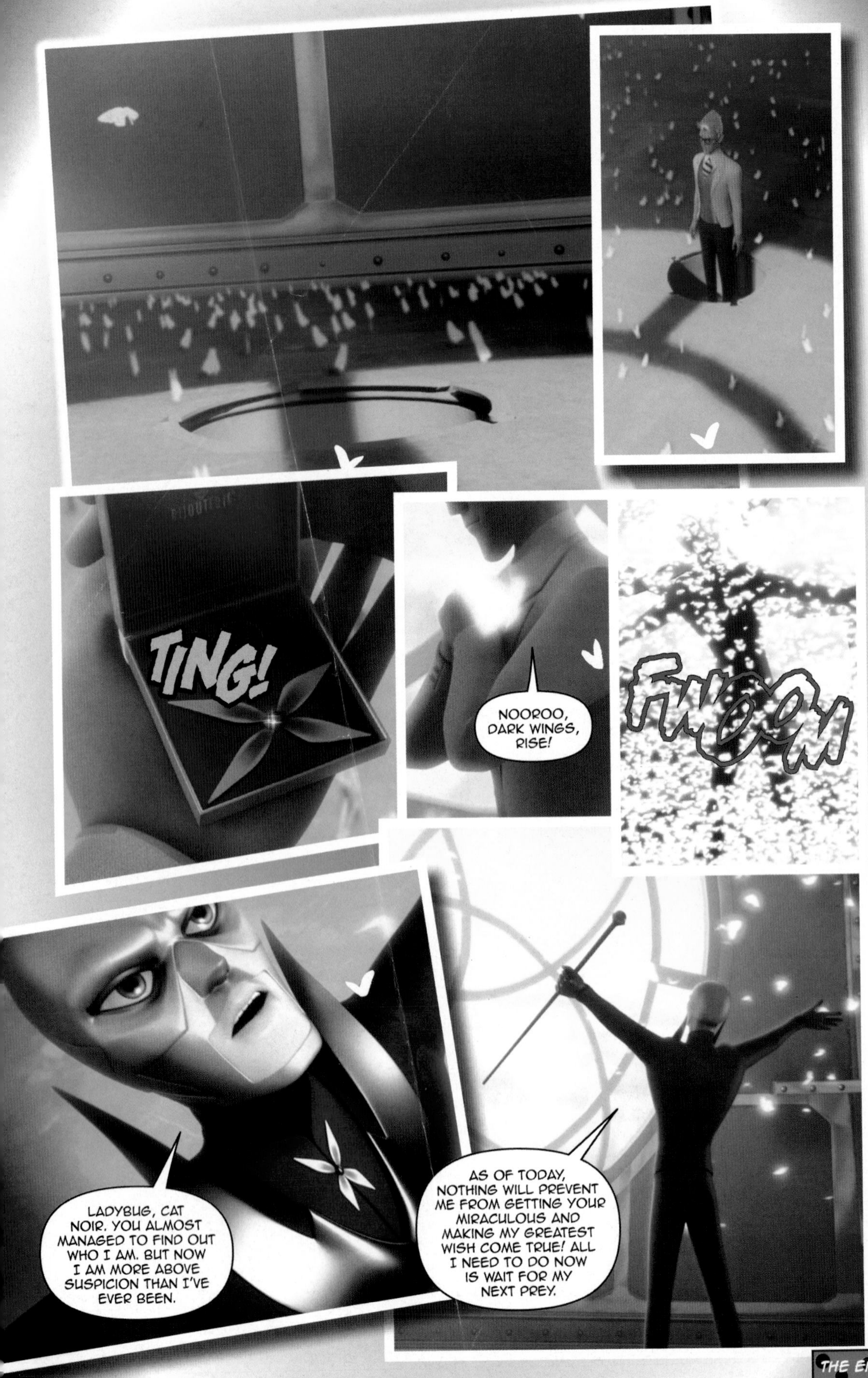
TING!
NOOROO, DARK WINGS, RISE!
FWOOM
LADYBUG, CAT NOIR. YOU ALMOST MANAGED TO FIND OUT WHO I AM. BUT NOW I AM MORE ABOVE SUSPICION THAN I'VE EVER BEEN.
AS OF TODAY, NOTHING WILL PREVENT ME FROM GETTING YOUR MIRACULOUS AND MAKING MY GREATEST WISH COME TRUE! ALL I NEED TO DO NOW IS WAIT FOR MY NEXT PREY.

THE EN

Prime Queen

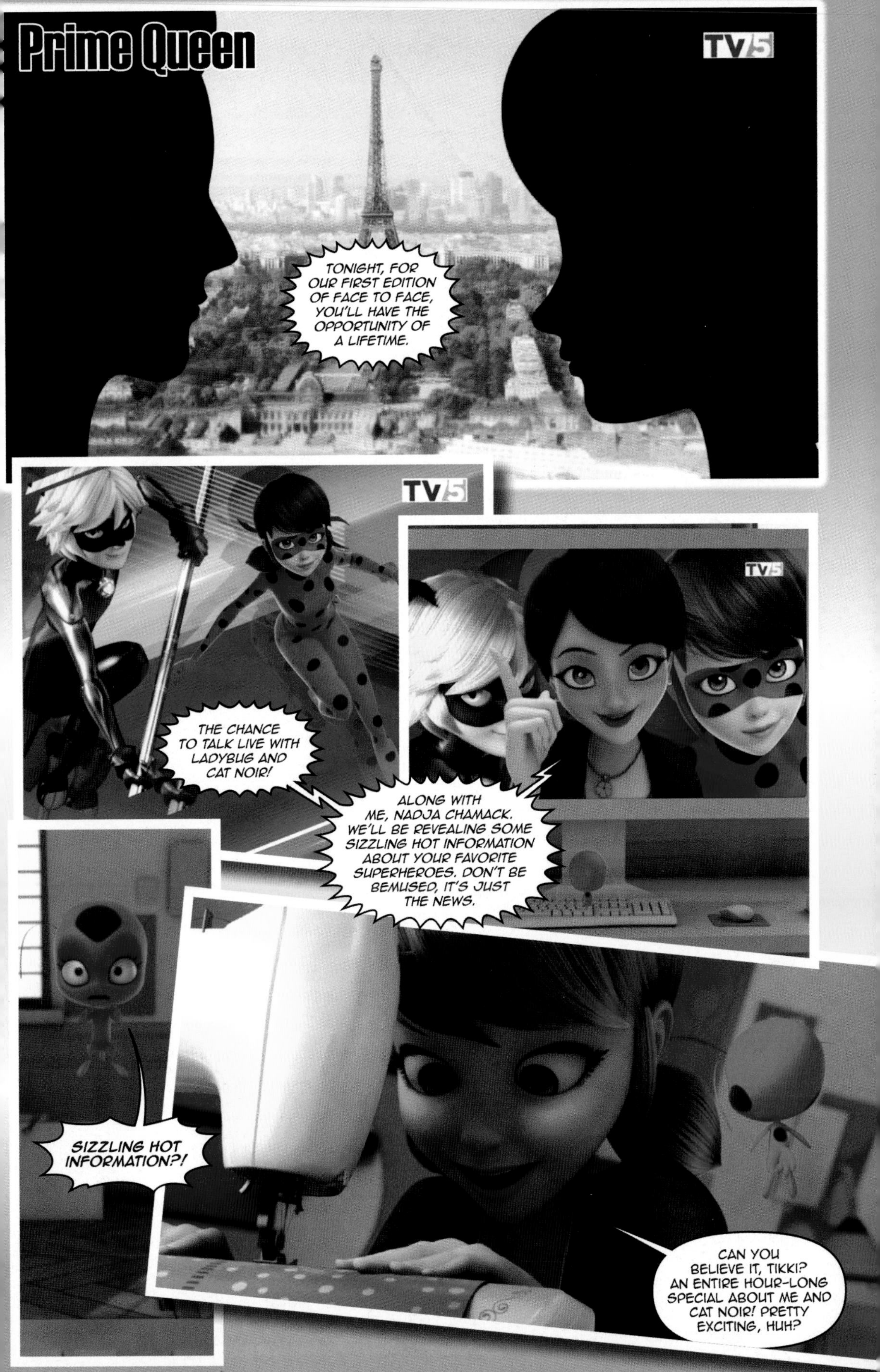
TV5
TONIGHT, FOR OUR FIRST EDITION OF FACE TO FACE, YOU'LL HAVE THE OPPORTUNITY OF A LIFETIME.
TV5
THE CHANCE TO TALK LIVE WITH LADYBUG AND CAT NOIR!
TV5
ALONG WITH ME, NADJA CHAMACK. WE'LL BE REVEALING SOME SIZZLING HOT INFORMATION ABOUT YOUR FAVORITE SUPERHEROES. DON'T BE BEMUSED, IT'S JUST THE NEWS.
SIZZLING HOT INFORMATION?!
CAN YOU BELIEVE IT, TIKKI? AN ENTIRE HOUR-LONG SPECIAL ABOUT ME AND CAT NOIR! PRETTY EXCITING, HUH?

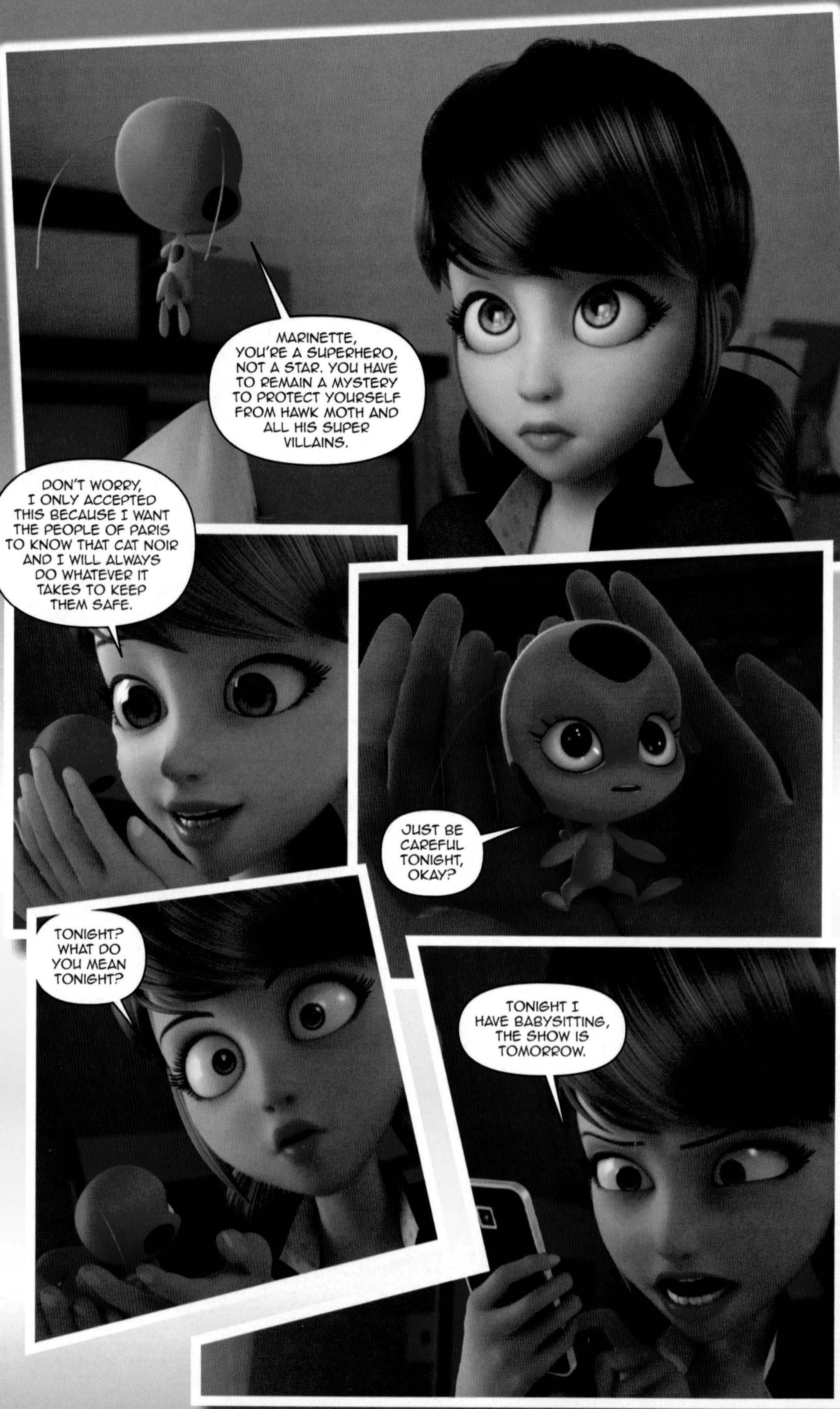
MARINETTE, YOU'RE A SUPERHERO, NOT A STAR. YOU HAVE TO REMAIN A MYSTERY TO PROTECT YOURSELF FROM HAWK MOTH AND ALL HIS SUPER VILLAINS.
DON'T WORRY, I ONLY ACCEPTED THIS BECAUSE I WANT THE PEOPLE OF PARIS TO KNOW THAT CAT NOIR AND I WILL ALWAYS DO WHATEVER IT TAKES TO KEEP THEM SAFE.
JUST BE CAREFUL TONIGHT, OKAY?
TONIGHT? WHAT DO YOU MEAN TONIGHT?
TONIGHT I HAVE BABYSITTING, THE SHOW IS TOMORROW.

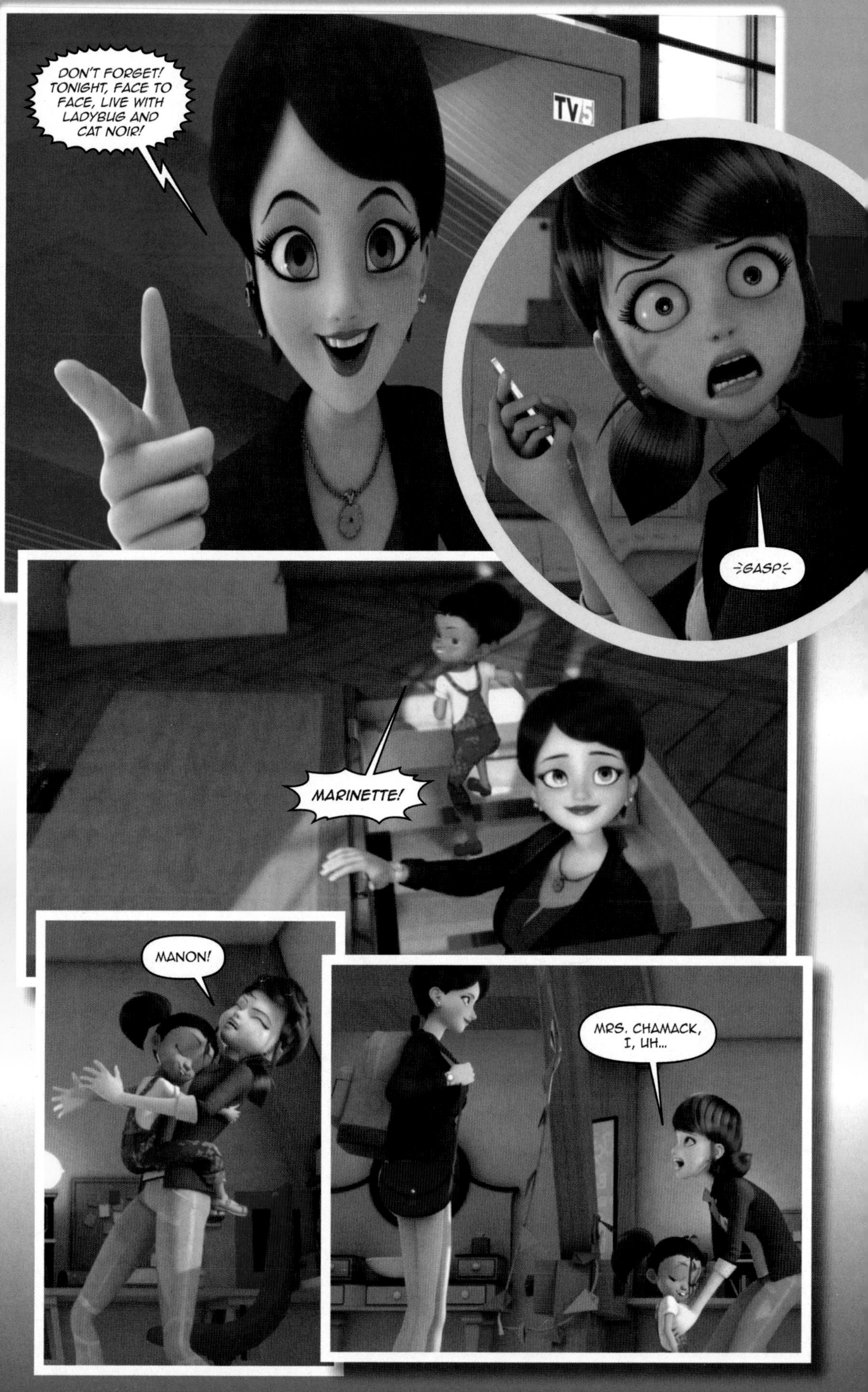
DON'T FORGET! TONIGHT, FACE TO FACE, LIVE WITH LADYBUG AND CAT NOIR!
TV5
GASP
MARINETTE!
MANON!
MRS. CHAMACK, I, UH...

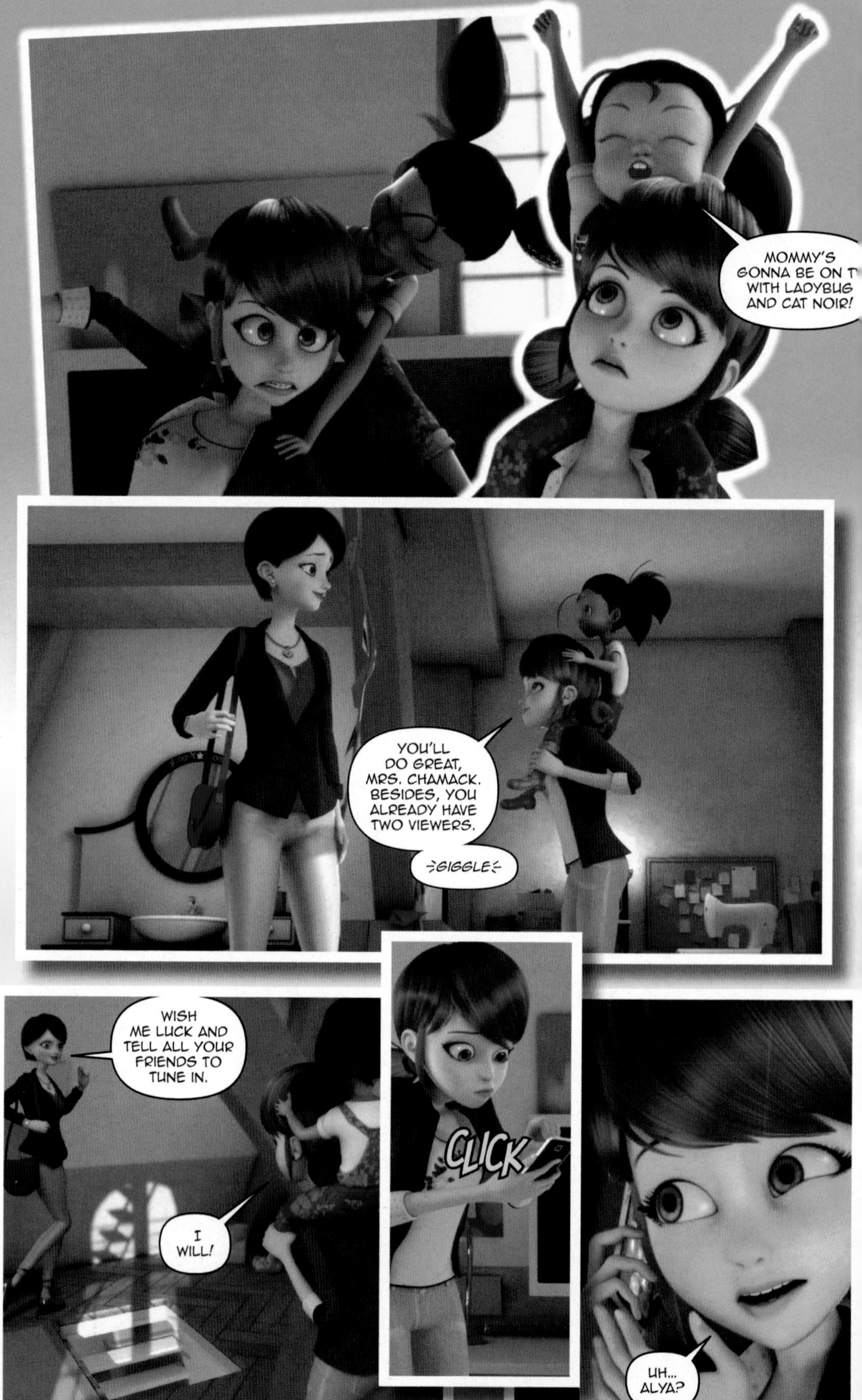

MOMMY'S GONNA BE ON T WITH LADYBUG AND CAT NOIR!
YOU'LL DO GREAT, MRS. CHAMACK. BESIDES, YOU ALREADY HAVE TWO VIEWERS.
GIGGLE
WISH ME LUCK AND TELL ALL YOUR FRIENDS TO TUNE IN.
I WILL!
CLICK
UH... ALYA?

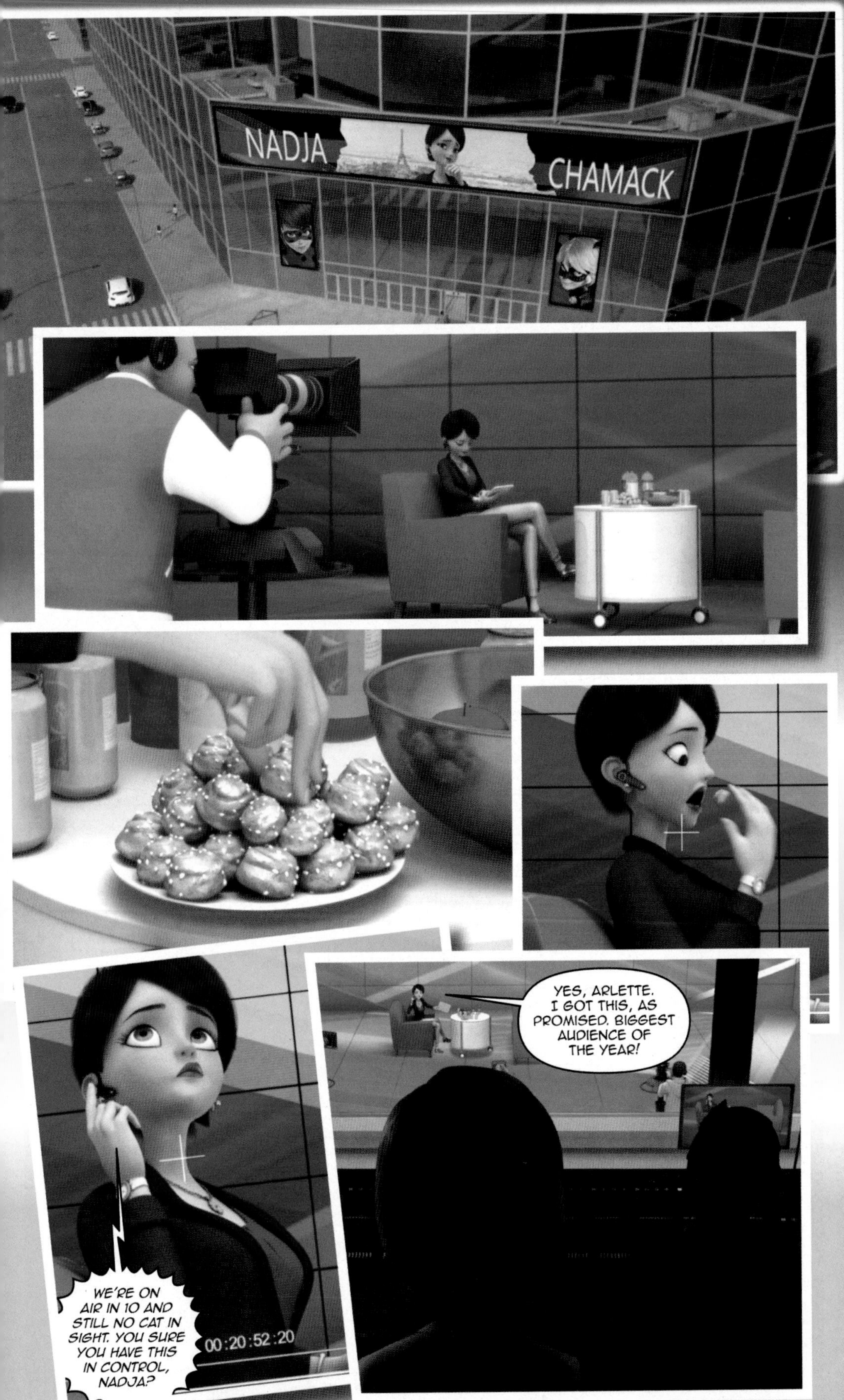
NADJA
CHAMACK
YES, ARLETTE. I GOT THIS, AS PROMISED. BIGGEST AUDIENCE OF THE YEAR!
WE'RE ON AIR IN 10 AND STILL NO CAT IN SIGHT. YOU SURE YOU HAVE THIS IN CONTROL, NADJA?
00:20:52:20

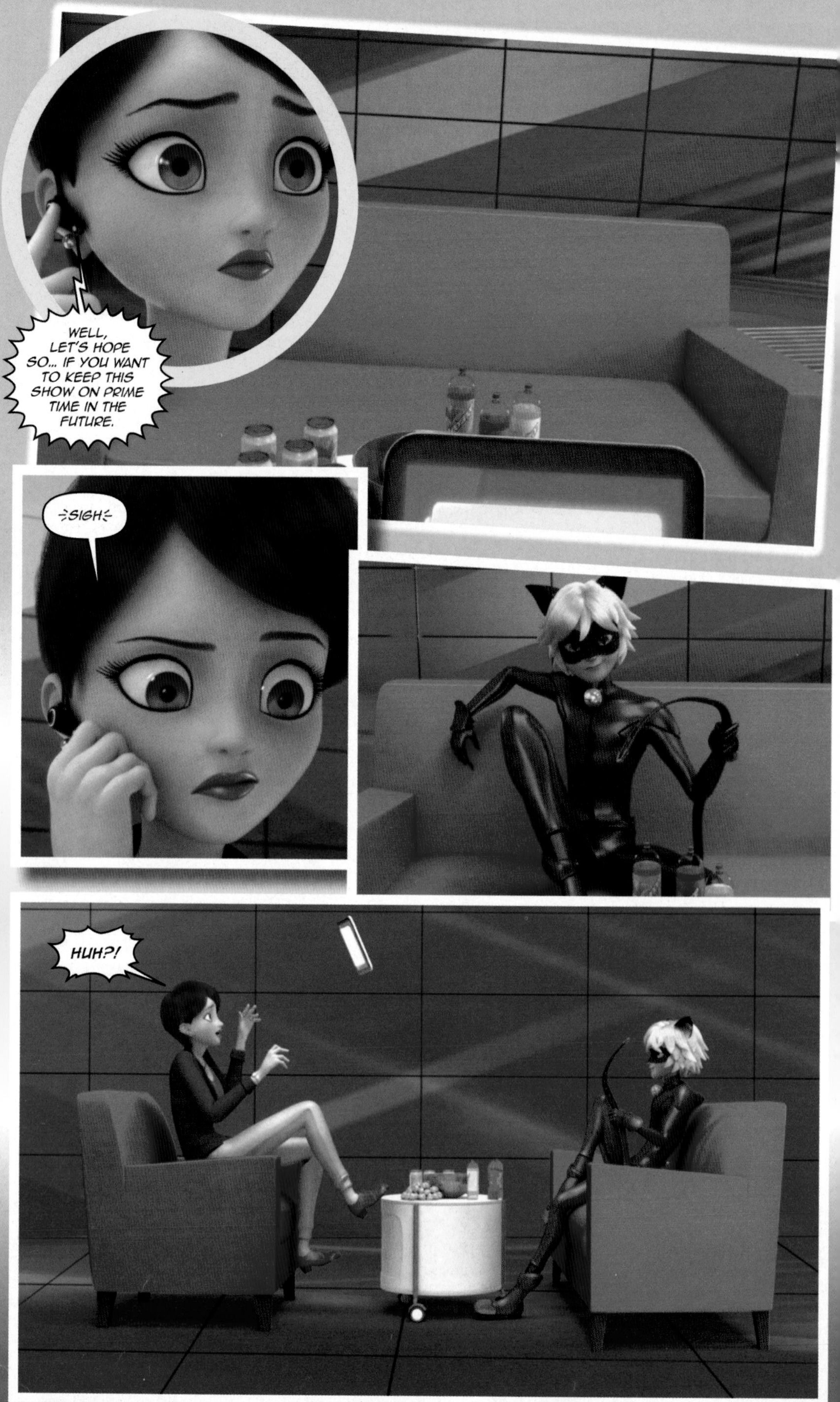
WELL, LET'S HOPE SO... IF YOU WANT TO KEEP THIS SHOW ON PRIME TIME IN THE FUTURE.
SIGH
HUH?!

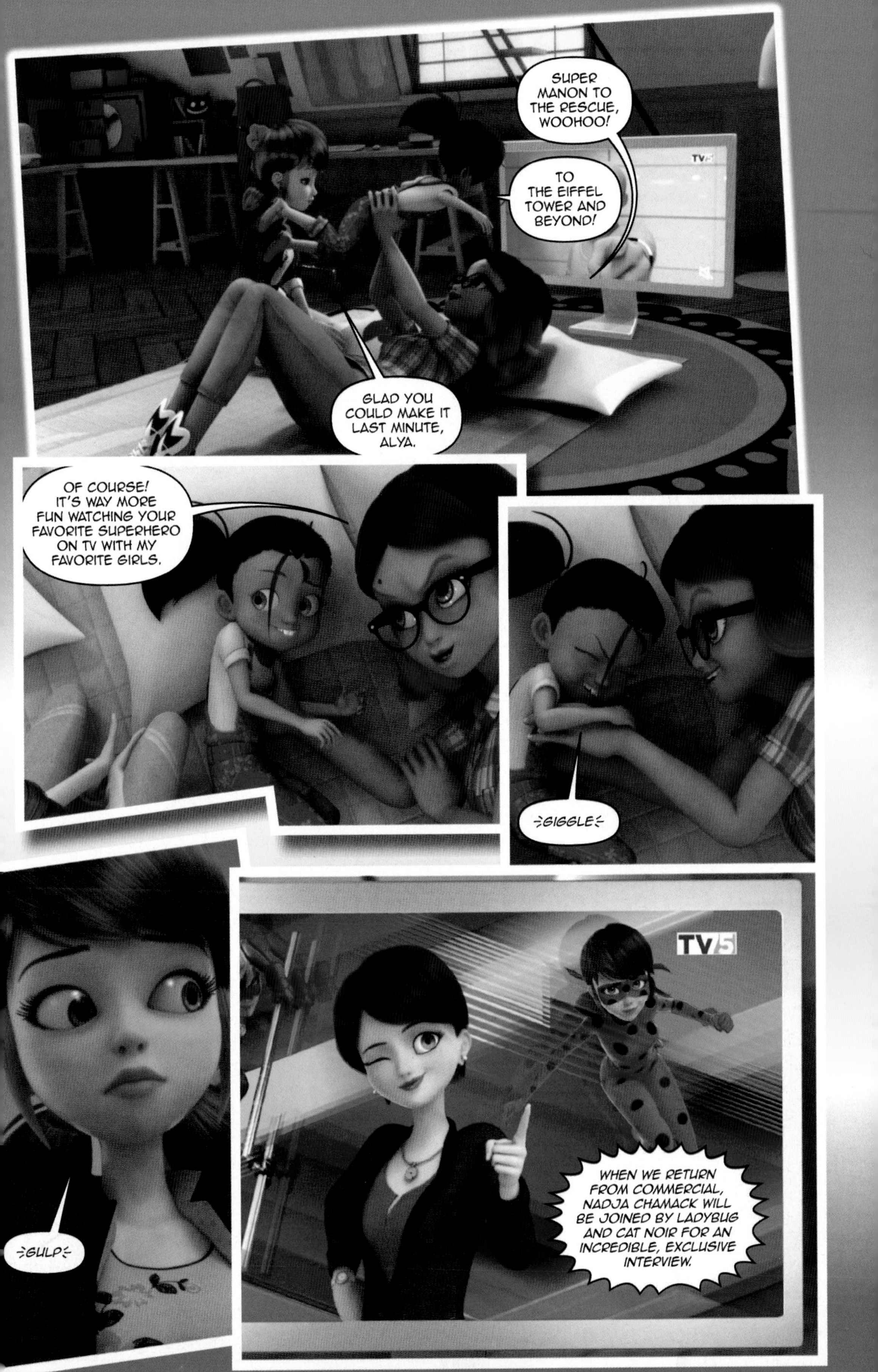
SUPER MANON TO THE RESCUE, WOOHOO!
TO THE EIFFEL TOWER AND BEYOND!
GLAD YOU COULD MAKE IT LAST MINUTE, ALYA.
OF COURSE! IT'S WAY MORE FUN WATCHING YOUR FAVORITE SUPERHERO ON TV WITH MY FAVORITE GIRLS.
GIGGLE
GULP
TV5
WHEN WE RETURN FROM COMMERCIAL, NADJA CHAMACK WILL BE JOINED BY LADYBUG AND CAT NOIR FOR AN INCREDIBLE, EXCLUSIVE INTERVIEW.

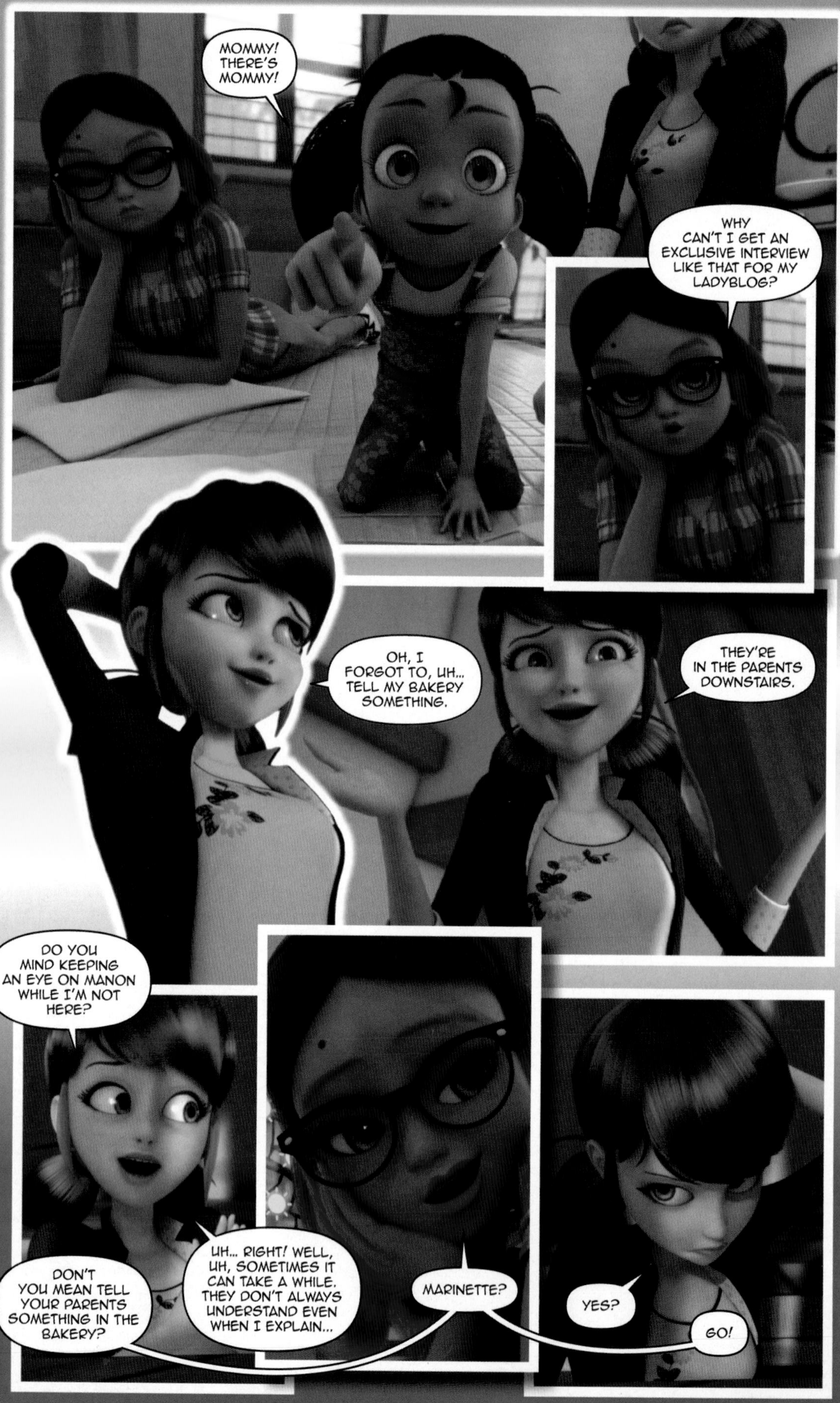
MOMMY! THERE'S MOMMY!
WHY CAN'T I GET AN EXCLUSIVE INTERVIEW LIKE THAT FOR MY LADYBLOG?
OH, I FORGOT TO, UH... TELL MY BAKERY SOMETHING.
THEY'RE IN THE PARENTS DOWNSTAIRS.
DO YOU MIND KEEPING AN EYE ON MANON WHILE I'M NOT HERE?
DON'T YOU MEAN TELL YOUR PARENTS SOMETHING IN THE BAKERY?
UH... RIGHT! WELL, UH, SOMETIMES IT CAN TAKE A WHILE. THEY DON'T ALWAYS UNDERSTAND EVEN WHEN I EXPLAIN...
MARINETTE?
YES?
GO!

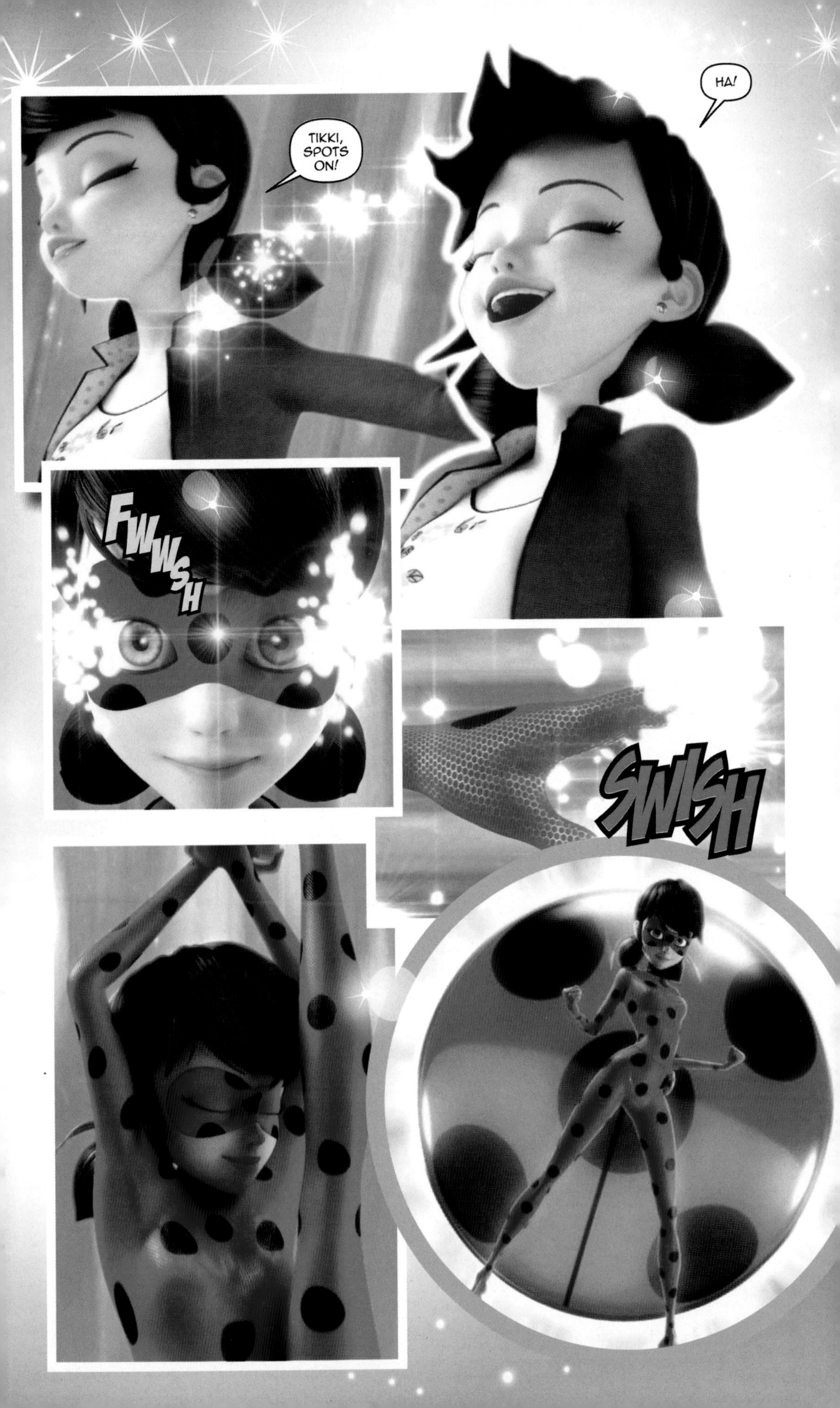
TIKKI, SPOTS ON!
HA!
FWWSH
SWISH

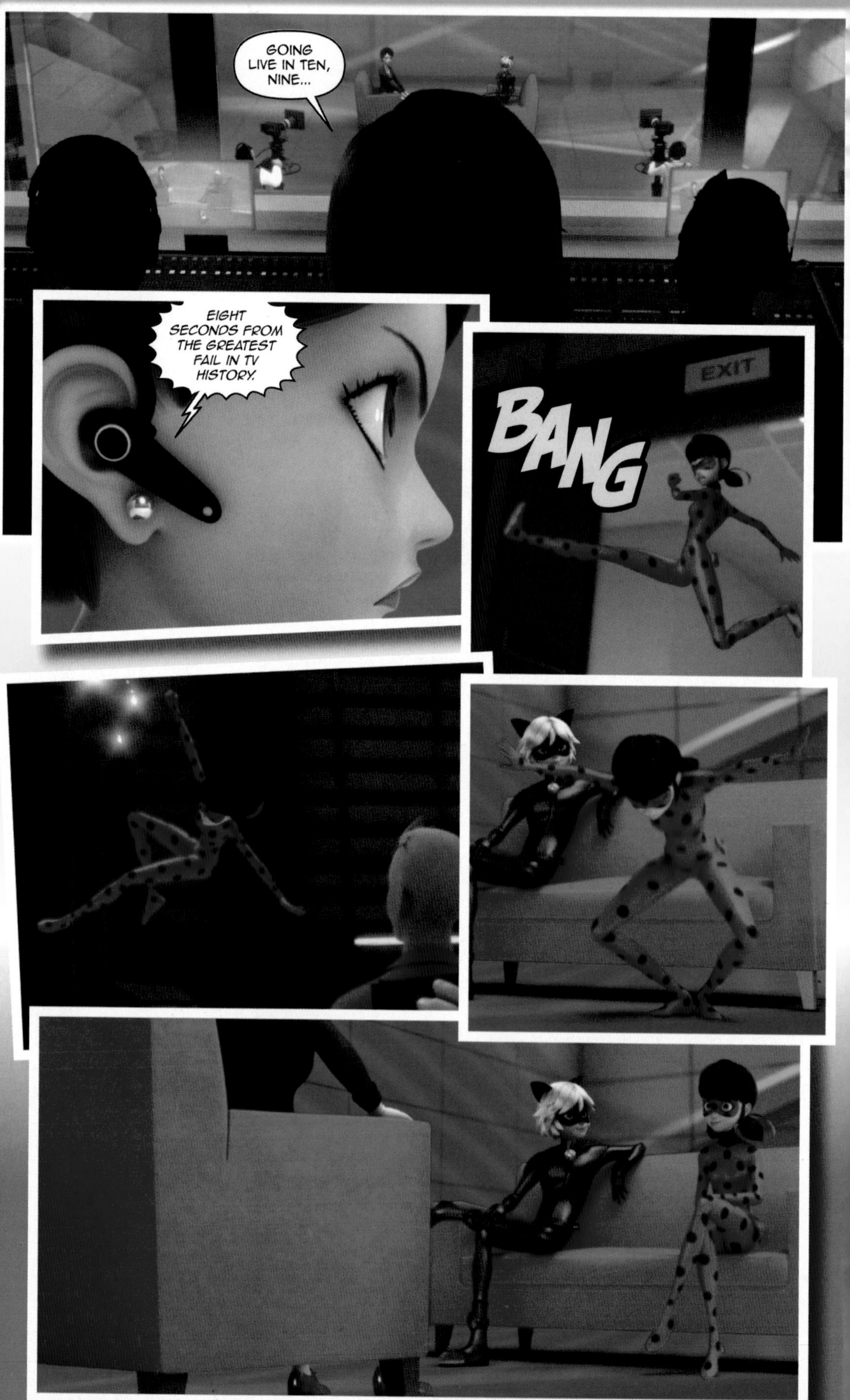
GOING LIVE IN TEN, NINE...
EIGHT SECONDS FROM THE GREATEST FAIL IN TV HISTORY.
EXIT
BANG

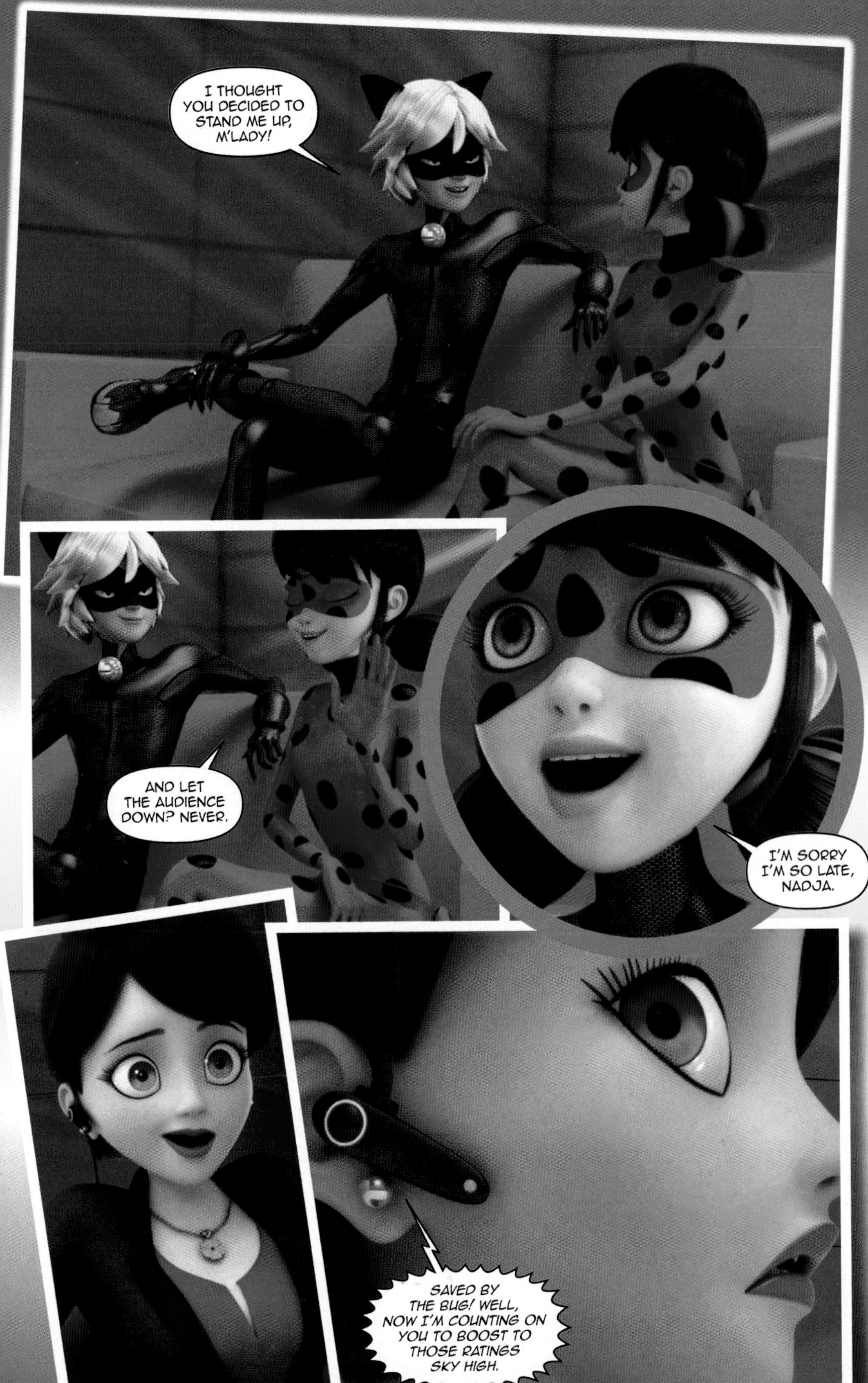
I THOUGHT YOU DECIDED TO STAND ME UP, M'LADY!
AND LET THE AUDIENCE DOWN? NEVER.
I'M SORRY I'M SO LATE, NADJA.
SAVED BY THE BUG! WELL, NOW I'M COUNTING ON YOU TO BOOST TO THOSE RATINGS SKY HIGH.

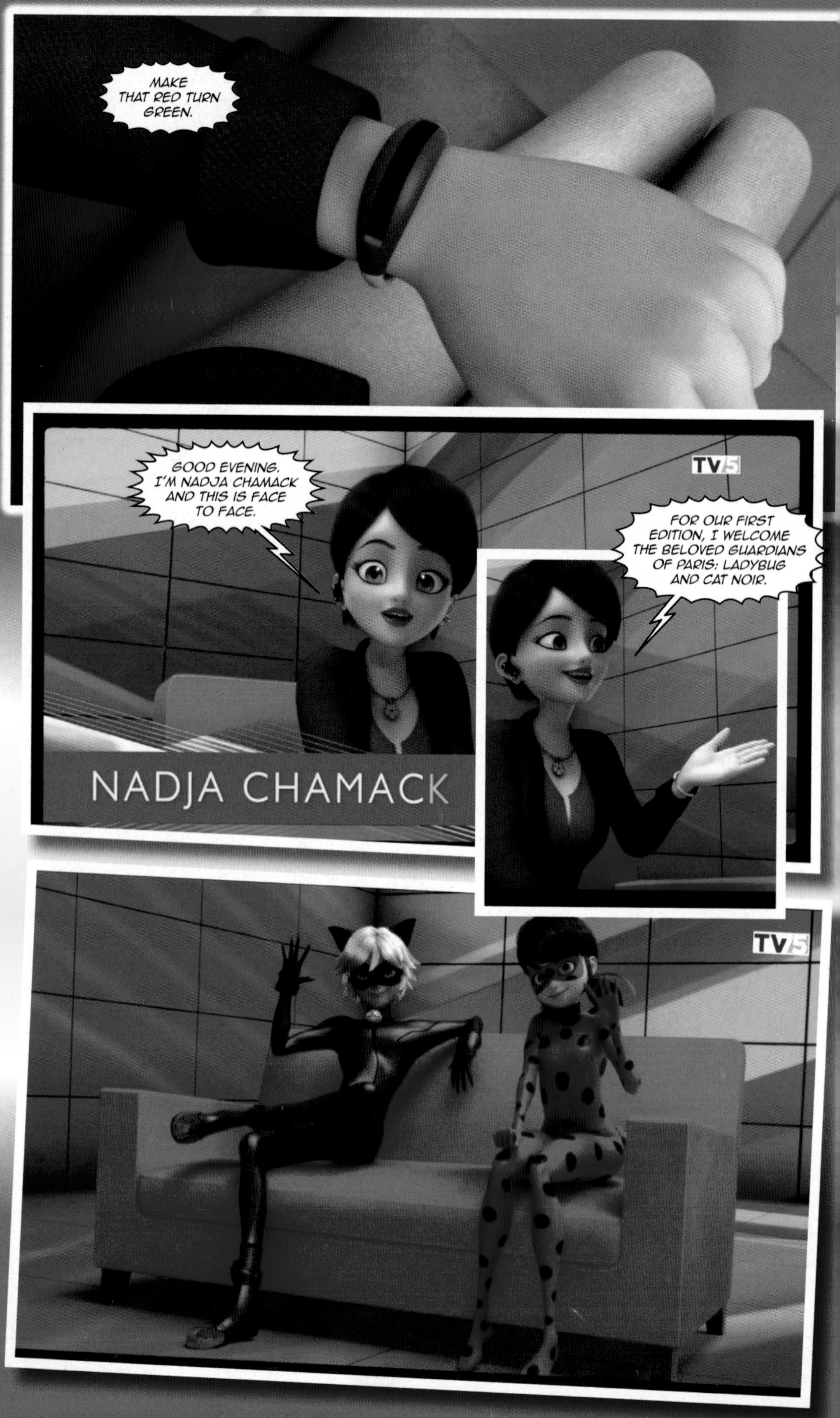
MAKE THAT RED TURN GREEN.
GOOD EVENING. I'M NADJA CHAMACK AND THIS IS FACE TO FACE.
TV5
NADJA CHAMACK
FOR OUR FIRST EDITION, I WELCOME THE BELOVED GUARDIANS OF PARIS: LADYBUG AND CAT NOIR.
TV5

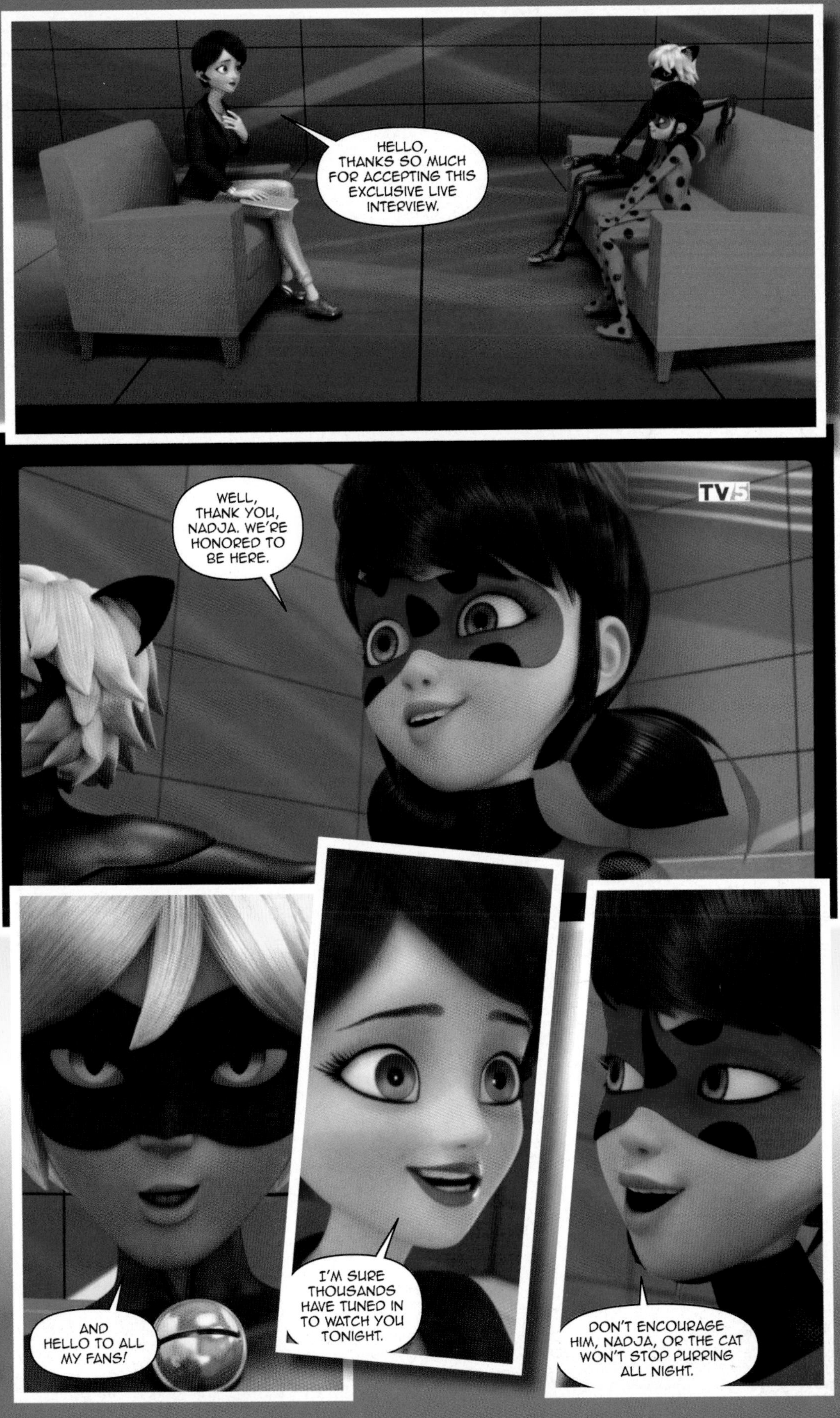
HELLO, THANKS SO MUCH FOR ACCEPTING THIS EXCLUSIVE LIVE INTERVIEW.
TV5
WELL, THANK YOU, NADJA. WE'RE HONORED TO BE HERE.
AND HELLO TO ALL MY FANS!
I'M SURE THOUSANDS HAVE TUNED IN TO WATCH YOU TONIGHT.
DON'T ENCOURAGE HIM, NADJA, OR THE CAT WON'T STOP PURRING ALL NIGHT.

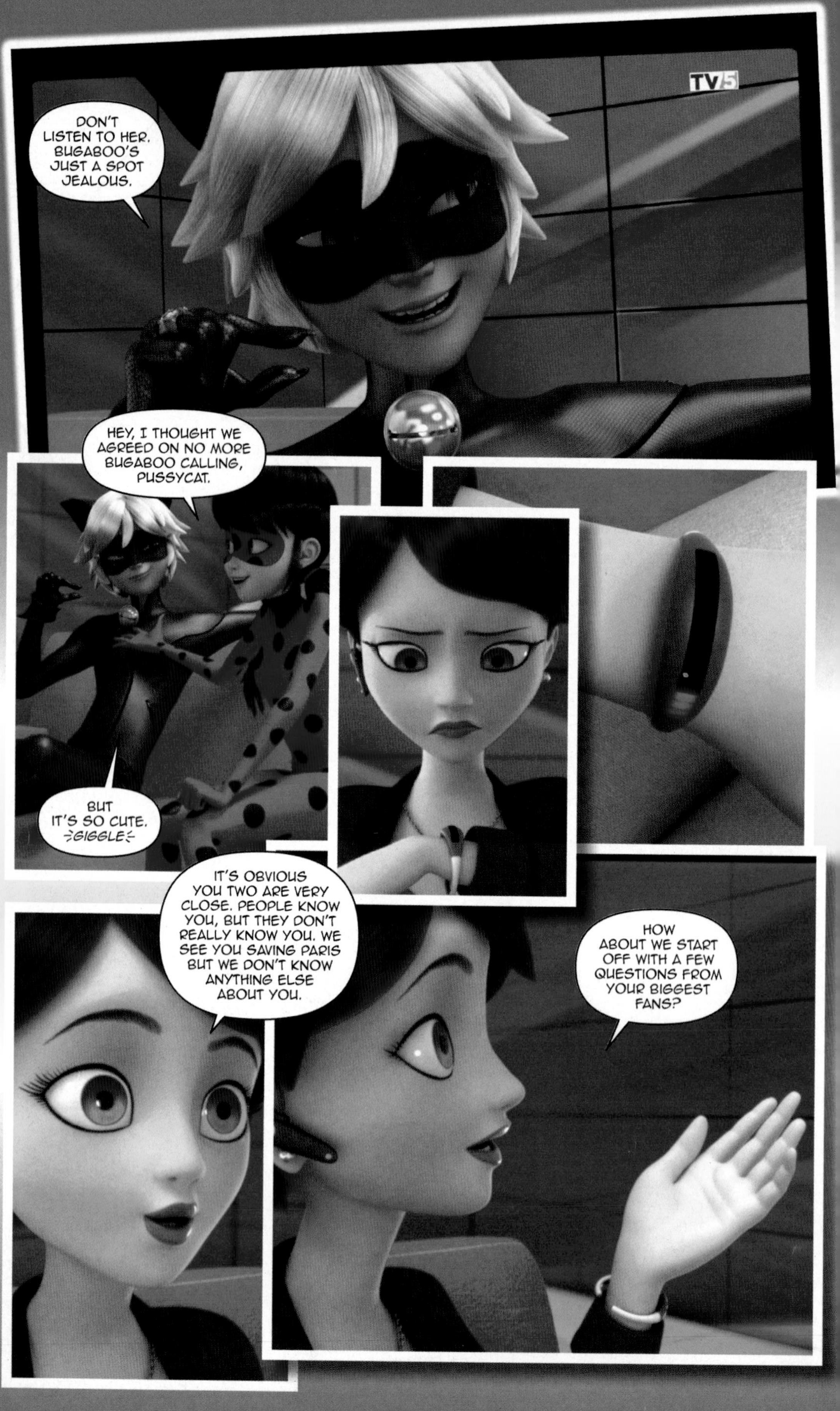
TV5
DON'T LISTEN TO HER. BUGABOO'S JUST A SPOT JEALOUS.
HEY, I THOUGHT WE AGREED ON NO MORE BUGABOO CALLING, PUSSYCAT.
BUT IT'S SO CUTE. -GIGGLE-
IT'S OBVIOUS YOU TWO ARE VERY CLOSE. PEOPLE KNOW YOU, BUT THEY DON'T REALLY KNOW YOU. WE SEE YOU SAVING PARIS BUT WE DON'T KNOW ANYTHING ELSE ABOUT YOU.
HOW ABOUT WE START OFF WITH A FEW QUESTIONS FROM YOUR BIGGEST FANS?

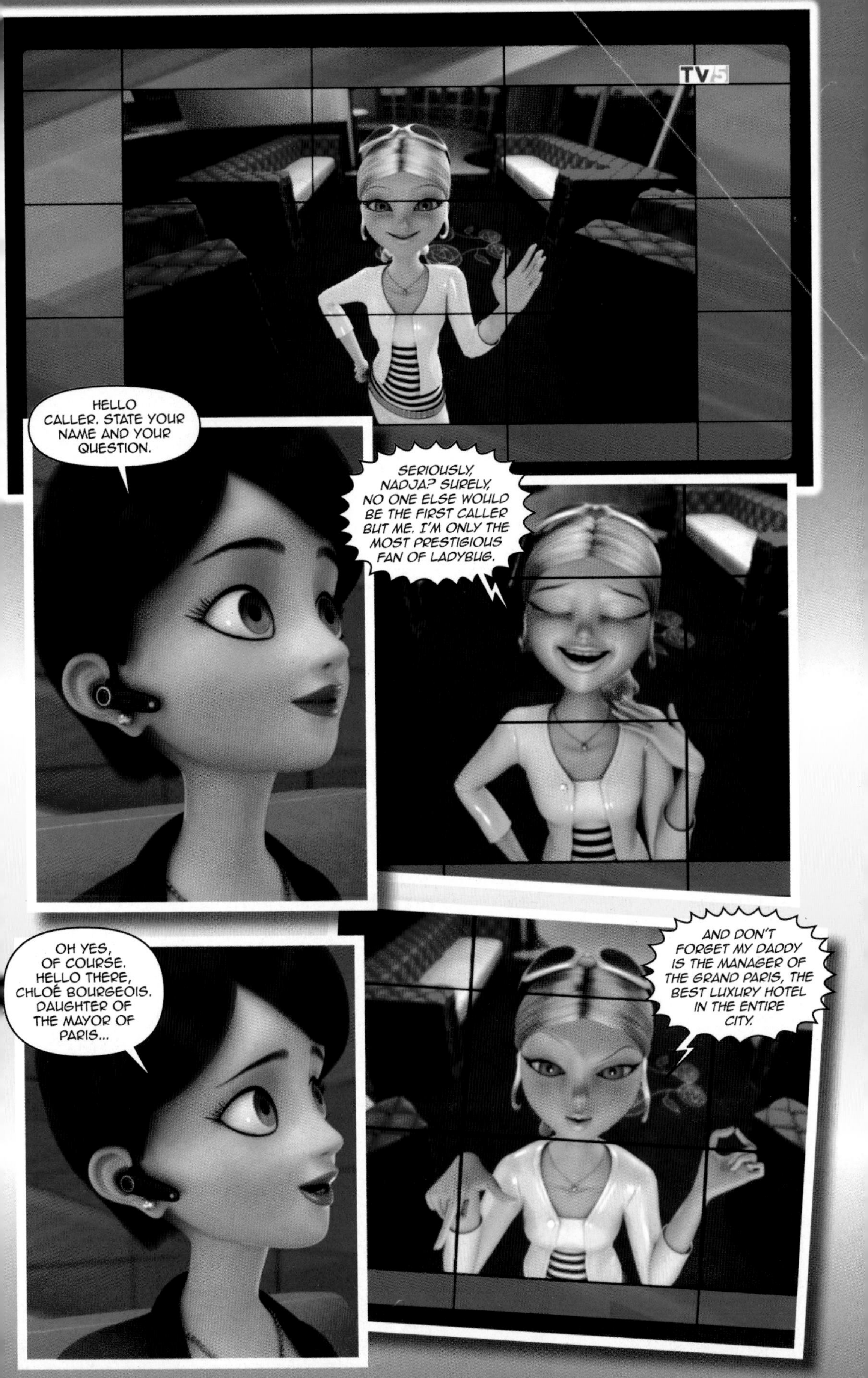
TV5
HELLO CALLER. STATE YOUR NAME AND YOUR QUESTION.
SERIOUSLY, NADJA? SURELY, NO ONE ELSE WOULD BE THE FIRST CALLER BUT ME. I'M ONLY THE MOST PRESTIGIOUS FAN OF LADYBUG.
OH YES, OF COURSE. HELLO THERE, CHLOÉ BOURGEOIS. DAUGHTER OF THE MAYOR OF PARIS...
AND DON'T FORGET MY DADDY IS THE MANAGER OF THE GRAND PARIS, THE BEST LUXURY HOTEL IN THE ENTIRE CITY.

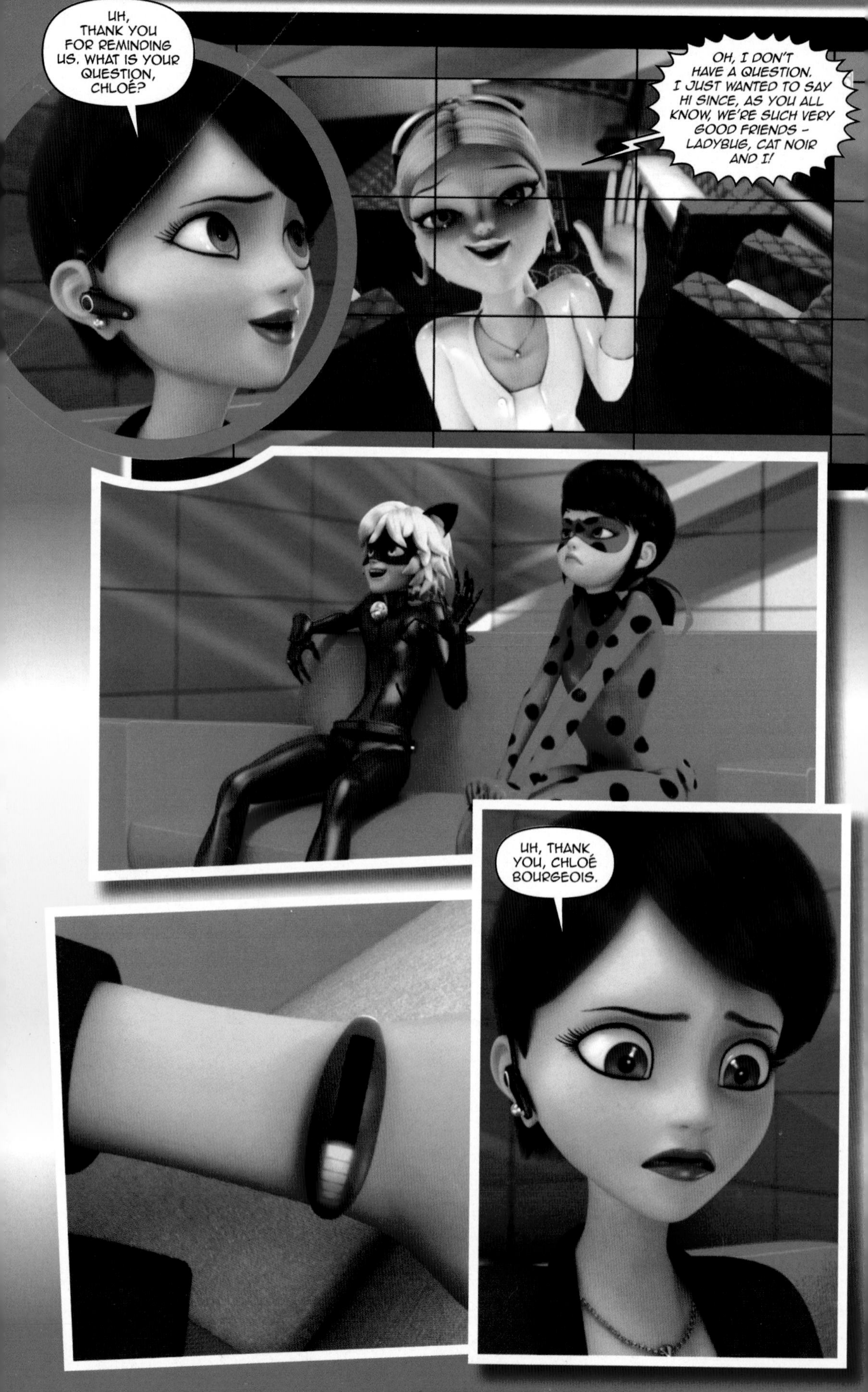
UH, THANK YOU FOR REMINDING US. WHAT IS YOUR QUESTION, CHLOÉ?
OH, I DON'T HAVE A QUESTION. I JUST WANTED TO SAY HI SINCE, AS YOU ALL KNOW, WE'RE SUCH VERY GOOD FRIENDS – LADYBUG, CAT NOIR AND I!
UH, THANK YOU, CHLOÉ BOURGEOIS.

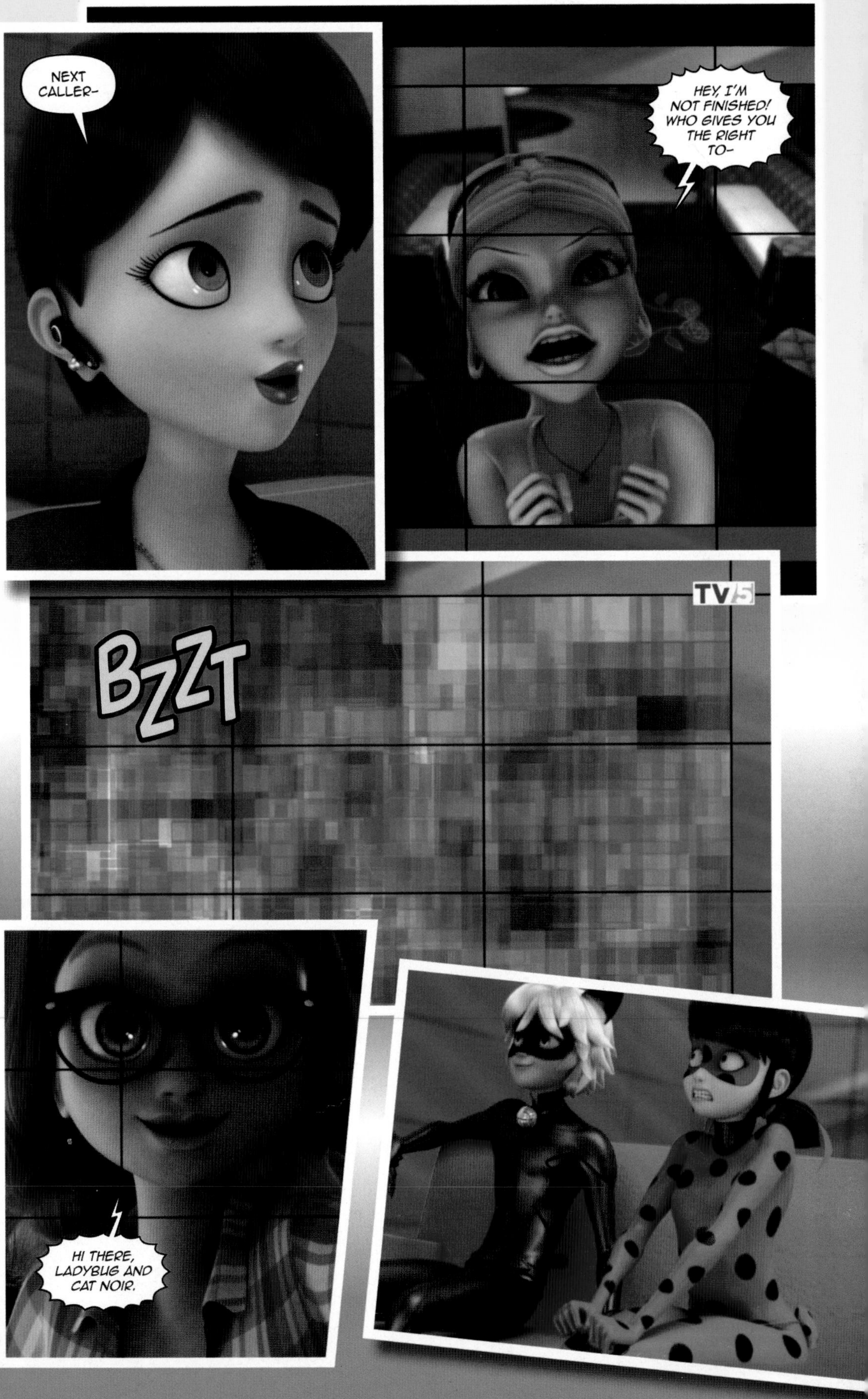
NEXT CALLER-
HEY, I'M NOT FINISHED! WHO GIVES YOU THE RIGHT TO-
TV5
BZZT
HI THERE, LADYBUG AND CAT NOIR.

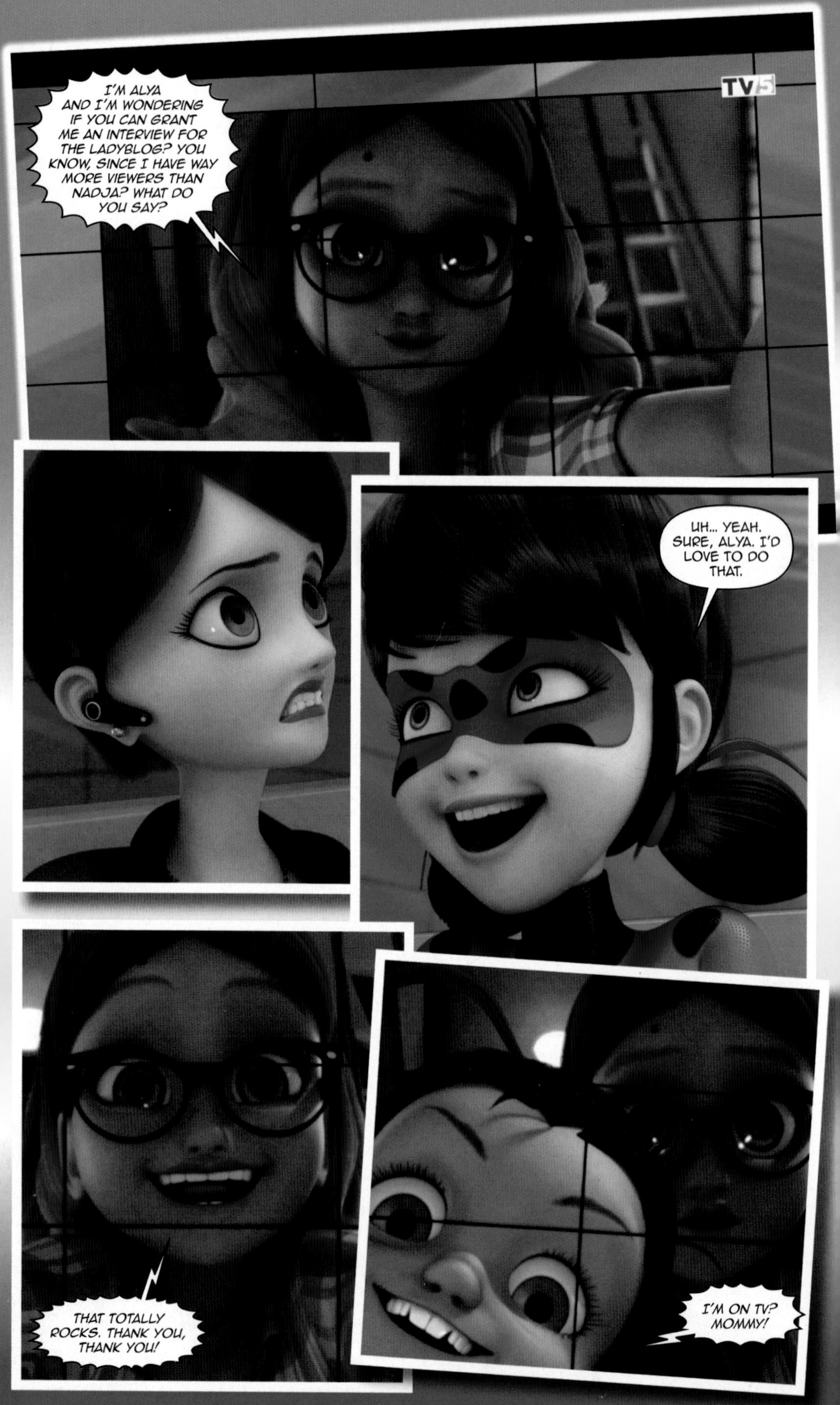
I'M ALYA AND I'M WONDERING IF YOU CAN GRANT ME AN INTERVIEW FOR THE LADYBLOG? YOU KNOW, SINCE I HAVE WAY MORE VIEWERS THAN NADJA? WHAT DO YOU SAY?
TV5
UH... YEAH. SURE, ALYA. I'D LOVE TO DO THAT.
THAT TOTALLY ROCKS. THANK YOU, THANK YOU!
I'M ON TV? MOMMY!

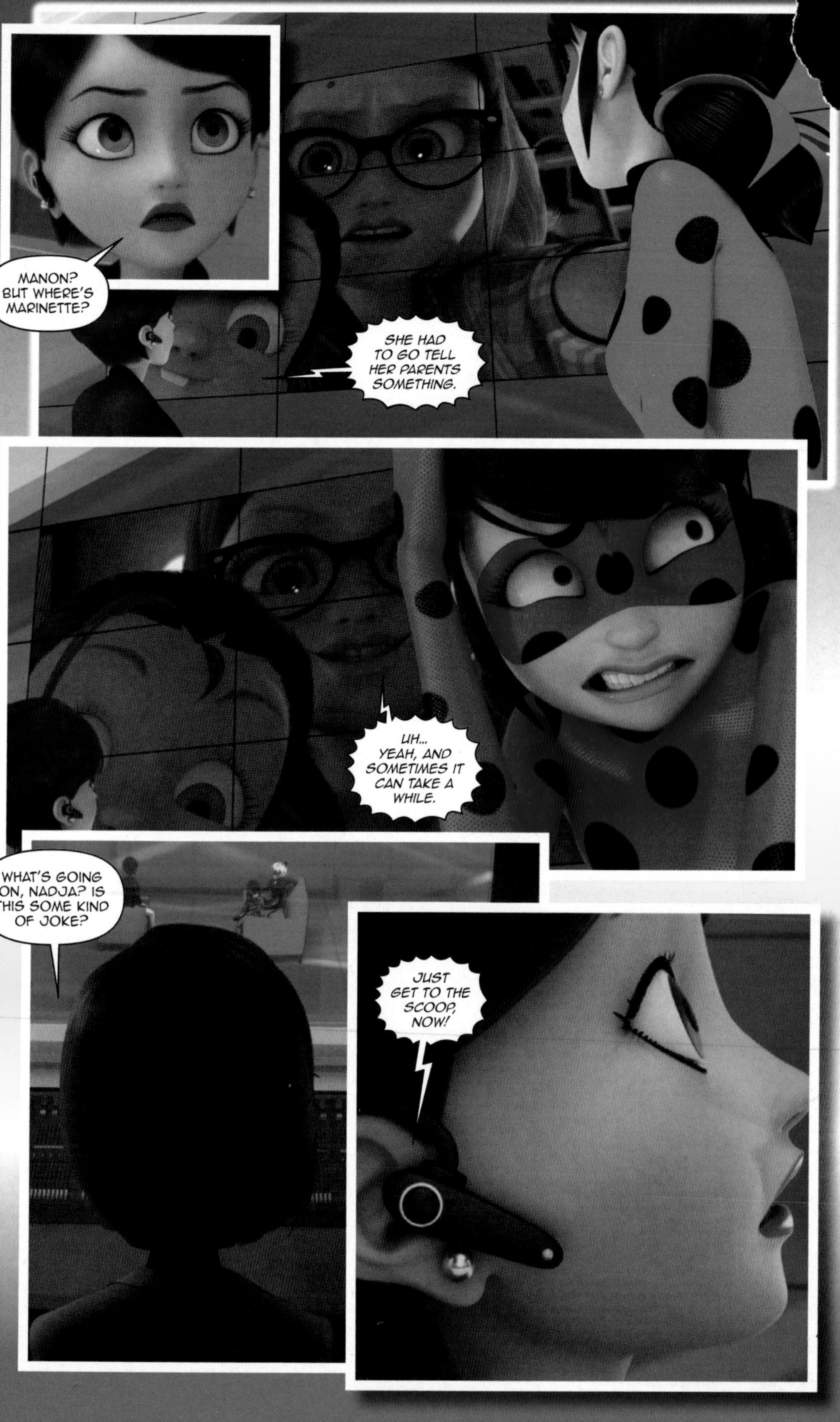
MANON? BUT WHERE'S MARINETTE?
SHE HAD TO GO TELL HER PARENTS SOMETHING.
UH... YEAH, AND SOMETIMES IT CAN TAKE A WHILE.
WHAT'S GOING ON, NADJA? IS THIS SOME KIND OF JOKE?
JUST GET TO THE SCOOP, NOW!

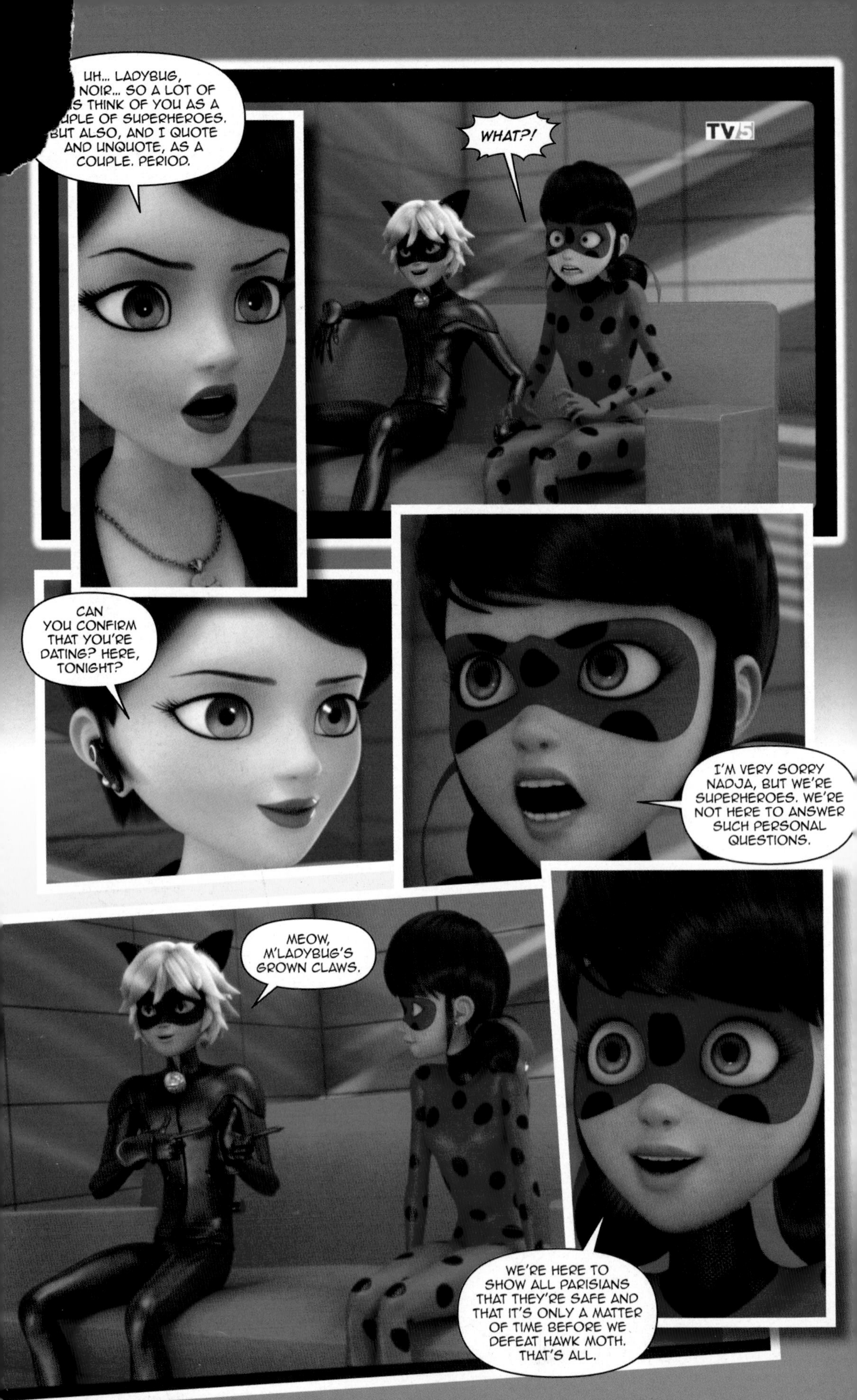
UH... LADYBUG,
NOIR... SO A LOT OF
S THINK OF YOU AS A
UPLE OF SUPERHEROES.
BUT ALSO, AND I QUOTE AND UNQUOTE, AS A COUPLE. PERIOD.
WHAT?!
TV5
CAN YOU CONFIRM THAT YOU'RE DATING? HERE, TONIGHT?
I'M VERY SORRY NADJA, BUT WE'RE SUPERHEROES. WE'RE NOT HERE TO ANSWER SUCH PERSONAL QUESTIONS.
MEOW, M'LADYBUG'S GROWN CLAWS.
WE'RE HERE TO SHOW ALL PARISIANS THAT THEY'RE SAFE AND THAT IT'S ONLY A MATTER OF TIME BEFORE WE DEFEAT HAWK MOTH. THAT'S ALL.

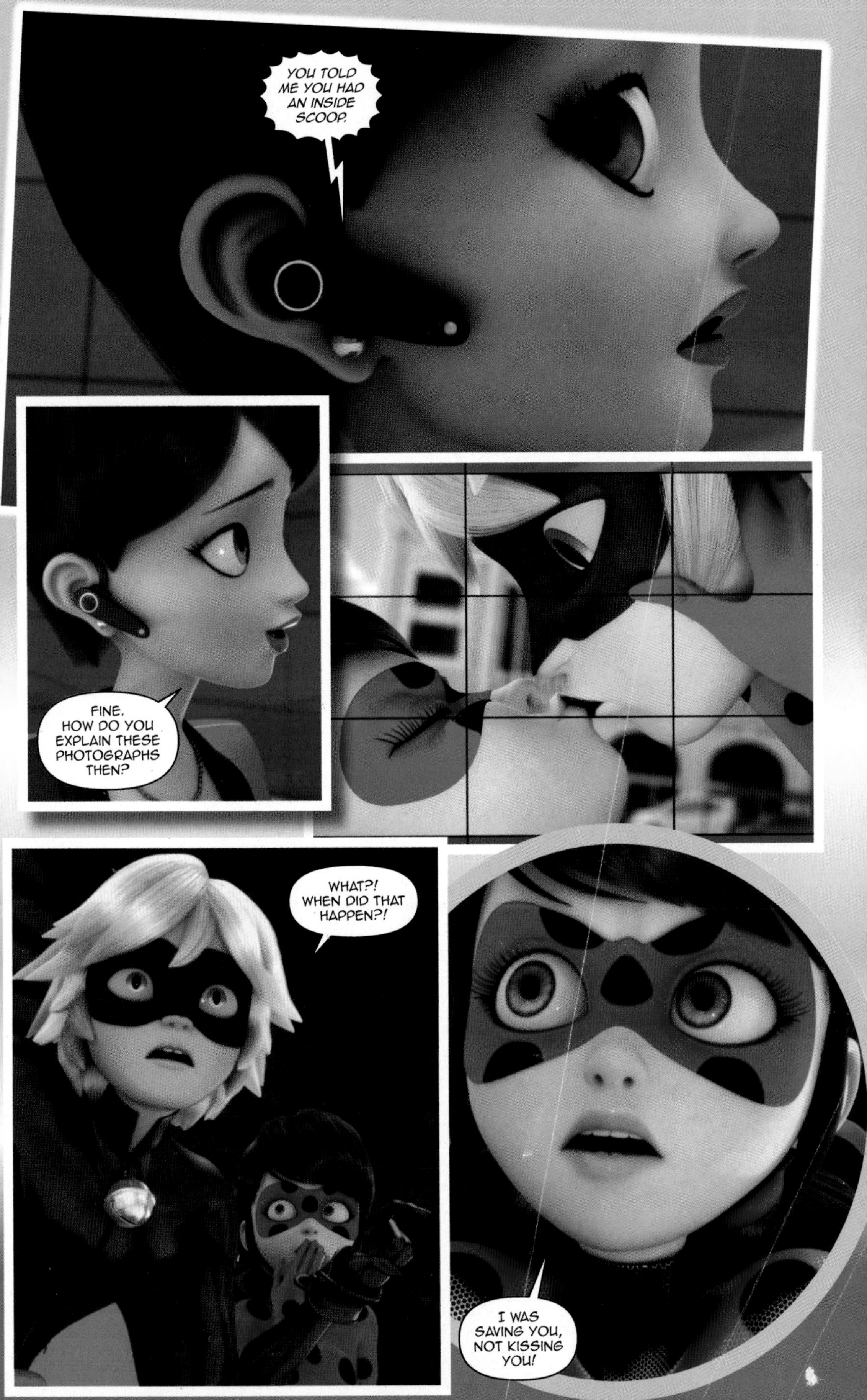
YOU TOLD ME YOU HAD AN INSIDE SCOOP.
FINE. HOW DO YOU EXPLAIN THESE PHOTOGRAPHS THEN?
WHAT?! WHEN DID THAT HAPPEN?!
I WAS SAVING YOU, NOT KISSING YOU!

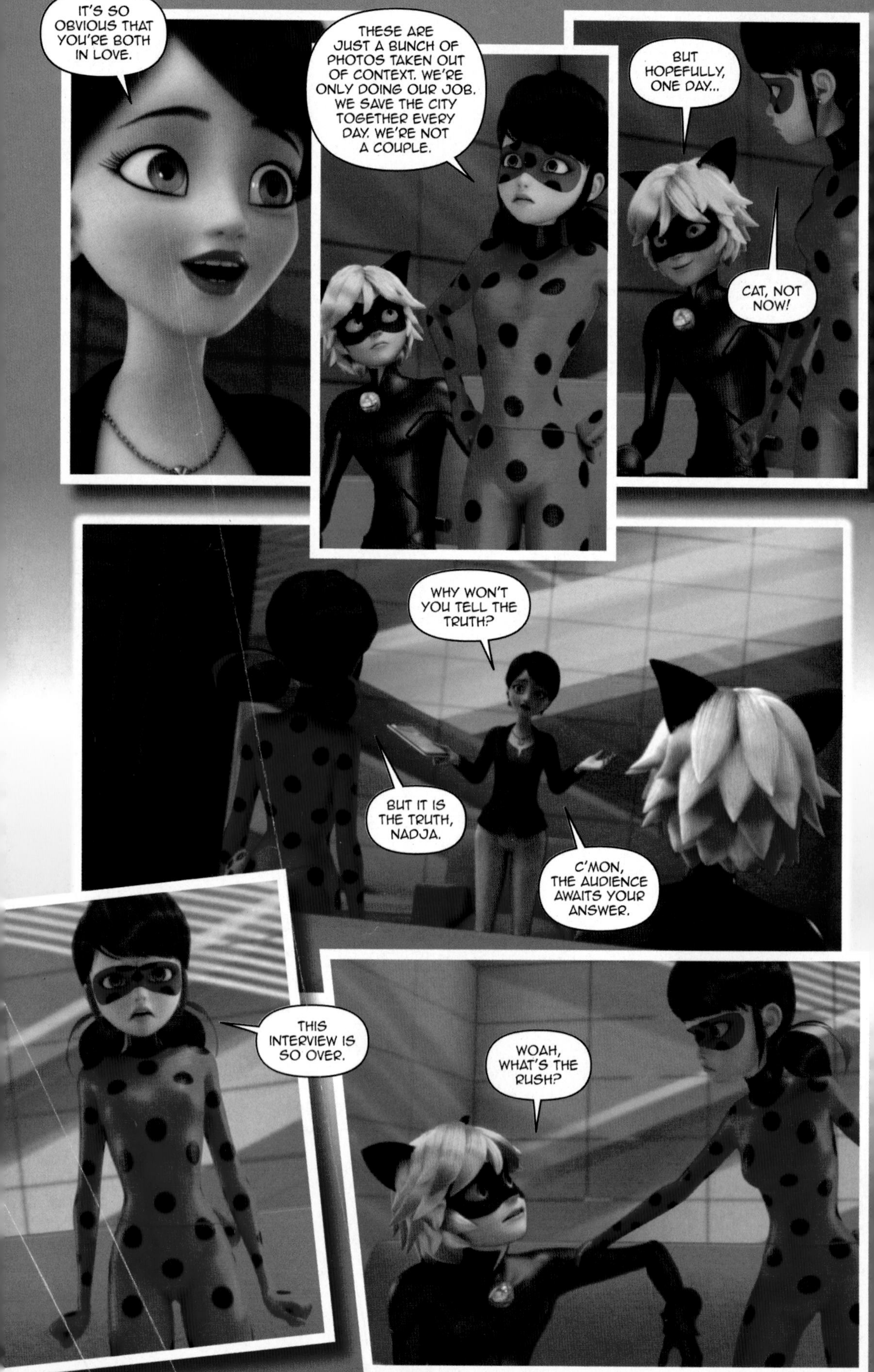
IT'S SO OBVIOUS THAT YOU'RE BOTH IN LOVE.
THESE ARE JUST A BUNCH OF PHOTOS TAKEN OUT OF CONTEXT. WE'RE ONLY DOING OUR JOB. WE SAVE THE CITY TOGETHER EVERY DAY. WE'RE NOT A COUPLE.
BUT HOPEFULLY, ONE DAY...
CAT, NOT NOW!
WHY WON'T YOU TELL THE TRUTH?
BUT IT IS THE TRUTH, NADJA.
C'MON, THE AUDIENCE AWAITS YOUR ANSWER.
THIS INTERVIEW IS SO OVER.
WOAH, WHAT'S THE RUSH?

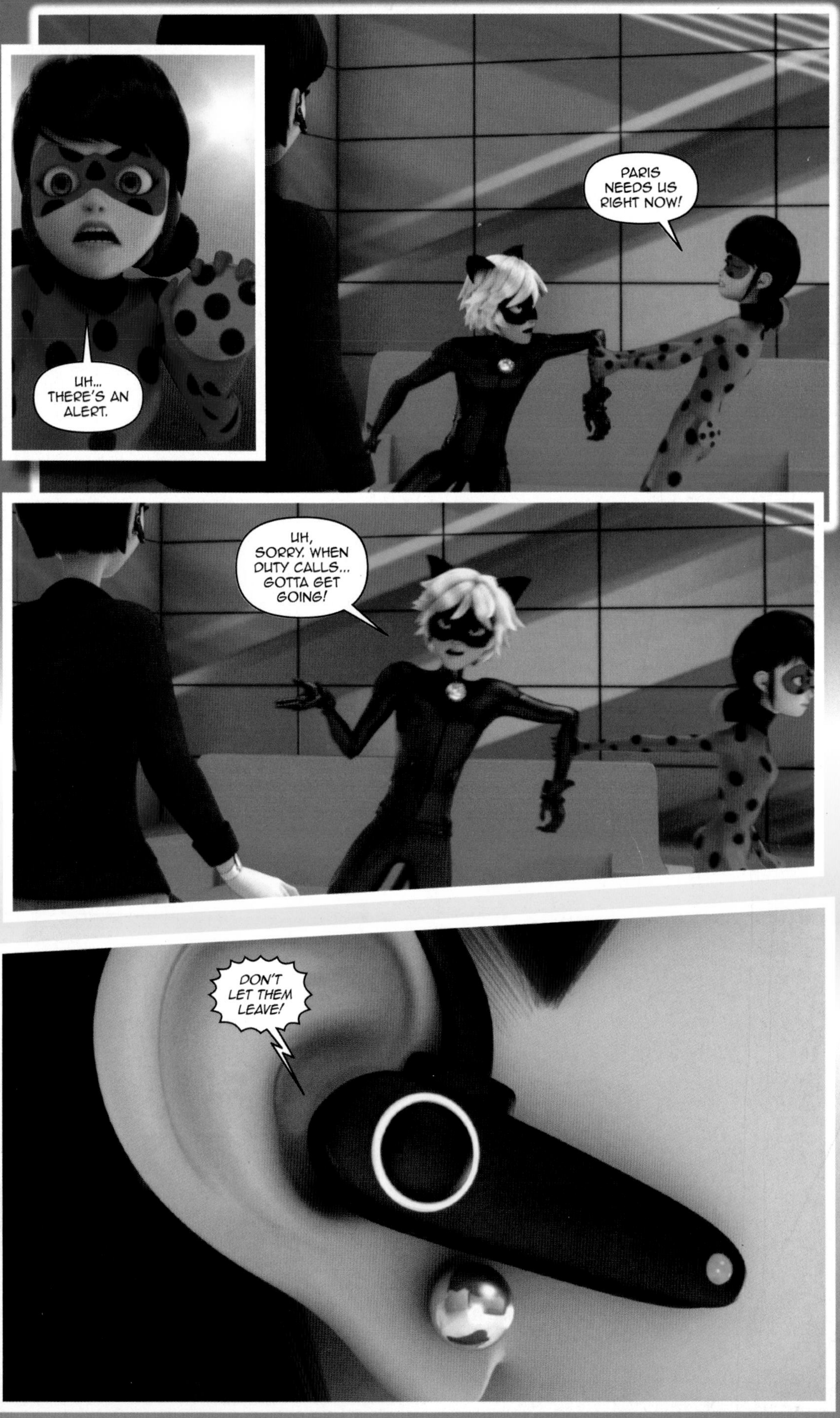
UH... THERE'S AN ALERT.
PARIS NEEDS US RIGHT NOW!
UH, SORRY. WHEN DUTY CALLS... GOTTA GET GOING!
DON'T LET THEM LEAVE!

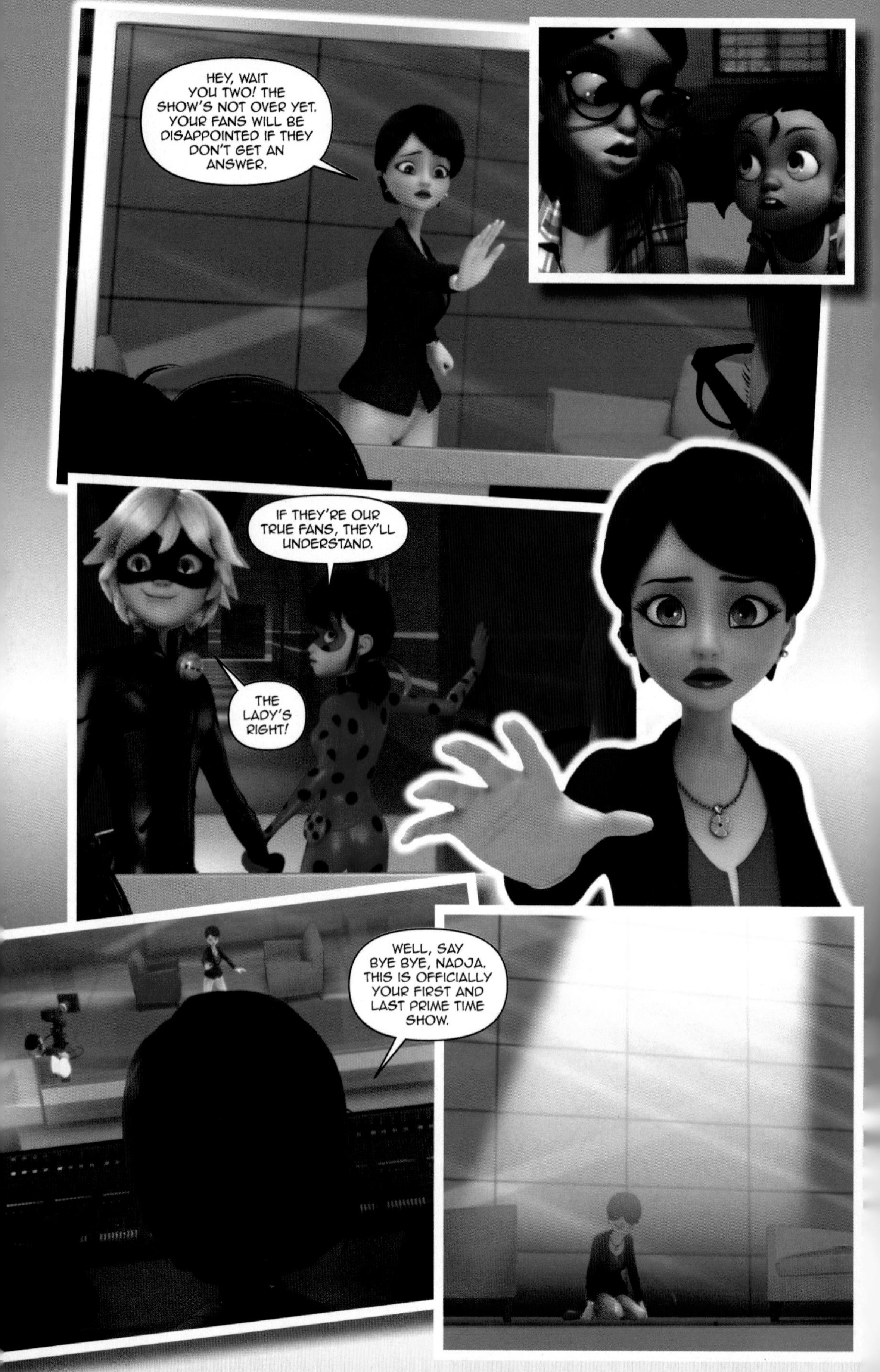
HEY, WAIT YOU TWO! THE SHOW'S NOT OVER YET. YOUR FANS WILL BE DISAPPOINTED IF THEY DON'T GET AN ANSWER.
IF THEY'RE OUR TRUE FANS, THEY'LL UNDERSTAND.
THE LADY'S RIGHT!
WELL, SAY BYE BYE, NADJA. THIS IS OFFICIALLY YOUR FIRST AND LAST PRIME TIME SHOW.

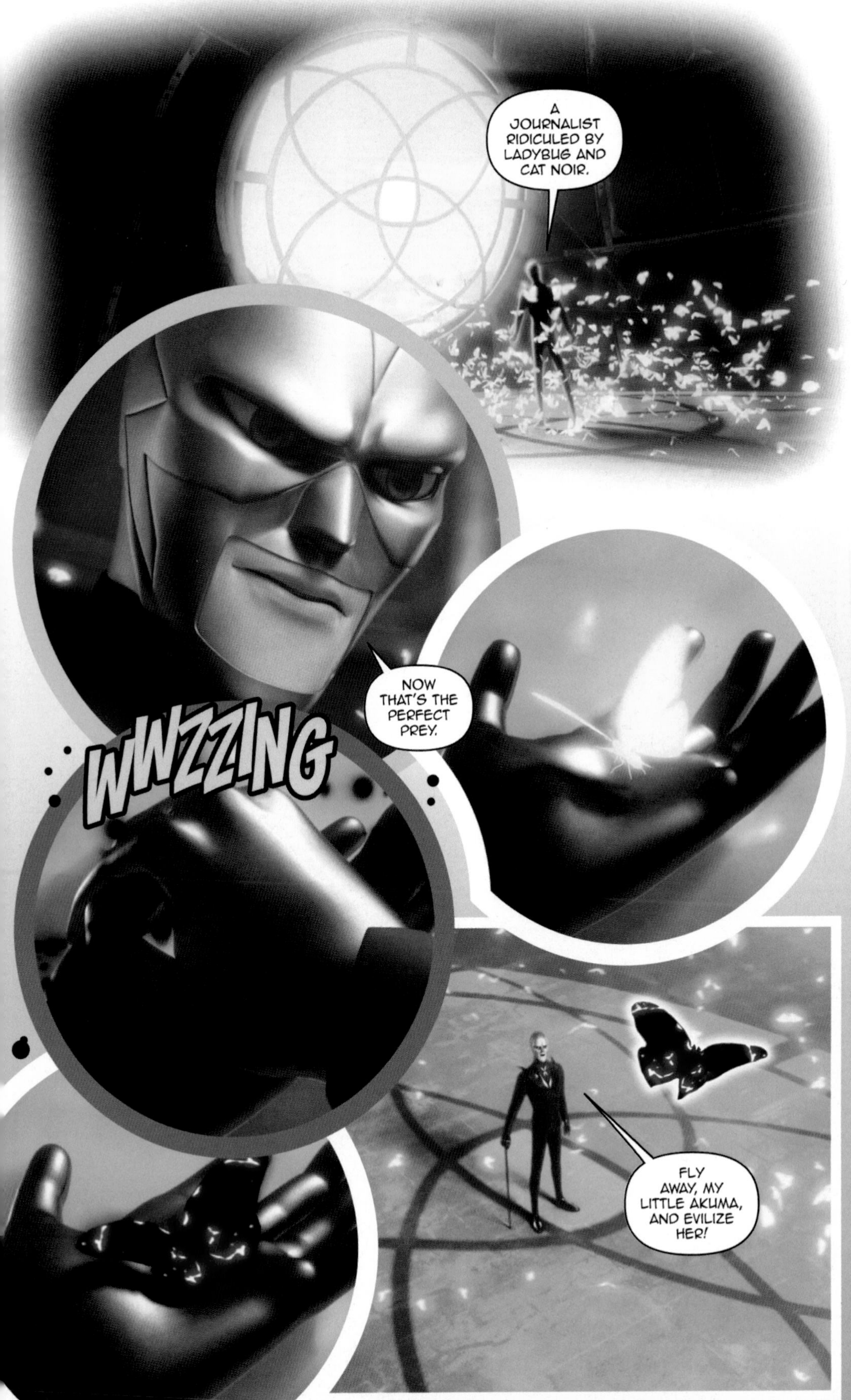
A JOURNALIST RIDICULED BY LADYBUG AND CAT NOIR.
NOW THAT'S THE PERFECT PREY.
WWZZING
FLY AWAY, MY LITTLE AKUMA, AND EVILIZE HER!

SOB SOB
FWUSH
PRIME QUEEN, I AM HAWK MOTH.
I SEE LADYBUG AND CAT NOIR HAVE DENIED YOU THE ANSWERS YOU DESERVE. STEAL THEIR MIRACULOUS AND YOU WILL GET YOUR SCOOP.
THE HIGHEST RATINGS WILL BE MINE.
GURGLE GURGLE

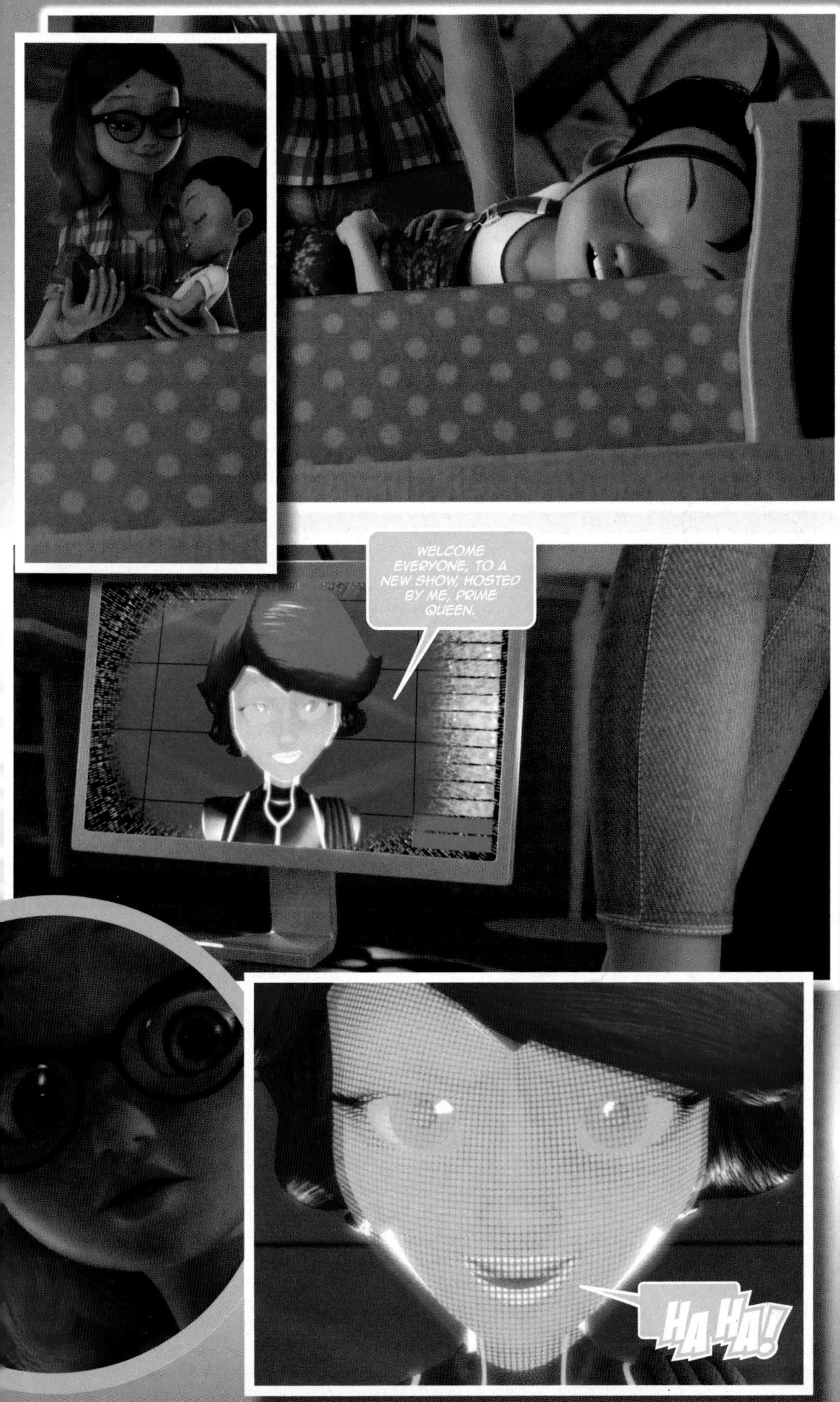
WELCOME EVERYONE, TO A NEW SHOW, HOSTED BY ME, PRIME QUEEN.
HA HA!

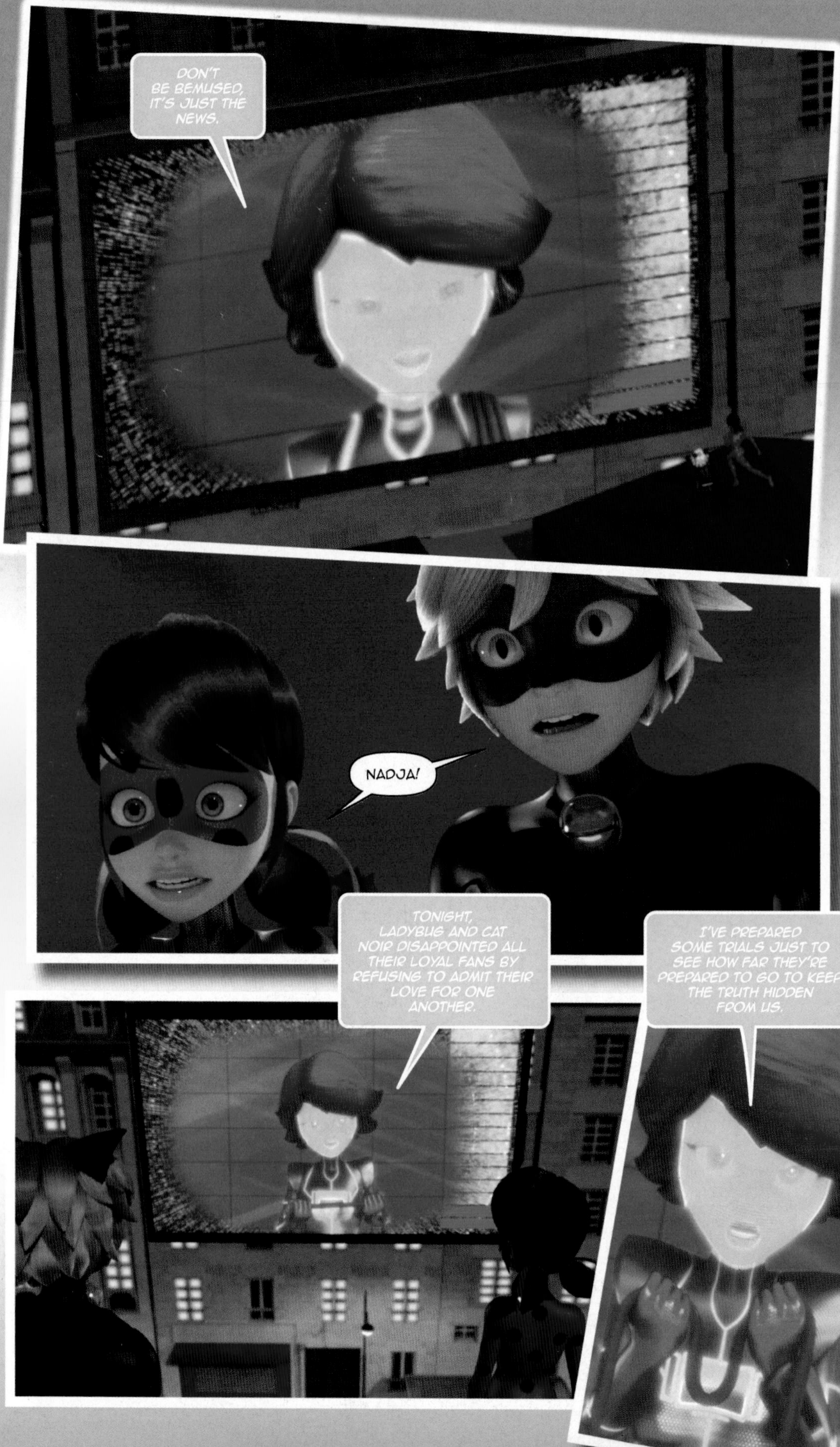
DON'T BE BEMUSED, IT'S JUST THE NEWS.
NADJA!
TONIGHT, LADYBUG AND CAT NOIR DISAPPOINTED ALL THEIR LOYAL FANS BY REFUSING TO ADMIT THEIR LOVE FOR ONE ANOTHER.
I'VE PREPARED SOME TRIALS JUST TO SEE HOW FAR THEY'RE PREPARED TO GO TO KEEP THE TRUTH HIDDEN FROM US.

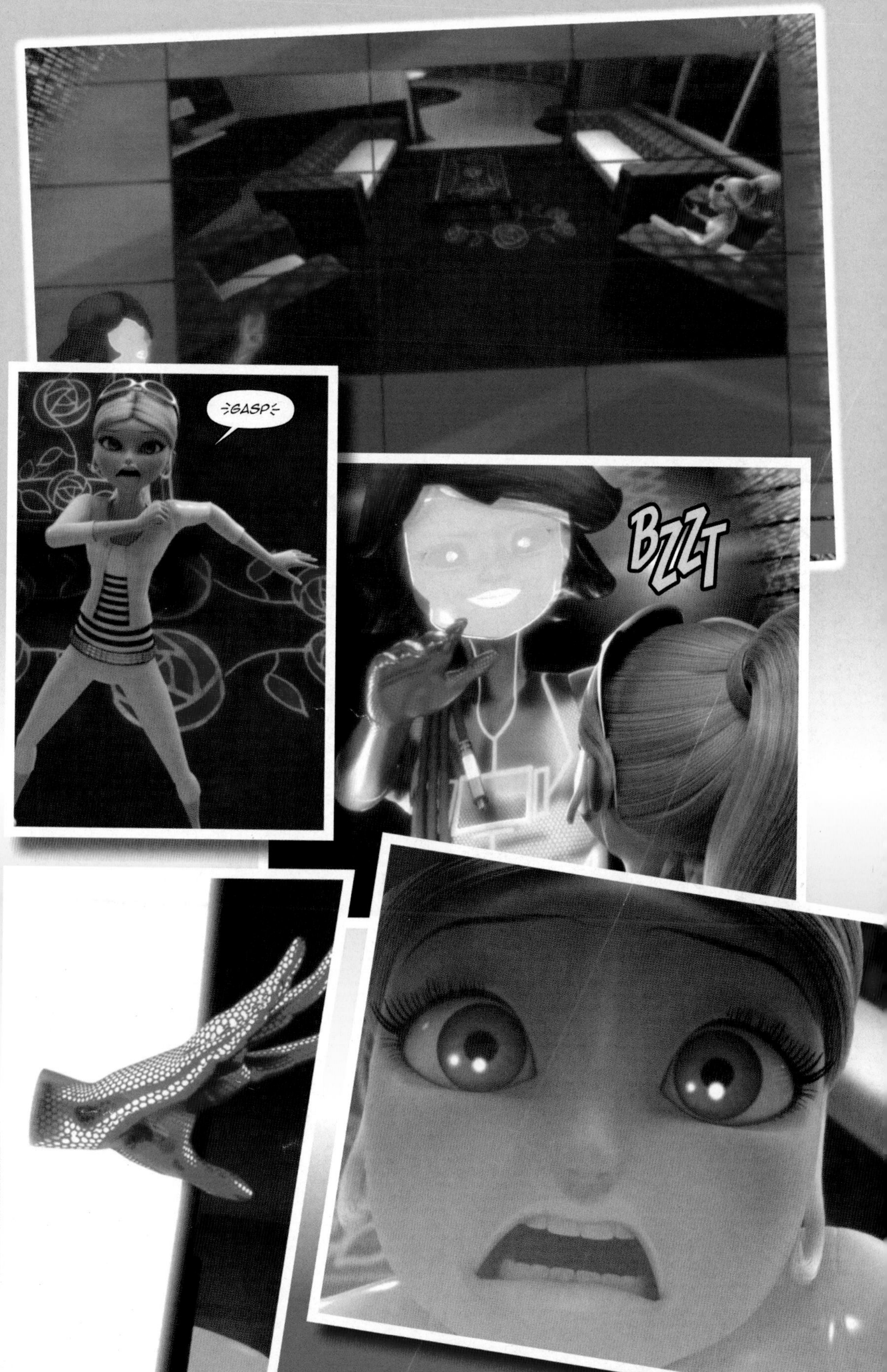
GASP
BZZT

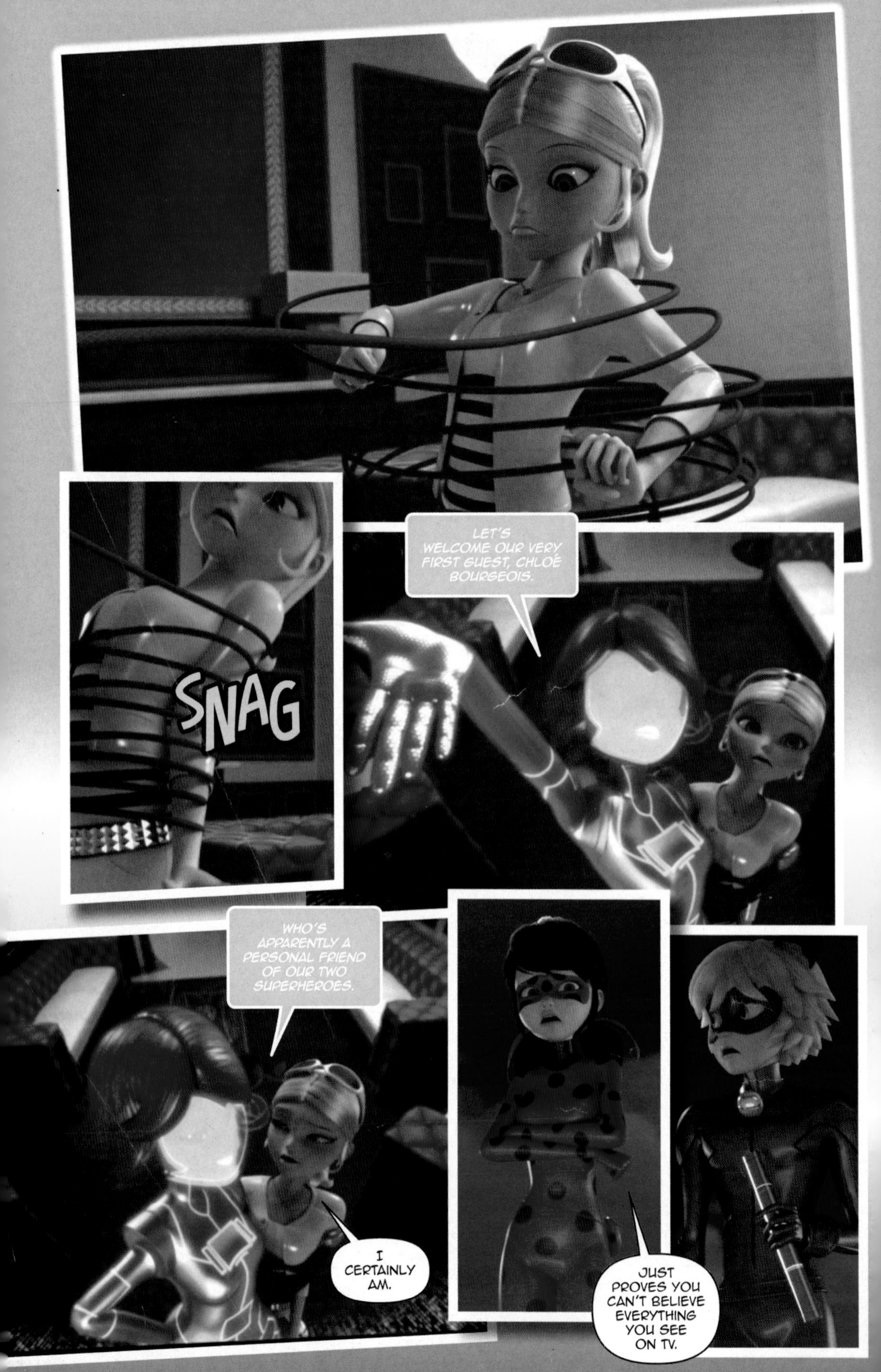
SNAG
LET'S WELCOME OUR VERY FIRST GUEST, CHLOÉ BOURGEOIS.
WHO'S APPARENTLY A PERSONAL FRIEND OF OUR TWO SUPERHEROES.
I CERTAINLY AM.
JUST PROVES YOU CAN'T BELIEVE EVERYTHING YOU SEE ON TV.

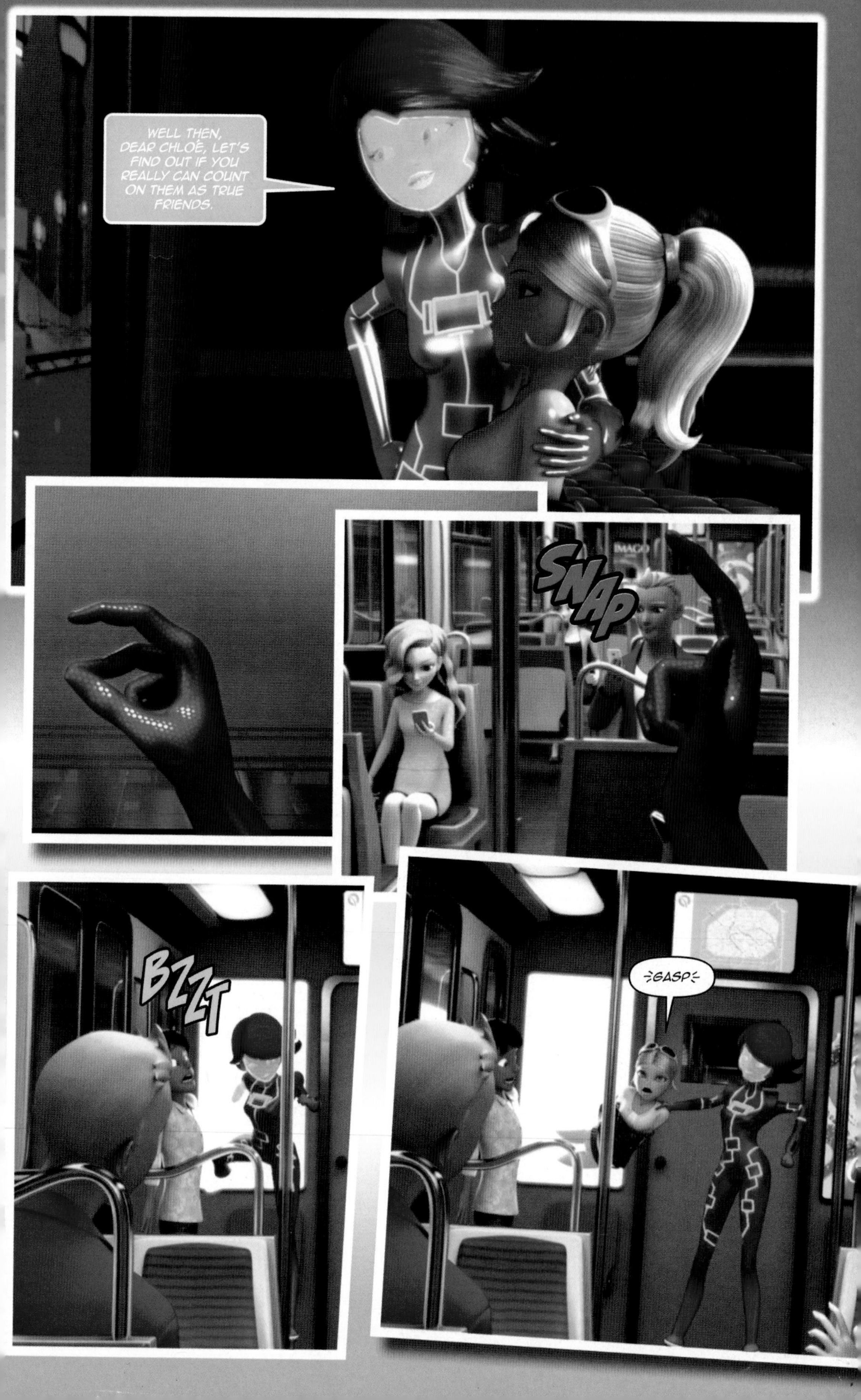
WELL THEN, DEAR CHLOÈ, LET'S FIND OUT IF YOU REALLY CAN COUNT ON THEM AS TRUE FRIENDS.
SNAP
BZZT
GASP

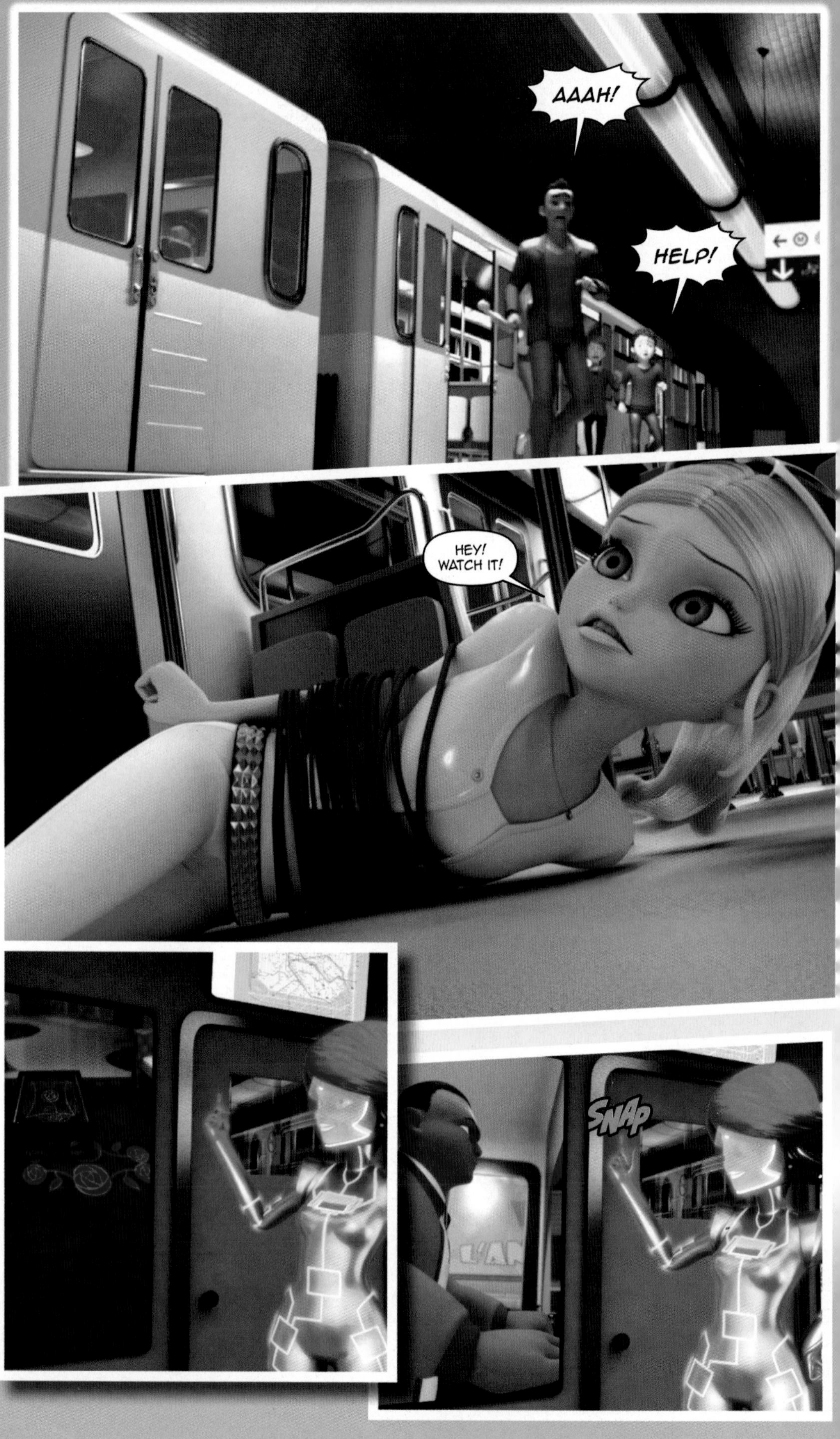
AAAH!
HELP!
HEY! WATCH IT!
SNAP

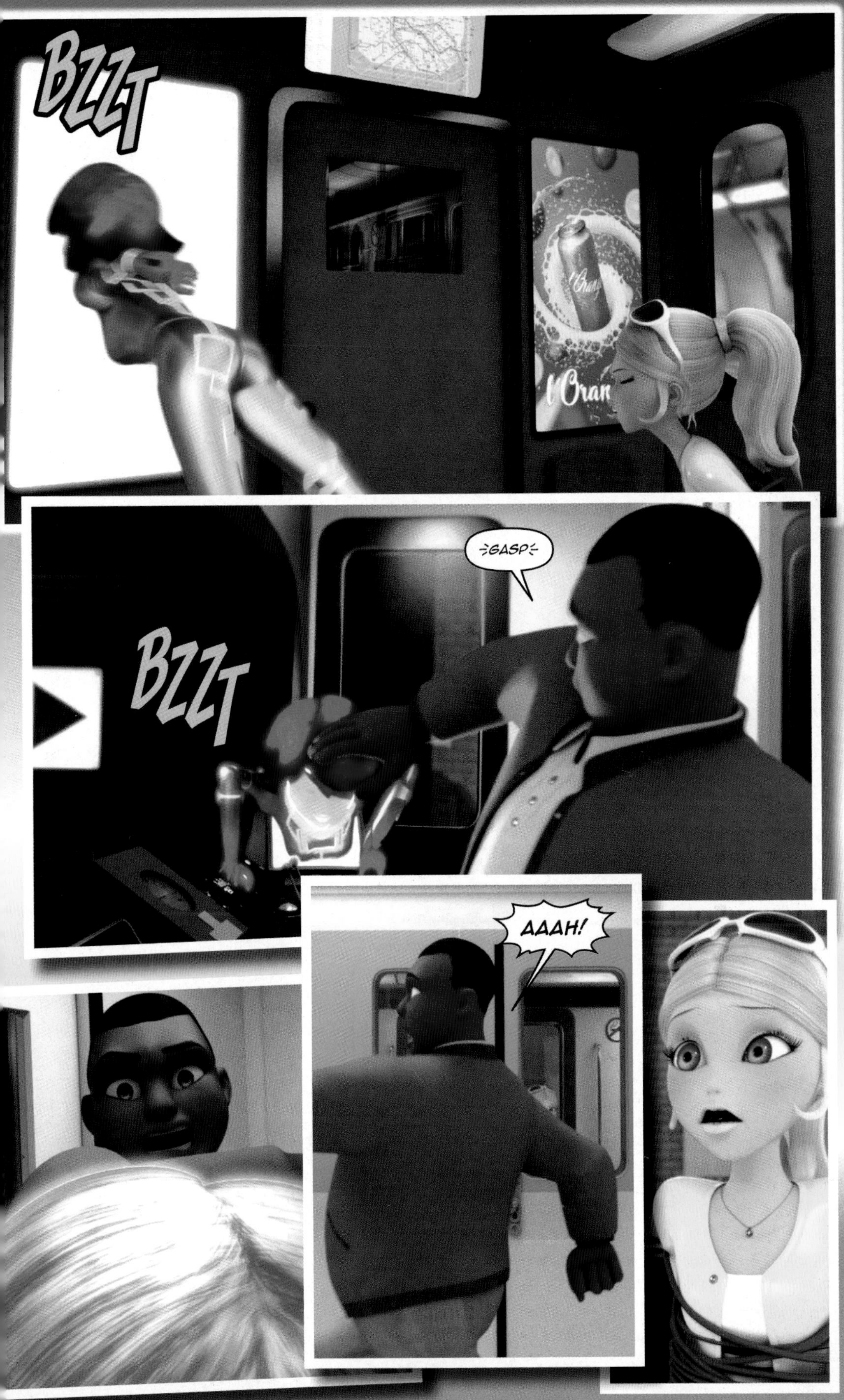
BZZT
l'Orange
l'Oran
GASP
BZZT
AAAH!

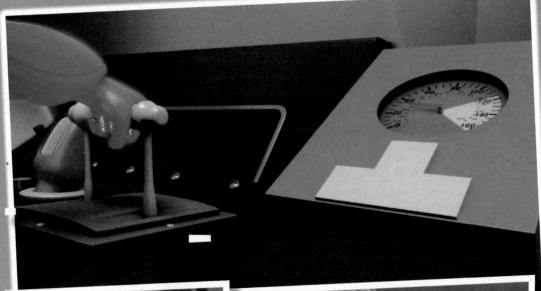

WHOA!

THIS CAN'T BE HAPPENING TO ME!

I NEVER EVER TAKE THE SUBWAY TRAIN! IT'S SO NOT... NOT ME!

OH... GROSS.

WELCOME TO THE SUBWAY OF SUSPENSE. IF IT REACHES 70 MILES PER HOUR YOU CAN SAY GOODBYE TO YOUR PRECIOUS LITTLE FRIEND.

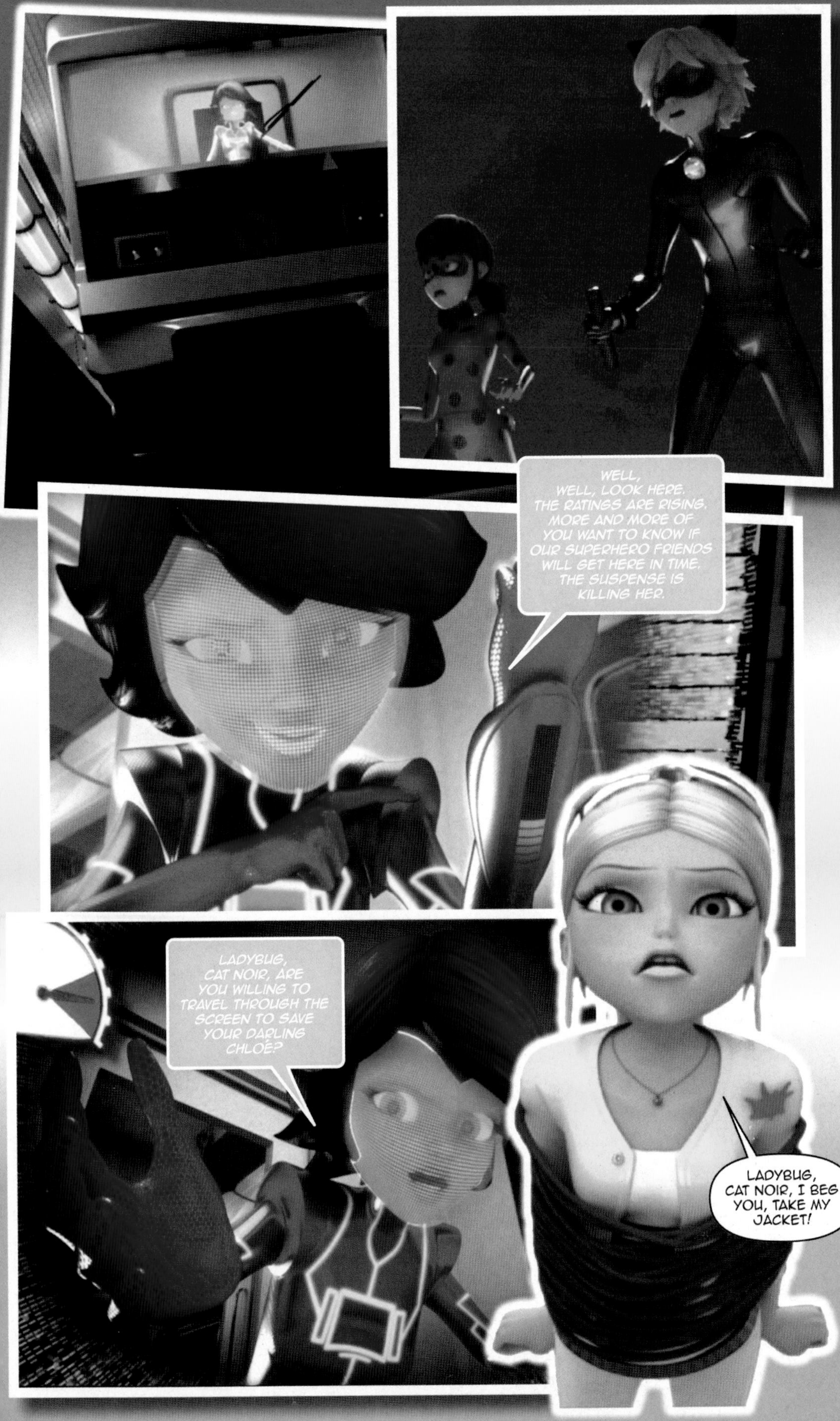
WELL, WELL, LOOK HERE. THE RATINGS ARE RISING. MORE AND MORE OF YOU WANT TO KNOW IF OUR SUPERHERO FRIENDS WILL GET HERE IN TIME. THE SUSPENSE IS KILLING HER.
LADYBUG, CAT NOIR, ARE YOU WILLING TO TRAVEL THROUGH THE SCREEN TO SAVE YOUR DARLING CHLOÉ?
LADYBUG, CAT NOIR, I BEG YOU, TAKE MY JACKET!

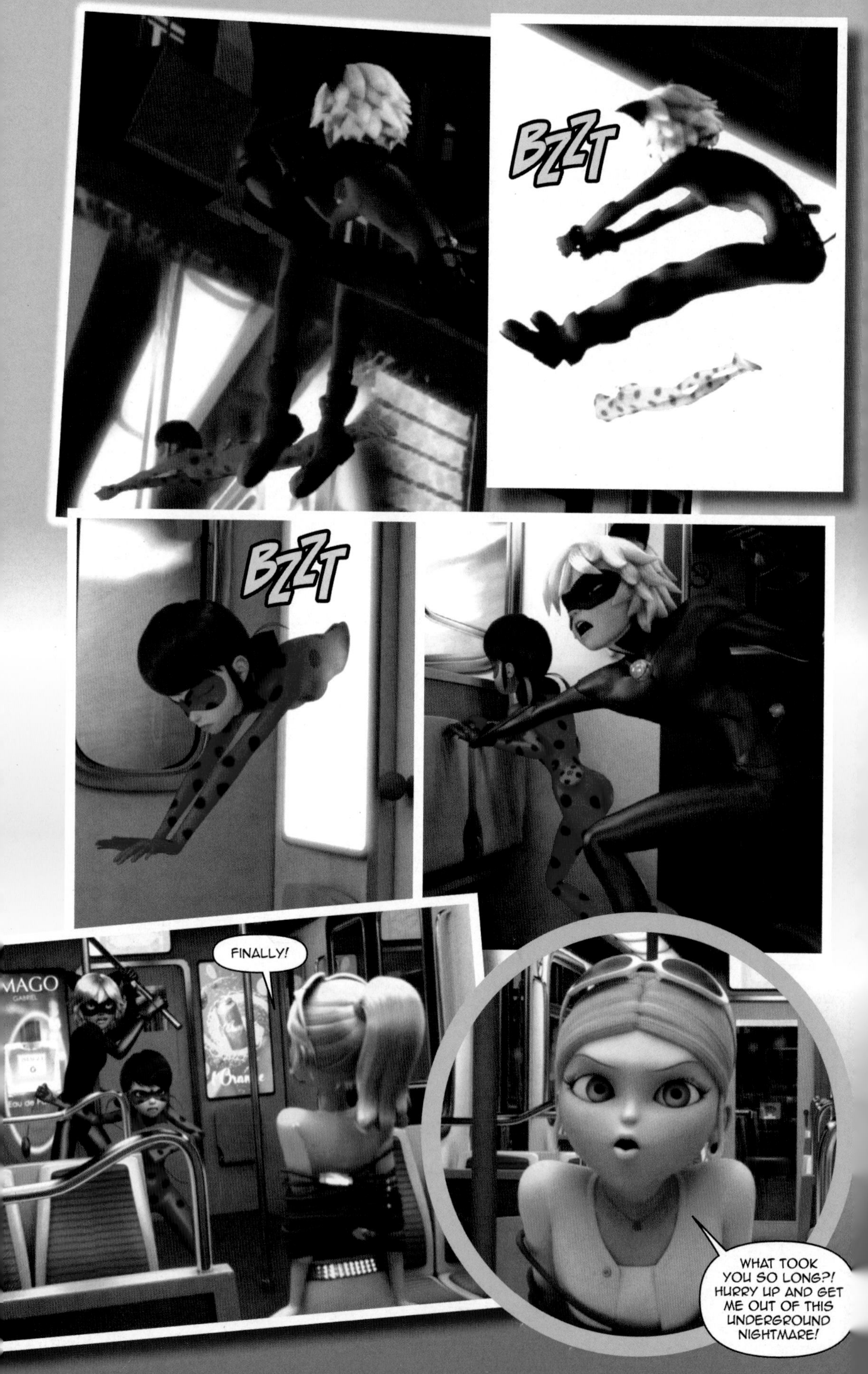
BZZT
BZZT
FINALLY!
WHAT TOOK YOU SO LONG?! HURRY UP AND GET ME OUT OF THIS UNDERGROUND NIGHTMARE!

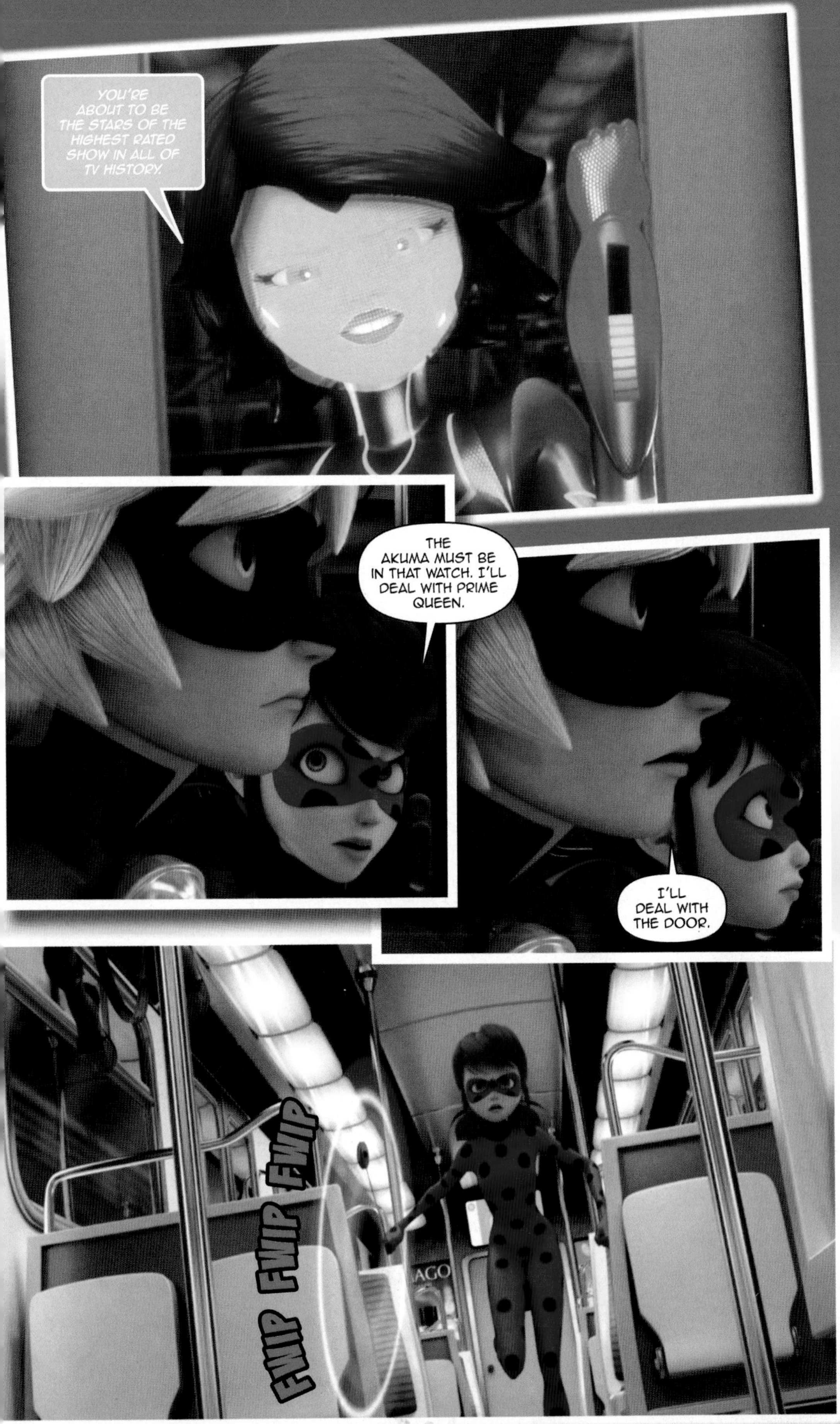
YOU'RE ABOUT TO BE THE STARS OF THE HIGHEST RATED SHOW IN ALL OF TV HISTORY.
THE AKUMA MUST BE IN THAT WATCH. I'LL DEAL WITH PRIME QUEEN.
I'LL DEAL WITH THE DOOR.
FWIP FWIP FWIP

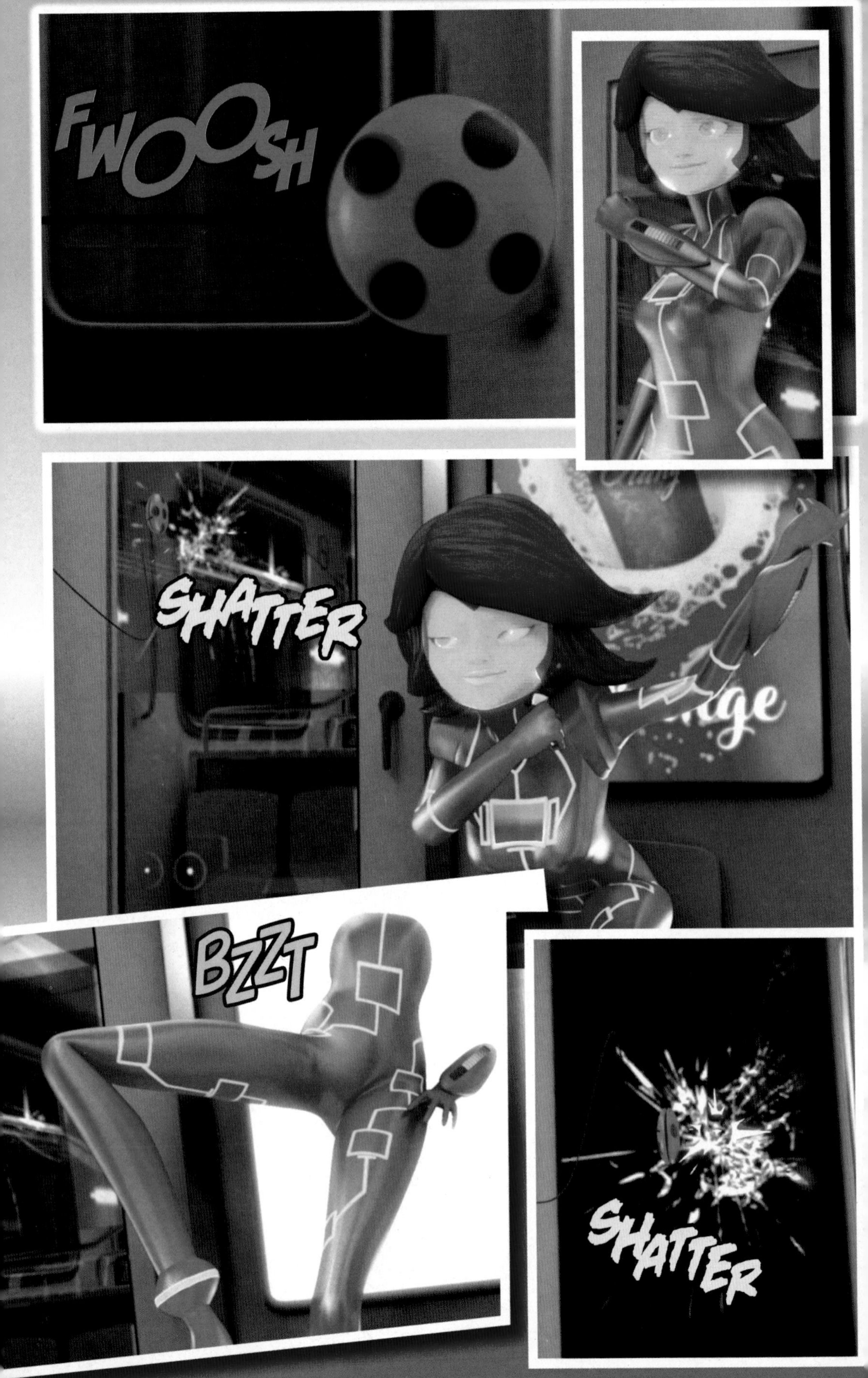
FWOOSH
SHATTER
BZZT
SHATTER

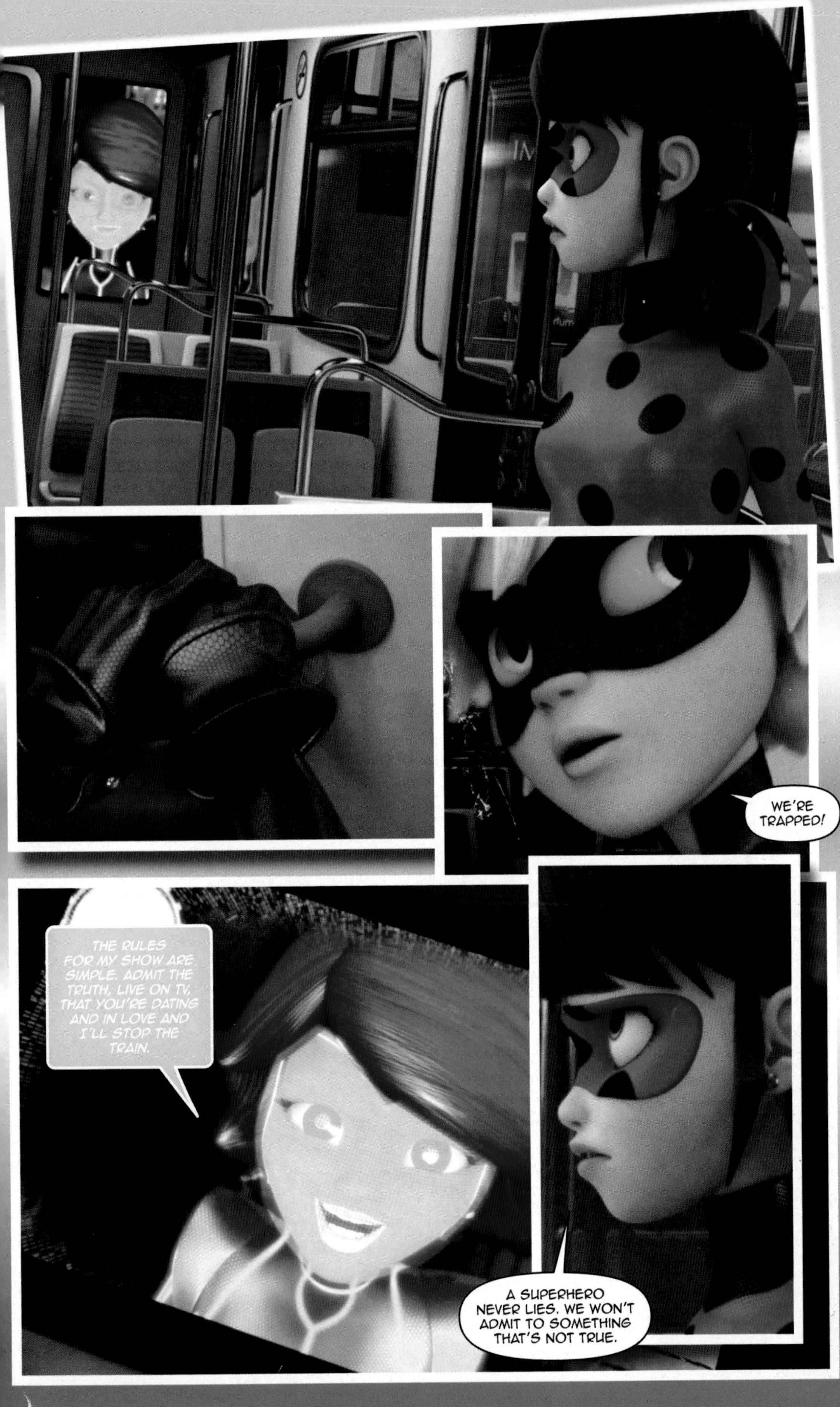
WE'RE TRAPPED!
THE RULES FOR MY SHOW ARE SIMPLE. ADMIT THE TRUTH, LIVE ON TV, THAT YOU'RE DATING AND IN LOVE AND I'LL STOP THE TRAIN.
A SUPERHERO NEVER LIES. WE WON'T ADMIT TO SOMETHING THAT'S NOT TRUE.

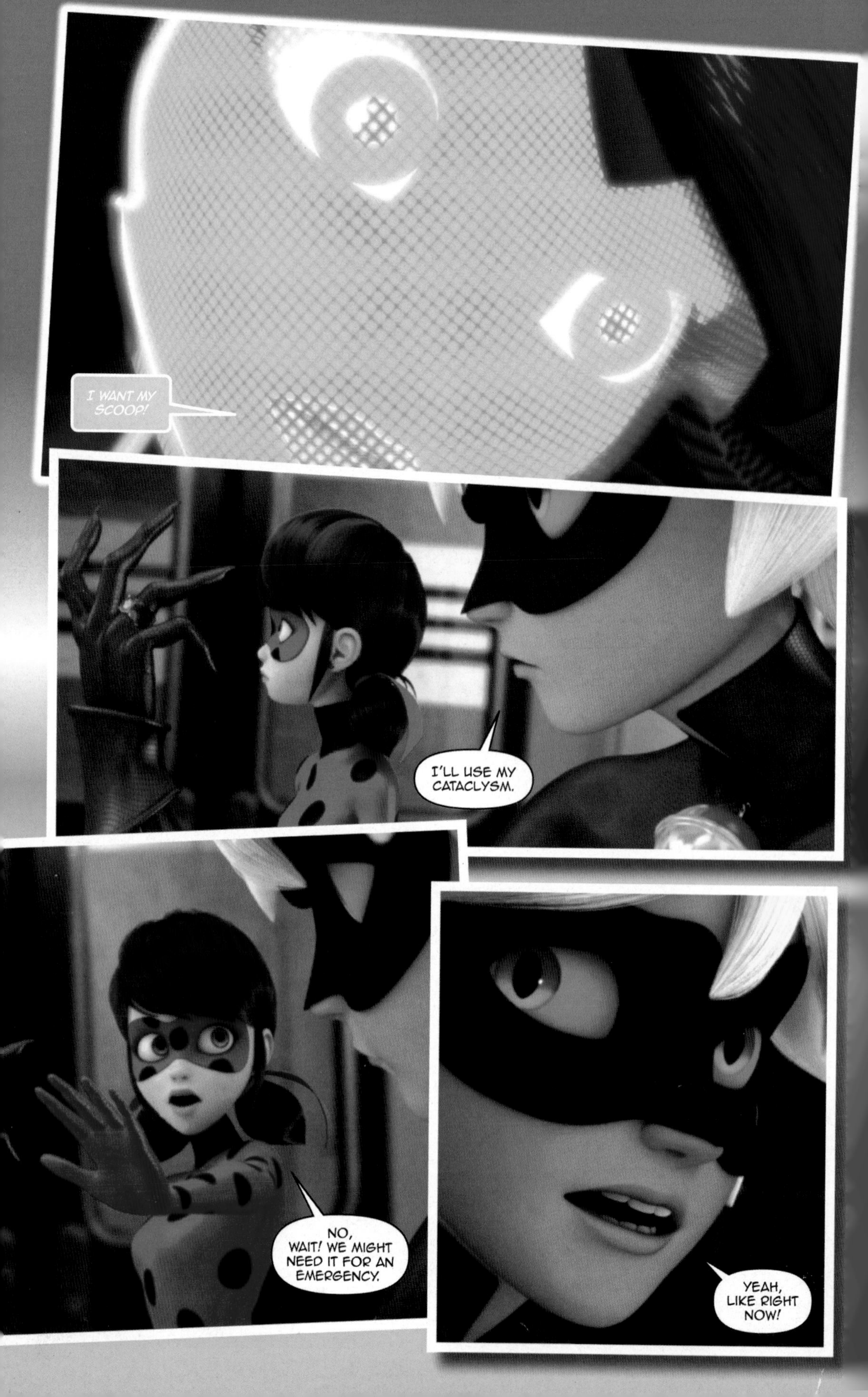
I WANT MY SCOOP!
I'LL USE MY CATACLYSM.
NO, WAIT! WE MIGHT NEED IT FOR AN EMERGENCY.
YEAH, LIKE RIGHT NOW!

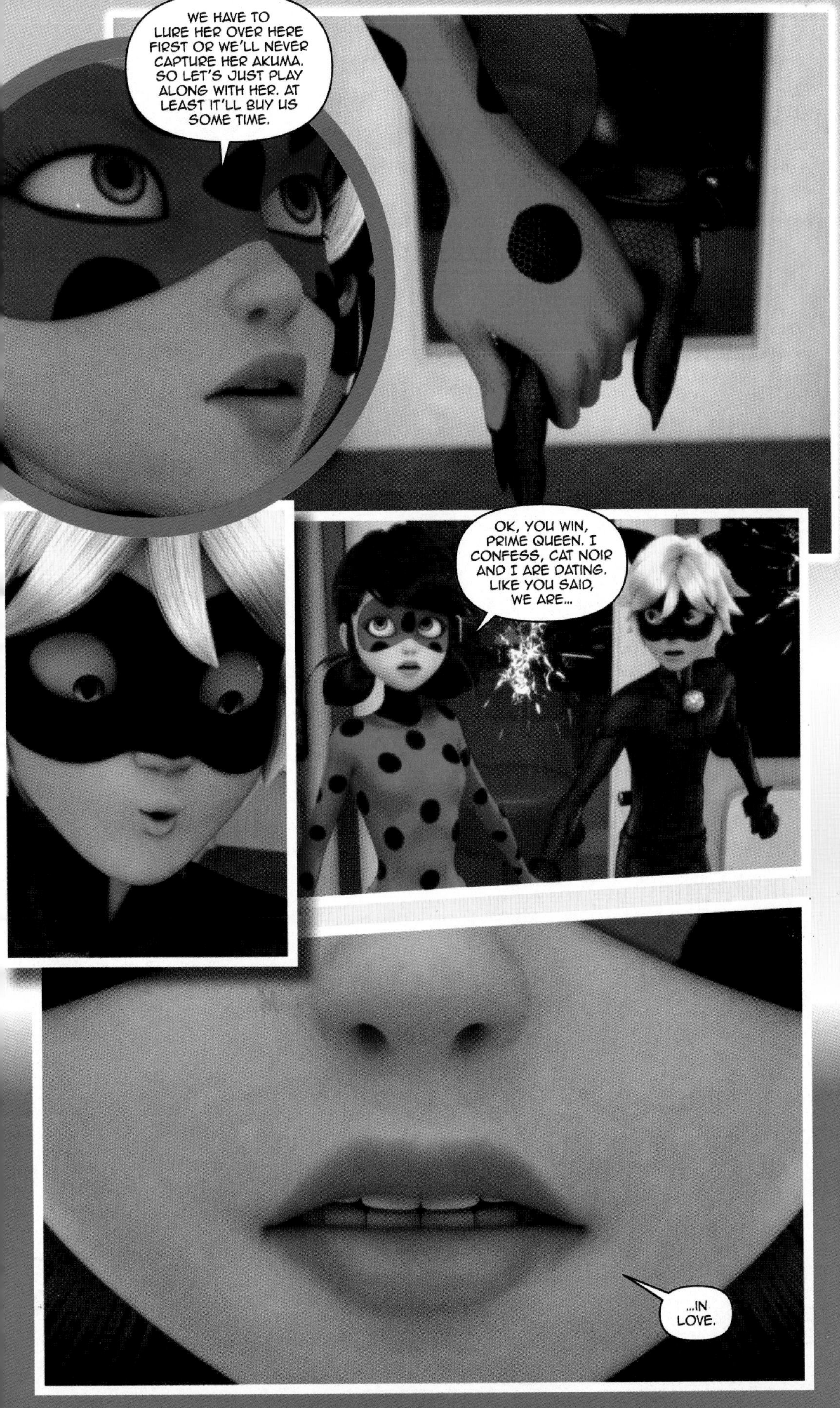
WE HAVE TO LURE HER OVER HERE FIRST OR WE'LL NEVER CAPTURE HER AKUMA. SO LET'S JUST PLAY ALONG WITH HER. AT LEAST IT'LL BUY US SOME TIME.
OK, YOU WIN, PRIME QUEEN. I CONFESS, CAT NOIR AND I ARE DATING. LIKE YOU SAID, WE ARE...
...IN LOVE.

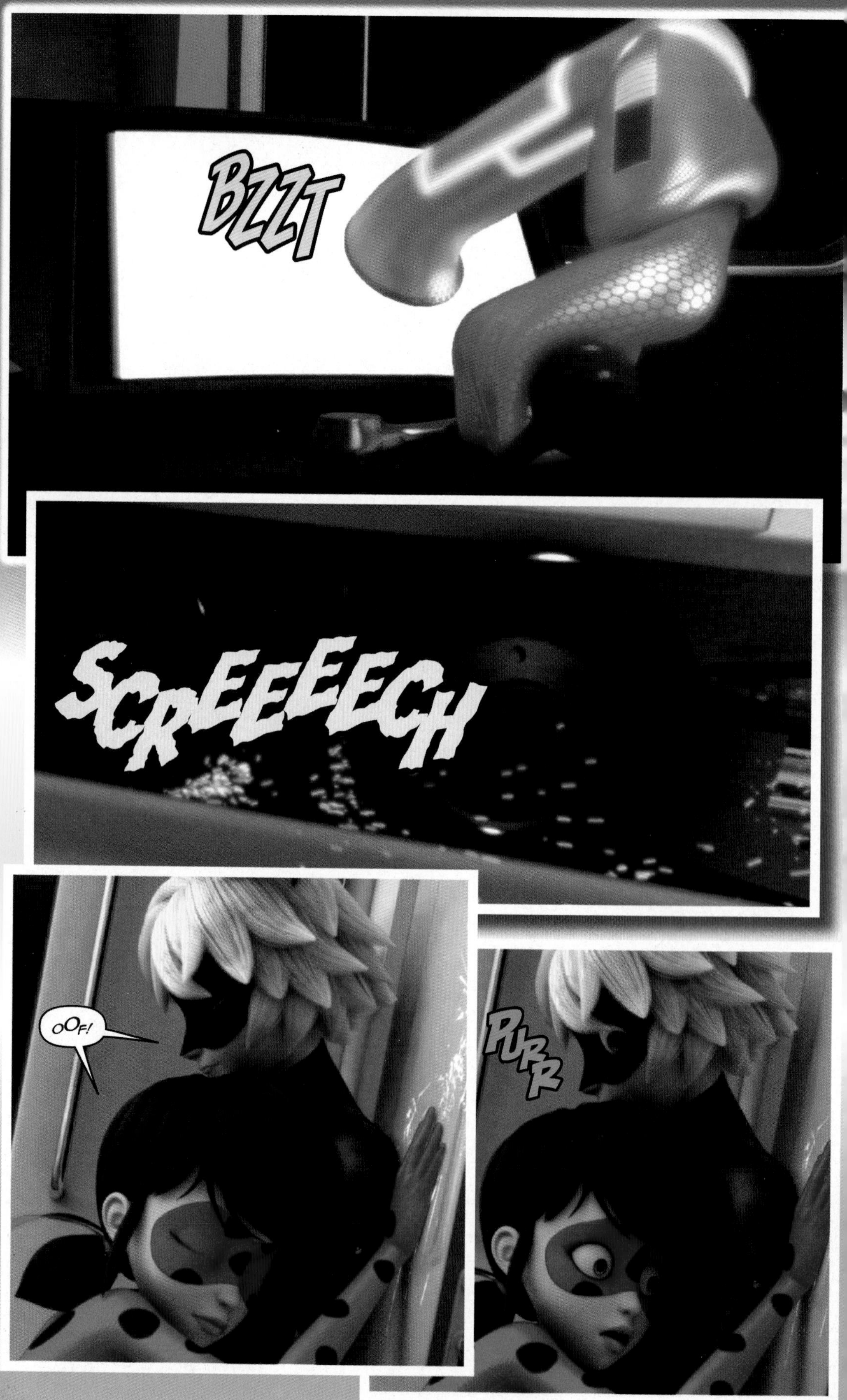

BZZT
SCREEEEECH
OOF!
PURR

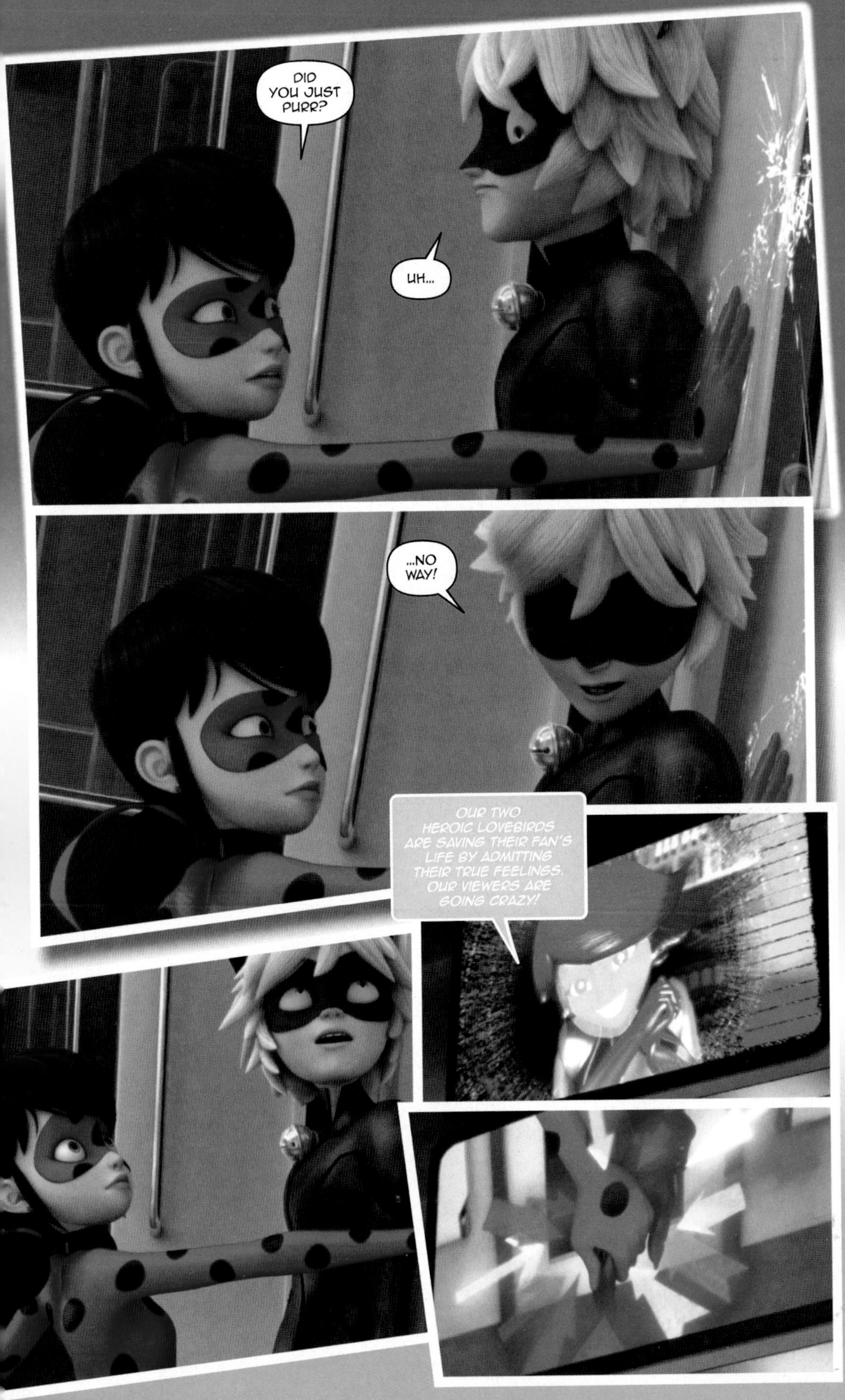
DID YOU JUST PURR?
UH...
...NO WAY!
OUR TWO HEROIC LOVEBIRDS ARE SAVING THEIR FAN'S LIFE BY ADMITTING THEIR TRUE FEELINGS. OUR VIEWERS ARE GOING CRAZY!

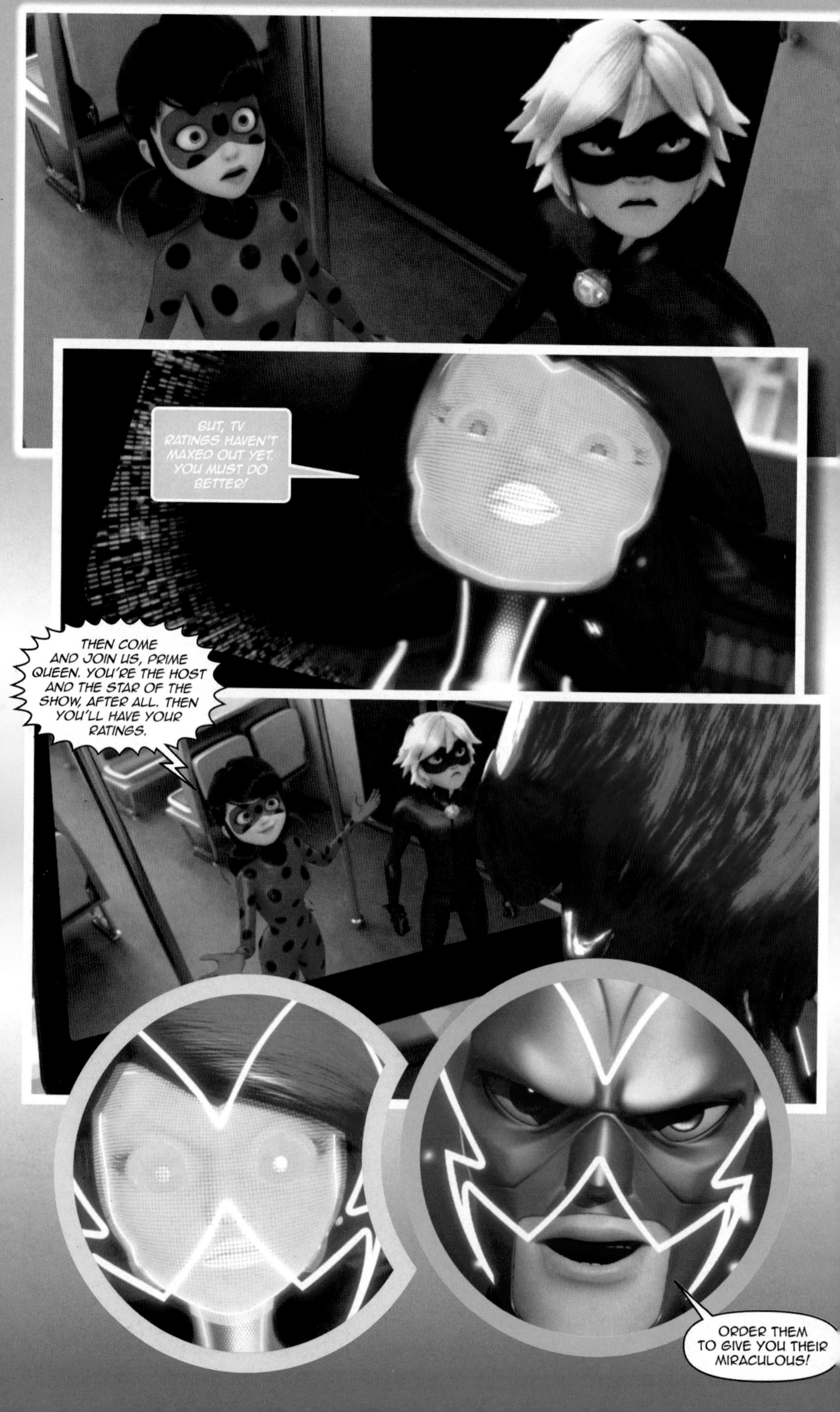
BUT, TV RATINGS HAVEN'T MAXED OUT YET. YOU MUST DO BETTER!
THEN COME AND JOIN US, PRIME QUEEN. YOU'RE THE HOST AND THE STAR OF THE SHOW, AFTER ALL. THEN YOU'LL HAVE YOUR RATINGS.
ORDER THEM TO GIVE YOU THEIR MIRACULOUS!

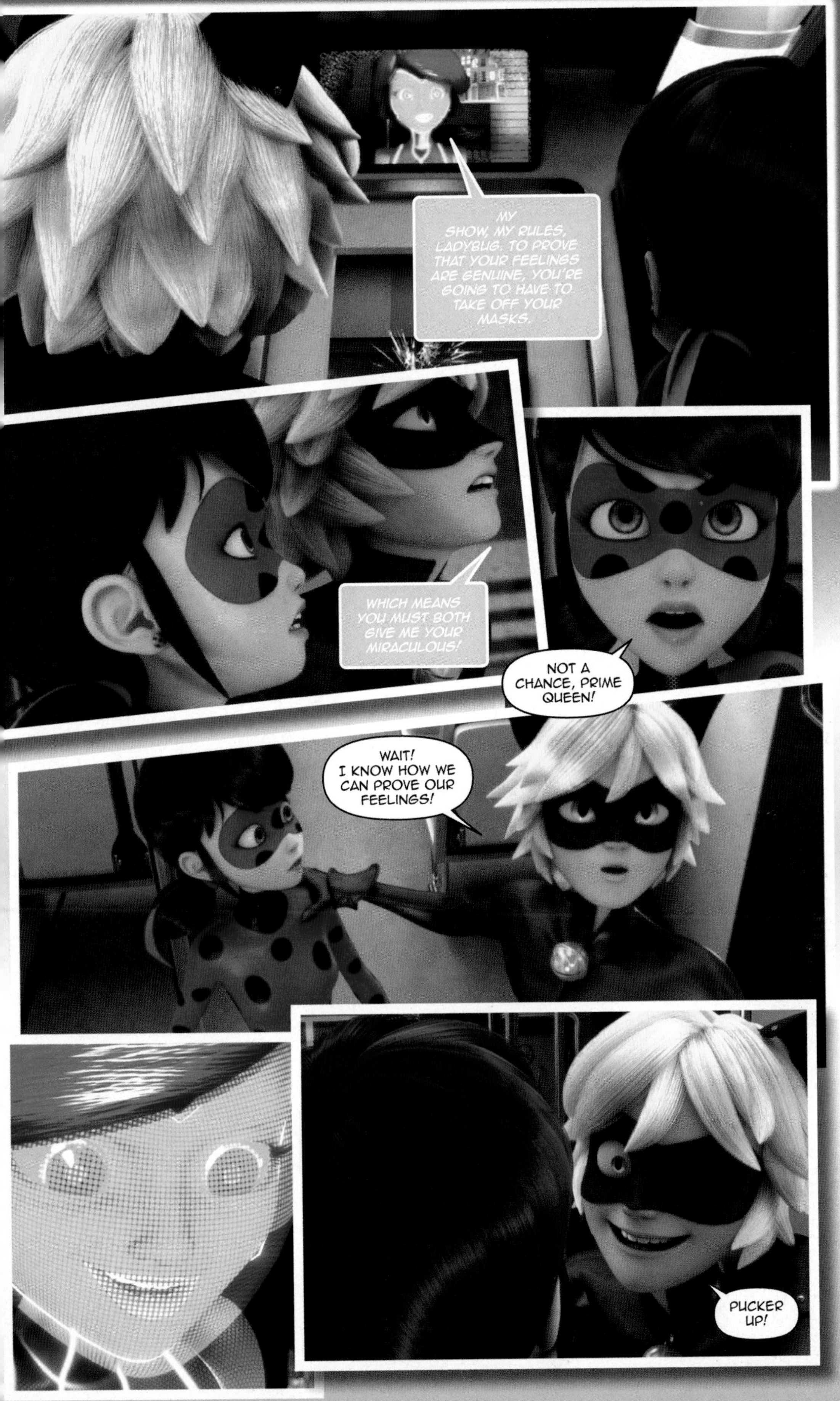
MY SHOW, MY RULES, LADYBUG. TO PROVE THAT YOUR FEELINGS ARE GENUINE, YOU'RE GOING TO HAVE TO TAKE OFF YOUR MASKS.
WHICH MEANS YOU MUST BOTH GIVE ME YOUR MIRACULOUS!
NOT A CHANCE, PRIME QUEEN!
WAIT! I KNOW HOW WE CAN PROVE OUR FEELINGS!
PUCKER UP!

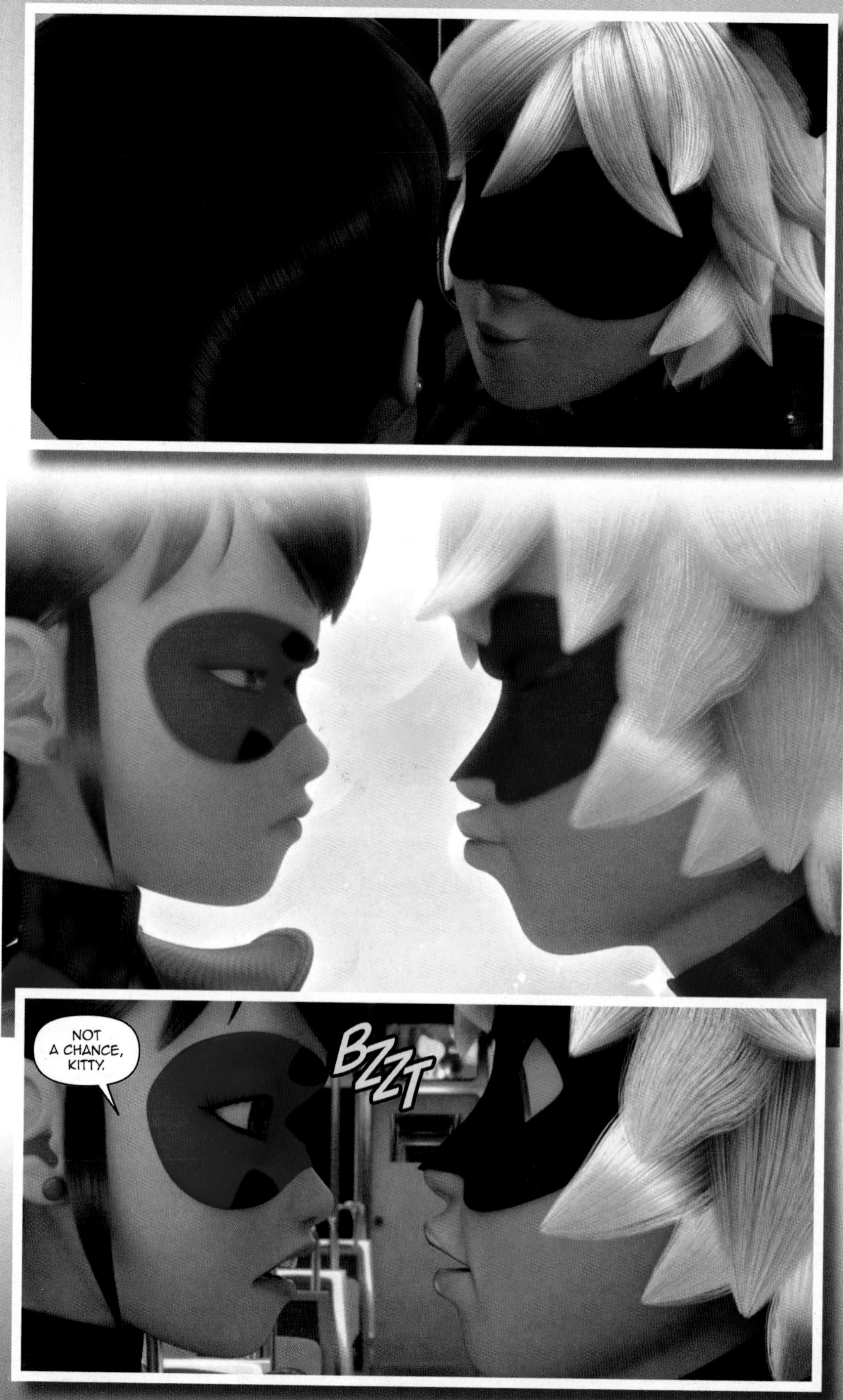
NOT A CHANCE, KITTY.
BZZT

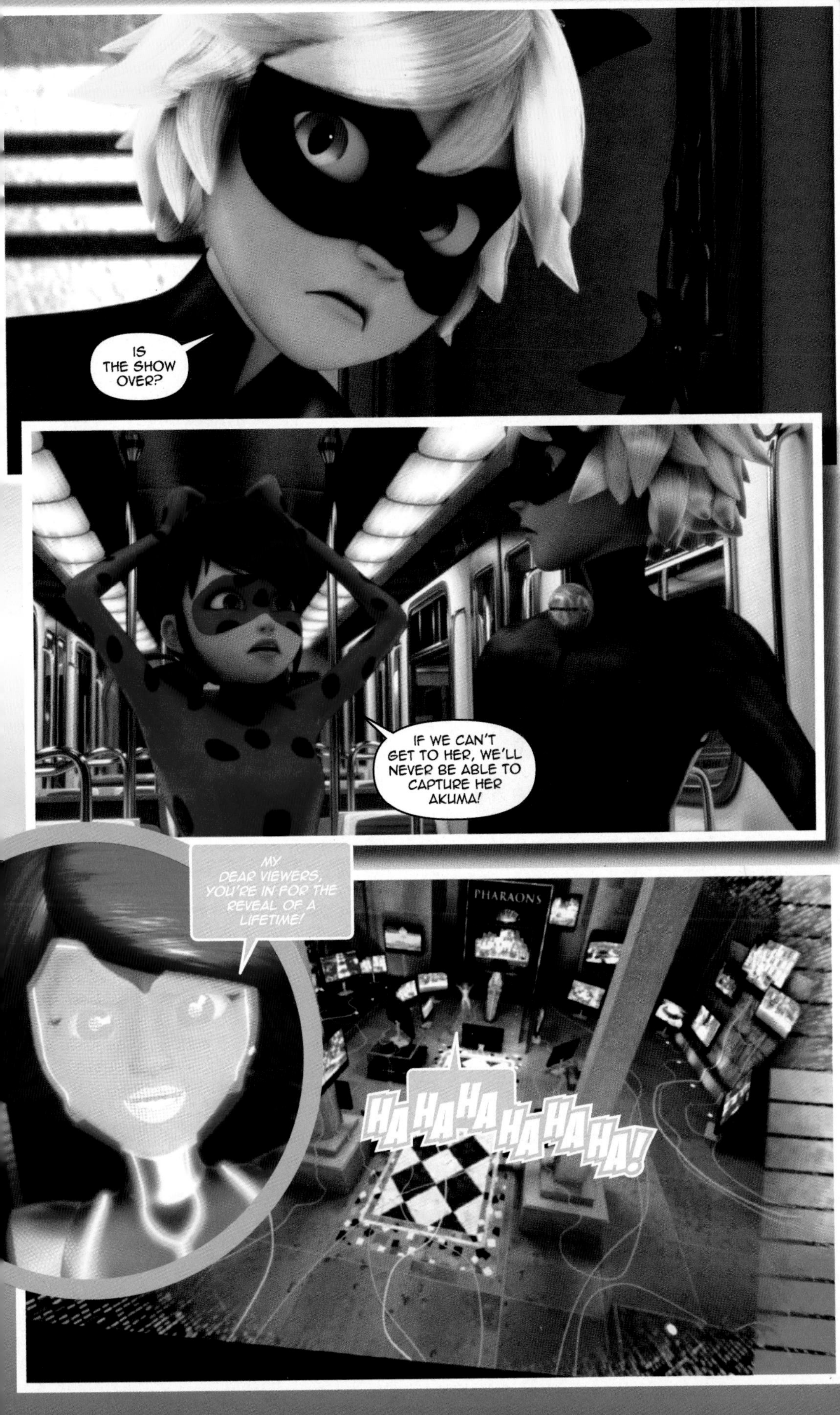
IS THE SHOW OVER?
IF WE CAN'T GET TO HER, WE'LL NEVER BE ABLE TO CAPTURE HER AKUMA!
MY DEAR VIEWERS, YOU'RE IN FOR THE REVEAL OF A LIFETIME!
PHARAONS
HA HA HA HA HA HA HA!

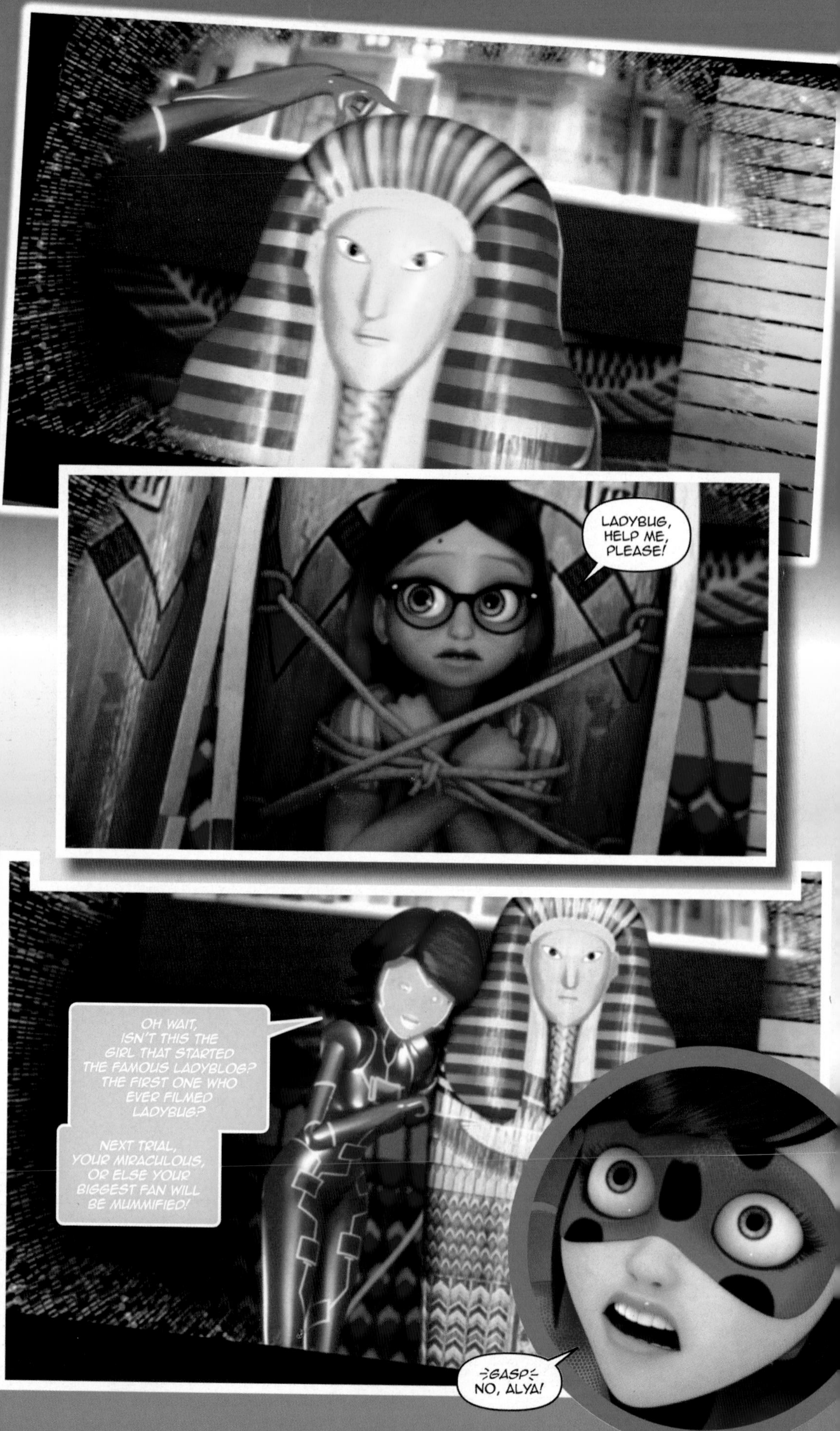
LADYBUG, HELP ME, PLEASE!
OH WAIT, ISN'T THIS THE GIRL THAT STARTED THE FAMOUS LADYBLOG? THE FIRST ONE WHO EVER FILMED LADYBUG?
NEXT TRIAL, YOUR MIRACULOUS, OR ELSE YOUR BIGGEST FAN WILL BE MUMMIFIED!
GASP NO, ALYA!

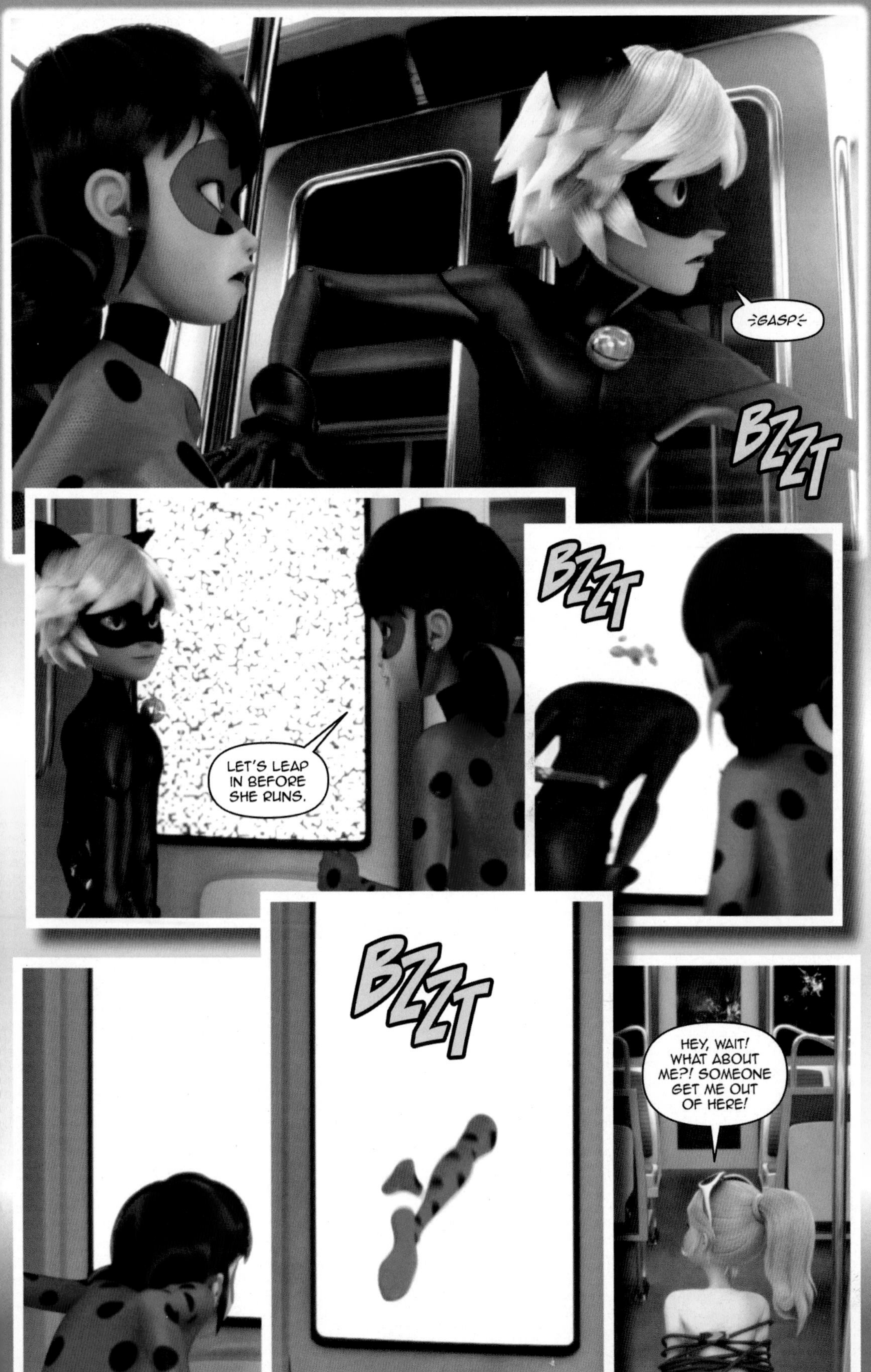
GASP
BZZT
LET'S LEAP IN BEFORE SHE RUNS.
BZZT
BZZT
HEY, WAIT! WHAT ABOUT ME?! SOMEONE GET ME OUT OF HERE!

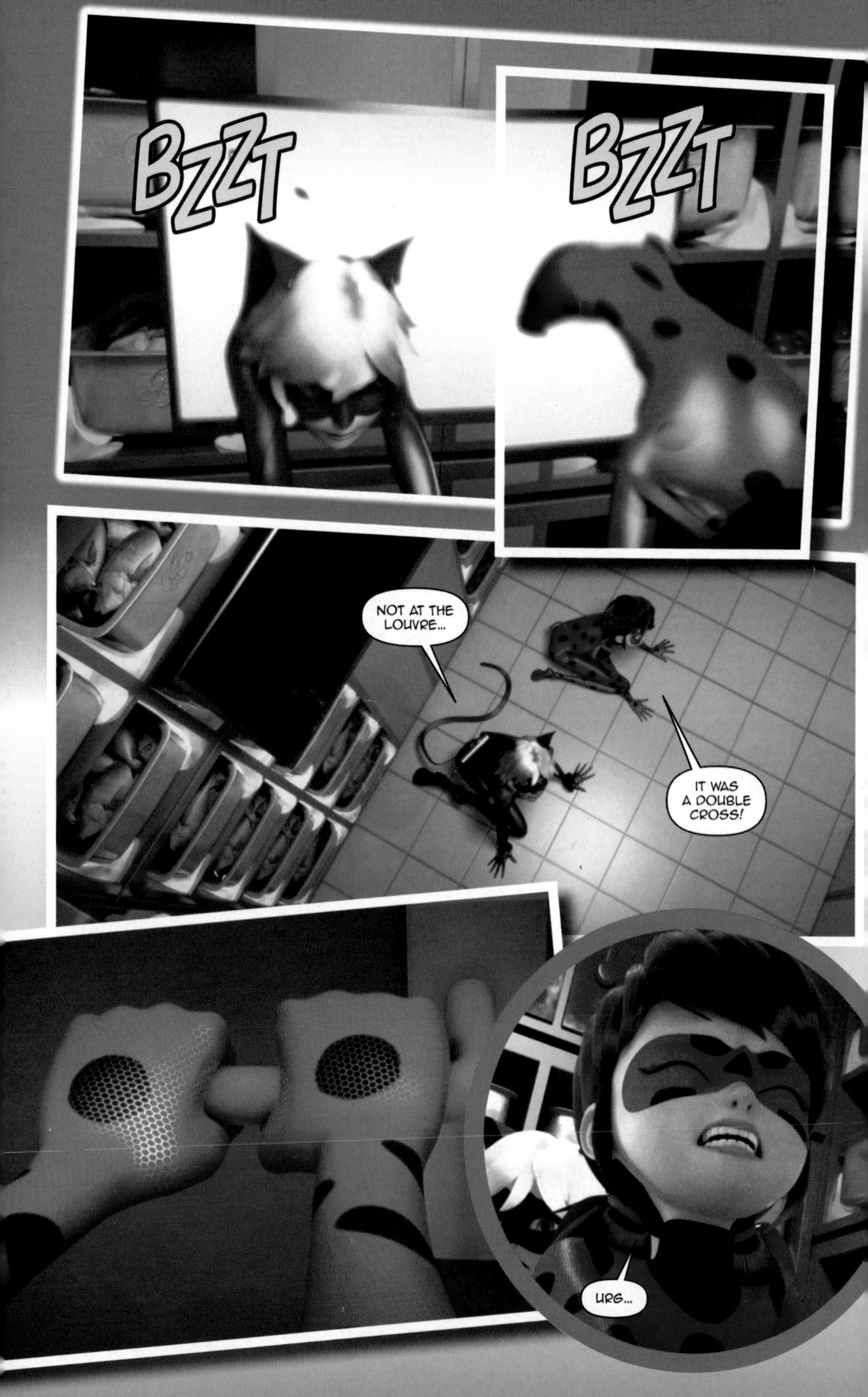
BZZT
BZZT
NOT AT THE LOUVRE...
IT WAS A DOUBLE CROSS!
URG...

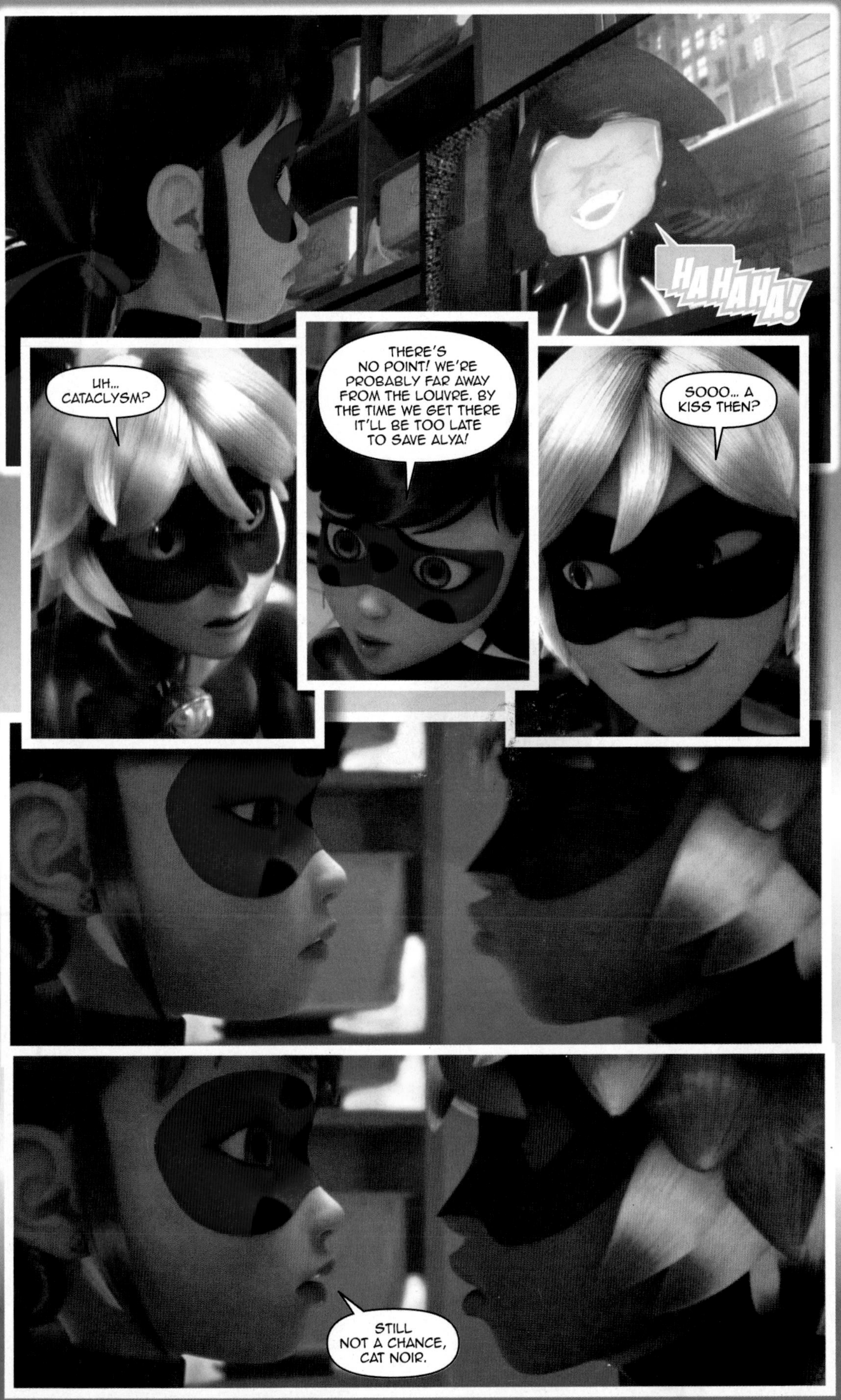
HAHAHA!
UH... CATACLYSM?
THERE'S NO POINT! WE'RE PROBABLY FAR AWAY FROM THE LOUVRE. BY THE TIME WE GET THERE IT'LL BE TOO LATE TO SAVE ALYA!
SOOO... A KISS THEN?
STILL NOT A CHANCE, CAT NOIR.

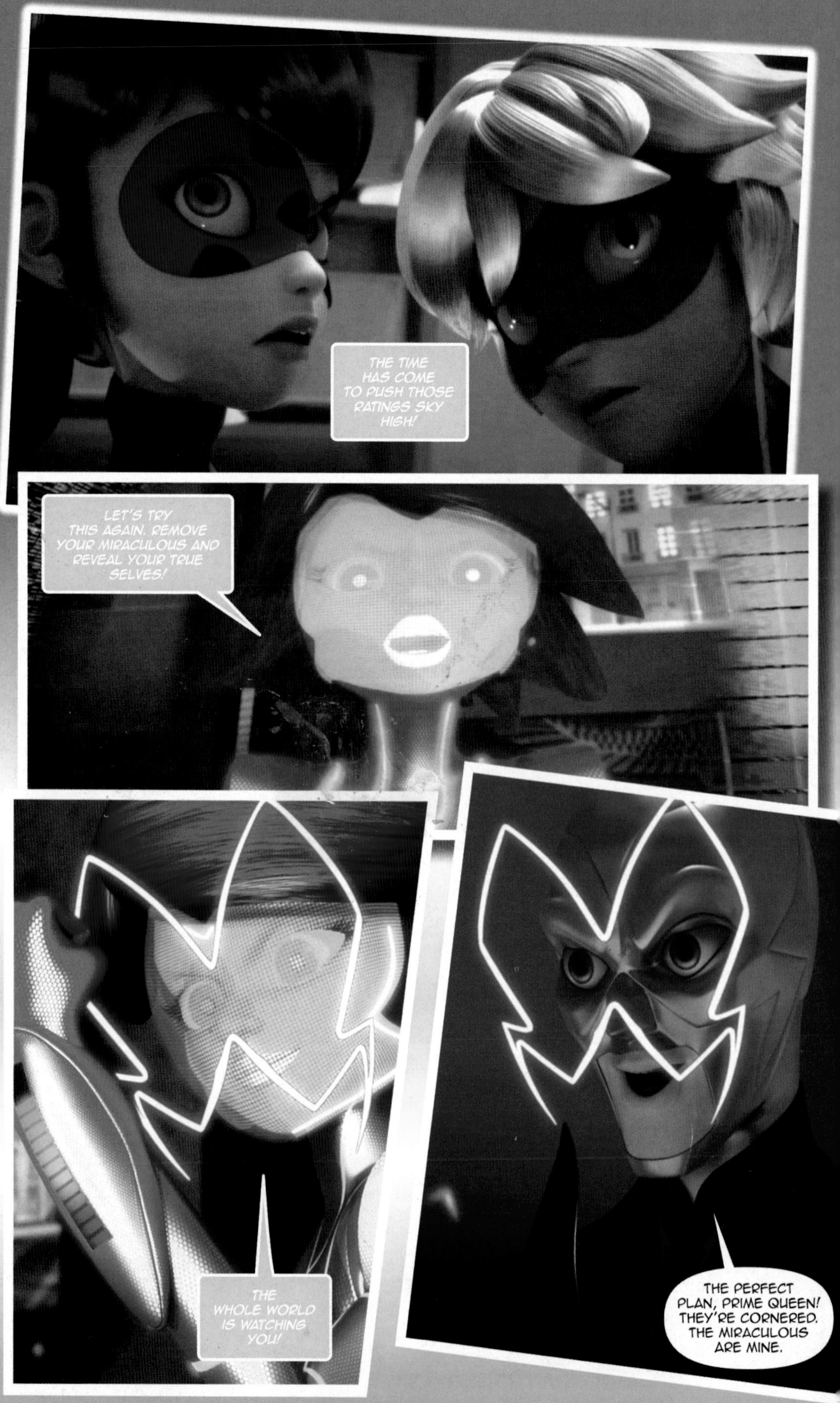
THE TIME HAS COME TO PUSH THOSE RATINGS SKY HIGH!
LET'S TRY THIS AGAIN. REMOVE YOUR MIRACULOUS AND REVEAL YOUR TRUE SELVES!
THE WHOLE WORLD IS WATCHING YOU!
THE PERFECT PLAN, PRIME QUEEN! THEY'RE CORNERED. THE MIRACULOUS ARE MINE.

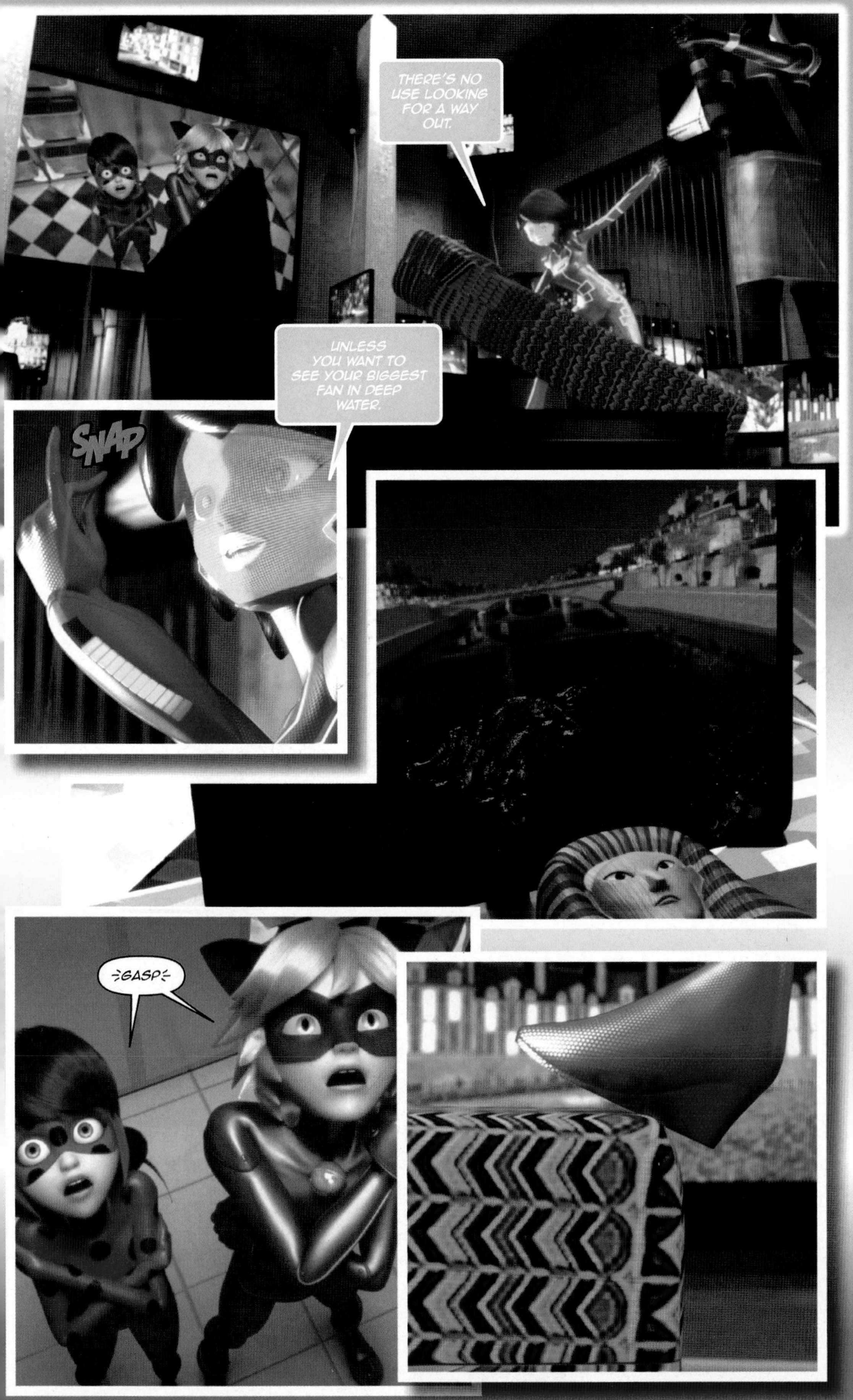
THERE'S NO USE LOOKING FOR A WAY OUT.
UNLESS YOU WANT TO SEE YOUR BIGGEST FAN IN DEEP WATER.
SNAP
GASP

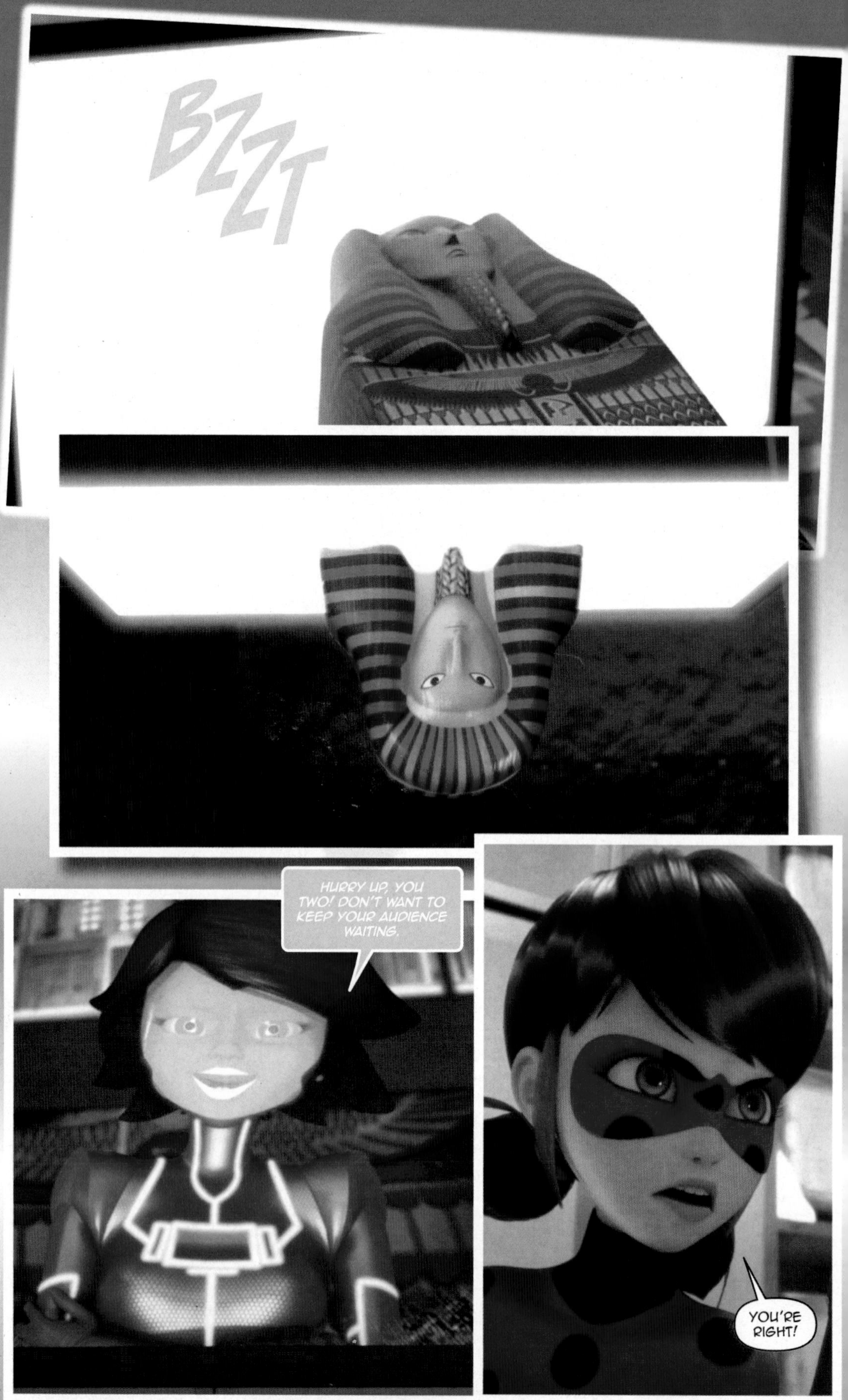
BZZT
HURRY UP, YOU TWO! DON'T WANT TO KEEP YOUR AUDIENCE WAITING.
YOU'RE RIGHT!

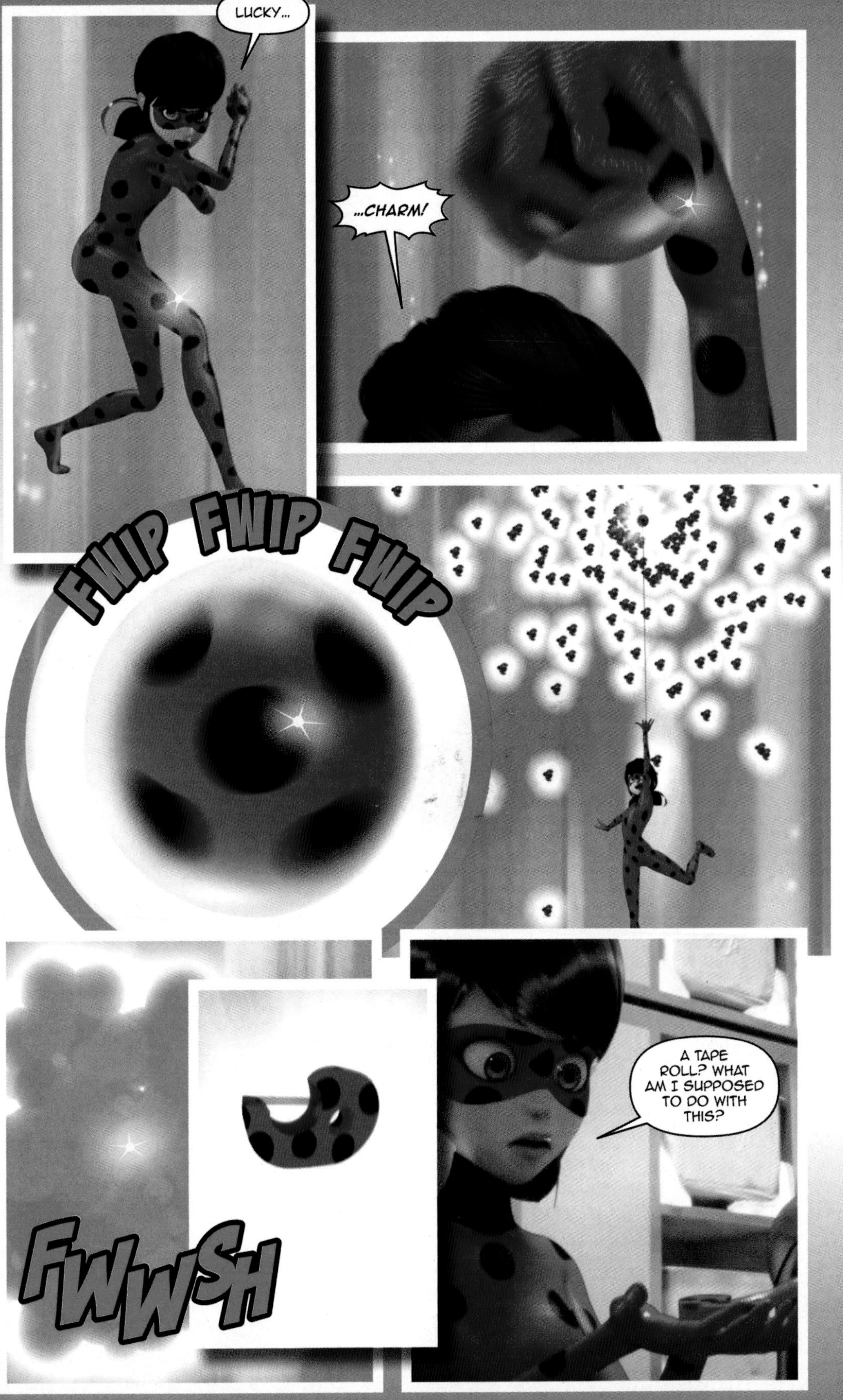
LUCKY...
...CHARM!
FWIP FWIP FWIP
FWWSH
A TAPE ROLL? WHAT AM I SUPPOSED TO DO WITH THIS?

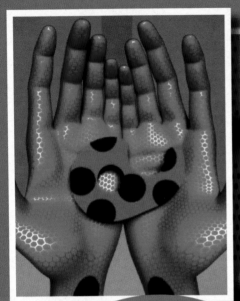

DING

DING

DING

OF COURSE!

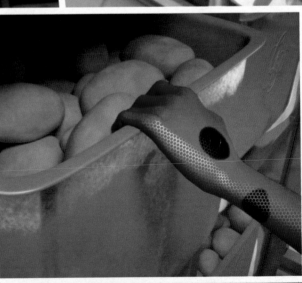

HURRY UP!
SHE'S ABOUT TO
PUSH ALYA IN THE
WATER!

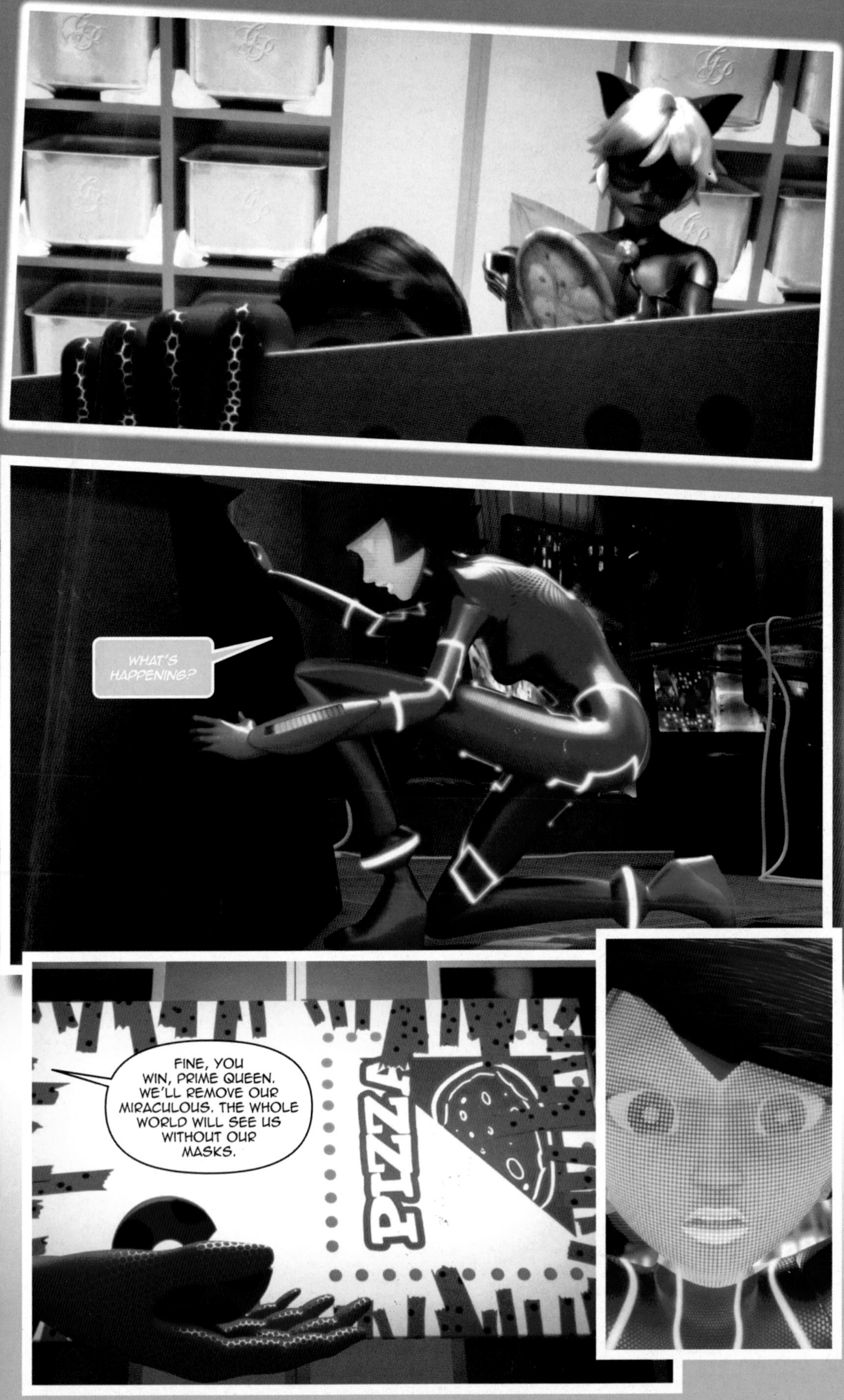
WHAT'S HAPPENING?
FINE, YOU WIN, PRIME QUEEN. WE'LL REMOVE OUR MIRACULOUS. THE WHOLE WORLD WILL SEE US WITHOUT OUR MASKS.
PIZZA

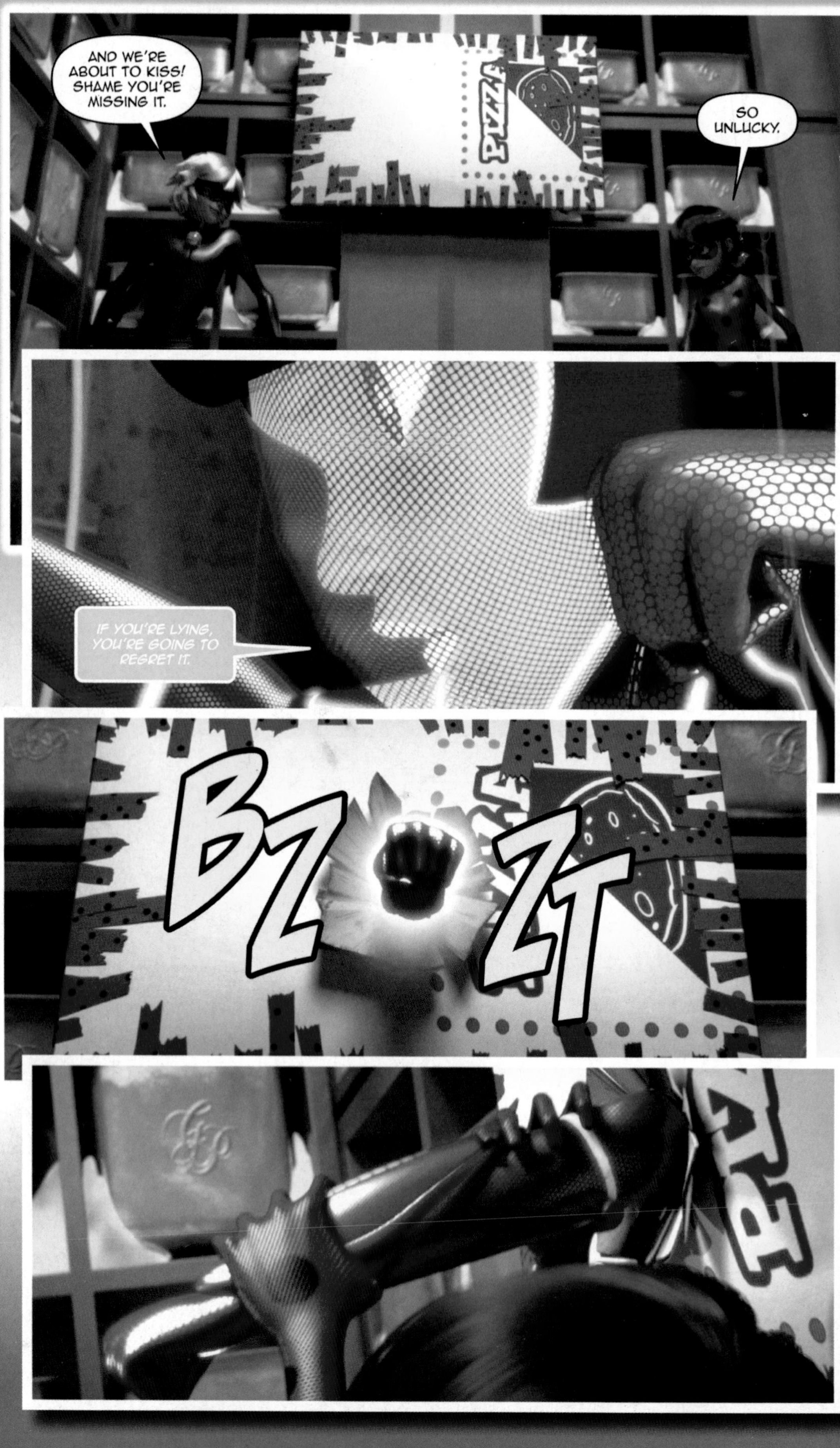
AND WE'RE ABOUT TO KISS! SHAME YOU'RE MISSING IT.
SO UNLUCKY.
PIZZA
IF YOU'RE LYING, YOU'RE GOING TO REGRET IT.
BZZT

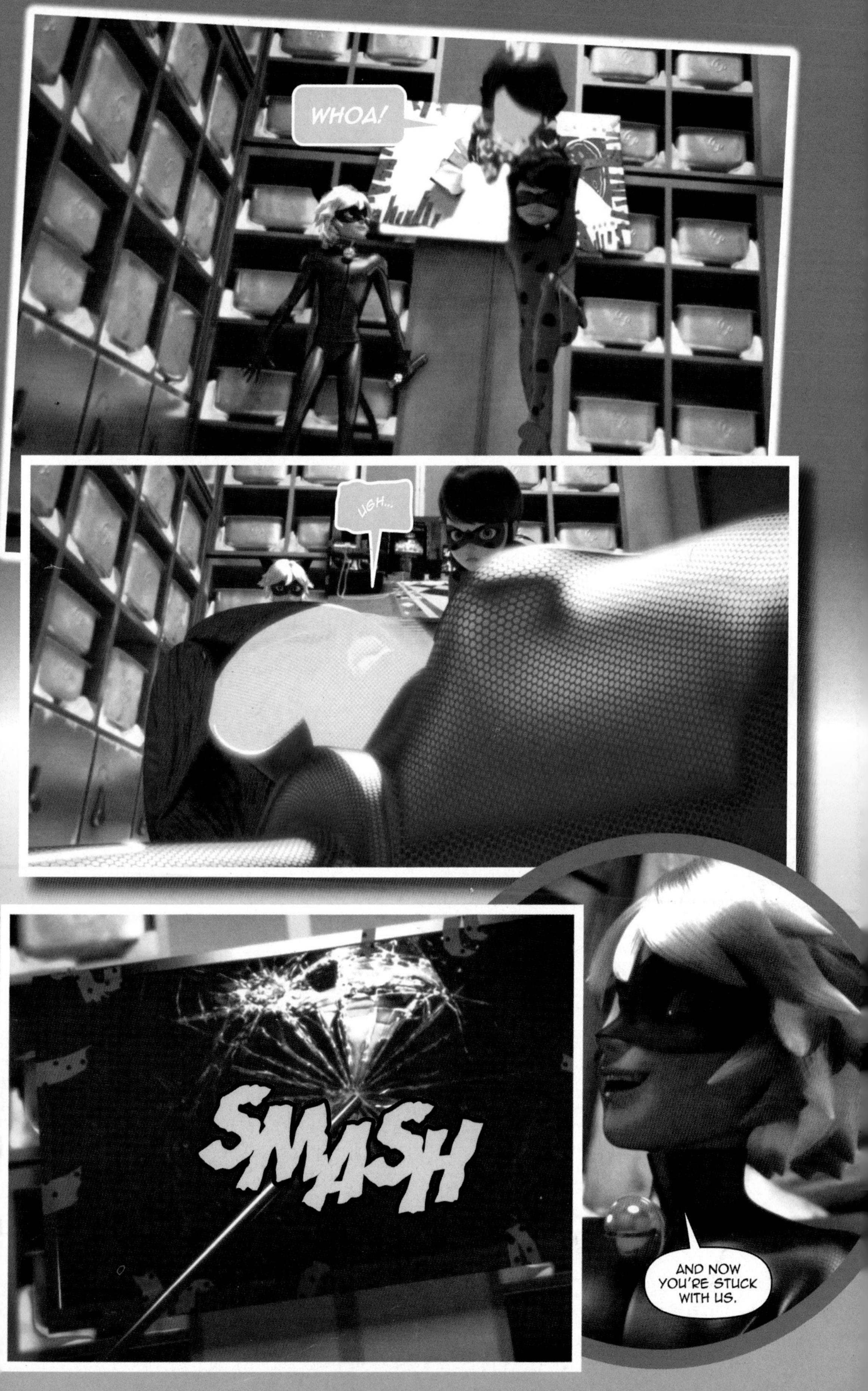
WHOA!
UGH...
SMASH
AND NOW YOU'RE STUCK WITH US.

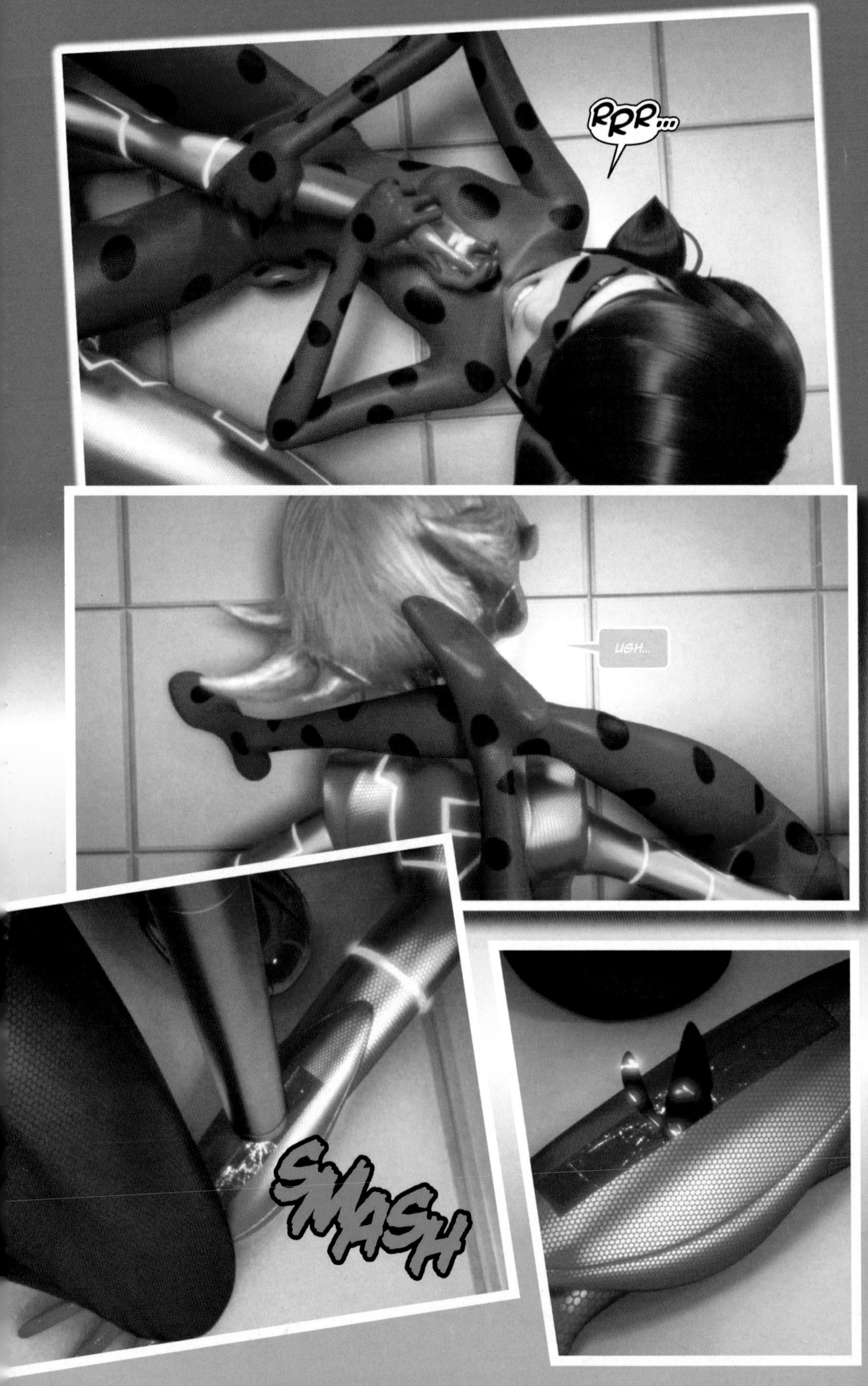
RRR...
UGH...
SMASH

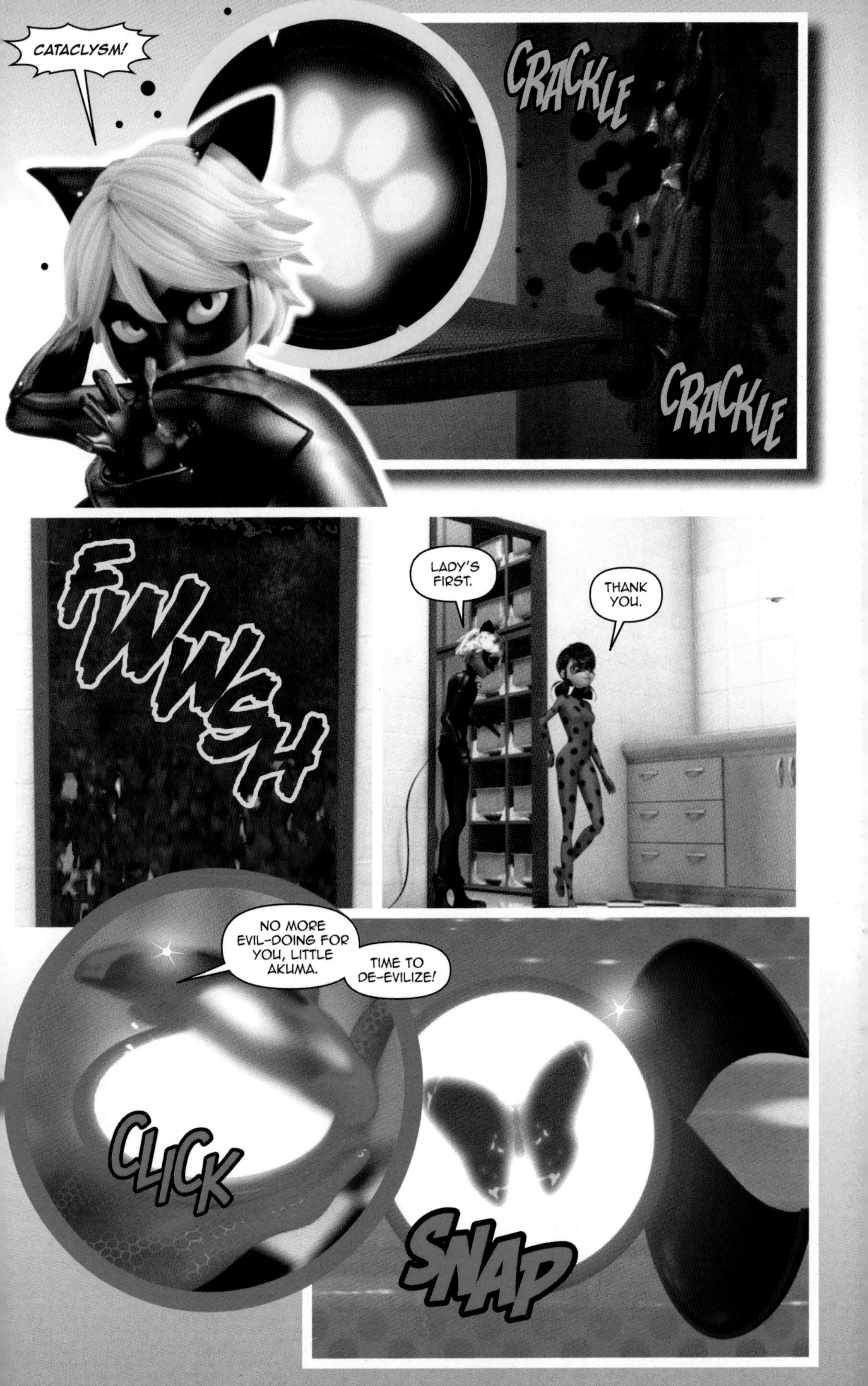
CATACLYSM!
CRACKLE
CRACKLE
FWWSH
LADY'S FIRST.
THANK YOU.
NO MORE EVIL-DOING FOR YOU, LITTLE AKUMA.
TIME TO DE-EVILIZE!
CLICK
SNAP

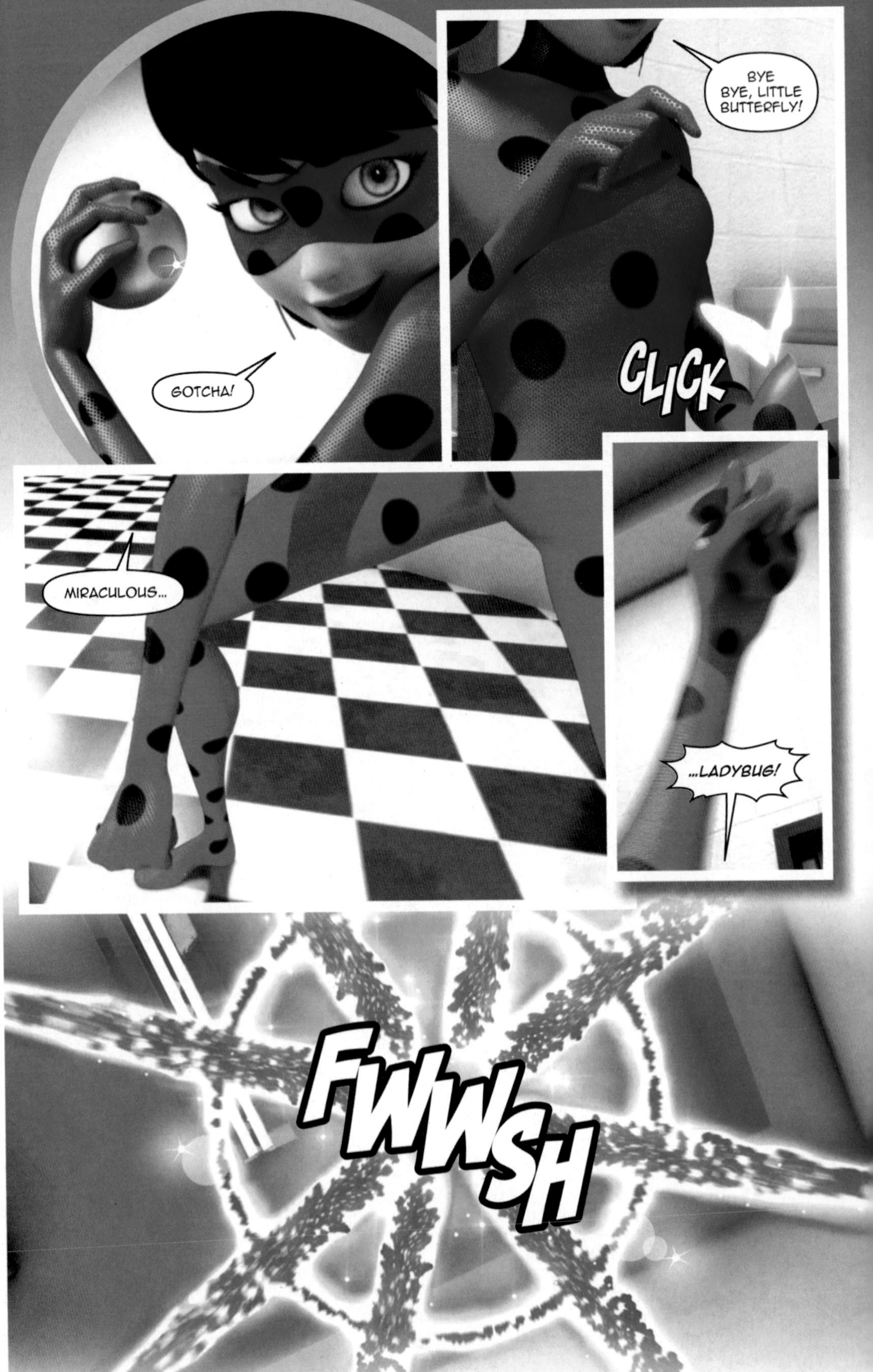

GOTCHA!
BYE BYE, LITTLE BUTTERFLY!
CLICK
MIRACULOUS...
...LADYBUG!
FWWSH

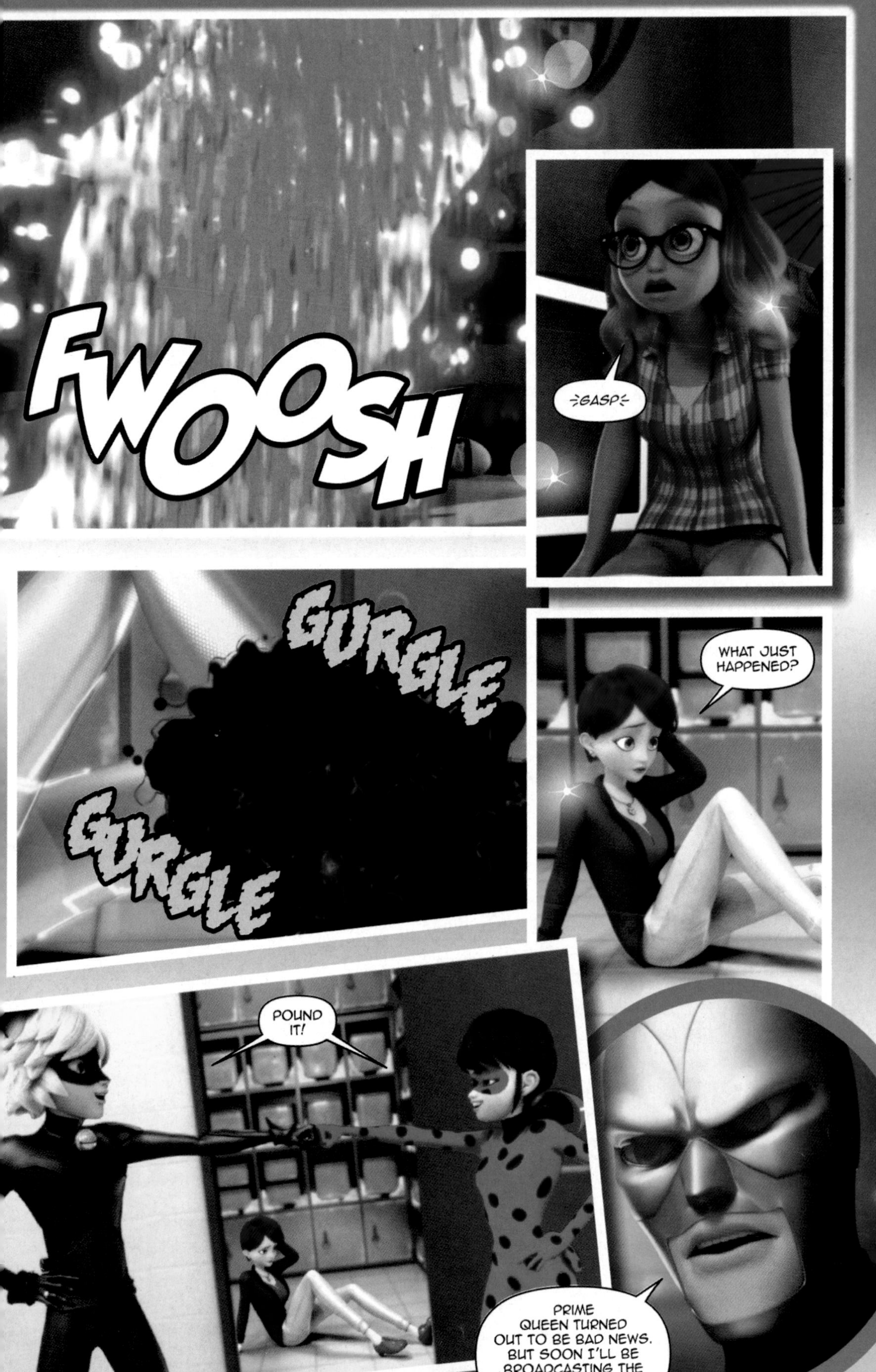
FWOOSH
GASP
GURGLE
GURGLE
WHAT JUST HAPPENED?
POUND IT!
PRIME QUEEN TURNED OUT TO BE BAD NEWS. BUT SOON I'LL BE BROADCASTING THE END OF LADYBUG AND CAT NOIR!

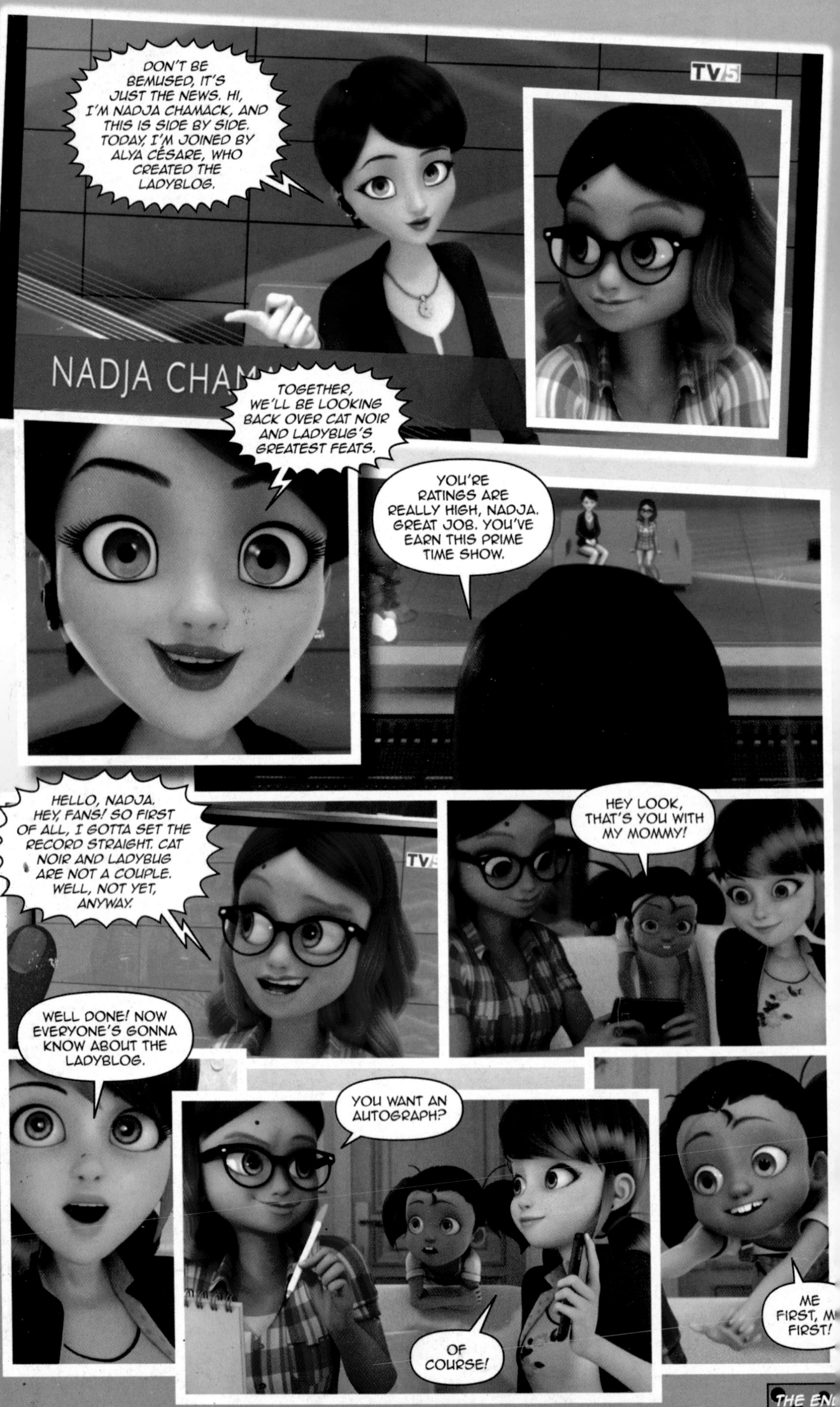
DON'T BE BEMUSED, IT'S JUST THE NEWS. HI, I'M NADJA CHAMACK, AND THIS IS SIDE BY SIDE. TODAY, I'M JOINED BY ALYA CÉSARE, WHO CREATED THE LADYBLOG.
TV5
NADJA CHAM
TOGETHER, WE'LL BE LOOKING BACK OVER CAT NOIR AND LADYBUG'S GREATEST FEATS.
YOU'RE RATINGS ARE REALLY HIGH, NADJA. GREAT JOB. YOU'VE EARN THIS PRIME TIME SHOW.
HELLO, NADJA. HEY, FANS! SO FIRST OF ALL, I GOTTA SET THE RECORD STRAIGHT. CAT NOIR AND LADYBUG ARE NOT A COUPLE. WELL, NOT YET, ANYWAY.
HEY LOOK, THAT'S YOU WITH MY MOMMY!
WELL DONE! NOW EVERYONE'S GONNA KNOW ABOUT THE LADYBLOG.
YOU WANT AN AUTOGRAPH?
OF COURSE!
ME FIRST, M FIRST!
THE EN